AN ANGRY SKY

A NOVEL OF THE PHONEY WAR

Also by Al McGregor
A Porous Border
To Build a Northern Nation
1917

AN ANGRY SKY

A NOVEL OF THE PHONEY WAR

Al McGregor

An Angry Sky:

A Novel of the Phoney War

ISBN 978-0-9950900-1-9 Kindle edition 978-0-9950900-3-3

Kobo edition 978-09950900-2-6

Library and Archives Canada Catalogue - TBA

Cover design: Quantum Communications

Al McGregor Communications
www.almcgregor.com

For all those who share an interest in history.

We did not make this war. We did not seek it. We did all we could to avoid it. We went so far in trying to avoid it as to be almost destroyed when it broke upon us.

    —Winston Churchill, Address to the Canadian Parliament, December 30, 1941

Contents

Chapter One: A Last Peaceful Summer

Southwestern Ontario
June 6, 1939

A distant flash of lightning and clap of thunder underscored the threat of a storm but the crowd surrounding the Royal Train remained stubbornly in place.

"Don't let thunder scare you," said a father lifting a toddler to his shoulders. "We may never have another chance to see the King and Queen. They don't often come to small towns like Glencoe."

"Is that the Prime Minister?" His wife's voice was almost lost in the murmurs from the hundreds of people at the station, "The man behind the King?"

"Looks like him and from the size of that gut he doesn't miss a meal."

"Shush!" Her whisper was fierce. Any reply was drowned by the shriek of a steam whistle. The Royal party took the cue, delivered a final wave and stepped back into the carriage.

For those aboard the train, the faces in the crowd began to blur. "The CNR is putting on quite a show. Massive new locomotive and special private cars." A middle-aged man reached across the aisle to a Canadian National Railway official.

"I'm Robert McLaren of the Willard Agency. Are you Williams of the public relations department?"

"I am and what else would you expect from a Royal tour but the very best?"

"I'm supposed to meet a friend," McLaren said. "A fellow named Evers Chance."

"One car ahead, I'll take you."

Williams tapped the shoulder of a black porter. "A scotch, George, and one for my friend."

"You must travel this route frequently to know a porter's name?"

Williams rolled his eyes. "All of the coloured staff are called George. But you know that. The Willard service ran a story on working conditions."

"Touched a nerve, did we?"

"I'm not going to discuss it. We try to accommodate journalists. You should be on the press train but the gentleman from London pulled strings," Williams grumbled and opened the door to the next car.

"McLaren! It's been far too long." Chance braced himself against the train motion and pointed to an empty seat.

Evers Chance had shed a few pounds; the hair was streaked with grey and he wore wire rimmed glasses but there was little to suggest a man in his sixties. McLaren wished he had taken a barber's advice to hide his own greying hair. To a casual observer the men would appear the same age, but McLaren was fifteen years younger.

"The refreshments," announced the porter, carrying a tray and two glasses. Chance seized one and passed the other to McLaren. "Good thinking, Williams. We'll talk later and I'll mention you in my report."

McLaren suppressed a smile. Chance never had sympathy for minor functionaries.

"It's been a long time, Robert. How is bachelor life?"

"I don't have much free time." McLaren slipped into the vacant seat. "My partner and I run a news agency. Our clients

2

are smaller newspapers and we're considering a radio division. But, I'm more curious about you. Is this trip a reward for service to the crown?"

The whistle interrupted as the train crossed a highway. The people standing by the track had a quick glimpse as the special thundered past. "I wish it were a vacation," Chance said as he rubbed his fingers on the edge of the glass, "but war clouds are gathering. We have to get Canada onside and wake the Americans."

"With a Royal tour?" McLaren knew his voice betrayed his skepticism.

"Have you watched the Prime Minister? William Lyon Mackenzie King is basking in the glory of the occasion. Britain has been concerned about his independent streak, to the point where a few nervous nellies fear Canada might remain neutral. When the Empire calls, Canada must answer."

"Surely, we make our own decisions."

"Oh, of course. Let Parliament decide but don't think the country can remain on the sidelines. Especially, if the old country is in danger."

"And the American visit?"

"We're making friends. When the British King meets the American President, he'll spell out the danger and a stronger bond will be established between the Palace and the White House."

"And you?" McLaren asked. His exposure to the world of intelligence had come through Chance and the Great War. In the intervening years, his friend paid for analysis of events in North America. "For this visit, I'm considered foreign office, but I maintain private ties in Europe."

Chance leaned closer. "I was sorry to hear you parted from Maria. I understand she's in France. I'd like to contact her."

For a moment, McLaren was silent. "Nothing dangerous?"

"One would hope not but let her decide."

Again, he hesitated. "I'll get the address for you."

"A radio message tells of a big turnout in Windsor," the public relations officer returned and informed them. "And, Michigan police collared that Irish fellow, so no longer fear of an attack on the King."

McLaren's eyebrows shot up. "Irish? A threat?"

"Royalty and Irish Republicans don't mix," Chance said, smiling. "We'll all breathe easier but don't get excited. No one is going to talk about it."

McLaren turned to Williams. "Have you been on the entire tour?"

"From day one, the arrival in Quebec City, across the west and back to Ontario."

"This is a bit of luck." McLaren said and reached into his jacket for a notepad. "A mysterious shipment arrived with the Royal party. Heavy crates came off a navy escort ship and were shipped under guard to Ottawa. Any idea how I would check that out."

Williams face began to flush. "No. No idea." He stammered and abruptly moved away.

"Gold." Chance spoke when Williams was gone. "Gold from the Bank of England. When war comes, Britain will need arms and ammunition. The Americans will demand immediate payment. The bullion will be stored until it's needed. But it's not a good day for reporters. No one will talk about that either."

London, England
June 9

With a single fluid motion, Dan Malone crushed the newspaper into a ball and fired it to a waste basket. "Another opinion piece from Lord Beaverbrook. He thinks no war this year."

Marcie Eaton brushed her blonde hair and studied the mirror before she replied, "Why do you care? His newspapers wouldn't hire you. Besides, most people hope Beaverbrook is right."

"If I don't find work we'll starve. We can't survive on your salary, even if male customers deliver large gratuities."

4

"Don't pretend to be a prude, Dan." She swung from the mirror to face him. "I only give the old duffs a smile and show a bit of cleavage. I don't mind and sooner or later you'll pick up work." She turned back to the mirror, mussed her hair and began to brush again. "The thought of war frightens me. Czechoslovakia wasn't worth fighting over and neither is Poland."

Malone slipped behind her to make faces in the mirror. She turned to face him.

"You're upset because London papers haven't offered work. All you have is a feeler from that Canadian news service."

"The Willard News Agency won't pay much."

"Is it money or ego? Is the Canadian offer beneath your station?"

She rose, dropped the housecoat to reveal a bra and panties and playfully danced beyond his reach.

"Later." She laughed. "I may learn something at work. Maybe one of the old duffs will drop a state secret. And you, my dear," she said, her hand lightly brushing his face, "must think of stories to impress Canadian readers." She giggled. "Dan meets a little princess. Forget the war horse and write about a pony."

Hyde Park, New York
June 11

Two special trains would soon depart for the final stage of the Royal visit. In hours, the trains would leave American territory, cross Quebec and end the continental odyssey on the dock at Halifax. Robert McLaren was about to board the first train when Evers Chance sauntered from the dusk. "The accommodation won't be as fine as with the Royal's, but you'll be ensuring their safety. If anyone dynamites the track, the members of the fourth estate on the pilot train will be blown to hell but the Royal party will be safe."

"That's re-assuring," Robert McLaren said and laughed. "Perhaps the dignitaries would offer a bottle of scotch for pain relief."

"I'll pass the suggestion along, but I won't be around. I'm off to New York to catch the flying boat."

"Something happening?" McLaren was instantly curious. "A new crisis in Europe?"

"No, I've seen enough. The tour is a great success. Everyone was pleased with the large crowds, but the private moments were more important. The King and the President hit it off. Franklin Roosevelt has a better understanding of the situation in Europe."

"Is war close?"

"To put it succinctly, yes."

"We've been thinking of expanding the news agency. Maybe it's time to speed up the plans?"

"That might be appropriate." Chance put a hand on McLaren's shoulder. "I'll also pay for any private intelligence sent my way. We can work as we did in the past."

On the platform across the track, two well-dressed young Americans watched the preparations for departure.

"See those men," said Tim Fulton, pointing. "The one guy is getting on the press train. I'll bet they're G-men. J. Edgar Hoover will have FBI agents everywhere."

"That's a figment of your imagination." Brad Wilson turned his attention to the second train. "I came to see the King and Queen, not to listen to crazy ideas."

"Be warned. Roosevelt is cozy with the Brits. He'll try to drag us into a war the same way President Wilson did in 1917. But this time will be different. We'll put America first."

"Why did you come? Why not simply ignore this latest King George and the little lady?"

"I wanted to see celebrities."

"The President lives at Hyde Park. Don't Franklin and Eleanor count as stars?"

"I'm no fan of FDR. He's had time to pull the country out the Depression, but thousands of men can't find work. It's time for new leadership."

"Anyone in mind?"

"I'll back anyone that keeps us clear of anything to do with Europe. Thank God, Washington refused to admit the Jews from that ship, the *St Louis*, the one, the newspapers made a fuss over. Cuba wouldn't take them, and neither would the U.S. or Canada. If they had been allowed in, thousands more would come. We don't want that."

Ottawa
June 16

"Good thing you took a cab, Miss. Looks like a shower." The driver manoeuvred through the midday traffic to the curb on Elgin street. "And, be glad you weren't here a month ago. A person couldn't move when the King dedicated the Great War Memorial."

The young woman plucked a bill from her purse and waited. "I can't afford a tip but if I get this job, I'll pay well in the future."

"Job interview, eh," the cabbie said, reluctantly surrendering the change. "Government work?"

"No, a position at a news service."

"Then I won't be expecting a tip in the future either. Newspaper folk are so tight they squeak. The building you want is on the corner."

Three flights up a grimy stairway brought her to the office of the Willard News Agency. "What do you want?" a receptionist, a gruff older woman, demanded.

"Wilma Fleming. I'm to see Mr. McLaren. I sent my reference letter earlier."

A short, thin man appeared from a hallway. "I'm Frank Willard, the co-owner. Robert can't make it," he said. "I'll handle the interview."

He led her through the newsroom where a pair of teletype machines hammered out the events of the day. A half-dozen desks were arranged in classroom fashion but only two appeared to be in use. A third was stacked high with newspapers. In a small inner office, he motioned to a seat. She saw his eyes dart across her body and pulled the light summer dress tight around her knees.

"I'm going to be honest," Willard appraised her from behind a desk. "I read your letter and the resume is pretty thin."

He flipped casually through the papers. "Wilma, eh? Got a second name?" he asked.

"Friends call me Sandy."

"Use that. It sounds more modern. Do you listen to radio much? Not Amos and Andy or music, I mean news broadcasts."

"The CBC or the Shirer reports from the Columbia System?"

"Yah. That's what I mean. We're going to branch into radio but most of the initial work will be transcribing, making notes on broadcasts. We want to study what the big boys are doing."

"I could do that."

"Don't get fancy ideas. Women are few and far between in this business."

"I would love to try."

Willard rose and walked to the front of the desk. "Can you type?"

"Yes. Well, I'm slow but it comes out fine, eventually."

"Ah damn, I need someone to step right in. And, we want someone who knows the parliamentary process."

"My father was a Member of Parliament."

"Why didn't you say so? He can give us a few leads."

"He died when I was a child. He lost a leg in the Great War, went to Winnipeg during the general strike and picked up a bug. My mom thought it was the Spanish flu."

Willard glanced again at the resume and tapped a pencil on the desk. "I didn't ask for the life story…"

8

An Angry Sky

"Mr. Willard." The older woman was in the doorway. "Robert is on the line from Halifax."

"Wait here," he ordered. Seconds later she heard Willard speaking. "She's the last one on the list, probably early twenties but has no experience. Only thing going for her is looks. A pretty girl, long legs, nice figure. But really, what's the rush?"

For few moments, there was silence.

"Ok. But you train her."

Several minutes passed before Willard returned.

"We'll try you. McLaren may be right; we may get busy."

"I have the job?" She wanted to be sure.

"Start on Monday."

"That's great."

"If it doesn't work, you're gone and in a hurry. And, a little sex appeal helps in this business. Work on that."

Paris, France
June 25

"Amazing." Evers Chance pulled his chair closer. "The lovely Maria, enchanting after all these years."

The reply was a shy smile.

"Early summer, a Paris café, a stunning female companion, what more could a man ask?"

The smile grew broader and her dark eyes flashed before she answered. "I was surprised to hear from you."

Maria, he guessed, was in her mid forties but looked younger. Dark hair reached to her shoulders and her skin was lightly tanned. She remained a classic beauty. He motioned to the waiter and watched as the wine was poured. "Robert says you write?"

"I pick up work with American magazines. Feature articles on European fashion or lifestyles. The work pays for my expenses and a freelance reporter is cheaper for publishers."

"And you are fluent in several languages?"

"I get by. French, a bit of German and the Russian I learned as a girl."

9

"Do you use the Russian. There's a large white Russian community in Paris."

"I met a few of them but their views are reactionary. Russia won't turn back the clock. But really, you were always well informed. You know that."

"Always delightfully direct," he said, laughing. "The lady hasn't changed."

"Oh, she has, but in ways that don't show. A husband, a failed marriage, I think it's made me," she paused, searching for the right words, "more mature?"

"The woman I remember asked a steady stream of questions."

She laughed. "A habit I haven't been able to shake."

"I hoped that was the case." Chance removed his glasses. "I need someone who can travel, observe and ask questions. The job would pay well."

"I was younger when we worked together before."

"I've grown to appreciate attractive, older, sophisticated females."

"Are you in the same business?"

"I'm interested in how the world changes and try to be well informed."

"I suspected a branch of British intelligence."

Chance lifted the glasses, holding them toward the sun, looking for a tiny speck. "Let's say, government work. It's better, safer, if you don't know the details."

"What would I be doing?"

"Readers may be interested in Germany or Poland, a woman's view. Nothing too deep, a breezy report on life for ordinary people. And, anything else you learn is relayed to me."

"And if there are problems, can you protect me?"

"We would try. You have a British passport. Are you still using Maria Dickson on travel documents?"

She nodded. "I could use the work."

"Tomorrow, a letter will be delivered suggesting a travel itinerary. With the letter will be an assignment from an American editor. You don't know him but I do. Check in with the British embassies. Passport control officers are usually helpful."

"I'll start to pack," Maria said and rose.

Chance too was on his feet. "One thing," he said. "An Edward Dupain may be in contact. Follow his instructions to the letter. It could be very important."

Ottawa
June 23

"Damn it, Sandy. Where have you been?" Frank Willard called from his office.

"Lunch," she answered. "You told me to go."

"Forget the excuses. I have to go out and a woman wants to talk to me, something about her relatives. Deal with it. Take a few notes and send her away."

"But I…"

"No excuses," and Willard slipped out a back door.

The visitor was a stout, middle-aged woman. "I wait for Mr. Willard," she announced as Sandy approached.

"He's been called away. I'm Wil… Sandy Fleming. I'm…a reporter."

"A woman." The woman sniffed and stiffened. "I not sure. You too young."

"Let's try. Why did you want to see him?"

"I am Mrs. Podborsky. Neighbor says Willard owns the news."

"He doesn't own the news, he writes it."

"Is same thing…yes? Please excuse. I learn English."

Sandy smiled to reassure her.

"I Polish." The woman sank into a chair. "Husband and I come to Canada in 1937 but Henry die. I want to bring my sister and her children. She on farm in Poland but was doctor. They alone. Husband no good, gone somewhere."

11

"Have you talked to the immigration department. It has to approve the applications."

"I talk to them and I talk to how you say? Commons people?"

"A member of Parliament?" Sandy suggested.

"Neighbors say I must grease the wheel? I offer money but they don't take."

"It's not money. The immigration process is often slow."

"I try to reach important people. Catholic friends get papers. Maybe they grease better."

The woman shook her head in frustration.

"Is same everywhere. People want to help until I say, we are Jews."

"I don't know," Sandy stammered. "But leave your address. We'll look into it."

"I need...how you say...rush? My sister worries about the Hitler. If Nazi come, not safe."

Berlin, Germany
July 5

"My trip came together quickly," Maria said as her eyes roamed across her friend's apartment. "And, I couldn't come to Berlin without seeing Elise and Karl."

"We had good times," Elise Munster offered a wane smile. Maria remembered her as outgoing and vivacious, now she was nervous and reserved. The apartment décor also signalled change. Once, Elise favoured a modern look to match a Bohemian lifestyle, but the furniture was old and showed signs of wear.

"I told Karl of the writing assignment and he knows of the magazine. He reads English language papers at the foreign ministry."

"I'm impressed," Maria said and settled into a plush wine-coloured armchair. "*Weatherbee Monthly* doesn't have a huge circulation. Most articles are political and rather dry. The magazine doesn't often publish articles that are light and breezy. But that's what they want from me."

"What will you write of Berlin?"

"I have good feelings about the city. The government and the leaders worry me."

"You shouldn't say that," Elise warned. "In the wrong company there could be trouble."

"I should overlook things like Kristallnacht?"

"Please, don't misunderstand. A mob was out of control and attacked anything Jewish. It wasn't right."

"Hitler did give the green light to beat Jews, destroy homes and burn synagogues."

"It's different when you live here. Foreigners don't understand."

"Berlin appears orderly, very peaceful. Where are the troublesome Jews?"

"Many have left the country. Others have been sent to work camps. The Fuhrer is resolving the problems."

"Listen to you!" Maria scoffed. "You sound like a Nazi."

"We adapt. How do you think we got this apartment? The Jews who lived here moved out. But don't worry, Karl and I had the rooms fumigated."

"This is the future?"

"Oh, let's not bicker. Don't spoil the visit. Come. We'll go for a walk."

On the street, Elise spoke quietly. "It isn't safe to talk at home. Karl was questioned at the foreign ministry after we had an argument. The apartment may have listening devices. Our quarrel may affect his hopes for promotion."

Maria froze and stared at her friend.

"No, don't stop," Elise warned. "Keep walking. Traffic noise covers conversation."

"Are you safe?"

"I think so. I feel bad about the apartment but what can we do. The former occupants are in the camps or maybe dead.

People disappear. And, no secret is safe even among friends or family."

"I didn't know it was this bad."

"Don't say anything more. Karl wants to talk. He'll meet you tonight."

"Every major city should have a Tiergarten," Maria said as she walked through the parkland with Karl Munster that evening. "The trees, the trails, the statues, a place to simply watch people."

Her companion appeared unimpressed. Munster had changed too. Once easy going, he now appeared stiff and reserved. "The timing of your visit is opportune." He spoke quietly, almost a whisper. "We need to get a message to the United States. Your magazine has influence. The editors know the right people in Washington. Tell them, Hitler faces serious opposition, from men in government and the army. He may be replaced. But, any foreign action, for example, a military strike would disrupt the transition."

"Karl, what are you saying? This is dangerous."

"German foreign policy would be unchanged but the barrier to honest negotiation would be gone. Our efforts will be compromised if foreign governments take advantage of any…uncertainty."

"But, what…" Maria's question ended as he raised his hand.

"I have to trust you. I have no other option. We can offer peace and security. But Washington must restrain the military elements in Britain and France."

The next day Maria walked brazenly to the entrance to the British embassy. She suspected the German sentry was under orders to observe all who entered and deter anyone seeking diplomatic shelter.

"Is there only one entrance," she said and waved her passport. "I was out last night and spilled wine. I'm going to be travelling and don't want trouble."

14

The guard glanced at the stained passport pages and allowed her to enter. Inside, she repeated the story for an embassy clerk and asked for the Passport Control officer. When he appeared, she added the name of Evers Chance and told of Munster's message. "I'm not surprised," he told her, "Hitler has opponents but we're not sure who they are, and I've never heard of the man you mention. The Germans may be trying to deceive us, but I'll pass it on. Where are you going next?"

"Chance suggested Poland and Danzig."

"I'll paste a note to the passport. A new document will take time, so I'll send it to Warsaw. Travel light. Be prepared to move fast."

"Is the danger that close?"

"Hard to tell but German propaganda is building a strong case against the Poles, the same way they built a case over Czechoslovakia."

Ottawa
July 10

"Walk with me," Robert McLaren said and grasped Sandy's arm as he threaded them through the evening rush of civil servants. "Let's find a quiet spot."

Had she done something wrong, she wondered, was the new job in jeopardy? "I'm impressed by your work," he set her at ease. "It can't be easy coming in with no experience."

"I enjoy it," she said as they found an empty bench. "A chance to meet new people and learn about the news industry."

She flipped off her hat and basked in the late afternoon sun.

"Frank was trying avoid that Polish lady," he explained. "But thanks to you, we might have a good story. I tracked down an influential Rabbi for more background."

"Is there a way to help?" She raised a hand to shade her eyes.

"It's complicated. It's not one family but a whole race. Hitler wants the Jews out. Those with money or important friends slip away but thousands, millions more across Europe, don't have that option."

"Why not go to Palestine, the Jewish homeland."

"Britain controls immigration and wants to keep the Arabs happy so only a few Jews are allowed in. Other new homelands have been suggested, perhaps Madagascar, the island off the coast of Africa, but that may be a pipe dream. Jews aren't popular."

"The antisemitism is here too. I don't have to look far to see signs saying 'no Jews' and the same thing happens to the coloured and natives. But that woman wants to bring her sister and two children. Three people don't make a tidal wave."

"The government fears even a few are too many. Immigration quotas are stacked against them. With the Depression and the lack of jobs, no one wants more competition in the workforce. If they did get in and needed public help, well, imagine the political storm."

"Do we do nothing?"

"If by we, you mean the Canadian government, I think the answer is yes. Our bureaucrats will hide behind the immigration barriers."

"And what about the news service?"

"Sandy, we're not big enough to rock the boat. And, the Rabbi urged me to wait. Jewish leaders are working behind the scene and publicity could upset the effort."

"I thought it might be an oversite or a wrong answer on a form."

"No, it's much bigger than that. Still, we can pull material together. I've had a letter from my ex-wife who has gone to Poland. I'll ask her to get pictures of the family. That will help if we eventually do a story."

"That's my streetcar," she told him pointing down the street.

"Don't be discouraged. These stories take time."

An Angry Sky

Eastern Poland
August 4

The knock on the cottage door went unanswered and Maria began to explore the yard. A hog's squeal came from a small shed and a figure emerged from the shadows, a woman, wearing the rough wool pants, preferred by working men.

"Are you Anna?" Maria called. "I've a message from your sister." The woman, suspicious of any stranger, froze. "I have a letter."

Anna spent several minutes reading her sister's note. "My sister knows your husband?"

"Yes, he's my ex-husband but we're still friends."

"My former husband and I are not friends, but what does that matter? You want pictures. Why?"

"For a news story. A picture will help if he writes about your case. It's common in the West."

"I know. I read western magazines and newspapers when I worked at the hospital."

"Yes, he said you were forced out of a medical practise."

"I have children," Anna said. "No pictures of them."

"People might be more sympathetic if they saw the children."

"A photo can also bring danger. My picture will have to do."

Maria returned to the car for the camera, waking the driver as she opened the door. She gestured at her watch and held up ten fingers. He nodded and slumped back on the seat.

"In front of the cottage," Maria suggested but Anna shook her head, "Someone might recognize the house."

"Who are you afraid of?" She asked and loaded the film.

"We don't know who to trust. And if the Germans come it will be worse."

"Where will you go?" Maria scanned the yard for an indiscrete background.

"Better no one knows," Anna said. "Even that driver might be a police spy."

Al McGregor

"We'll put cows in the background. Cows won't talk."

Anna brushed hair from her eyes and spoke softly. "Tell my sister I will finally see Paris." She squared her shoulders and stared into the camera lens.

"Do you have money and documents?" Maria motioned her a step to the left.

"We have exit visas, but no country wants Jews, legal or not. I am selling the farm, but no one will pay much. Buyers sense desperation."

"Who would buy it?"

"Jews, Poles, what does it matter? Most have seen hard times before and will stay. I believe no one is safe. So, I take my son and daughter and run."

Anna continued to speak as Maria snapped pictures. "Maybe I will see the photo's later. Canada wants farmers. My experience could help."

"Tell them about the medical training, too. That country needs more than farmers, despite what the immigration department says." Maria took Anna's hand, seeing the shock as the hundred-dollar American bill slipped into her fingers. "It's not much. But it may help."

Anna waved good-bye as the car travelled down the rutted lane way.

"That one is leaving soon," the driver announced. "She tried to sell pigs to the village butcher. She is going to France."

"Now that's odd," Maria shifted to wave at the figure disappearing in the dust. "She talked of Switzerland."

London
August 26

Evers Chance rolled the brim of his hat through his fingers trying to disguise his impatience. "Only a minute," the uniformed secretary informed him, but a half hour passed before he was ushered past the guards.

"Good to see you," said Stewart Menzies, the deputy chief of British intelligence, as he rose by his desk. The two men had known each other from the early stages of the Great War. Menzies had been steadily promoted and office chatter suggested he would soon lead the foreign intelligence section, MI6. "Have a look." He pushed a document across his desk. "The official notice of a Russian-German non-belligerence agreement. Hitler no longer has to worry about a threat from Moscow."

"A neutrality pact," Chance said and scanned the page. "That won't last."

"Doesn't really matter, I suppose, but it is a damn shame our government dropped the ball. We could have done the deal with Stalin."

"It certainly adds a darker hue to the war clouds."

Menzies glanced at another slip of paper. "We appreciated the information on the pro-German feeling in Danzig and especially the hint of opposition to Hitler. We've heard this before but it's odd. We don't know the man involved. The report came from one of your private agents?"

"Yes, one of my amateurs. She's in Poland. I'll get her out soon. My men in Eastern Poland will stay. I've followed the old communist strategy. Get your people in place early and don't use them till absolutely necessary."

"I know you protect them. However, I may soon demand the names and contact information."

"But not today." His reply suggested Menzies would face a challenge.

"Oh, all right but stay in touch through Martin Downey. The two of you are well acquainted?"

"We are but I'll be away for a while. I'm off to Paris."

"Fall is a lovely time to see France but the French are on edge. The Louvre has closed."

"Why? The Germans won't march in tomorrow."

"The French fear air attacks. The artworks are being moved to safer locations." Menzies appeared to be considering his next words. "You've been at this game since the first war. I wonder how long old timers will survive amid the influx of new men and new ideas. The old order is changing." The meeting appeared over but Menzies moved from behind the desk. "That amateur, the woman you mentioned. Take special care. She has that Nazi friend. It may be innocent but watch your back."

Ottawa
August 27

"Something's up," Robert McLaren announced as he returned to the office. "No one on the Hill wants to talk. Other reporters are getting the cold shoulder, too."

"Don't be silly," Willard laughed. "A long weekend is coming. No one wants to bother with a reporter. Especially one who thinks war is coming."

"More men in army uniforms were on the streetcar this morning," Sandy set aside a newspaper. "And they were very quiet. Soldiers are usually a loud bunch."

"Excuse me, Mr. McLaren, a phone call," the receptionist said as she hovered in the doorway. "The gentleman says it's important."

As McLaren left the room, Willard called after him, "Keep it short. We've got to make a decision on radio."

"The new equipment?" Sandy asked Willard. Her summer had been spent transcribing radio broadcasts. "Earphones would make my job easier. The static can be so bad I have to put my head against the radio."

"We wouldn't want your hair messed."

"I wasn't complaining…"

"It's on!" McLaren called from the hallway. He began to speak as he re-entered the room but stopped and swung the door closed. "Keep this between us. The army has ordered mobilization, no big public statement, instead, private telegrams will be sent to units across the country. Regular forces first and the reserves over the next few days."

For a moment, the room was quiet with the only sound carrying from the street below.

"We could break the story," McLaren suggested.

20

"And the police could break down the door," Willard countered. "Let the government announce it."

"The Toronto and Montreal papers won't wait."

"The Toronto and Montreal papers can afford lawyers. Besides, what is there to mobilize? Mackenzie King and R.B Bennett before him starved the armed forces."

"We should publish," McLaren argued.

"No," Willard wasn't budging. "We can't upset the powers that be as we're moving into radio."

"The story will leak," McLaren predicted and rocked on the edge of a desk. "Eventually the smaller papers will notice the activity at local armouries."

But from Willard's frown he knew he was beaten. "If we won't publish, I'll pass the word to a friend in Toronto. His paper will publish, and he'll owe me. And Frank, call your political friends. Tell them we held off for the good of the nation. Maybe we'll get better treatment in the future."

"Consider it done."

"And, I'm going to telegraph Malone in England," McLaren said. "No more piece work. He's full time."

"That's more expense!"

"Live with it, Frank. Live with it."

Berlin
August 30

The carriages overflowed as Maria joined the crush fleeing Warsaw. Foreigners were confined to a special car and after crossing the German border officious trainmen closed the window curtains. A youngster peaked around the cloth and described roads jammed with soldiers, horses pulling heavy guns and lines of tanks. In Berlin, the station was bedlam as soldiers crowded into eastbound trains.

On a whim, she called Karl Munster and arranged a meeting in the Tiergarten.

"Karl, I came from Warsaw. Everything points to war."

21

His reply was terse, tinged with sullen anger, "It's the filthy Poles. The Fuhrer is a peace-loving man and agreed to negotiations but the Poles are stalling, and time is running out."

"But what about the plan to overthrow Hitler?"

"Keep your voice down," Munster snarled with a tone that frightened her. His fists clenched and for a moment she thought he might strike her. "The Fuhrer is our leader. Any faults are overlooked in a crisis. Germany doesn't want to fight. Send another message to Washington. The Americans must urge restraint."

"What about you?"

"If we must teach the Poles a lesson, I will play a part. I have been training with a new SS unit, the Einsatzgruppen."

"And will Elise be happy as an army wife?"

"She no longer matters." The ugly tone never left his voice. "The filthy bitch lied. I ordered a review of her ancestry. Her grandmother was one quarter Jew. For me, Elise is as good as dead."

"I can't believe it. You loved her once, I saw it."

"We both know love can pass. She's been sent to a camp. If she works hard, she will be released, but nothing can remove that Jewish stain."

The hotel clerk beckoned as Maria crossed the lobby.

"An urgent message ma'am, a call from an Edward Dupain. He says a ticket for the Paris train is waiting at the station."

The conversation with Munster had upset her, and for a moment she was confused.

"Very nice man," the clerk sensed the uncertainty. "He wasn't sure you would remember him and said he was a friend of a Mr. Chance. If I was you, I would collect my bag and go. The Gestapo are showing a special interest in foreigners."

The journey from Berlin to Paris was delayed repeatedly. In German territory, trains moving east took the right of way; carriages filled with troops, countless boxcars and cargoes covered with tarpaulins. Her train was hours late reaching Paris but the moment she stepped to the platform a young man approached. "Maria Dickson?" he asked and when she nodded, simply said, "Follow me." A car waited nearby, and she saw Chance motion to the seat beside him. Before she could move loud voices erupted.

"Bye-bye, Mommy," someone called, the words followed by a chorus of laughter from other young men. "John will be good. Don't worry."

She ignored them and slipped into the car.

"New friends?" Chance asked.

"Uncouth, loud, and obnoxious." She slammed the door. "My train was the last from Berlin. That group had special documents, courtesy of the American embassy. The tallest one, John, spent the trip detailing a tour of the fleshpots of Eastern Europe in vivid detail. He was so loud I heard everything. Finally, I told him to grow up."

"And the advice was not appreciated," Chance guessed.

"Not in the slightest. They're well-to-do college brats. One of them said I shouldn't speak that way to a Kennedy."

Chance squirmed to peer at the men. "Might be Joe Kennedy's son, the American Ambassador in London. Old Joe made a fortune in booze and claims to be a close friend of the President. He's reputed to have a way with Hollywood starlets. Like father, like son."

"Nothing excuses that man's behavior."

"The flat is about 20 minutes away," Chance said. "You should rest. We can talk in detail tomorrow."

"I don't have much to tell. Polish forces were mobilizing and foreigners in Berlin are getting out. It won't matter in the grand scheme of international politics, but my former friend turned on his wife because of a Jewish ancestor. Most German's appear resigned to whatever comes. The bone-fide Nazis expect to win the war in a few weeks."

"Quick and decisive." Chance turned to study the people on the street. "Paris and London don't want war, too many bad memories from the last go around. We squandered a whole generation."

A breeze stirred the curtain and drew her to the window. Below, Paris streets appeared normal although thick black newspaper headlines told of army mobilization. Maria perched on the sill watching as afternoon turned to evening. She had slept most of the previous day, waking only when Chance called to tell her of the invasion of Poland and to cancel their meeting. By morning, she roused to walk, to enjoy the sunshine and returned with freshly baked bread and a bottle of wine. Through the afternoon she read and listened to radio bulletins.

"Are you rested?" Chance asked when he arrived.

"I went shopping although I didn't need much," she said. "Whoever stocked this place planned for a siege."

He chuckled. "I keep this to get away from the world but with the threat of war, I'm not sure how long I will be able to use it. The Germans hit Poland with a vengeance. Their army has pushed well past the frontier."

"Why would the Poles attack a German radio station? They must have known where it would lead?"

"That was German propaganda conceived by their ministry of enlightenment, a trick to deceive the world. The bodies of concentration camp prisoners, were dressed in stolen uniforms and displayed to bolster the story of an attack that never happened."

She shook her head in frustration. "I'm already tired of deception. When will Britain and France send troops to Poland?"

"Probably never. The British army isn't ready. The French may threaten the German border, but France isn't ready either. The Poles are on their own."

Nervous energy drove her to the kitchen and moments later she returned with two glasses.

"I keep thinking of the packages I took to Poland. What was in those letters?"

"Instructions and you should forget where you went."

"It's not easy. I met a woman. I didn't tell you. She has relatives in Canada and wanted to get away."

"She did. I have some influence. For now, Anna and the children are out of harm's way."

At first, Maria was pleased but surprise quickly turned to anger. "You had me followed."

"A necessary step. The family is safe. And, I had to know you could handle the work."

"Bastard!" The anger exploded and she threw the wine in his face.

He lifted a handkerchief from his pocket and dapped calmly at his cheek. "A waste of good wine," he said and removed the jacket. "You need time. Go to Normandy and get away from all this."

"Bastard! You know about the farm, too! Have you been watching me all these years?"

"No, only since you agreed to this assignment. The Norman house is lovely, I hear."

"Do you know everything? Do you and your friends watch while I'm in my bath."

"I haven't. Although, I'm sure it's an enchanting sight."

"How could you?"

"My associates and I had to know. I told them about your background and how we worked together in the Great War but the German connection, with Munster and the foreign office, raised suspicion."

"You missed something. He's transferred to the SS, an Einsatzgruppen force."

"Hmm." Chance retrieved a small pad and pen to jot a note. "I've heard of them but I'm not sure what they do."

"I wouldn't tell if I did know."

"So, you don't know. We'll look for answers elsewhere. How do you know that couple?"

"Whose business, is it? I'm sick of questions? I'll look out for myself. I've done it for years."

"And done a fine job but it won't be as easy in the future. Money for example will be harder to come by. I can arrange funds."

"Am I to be a kept woman?" she demanded. "Damn it. What are you suggesting?"

"I never thought of you that way," he chuckled. "Nice thought but I doubt it would work out. In all honesty, we're not sure what we need. I'll keep you safe, and…" he chucked again, "I can provide for you in the manner to which you have been accustomed. The other choice might be rather dull, a return to Canada? Maybe writing for a women's journal?" He retrieved the jacket, tossed it over his shoulder and moved toward the door. "Take time to think?"

His hand was on the doorknob when she spoke.

"No! I don't want to go to Canada and yes, I need time."

"Go to Normandy. I'll see you in a few weeks."

"Bastard!"

"A couple of small points and I'll leave. How do you know those Germans?"

"What are you asking? Do you think I'm a fascist? We met in the twenties when Robert and I toured Europe. We were friends, good friends, nothing more."

"I thought as much. The other question is Robert? Why did you break up?"

"Ah God. Are you a nattering old busybody? Do you want to know about our sex life? We broke up. We fell apart. We fell out of love. That's all there is."

Chapter Two: First Blows

London
September 3

"Come on," Dan Malone adjusted the radio dial. A few words were lost in static before he heard the British Prime Minister... *"This country is at War with Germany..."*

The next words were lost as the static returned. "Damn! Damn! Damn!" He slammed his fist on the receiver. The reedy voice of Neville Chamberlain echoed from other radios in the apartment building, but the words were indistinct. Angry, he switched off the set. Marcie would be back soon. The shouts from last night's fight must have shocked the neighbors and all because, she refused to evacuate to the country. In her estimation, London was perfectly safe. Their preparations were made. Extra canned food was in the cupboard. The blackout curtains up and the gasmasks ready. He heard the door open and saw Marcie in tears.

"I didn't think this would happen. Lord Delmer at the club said negotiations were to start. He was so sure," she said. "A Swiss businessman brought a message from Goering and he's a top Nazi."

"I know. Those stories have been swirling around." He wrapped his arms around her.

"Maybe the war will be short.'' She said hopefully, "Someone can arrange a ceasefire."

"Every war is supposed to short. We have to be prepared for what comes."

"I'm not going away." She broke the embrace. "My place is here. With you." Their earlier argument began the same way. He had urged her to return to her parent's village. A sleepy hamlet was less a target than the sprawling metropolis. "Those barrage balloon things are going up all over the city," she told him. "But I can't see what good they will do."

"The balloons are to stop low level attacks, but bombs will fall. The War Ministry believes bombers always get through."

"We're all crazy. People cut short summer vacations and came home because of fear of war. And when they got home, they sent their children back to the country, to small towns and to farms. I didn't see any kids this morning. Maybe, they're in the country, or Scotland or Canada."

"Where they will be safer."

"I'm not a child and I'm not going. And, I'm not going to the shelters. Imagine, crammed in with people belching and farting. I'm not going into one of those." He slipped his arms around her again. He hadn't told her of the thousands of coffins quietly ordered for use in major cities. "A friend has a personal shelter," she said. "But it doesn't sound like much, an Anderson shelter, a piece of metal stretched over a hole in the ground. I'd rather go to the cellar."

"Alright." He gave in. "More tape for the windows will reduce the risk of flying glass. And the black out curtains must be closed at dusk. I don't want an air-raid warden charging in when, well, we're in the middle of something."

She relaxed as she caught his meaning. "Now that sounds better! Everyone says coal will be rationed. We'll spend our time under the covers to keep warm."

"Marcie. It's not safe…" he tried one last time.

An Angry Sky

"The club has a strong shelter. I'd be safe there. And at home, I only have to keep you under control."

She dabbed at her eyes. "I'm staying...but what's that noise? An air-raid siren?"

Ottawa
September 5

"The sirens put the fear of the Lord into Londoners," Frank Willard snickered. "The air-raid warning, only minutes after the declaration of war, was a false alarm. A private plane winging back from France set off a panic."

"No one was taking chances," Robert McLaren said. "A fellow from External Affairs says the staff at Canada House never heard the all clear. They were in the shelter for hours, could have smothered and no one would have known."

"Hee...hee," Willard chortled. "So much for the coveted overseas posting. The consulate staff will be begging for jobs back in Ottawa."

"Yes, far from bombs and sirens," McLaren agreed as he cut a clipping from the morning paper. "This ship torpedoed off Ireland, the *Athenia,* was bound for Montreal. Canadians must have been on board. I'll have Sandy make some calls."

"Not that big a story," Willard leaned back in his chair. "First reports say most of the passengers were rescued."

"We should hire a reporter in Halifax," McLaren suggested.

"No way." Willard sat up. "We're already spending too much."

"*You* bought the radio equipment." McLaren set the scissors aside and leafed through the rest of the pages.

"Radio is the future," Willard told him. "But our future is delayed. The New York sales rep says the equipment won't come for a few days. The American army is using its clout and claiming priority on rail shipments."

"That's odd," McLaren said. "I wonder? The U.S. is neutral and won't sell arms to belligerents but could ship guns, ammo and whatever to Canada until there's a declaration of war.

29

Maybe the delay in recalling Parliament is a plan to build up war supplies?"

"More likely an unintended coincidence," Willard settled back in the chair. "King wants Parliament on record in case things turn sour. He wants to take the credit or spread the blame. And he won't hurry."

McLaren folded the paper. "We should talk about Sandy. The probation period is up. We should boost her salary."

"Oh, don't be silly. She's lucky to have a job." Willard chuckled again. "She'll accept a few months on a starting wage."

New York
September 7

Tim Fulton admired the view from the observation deck of the Empire State Building. The war appeared to have little impact on the harbour in a 'neutral' America. Ships came and went, and the loading docks were busy. Still, he suspected customs officers would be paying close attention to shipments for Europe. His suspicions had been fuelled by a German Consul stationed in New York.

"Lovely view, isn't it." Erich Schmidt lifted a small set of binoculars. "And an excellent site for our meeting. The FBI no doubt has stepped up a watch on my consulate." Fulton glanced quickly at the other people on the deck. Schmidt laughed. "One hopes that J. Edgar Hoover is also watching the British, the French and the Poles."

"The German army isn't making friends," Fulton turned to stare out over the harbour. "I don't often agree with President Roosevelt, but he was spot on in calling for restrictions on bombing cities."

"These things can't be helped," Schmidt spoke softly. "The Poles are devious. Bombing is the only way to reach them in their lair. What does it matter if Warsaw is damaged?"

"And, I'm trying to counter stories of bloodthirsty Germans. Why would a submarine attack a passenger ship? Thirty Americans died on the *Athenia*. It raised bad memories of the sinking of the *Lusitania* in the Great War. And, a little Canadian girl was one of the victims. She was no threat to the Reich."

"Tim, Britain declared war on Germany. Churchill ordered that attack to make us look bad."

"Don't start that," Fulton warned. "That kind of claptrap is intolerable. No one believes it."

Schmidt raised the binoculars to survey the harbour. "It must be hard to identify a ship, especially at dusk or in darkness. I too, can't believe the British would kill their own people so we may learn later it was a mistake, a commander who mistook a passenger vessel for a war ship."

"Later? Tell the true story now."

"The Fuhrer will decide. I can't say when. For now, Berlin blames Great Britain."

"But the German story stinks. If you want to sway American public opinion, you must do better."

Ottawa
September 9

"She should be back any minute." Frank Willard looked across the newsroom to Robert McLaren. "I'd feel better if you were in the Commons to cover the debate. Sandy might miss something." He hunched over the typewriter and pecked for a moment. "How does this sound? The decision for war was a signal the country supports Prime Minister William Lyon Mackenzie King and the Liberal government."

"Boring and predictable," McLaren told him. "Maybe, something about the drama of the moment."

"What drama? King waited for almost two weeks to recall Parliament but there was no doubt of what the House would do." Both men hesitated at the sound of clicking heels as Sandy burst into the room. "I couldn't find a telephone," she panted. "The war declaration was approved."

"Fine, was the vote unanimous?" Willard asked, his fingers poised above the keyboard.

31

"I don't think so." She gulped for air. "One member, Mr. Woodsworth stood against it."

"Ah, never mind him. He's a pacifist and a socialist. But did the rest of his Co-operative Commonwealth Federation vote no or only him?"

She hesitated.

"Only him but I don't think there was a recorded vote. I mean Woodsworth was clear, but a couple of Quebec MP's appeared uncertain. I wanted to talk with other reporters but since we don't have membership in the Press Gallery, I had to sit in the visitors' section."

"Don't start the Press Gallery argument." Willard's fingers continued to hover. "Membership costs too much. Besides, it's nothing but an old reporters' club."

"I'm explaining why I took so long. The House approved the declaration. I'm certain of that but I don't think there was a roll call."

"I'll keep it vague," Willard decided and began to type.

"It takes guts to stand alone as Woodsworth did," McLaren told them. "After the debacle over conscription in the last war, French speaking members must have reservations. Maybe that explains the way the vote was handled. A chorus of yea's instead of a recorded vote, quiet opposition could pass unnoticed."

"I did my best." Her voice choked as she defended herself.

McLaren's words brought immediate relief. "Reporters can spend years watching antic's in the House and be baffled. The important thing is the result. We're at war."

Eastern Poland
September 18

German scout cars blocked the streets as soldiers herded residents to the village square. Colonel Karl Munster tapped a riding crop against a glove and surveyed the crowd before speaking quietly to a lieutenant. "Do we have them all?"

"We think so. A small village has few hiding places."

An Angry Sky

Munster squared his shoulders and loosening the cover on his revolver. "Achtung! Achtung!" He shouted, clicking the heels on his leather riding boots. The crowd slipped into a restless silence. "The German army came to restore order," he paused, waiting for their full attention. "And what do we get? As my men were rounding up Jews for re-settlement someone threw a rock. Criminal acts must stop. Where is the mayor?"

He waited until an elderly man stepped forward.

"I warned you to control the people?"

"Yes, Herr Colonel and we helped identify the Jews."

"And did you also ensure that valuables were collected and brought to the village office?"

"Yes. When the Jews were evicted, we scoured each house but didn't find much."

"Odd," Munster raised his voice. "My men think townspeople kept household goods for themselves."

"I know nothing of that," the mayor answered.

"Turn around. Face the people," Munster ordered, and as the mayor turned, lifted his revolver. "Orders must be obeyed."

The gun was inches from the mayor's neck. Munster smiled at the shocked faces and pulled the trigger. The mayor pitched forward, dead before he hit the ground. "Johan!" A woman screamed, ran from the crowd and threw herself on the body. And, for a second time the revolver barked.

The lieutenant swayed in shock. "Was that necessary?"

"I decide what is necessary." Munster holstered the gun. "Burn the village."

"But sir…"

"No buts! Burn every building. Drive the people into the countryside. Those that survive will convince others to obey. And when there is nothing but ashes, load the men and move west."

"But we were going east?"

"No more, back to the west. Our Russian allies will occupy this area."

"Our unit lost a dozen men to pacify this region."

33

"No arguments!" he said. "Eastern Poland has been given to the Red Army."

Near Le Havre, France
September 23

The directions led him along a rural road to where a rutted path snaked through a small forest and crested a hill. Across a narrow valley, was a house and a ramshackle barn.

"I wasn't expecting company," Maria's voice carried from an open window, "and certainly not you."

"A pleasant surprise, I hope." Evers Chance raised his cap. "I came to make amends. Our last parting was less than amicable."

"That's true. But I was raised to be a gracious host," she waved him inside. Light streaming from the large windows showed a couch and several chairs, arranged in front of a stone fireplace. Maria disappeared through a door he suspected led to the kitchen. "It doesn't look like much," she returned with two cups of coffee. "I stumbled across this in 1937, rented for awhile and bought it last summer. The land is more impressive than the buildings. I have fifty acres, a small pasture and the forest you passed on the way up."

"And you work this, alone?"

"And why not?" Despite the stern tone her face began to relax. "Men underestimate me."

"And, at their peril." He smiled. "I won't make that mistake…again."

"Oh. He's humble, today. Does he want something?"

He ignored the question and instead said, "I'm intrigued. Tell me how you found this oasis."

"In Canada, we had a summer house on a lake. I couldn't find that in France and this was the next best thing. The ocean is a few miles away. If I need company, I go to Le Havre or Paris. Or in a few hours, I can be in London."

"And this is the studio? Do you paint? Or write?"

An Angry Sky

"Painting frustrates me," she confessed. "My work looks like an impressionist's breakfast and that's not what I aim for. So, I write. Magazine articles mostly, which you've seen."

"No, racy novel, hidden away?"

She smiled. "Not yet."

"And the farm? I fully appreciate your ability, but it must be hard work."

"Not so hard. I hire help. A farmer with two strong sons lives nearby."

Chance stood and stretched. "Can we walk? Show me the estate?"

The stable had seen better days. Stone walls formed a foundation, but one section of roof was open to the sky, evidence of a rogue wind. The mows were half filled with hay and straw while a few chickens poked for insects.

"Basic shelter," she led him through the barn. "The cows are on pasture. The roof will be fixed this fall." She proudly pointed to a chicken roost. "I have fresh eggs. I can make an omelette for lunch?"

"I'd like that." He followed as she stepped into the sunshine and pointed down the valley. "I enjoy exploring in the woods and found a small cave tucked into a ridge."

"You sound happy?"

"I'm as happy and content as I was meant to be."

"I've always wondered," he hesitated, "you and Robert appeared so good together?"

"Back to that are you? I'm not sure it matters but, yes, we were good together, for awhile." She rested on the remains of a stone fence. His eyes were drawn to the legs, sprouting from rubber boots and rising to gracefully disappear under a yellow cotton dress.

"I thought I was a pregnant once. And that's when things began to fall apart. I wasn't, you see. The doctor diagnosed a false pregnancy brought on by nerves. And, right then, I decided I didn't want a child."

For a moment she appeared lost but then continued.

35

"Maybe it was the war. We all saw it. The violence in Russia, in France or malnourished toddlers in the slums, even in peacetime. Robert had his own demons, the memories of the battlefields in Flanders. He had nightmares and...."

"That was common," he told her. "It's hard to keep the ghosts away."

"I suppose," she said and turned to stare off down the valley. "I was very careful and often rejected his...advances...and gradually our marriage disintegrated. He's quite conservative and prefers the little woman to simply tend the house. As you might guess, I didn't accept that. We drifted until the gulf was too large to close. We tried but it didn't work."

"But stayed together, in the eyes of the law?"

"He didn't want to go through the public censure that came with divorce in Canadian society. Do you know one of their grounds for divorce is bestiality? Neither one of us wanted to go through the process so legally we're married."

"I'm beginning to understand."

"Robert says we escaped the worst of the Depression, but we lost money. My inheritance, that legacy of a Russian father and Arab mother, pretty much disappeared. It was cheaper to remain together."

"That too is common enough," Chance nodded as Maria continued. "Robert threw himself into his work. He's a great reporter but cares for little else. Frank Willard needed help with the news agency. Robert thought it was a good opportunity although I've never trusted Willard."

She paused, considering how much to share. "He made a pass at me once. The man is a pig! He can't be trusted but Robert doesn't see it. When Europe beckoned, I left. I make enough to get by, and Robert provides small support payments."

Her smile faded. "Is that enough or do you want more salacious details?"

"I didn't mean to pry, or honestly, yes, I guess I did. I knew you both. I wanted to understand."

"And do you?"

"I think so."

"It's my turn." She met his eyes. "Have you spent all these years with British intelligence?"

He sighed and sat beside her on the fence.

"After the Great War, I returned to the import-export business. I maintained a few ties to government and arranged a few writing assignments for people like Robert. We needed to know what North America was thinking. But most of my work was on the continent and in the early '30s I started to see more shipments to Germany, the type of material used to build weapons."

"Did anyone care?"

"Not at first. No one wanted to rock any boats. The appeasers thought it possible to make a deal with the Fascists and some still do. My commissions were relatively handsome, and I used the money to build a network of informants. Businessmen pay for reliable information and I have a working relationship with the British government. While I accept their money, I consider myself independent."

"Which explains the packages, I delivered in Poland?"

"Yes, money and instructions on ways to communicate. Each of them found a parcel, by the way. Face to face meetings would have been dangerous."

"And what are they telling you now?" She asked. "French radio bulletins predict Hitler will fail to take Warsaw."

"There won't be much left of Warsaw to take. Bombers are decimating the Polish cities and the Russians are coming in."

"What?" She sprang to her feet. "The Russians? Germans won't be able to withstand the Red Army. This little war must be almost over."

"Oh, I wish it were so, but no. The Russians and Germans have a secret arrangement. Russia gets Eastern Poland to use as Stalin pleases."

She sank back against the fence as Chance continued.

"The German's are using brute force. Anyone who shows the slightest resistance is shot and anyone that might show resistance in the future is eliminated. The upper crust, the Polish leadership, is being destroyed. Men like Munster and the Einsatzgruppen are engaged in a form of terror, so blatant and cruel that regular officers in the German army are complaining."

Maria shuddered. "The Jews get the worst of it," Chance continued, "But any who don't fit the vision of a perfect Aryan, are ground to dust. It's bloodthirsty and ruthless and the contagion may spread. If the German army marches on France, well, you'd be safer in England."

"I...I...don't know what to say."

"Hitler will digest his latest conquest. But after a few weeks, or at most, a few months, when his army is resupplied and the men rested, he'll move again. He won't go east. He'll attack in the west."

"I don't know what to think?"

"I can arrange lodging near London."

"But I have the farm?"

"Decide soon. There could be a peaceful solution, but I really don't think this war will end with negotiations."

Maria ran her hands through her hair.

"Damn it, Chance! I don't know what to do?" She found herself sobbing on his shoulder and felt his hand stroke her hair.

"For your own good, come to England." He grasped her shoulders and gently twisted her toward him. "I want to keep you safe."

Near Montreal
September 27

Frank Willard at the wheel was what her mother would have called a 'holy terror' and Sandy wished she was on a train. A chance to cover her first election was welcome but not at the risk of life and limb.

"Asshole," Willard snarled, passed a slower car and returned to the proper lane seconds in front of a large truck.

Sandy's eyes shifted from the highway to the safety of the passing landscape. The trees were changing colour as fall approached. Despite the cooler air, she kept a window half open, fearing the smoke from his cigar would bring on nausea.

"With this traffic, we'll be late." Willard stamped on the brakes as the car ahead slowed. "I've going to meet an old friend, a printer, in Montreal. With the war, the governments will demand millions of new forms and documents. I'll collect a few dollars if I steer him in the right direction. When that meeting is done, we'll work on the election."

He glanced across the car. Sandy appeared intent on the low clouds that hung over the Gatineau Hills. Her coat was tightly fastened, and slacks touched the floorboard."

"I hope you brought a dress. Men open up when they speak to a well-dressed woman, especially one who speaks their language."

"My French is passable," she answered. "I get by but I'm not bilingual."

"Knowing French helps us navigate in Quebec. I have to hand it to Premier Duplessis. The whiff of corruption in his government grew to a stench and he calls a snap provincial election. Distract the voters. Forget corruption, he says. Worry about conscription."

"I don't understand." She saw his one hand was on the steering wheel, the other on the floor mounted shifter. The cigar, now dead, was clenched between his teeth. "The Prime Minister says there will be no conscription. And the other parties agree. Men who join the armed forces don't have to serve outside of Canada. But if they want to volunteer to go overseas, they can."

He popped the dead cigar in the ashtray. "That's what King says. The election will show if Quebec believes him."

"We don't need conscription," Sandy persisted. "A flood of men are signing up, all volunteers."

"Same as in the first war." Willard rapped the car horn repeatedly in a vain attempt to clear the traffic. "Canada didn't need conscription until the volunteers stopped coming forward. And, when conscription was imposed, Quebeckers ran for the hills or took to the streets. Four people were killed in the riots in

Quebec City in 1918 and that was the official count. I think more died and the government covered it up."

"My dad ran in the '17 election and opposed conscription," she told him. "And he ran in rural Ontario. The anti-conscription movement wasn't confined to Quebec."

"So, they say," Willard shifted to a lower gear. "But, take a close look at today's army. Some men don't pass muster. Volunteers came forward for one reason, grub, three square meals a day. Many haven't eaten so well since the Depression started."

"But they're signing up."

"And the Prime Minister likes that. He likes anything that will keep the country together. And, I hear that three of his cabinet ministers from Quebec are ready to take on Duplessis. They'll threaten to resign from the Federal House if Duplessis is re-elected."

"And, what would that accomplish?"

"Without strong Quebec voices the Commons might lean toward conscription. A Liberal win keeps Quebec men safe. A vote for Duplessis increases the risk of a spell in the army."

The traffic ahead began to slow.

"Oh damn. Get off the road, louse." He shouted and slammed his fist on the horn. "By the way, Montreal hotels are almost full. We may have to share a room." And, as if to reassure her, he reached to pat her leg.

"It's ok." She smiled, "My friends have extra space. I told them I might come."

"Damn!" Willard snarled and tramped the gas peddle.

Washington
September 30

Tim Fulton took a deep breath. Weeks of effort had produced a meeting with a man reputed to be a Washington power broker.

"Congressman, the Canadians don't have the oil supplies to fuel themselves and British convoys for England. I have proof American tankers are making secret deliveries." He opened his briefcase. "Here's a list of the ships that mysteriously sailed to Halifax. Fuel from American refineries and shipped in American vessels, is a violation of the neutrality act."

"Uh-huh," the Congressman mumbled as his finger ran down the page. "The oil companies own the tankers, not the U.S. government."

He peered over the top of his glasses. "Do you work alone, Mr. Fulton? Ordinary citizens don't produce this sort of detail."

"I want to keep the U.S. out of this war and have like-minded friends along the east coast."

"And would these 'friends' be part of the German Bund or Nazi sympathizers?"

"I get information anywhere I can. It shouldn't matter. If the U.S. is neutral, we can't play favourites."

"I think, Mr. Fulton, you are ahead of yourself. A few tanks of fuel oil are not going to carry us into any European quagmire."

"But it's not only fuel. Under our rules, new war planes can't fly across the border. Instead, planes are flown to air strips near the Canadian border and are met by a man with a team of horses. With a chain or a few ropes, he hauls the plane to the Canadian side where a British pilot takes over."

"Proof? Pictures, signed affidavits, a bill of sale?"

"No, I don't have that."

"Then there's not much I can do. My concern is the economy. I want men working. If that means producing armaments, so be it and if that means quietly selling material, so be it. Business leaders are smart. I suspect there are sales to both sides. But, rest assured, we're a long way from sending Americans to fight."

Cliveden Estate, England
October 15

"Marcie don't fuss, you look marvellous."

She nervously ran her hands across the light blue dress. "It's not my sort of gathering," she said as they navigated a manicured pathway, "a bit posh."

"Nonsense," Dan Malone reassured her, as he had throughout the drive from London. "The same sort of people visit the club every day."

"But at the club I serve them, I'm not an invited guest." She squirmed to be sure the last wrinkle was gone. "Lord, look at this place. The Thames across the way, the gardens and the size of the house."

"Take it all in," he advised. "A representative of an obscure Canadian news agency is not often invited to Cliveden."

Moments later, Marcie's gasp signalled more trouble. "Dressed formal," she whispered, "except us." He scanned the reception room. Ladies in formal attire, men in tuxedos but most men in uniform.

"I couldn't help but overhear." An older man in a clerical collar moved beside them. "The dress codes are less rigid today. A humble vicar was once expected to use finery suited for a bishop, but no more. I'm Vicar Duncan. What brings a charming young couple to this gathering?"

Marcie spoke before Malone could open his mouth, "An invitation from Lady Astor. We aren't crashing the party." For an instance Duncan was silent then began to snicker.

"I'm Dan Malone. I'm a Canadian reporter and this is my companion, Marcie Eaton."

"Ah," the Vicar nodded. "Nancy Astor enjoys colonials. Cliveden served as a hospital during the first war and has been offered to Canada as a hospital site again. Let's hope it's not as busy as the last time."

"What's Mrs. Astor like?" Marcie asked. "I know she's American, but I hear these stories about the Cliveden set and her influence. Do appeasers and fascists really hold secret meetings here?"

"Oh, nothing of the sort," the Vicar smiled, "Nancy enjoys hearing all opinions. Marvellous lady. American through and

42

through, a free spirit. She says what she thinks and...Excuse me. I must speak to this dear soul."

The Vicar reached for the gloved hand of an elderly woman. "Lady Evelyn. Nice to see you," he said. The response was a frosty nod. "This young couple is from Canada," the Vicar explained. "Mr. Malone and Miss Eaton."

"Related to the department store Eaton's?"

"No, Dan's from Canada. I'm actually English," Marcie told her. "My family lives near Birmingham."

"Pity!" She dismissed them. "Vicar, what do you hear of peace talks? I think Hitler can keep Eastern Europe. We wouldn't want it anyway. And, give up the African colonies we took in the last war. That should satisfy him. We've more in common with Germany than we admit."

The Vicar smiled and tried to lead the couple away, but Lady Evelyn grasped Marcie's arm. "Do dress properly another time, young lady. Appearance is so important."

"Oh, for heaven's sake," another woman closed in. "Don't mind her. The clothes are clean, and you wear them well. That's good enough. I'm Nancy Astor, delighted to meet you."

"A pleasure, ma'am," Marcie offered a small curtsy.

"That's not necessary. I'm glad you came. And Mr. Malone, I have yet to hear of the Canadian intentions for Cliveden?"

"Ottawa takes it's time making decisions."

"I doubt it's Ottawa, more likely Willie King can't make up his mind." She smiled. "We'll meet again, when decisions are made."

"Yes, ma'am. A pleasure ma'am."

"And bring the young lady when you come again."

"Fascinating, isn't she." The Vicar spoke quietly, "Who would have thought an American could conquer British society and become the first women in the British House of Commons. But there she is and larger than life."

"Her husband's money helps." An army officer laughed. "Good to see you, Vicar."

The Vicar smiled and the officer moved on. "Damned if I can remember his name but he's an excellent polo player."

"I'll reintroduce myself, Vicar," another uniformed man shook the Vicar's hand. "Harry Cranston."

"Harry," the Vicar smiled, "and what's this, wings on the uniform, an air commodore?"

"On no sir, a humble pilot."

"Seeing much action," the Vicar motioned Dan and Marcie closer.

"Coastal Command sees action, attacking German ships in the Channel but Bomber Command is in a leaflet war. The pamphlets we drop over Germany are supposed to destroy enemy morale but instead hurts ours. One pilot was reprimanded because the crew didn't cut the cord that bound the flyers. His superiors feared someone on the ground could be hurt."

"Pamphlets?" Malone asked. "Not bombs."

"Oh no. Not bombs. Nobody wants to upset the apple cart. Hitler might retaliate and we wouldn't want that. The Phoney War is one concept on which we all agree. The French talk of 'Drole de Guerre', an odd war and to Germans, it's 'Sitzkreig', the sitting war. Americans call it, 'the Bore War'."

"Harry, I like it this way," the Vicar patted his shoulder. "I did too many funeral services the last time."

"Excuse me. An urgent message for the Admiral." A young naval officer pushed through the reception area.

The chatter soon faded along with the colour of the Admiral's face. "I'm afraid, I must go."

"Bad news is it?"

"Extremely. The BBC will release a communique soon. A German sub penetrated Scapa Flow overnight."

"Scapa?" another guest spoke, "the home base of our fleet. I'll wager the Nazi was shot to pieces."

"Unfortunately, no. The sub escaped and the bastard sank the "*Royal Oak.*""

"Oh my God."

"Over 800 men and boys went down with her."

"Boys?" a guest asked.

"Young gentlemen in training for a career at sea. A few of them might be only 14 or 15. It's no Phoney War to those parents."

Montreal
October 25

Sandy Fleming continued the telephone diction.

"Political observers believe the energetic support of the Federal party helped ensure the surprise election victory for Quebec Liberals. The results are a vote of confidence in the Mackenzie King government."

She glanced again at the copy, "That's Period. Full stop. And thirty."

"Got it." The voice of Robert McLaren in Ottawa came through the scratchy telephone connection. "Sorry we had to send you off alone but a fine job. And, your byline is going on the story."

"Gosh...thanks." Sandy was pleased. "I'm going to get something to eat and a good strong drink before my train leaves."

"Bring us the bill," he laughed but, in the background, she heard another voice.

McLaren came back on the line. "Mister Willard says the company will reimburse for food and not alcohol. The man can be insufferable."

The phone call completed she sat thinking over the day. Quebec Liberals had easily won control of the National Assembly, but the popular vote suggested the conscription issue might not be dead.

"We could wait for the train together," a man's voice said.

The first instinct was a sharp rejection, but she immediately reconsidered. First, an army uniform caught her eye and second, the man who wore it. In his mid twenties, tall, muscular and sporting a thin moustache.

45

"My train leaves," she glanced at her watch, "in just over an hour." Minutes later they sat in a nearby tavern.

"I overheard the telephone conversation, so I know you are a reporter. I'm Michael Godbout. My commander would not like me talking to the press."

"Thanks for being brave." Sandy smiled. "I didn't want to be a lone female in a tavern. And, I'm not good identifying uniforms?"

"Then consider me, a humble soldier and proof of the inconsistencies in our culture. My regiment is from Eastern Quebec, which some people claim is peopled by English haters."

"You don't appear to be a firebrand."

"It takes all kinds, mademoiselle. As a soldier, I follow orders. I should have few opinions."

"But you obviously do. I'm trying to understand the election result."

"Ah, that would take more time than we have tonight."

"Tell me a little. Why did Quebec vote as it did?"

"Who knows? It might be that Ottawa Liberals poured in money and gave away bottles of good whisky. Or, the result may have been a message to Maurice Duplessis and the 'Union Nationale' that their time was up. Or, perhaps the local priests said to vote Liberal. In Quebec, the church is as powerful as the state."

"I thought the vote was about conscription."

"Not that alone. We fought conscription over twenty years ago. If the government wants men, it will take them."

"But the war…"

"Phoney war," he corrected her. "The talk of negotiations, if true, could lead to an armistice. If needed, men will come forward but without the chest thumping patriotism of English Canada. Quebec has no love of Empires: British, French or German."

"And what about democracy and what Hitler is doing?"

"Abstract concepts when a man is trying to put food on the table," he said.

"Is that an odd view?"

"I am an odd military man. I wanted a job. When I signed up, four years ago, I expected peace and a paycheck."

"And now?"

"I am about to ship out."

"Overseas?" she asked.

"Oh, I hope not. We may relieve a British unit in the Caribbean or in Newfoundland. The only certainty is that I'll see more of the world than a poor kid from Quebec might hope to."

"I hope you stay safe."

"I do too."

Chapter Three: The Phoney War

Near London
November 4

The ferry was late, the result of delays in boarding, a mix-up in communications with the British destroyer that provided protection and the rough water on the English Channel. The beep of a car horn drew Maria's attention to where Evers Chance waited by a parking area.

"Was the crossing frightful?" he asked.

"I've had worse." She eased into the car passenger seat. "I'm wondering what you have planned. The message was pure Chance, nothing in it would give away secrets."

He laughed before putting the car in gear. "My landlord has a spare room. We'll share the kitchen and facilities, but I'll be away a good part of the time. Have you made a decision?"

"I'm going to stay in France" she told him. "Everything suggests the Nazis must be stopped."

"I expected as much," he said. "And, I've arranged for self defence training and a few other things."

"I'll be busy," she said flippantly. "Maybe, I can learn about explosives and wipe out the German Headquarters?"

"Definitely not! The people I recruit, observe. The army can send men to make things go bang. My people are separate. But, there's always a risk."

"That warning has been repeated time and again in the past few months and I'm still here. The training? What's involved?"

"A few tricks to keep the body whole and a few lessons with a revolver."

"All the while maintaining feminine decorum?"

"By all means. That, and the ability to blend into a crowd and stay calm are important assets. A couple of weeks should cover the basics."

"So common place," she glanced his way. "Like now, a couple out for drive and underneath, deadly serious." She paused. "Does it get easier, with time?"

"It's a job. I find I have the necessary skills."

"Any time for friends?" she asked.

"Only a few."

"I found women's underthings in the apartment in Paris. Do they belong to a friend?"

"Hah. I'll take that up with the cleaner. Other people also use that address."

"Oh. That was evasive. Perhaps, I'm onto something."

He merely smiled and let the silence fight the sound from the car engine. In a few minutes she was asleep.

She woke an hour later as the car slowed.

"A small problem," he told her. "We're being followed."

Maria began to turn to the rear.

"No, don't look. It's a fellow I know and the local constable. I don't want them to meet you. Just play along."

He parked outside a small hotel, swung an arm around her and ran a hand through her hair. "Let's go, Beverley," he called as he opened the car door and froze in apparent surprise. "Martin Downey and Constable Wells. Constable, you should keep better company."

Al McGregor

"I needed local police to find you." Downey sounded angry. "We need a word."

"I'm busy," Chance replied. "Maybe later." He rounded the car and opened Maria's door. "Man's got the right to a good time."

"No! Now!"

Chance helped Maria from the car, bent to lightly kiss her lips and nuzzle her hair. "Keep your face turned away," he whispered before playfully slapping her rear.

"Now!" Downey repeated.

"Ah shit. Go book a room Bev. I'll be in directly." He whistled in appreciation as she walked to the hotel.

Downey edged nearer so the constable couldn't hear. "Do you have anyone in the Netherlands? The Germans who want to replace Hitler are anxious for a chat."

Chance shook his head. "No, I don't have Dutch associates and I'd be damned careful about meeting any German close to their territory. A Nazi is a Nazi."

"Thanks for that insight." Downey shrugged and returned to his car. "We can go...unless you have something, Constable?"

"I do. That woman. I don't want whores flaunting their wares in my town."

"Constable," Chance smiled and turned toward the hotel, "whatever happens will be based on pure affection."

"Can you tell me anything?" Maria asked a few minutes later.

"Someone in the foreign office thinks he can end the war," Chance answered. "Whether that's possible is another matter. I don't put much faith in it. I can't say more."

"Somehow, I expected that. On another matter it's been a long time since anyone whistled at me. And that kiss was gentler than I would have expected."

He was silent but for only a moment. "Was nice, wasn't it? And your ass was firmer than I expected."

Kingsmere, Quebec
November 12

A uniformed police officer checked identification before pointing to a winding path. "Stay on the trail. He's at the house."

"I'm nervous," Sandy said as a gate closed behind them.

"The Prime Minister doesn't bite," Robert McLaren smiled. Someone had swept a track through the leaves that had fallen on the driveway. Kingsmere, the Mackenzie King estate, was a sprawling acreage of trees and rocks less than an hour from Parliament Hill.

"King suggested I bring you. The article on the Quebec election caught his eye. I suggested Laurier House, but he prefers Kingsmere."

"Was this a family cottage?"

"He found the property years ago and in true King fashion, very cautiously, expanded. With almost five hundred acres, he doesn't have to worry about undesirable elements appearing on the doorstep.

"Do I look alright?" Sandy ran her fingers through her hair.

"Quiet," he urged as a warbling, off-key voice began to sing a hymn.

"Oh, for recording equipment," McLaren spoke softly before calling a greeting.

The reply came from a veranda where the Prime Minister abruptly ended his recital. "Hello, Robert. And, Miss Fleming. A pleasure to meet you." She fought the urge to laugh. Brown suspenders covered a stained work shirt and held his pants near chest level.

"Let me get a coat." He reached inside the door and plucked an old suit jacket from a hook before leading them on a tour. In the next few minutes he told of developing Kingsmere, of plans for future renovations, of friends who lived near by and how an attempt at farming was thwarted by thin top soil and the rocks of the Gatineau.

"And Miss Fleming? Your father was a Member of Parliament. It's a pity I never met him."

"He's been gone almost twenty years. My recollections are hazy. He wanted to work with veterans. That's what drew him to Winnipeg at the time of the general strike. Spanish flu killed him, and his death hit my mother hard. She died a few years later."

"Sad, very sad," King reached down to lift a branch that had fallen on the walkway and heaved it under a neighboring tree. Before she could say more, he pointed to large blocks of stone, embedded in a field. "The Ruins. I collected bits and pieces of Ottawa's past, foundation stones and ornaments. That bay window was rescued from the wrecker's hammer. I find them alluring."

From the corner of her eye she saw McLaren shrug.

"Step to the opening," King urged. "Look toward to the sky, as a homeowner might have when the window graced a house."

Behind King's back, McLaren rolled his eyes.

She stifled a giggle and tried to concentrate. Her eyes rose toward the sky and the wispy clouds. "When I was a child, I saw clouds as castles, with big towers and knights on horseback."

"What do you see today?" King prodded.

She took a deep breath and tried to ignore McLaren's grin. "To the right," she pointed, "an angel blowing a trumpet."

"Yes, I see it too," King was impressed. "Signs from the almighty appear daily but we often fail to grasp their significance."

Sandy leaned forward and placed her hands on the windowsill. "My mother said I had too much imagination."

"That's not a problem. A sensitive soul is critical in today's world. Not all young people are open to the unknown and unseen. Do you ever hear your father's voice?"

"I'm not sure I'd know it," she confessed. "I was very young when he died. My mother felt his presence. She always set an extra place at dinner."

"Families which suffered a loss during the first war felt that was a way to remember the departed. My family is on the other side and they guide me. We can speak of this again. But the afternoon is chilly. Let's go inside."

The house was warm, and a small fire crackled in the fireplace. King opened a door and a small terrier dashed into the room.

"Behave, Pat." King patted the dog's head. Pat sniffed the guests, rejected McLaren and settled at Sandy's feet. "Pat is a tried and true companion," King explained, "I don't know what I would do without him." Sandy bent to rub the dog's ears and stomach. "I'm forgetting my hospitality," their host apologized. "I can offer tea but have no alcohol in the house. And, I don't smoke. One of the few characteristics I share with Mr. Hitler."

"We're fine," McLaren spoke for them both, "but I did want to ask about the war. Everything will be off the record."

"As it must be," King settled into a chair near the fire. "At times I know little more than the papers."

"Oh, I doubt that," McLaren laughed. "Our previous conversations have been very enlightening. A Canadian Expeditionary Force, is it about to sail to England?"

"Amazing what a reporter hears," King smiled. "A small force will be dispatched. The men can train in England, no fighting, thank heavens. About twelve thousand will be going, sometime over the next few weeks."

"Will this force be the extent of our contribution?" McLaren asked.

"It will if I have my way. We must avoid heavy causalities. Great Britain will always want men, but Canada may not send them. Miss Fleming's work on the Quebec election shows the conscription issue is still alive. And, we have enough volunteers. We're scaling back recruitment. I hope for a peaceful settlement."

"And in the meantime?"

"Canada will fulfill her obligations. The British need air training facilities. We're a natural and a safe location. The rate of injury or deaths should be very limited. The British may try to stick us with the entire cost, but I promise you, we will not overspend."

On the drive back to Ottawa, Sandy was perplexed. "I really didn't know what to make of his conversation at the ruins. I wondered if I missed something and as we were leaving, he whispered we'd talk again. I'm used to men and 'come-ons'. It wasn't that."

McLaren chuckled. "Long ago, he was considered a ladies man. Today, his private life is…very private. He keeps a few long-time friends. Julia Grant, the former President's granddaughter came to visit earlier in the summer."

"But why would he want to talk to me?"

"Maybe he wants to hear what you think of the war effort?"

"We both know that's not it."

"If you begin to speak of Rex, as his friends do, I'll start to wonder."

"Rex…oh… like a king. I would have expected, Mac-as in Mackenzie."

"Or Willie?"

"Could he be a weird Willie?" Sandy wondered aloud. "What a strange little man."

Ottawa
November 13

Delivery of the radio equipment was repeatedly delayed, and construction of a new studio and control room took longer than expected. But finally, the Willard Agency was to join the broadcast world. "Not much to look at," Sandy said as she glanced into the studio to see only a microphone on a table and a single chair.

"It's all we need," Frank Willard explained. "We're not producing high end drama or recording choirs. If we have a guest, I'll bring an extra chair. My sister's boy, Casey, is wiring the control board. He's a natural with electronics and we do have to watch the costs. I thought the newspaper owners were cheap, but radio executives are worse. I practically gave the service away to win a few clients."

"I've got it," Casey called from under the control panel. "I had to make an extra hole for the cable. A few more minutes and we should be in business."

Sandy had seen enough and returned to her desk in the newsroom. The room was cold as Willard demanded lower heating costs.

"Mr. King misled us." McLaren rolled his chair across the space between them. "He said the army had enough men but that's not the whole story. They've run out of uniforms. No more men until that problem is resolved."

"Maybe, the men won't be needed. Peace could break out." Sandy shivered. "But I could sure use a heavy army coat." McLaren in a full suit didn't appear to notice the chill. Tomorrow, she decided, she would wear slacks and retire dresses for the season.

"Robert, come take a look," Willard beckoned from the control room door. Inside the room, McLaren found Willard and Casey on their knees. Their heads under the panel.

"Look at this," Willard whispered, "Casey cut too large a hole. Check the view." He pushed the youth aside to make space. The opening faced Sandy's desk. Her long bare legs were stretched out, toes wiggling in a vain attempt for warmth.

"Aren't they something," Willard giggled.

Before McLaren could reply Casey chimed in. "I've been watching her. She's wearing one of those filler bra's or her boobs are growing."

Sandy began to rub her legs to increase circulation, first a slow movement and then more rapidly. Willard was spellbound.

"Fer Christs sake," McLaren backed away, "Give the girl some dignity. Casey, plug that hole."

"Ah, come on. Uncle Frank enjoys the view."

"Plug the hole," he said. None of us are adolescents." He stormed away.

Willard reluctantly rose. "Do it Casey. McLaren can be a royal pain. One of these days he'll get his comeuppance. He acts as if everything was a matter of life and death."

London
November 20

A single shot and two more in quick succession.

"Squeeze gently. Don't jerk." The instructor rarely spoke and when he did the words came in a volley, "Steady the pistol. That's it. We're done."

"Thank you, Rupert. Perhaps we'll meet again."

"Doubtful ma'am," and with that he walked away.

Maria turned to Chance. "Who trained him?"

"Rupert? He learned on the street, well, maybe a bit in the army but mostly on the street."

"I've never heard gunfire on the streets of English towns."

"Didn't say English streets. He spent time in Asia." Chance smiled. "But forget him. He likes it that way."

"I never expected to take a course in weapons, or Morse code. When do I learn silent killing?"

"With luck, never! I'll fix dinner. You can freshen up."

An hour later Chance sat by the fireplace apparently lost in thought and didn't notice as she slipped onto the room.

"That doesn't happen often. I surprised you."

He came to his feet. "Only minutes to dinner. We're having lamb chops."

"Suits me." Maria's swept a lock of hair from her face. She wore a simple skirt and woolen sweater. "I'm glad to sit without fear of Rupert's rage."

Chance slipped back into the chair. "Sorry if we pushed you hard but facilities are strained. Later we'll have special schools but for now, one on one is best."

"I haven't had time to think. Has anything happened in the world?"

"We're still at war."

"With the Germans?"

"At least until they quit and go home."

She laughed, glad to finally relax.

Chance stirred the fire. "You don't have to go back to France. We could find something here."

"After all this work, this training? I thought we had agreed on my role."

"New trouble, I'm afraid. The Gestapo managed to pluck a couple of agents from under our noses at a place called Venlo on the Dutch border. The agents were well acquainted with people in Holland, so that entire network is compromised. It raises two issues. First is the danger."

"I've thought this through," Maria answered. "I want to go back. Besides, a diplomatic breakthrough could end things peacefully."

"Ah, that's the other issue. Venlo frightened our people. Secret talks will be difficult if not impossible. And, the Nazi security apparatus is on high alert. A bomb exploded at a beer hall in Munich, only minutes after Hitler left the building. An attempted assassination is another reason to ferret out any German opposition. In the last few months, everyone from prominent politicians, to businessmen and even the Pope have tried to find a peaceful solution. Nothing worked."

"Who knows about me?"

"No one knows much. The trainers don't know where you are going. I hinted at South America."

"Then, I'm not worried. I can get out if I have to."

"It may not be that simple."

"I'm going back." She crossed her arms. "It's settled."

Chance sighed, walked to the stove, opened the oven door, sniffed, and closed it again. "A few more minutes," he told her, moving across the room to retrieve a small paper bag. "I brought an American passport for you. If the Germans invade France and are successful, the American documents will ensure better treatment than would be expected for a British national. And, to my eye, America will be neutral for a long time."

"And where will you be?"

"You may see more of me than you expect. And, that Washington magazine will want more articles."

"All very well planned, almost a private war." Maria shook her head in amazement, "I should have expected it."

"I've always preferred to work alone. It avoids complications from relationships. What about you? Have there been no other loves but Robert? I mean, is there anyone else in Europe who knows you well and might suddenly appear?"

"I've had friends, grew close a couple of times, but it never felt right, so no."

"Those men were damn fools."

"That's generous," she laughed and again ran a hand through her hair. "I sometimes feared something would surface from my past. The work I did in Russia. The righteous might be shocked."

For an instance his mind flashed back. A young beauty recruited in exchange for escape from revolution. A fleeting glimpse of naked breasts fuelled the fantasies of the nobleman before a doctored drink cooled his passion. And while he slept, Maria rifled his files.

"Nothing to worry about," he assured her, "I was there. Everything was done for King and country."

Suddenly, he was aware of how close she was and almost by instinct his hand reached to stroke her cheek. He caught himself before he touched her.

New York City
January 1, 1940

The strains of Auld Lang Syne faded, and the voice of Guy Lombardo came through the radio. "A Happy New Year. The Royal Canadians wish you a happy 1940."

"Americans should be on American radio on New Year's Eve," Tim Fulton handed his coat to the hat check girl and waited for a ticket. "A pretty thing like you should be dancing."

"A girl has to make a living," she lightly tapped the cup where tips were collected, "I'll dance next year."

"I'm meeting a friend," he said, dropping a few coins in the cup. "A Mr. Schmidt?"

"The Green room, down the hall and turn right." Fulton followed the directions, showed his invitation and collected a glass of champagne from a passing waiter.

"A late arrival," Erich Schmidt smiled a welcome. "I thought it best to use my name for the room. An FBI informant or another low life might misunderstand."

Fulton recognized several of the other guests.

"We are among friends," Schmidt assured him. "And, our people are alike, in many ways. Americans prefer an orderly society and the right sort of people." He motioned to a black waiter carrying a plate of appetizers. "The only coloured are kitchen staff and the club will not admit Jews."

Fulton had no time for small talk. "Is there news from overseas?"

"Germany offered a peace plan but the French and British do not appear ready for negotiation. The atmosphere has been poisoned by absurd rumors of opposition to the Fuhrer. Every officer swears personal loyalty to Adolf Hitler. And an oath is a matter of honor."

"I'm afraid America is more concerned with cash than honor," Fulton replied. "The British and French are placing orders for weapons. Factory owners smell money. And, there are what are called...interventionists. They oppose anything with a hint of Fascism and are well organized."

"Is it all about money? What of the historic ties with Britain?"

"Overrated. Most Americans don't like British. We were suckered into the first war and Brits always manage to offend us. Remember the abdication crisis. That was a snub. An American girl, Wallis Simpson, wasn't good enough for English society. And the rightful King gave up the throne to be with her."

Schmidt nodded. "It helps to speak to someone who truly understands America."

Al McGregor

"I'm glad to help," Fulton smiled, "and let me offer a bit of advice. Fight the British and French, if you must, but avoid anything that attracts American attention. The President's term is almost over. Keep a low profile for a few months."

"We forget democracies have these tedious elections. The ambassador to London, Joe Kennedy, would like to be President? We could work with him."

"He's more important where he is. The British Prime Minister Chamberlain needs help to keep the warmongers in check."

Schmidt smiled. "No matter; 1940 will show that Germany is unstoppable."

Ottawa
January 20

The waiter smiled as he navigated the tables. The middle-aged man seated with the attractive young woman could be a large tipper, since men tried to impress younger companions. The girl was pretty, brown hair cut short, well dressed, a shapely figure, but her eyes darted furtively around the room. "A menu?" he asked politely.

"No, not yet." The woman answered for them, "Maybe later." Sandy Fleming toyed with the cutlery as the waiter left. "I need to talk to someone, and it couldn't be at the office because Willard hovers over me. I can handle him, but I have another delicate issue."

"I'm all ears." Robert McLaren told her.

"I had a strange invitation the other night," she began. "Mr. King remembered our visit. He thinks I have an interest in spirits, in spirituality. My school friends played with a Ouija board but that's as far as we went. Mr. King goes much farther."

She glanced around the room before she continued.

"He invited me to dinner at Laurier House. He has a portrait of his late mother with special lighting and candles, as if she were a deity, a display suitable for a saint. The devoted son told

60

me all about her, actually kissed the portrait and took me to another room where he praised his grandfather."

"The rebel," McLaren nodded, "William Lyon Mackenzie, who led the revolution of 1837."

"He has a poster offering a reward for his grandfather's capture."

"He's devoted to the ancestors. Family had a big influence on his life."

"It was strange, and I understand family pride but there's more. Two other women arrived. One was a lady from Kingston who claims to communicate with those who have passed on. The other was a friend of Mr. King. Both of them knew what was going to happen."

"This is getting interesting. Let's hold off on food."

"We put our hands flat on a table and were supposed to concentrate and a weird tapping sound came from under the table. It wasn't just one tap for yes or two for no. It was like a telegrapher working his key, a series of thumps. The Kingston lady thought Mr. King's mother was trying to reach us."

"Are you ready to order?" The waiter had returned.

"No. We'll call when we are ready." Her reply was curt, and she waited to be certain he was gone.

"King paid rapt attention," she began again. "Another messenger from the other side warned him to be strong and that attempts would be made to destroy his career."

"Had you been to a séance before?"

"Definitely not and I'd have kept this to myself but a couple of days later the Ontario Premier came out against the Prime Minister for not doing enough in the war. Isn't that an attempt to destroy him, at least politically?"

"Did she specifically name Mitch Hepburn."

"No, but it was a strange coincidence."

McLaren tried to make sense of it all. "This clairvoyant, this spiritualist, predicted someone as going to undermine King. All kinds of men oppose him. The war effort is under constant scrutiny. One prediction is not enough to get excited about."

Al McGregor

"I know, I know but I had to tell someone. And something else. She said King would lose a valuable advisor. She hinted a death was imminent. That upset him. He stopped the session right there."

"Will you be invited back?"

"I don't know. It was so strange."

"People dabble with spirits as a form of entertainment, but I never put faith in it. Strange stories emerged in the Great War, dead soldiers returning and other unexplained phenomena. Mysticism, spiritualism, people are drawn to the hope of communication with those who have passed over. I've heard of table rapping or sometimes a spirit takes over and speaks through a medium, a person who communes with the other side."

"He made us promise to treat everything as confidential. That promise was meant for me and I've broken my word."

"Don't worry. The secret is safe."

"It feels silly but scary, too."

Ottawa
February 7

"King may pull this off," Frank Willard laughed as he flipped through the newspaper. "His snap Federal election call caught the opposition by surprise. Another Liberal, Mitch Hepburn says the government isn't doing enough for the war effort, so King says let the people decide. Conservatives counter with a call for a national government, a coalition which raises bad memories of the first war and of conscription. I think, the Tories have already lost."

"The election is weeks away," Sandy reminded him. "Everyone thought Duplessis would win in Quebec and that was wrong."

"Don't be naïve." Willard snorted and tossed the newspaper aside. "King wouldn't call an election if he didn't expect to win. The only thing that could save the Tories is a massive German attack, and with the frightful European weather, that's unlikely."

"It's not fair to write off the opposition? The Conservative leader, Robert Manion may surprise us."

"Not a hope. Manion will have trouble hanging onto his own seat down in London, Ontario. King will win a large majority."

A ringing telephone interrupted the conversation and Sandy answered. In a few seconds, she moved to a typewriter and rolled in a sheet of paper. "It's Robert, something urgent," and began to repeat his dictation.

"Canada's Governor General Lord Tweedsmuir has been rushed to hospital. His condition is believed serious. Lord Tweedsmuir has close ties to the highest levels of the British government."

Willard tore the sheet from the typewriter and began to send the dispatch through the system while Sandy stayed on the phone.

"Yes," he heard her say, "full biography on file under the name John Buchan. Not for publication, condition critical."

Suddenly her face turned white and her voice was strained, "And you will file on his 'Advisory' role to the Prime Minister."

McLaren had more to say and when she replied her voice quavered, "Yes, I know. I thought of the spirits too."

Ottawa
February 14

"The military guard of honor begins the slow procession from Saint Andrew's Church as Ottawa bids farewell to Governor General Tweedsmuir."

The sound of the radio broadcast abruptly faded. "Damn," Frank Willard hissed. Sandy reached for the volume but before she could touch it, the voice of Robert McLaren returned.

"Thousands of people have lined Wellington street to watch the cortege pass," he said. "A special train will carry the remains to Montreal for cremation before the ashes are returned to England. This is Robert McLaren reporting for the Willard Radio Division."

"Cut it." Frank Willard made a slashing gesture across his neck.

The sound engineer nodded and twisted a dial before he spoke, "I'll collect the gear from the street and finish in the office later."

"Don't miss anything. That equipment is worth a lot of money." Willard stood and scratched his stomach. "People tell me radio is the future, but radio will never replace the newspaper."

"I thought the broadcast was quite good," Sandy said. "Almost like being there."

"I found it boring. I'm not sure McLaren has a voice for radio. Like silent film stars, he's making a difficult transition to talkies."

"The Canadian Broadcasting Unit had all kinds of people working on their program. Robert was alone and don't forget his interviews with the doctors, as Tweedsmuir was failing."

"I prefer a deep, mellow voice. Don't get me wrong. He wrote a great piece on Tweedsmuir, his novels and the book made into a movie, the Twenty-Six steps…"

"Thirty-Nine," Sandy corrected him, but Willard rambled on.

"Tweedsmuir had connections to the rich and powerful and had private intelligence meetings with President Roosevelt. Who knows what secrets he took to the grave?"

"Mr. Willard?" The engineer dressed in overcoat and boots, waved a sheet of paper. "I'll leave my invoice. Prompt payment would be appreciated."

"Ninety days, my friend. Ninety days for all my bills." Willard abruptly turned his back and waited for office door to close.

Sandy sorted the afternoon mail until she heard Willard approach and felt his hand on her shoulder.

"How about something special for Valentine's day?" He was much too close. The smell of stale cigar smoke was overpowering, and his fingers played with her collar.

An Angry Sky

"Not a good idea. I'm coming down with a cold. I better leave early."

The fingers fell away as he stepped back.

"I don't pay for sick time. I'll deduct it from your pay."

London
March 4

Dan Malone crushed the remains of a cigarette and pulled another from the pack, but before he could strike a match, a hand tapped his shoulder.

"Step into the doorway to light that." He faced an elderly air-raid warden. "German pilots have good eyes. In the blackout the flame looks like a bon fire."

He shone a light on Malone's face. "Not from around here, are you?"

"The German's can see that light too." Malone blinked and raised his hand to shade his eyes.

"Needed a good look." The flashlight blinked out. "Not many civilians on the street this time of night."

"I'm meeting my girlfriend," Malone turned into the doorway and struck the match. "She's on the tube."

"The protective services can't be too careful. Let's see identification." Before Malone could reach for his wallet, Marcie emerged from the underground station.

"That's her. I don't like her on the streets alone. As you say, we can't be too careful."

"I wouldn't be concerned in this area, but other parts of London are not as safe. Germans aren't the only threat in the blackout."

"Oh Dan, have you been arrested?" Marcie laughed. "I can take over now, sir." She flashed a smile and began to guide Malone down the street.

"Wait. Identification?"

After a cursory examination, the documents were returned.

"Canadian," the warden observed. "Learn how we do things in this country. Don't go flouting authority."

65

Al McGregor

"I'll see he minds," Marcie smiled again, and the English accent reassured him.

"On your way, then," he slipped the light into his belt and moved off.

"Good Lord," Malone whispered, "The British Gestapo."

"Oh, never mind," she took his arm, "I'm asked for papers all the time." Her lithe figure and blonde hair attracted attention in the blackout or in sunshine.

"Did you have an interesting day?" he asked.

"A day like any other. I smiled. I giggled and collected a few generous tips."

"With the age of the men at that club, there may have been heart palpitations. Be careful. Don't kill the clientele."

"Oh, don't I know it. Old General Dalton gave me a tip for prompt service. I think he fancies me."

"The man must be ninety."

"But very active and well connected. He's convinced peace talks are underway. The old guard would, however, prefer a nice little battle before the diplomats bring the war to an end."

"Stop!" Malone grabbed her as a car sped by on a cross street. "The fool is driving too fast. That light from the shielded headlights is next to useless."

"Come on," she stepped off the curb without another glance and marched through the intersection. "That's the way it's done. And, if you are hit, hope for a Bentley or a Rolls. Smaller-car owners may not have the wherewithal to settle an accident claim."

The busy streets of a few months earlier were strangely quiet. Popular clubs had initially been closed by government order and while the restrictions were lifted fewer people spent a night out. Cynic's claimed more people had been injured by accidents in the blackout than in war time action.

"And what did you do today?" She brushed against him.

"The agency is pre-occupied with the Canadian election. Another item on training for the Canadian troops didn't excite them. But…I may be going away for awhile."

66

He felt her miss a step.

"Go on." In the dim light he could see only the silhouette of her face.

"An excursion to see the forces in France. I'll be writing feature stories, less dangerous than strolling in the blackout."

She walked faster.

"Marcie," he trotted to catch up. "I've got to do something. If I'm not working as a reporter, I could be in the service."

"Then go to France. I prefer a reporter to a soldier."

"The trip would be short. With all the speculation on peace talks, I may meet the British Expeditionary Force coming home."

In the distance, Big Ben began to strike the hour. She took his arm and for an instant reminded him of a child reciting a nursery rhyme.

"War. War. War. The war is a bloody bore.

And, please God, keep it that way."

Ottawa
March 28

"More evidence of a Phoney War. The Prime Minister is going on vacation." Frank Willard laughed and cleared the clutter from his desk.

"King will stop for a meeting in Washington during his trip south," McLaren said. "But there's no sense of urgency. He has a big election victory, a clear majority. Imagine what he can accomplish if he doesn't fritter away the opportunity."

"I'd bet on frittering," Willard laughed again. "But the conscription question is resolved, for the time being. Quebec gave King the seats he wanted."

"We'll see a big push on the Commonwealth Air Training Program now," McLaren predicted. "Setting up over a hundred bases and air strips will take time and money."

"But they may not be needed," Willard glanced at another file and dumped the contents. "The British appeasers are hinting of negotiations."

"Chamberlain is the appeaser in chief," McLaren agreed, "and maybe he's on the right track. With a breakthrough in talks, no one would have to resort to force. Everyone remembers the carnage in the last war. Although with the size of the French army and the British Expeditionary Force, one might expect the combined force could simply march and take Berlin."

"So, what will we concentrate on in the next few weeks?" Willard had found a box of toothpicks amongst the papers and began to work on his teeth."

"The air training programs. Many of the bases are in Ontario and easy to reach. Malone is going to France. If he can track down a few Canadians in the Royal Air Force, we could do a series on air power."

Le Havre
April 12

A newborn wobbled to its feet. Maria tiptoed forward, guided it to the cow's udder and stepped back reassured as the calf began to nurse.

"I never would have believed this," the voice of Evers Chance startled her. "A mistress of the barnyard."

"What a surprise." She ran to throw her arms around him. "I am so glad to see you."

"And you are as striking as ever."

"Flattery works," she laughed. "My farm work is done. Can you stay long?"

"Only a short stop. I've business in Paris."

Inside the house, she kicked off her boots and lead him to a coach by a roaring fire. "That calf is the third this year and I have twice as many chickens as last fall. Rene, the farmer up the road, predicts a growing demand for meat with the German border closed."

Chance smiled. "I never saw you as a war profiteer."

"That's a stretch but I have the time and he has the expertise. His youngest son is fourteen and I pay for his help. The other

68

son has been conscripted for the French Navy, on a battle cruiser, I think... *Bretagne?"*

"One of the mainstays of their fleet but other's pay more attention to naval affairs."

"I heard the radio reports this morning. The Nazis are pressing Denmark and threatening Norway."

"Again, my associates have a better feel for the northern climes. I have trouble keeping up with Western Europe."

"Don't play dumb," she said. "Are we heading for a shooting war or an armistice?"

"I'd be rich if I had a dollar for every peace rumor. Unfortunately, the peace feelers have been much less than productive."

"Then why hasn't the fighting started?"

"The Nazis need to re-equip while the British and French, after years of neglect need to build their armies. Still, each morning I expect to hear the Germans are advancing across Belgium or France. I would feel better if you were in England or North America."

"No. We've settled that. I'd have nothing to do in England. In North America I'd be knitting socks. The odd tidbits of information I pass on may be useful and I feel part of the war effort."

"If Europe explodes," his voice was resigned, "the situation will quickly become confused...untenable."

"Don't worry. Maybe later, I'll change my mind. It has happened." She laughed. "Not often, but it has happened."

He studied her face, trying to memorize all that he saw. "I'll make arrangements for supplies. I'll see you are well prepared."

Berlin
April 24

A line of trucks snaked toward the army camp. A lone staff car threaded through the traffic, the blaring horn, a signal of the apparent importance of the passenger. "Heil Hitler!" an orderly barked as the Colonel arrived at the headquarters. "A special delivery package has come, perhaps details of our next objective?"

Karl Munster offered a cold stare before he spoke. "At the proper time we will learn our assignment, Corporal, until then, we continue with the routine. See if my new revolver has arrived."

Jurgen Heinzman clicked his heels. He had been assigned to Munster only a week earlier and was trying to understand this new master. The Colonel lived by rules and regulations and was said to have been ruthless in the Polish campaign.

Fifteen minutes passed before Heinzman, revolver in hand, returned. The Colonel sat rigid. The package was open. On the desk was a single sheet of paper covered by a thin layer of dust. "Not orders, Corporal, a personal matter." Heinzman presented the new luger. Munster hefted the weapon before gently stroking the barrel. Several minutes passed before he remembered the corporal. "Sit." He waited impatiently as Heinzman brought a chair. "I have a suspicion that the men have the wrong impression of me. What do they say?"

"Uh…" the corporal stammered, thinking frantically of a reply. "…Uh…that the Colonel was very brave and completed the Polish campaign with…uh…with rigid discipline, and uh…they say he is devoted to the Reich."

"But there is more?"

"They wonder why you are ignored by other officers. Is it something you did, or do you prefer it that way?"

"Corporal. I will tell you. Share it with the men. I will need their complete confidence for what is ahead."

"Yes, Herr Colonel."

"I have a stain on my record, not the army or party record, a personal problem. My wife lied. She claimed to be pure Aryan, but her grandmother was part Jewish. Of course, I immediately divorced her. She was sent to a camp for re-education, but Elise was head strong. To make a long story short, she died."

The corporal waited in silence.

"The envelope—contains her ashes. And, as the Reich requires, I will pay the cost of cremation. Assure the men, nothing will keep me from performing my duty."

Munster lifted the envelope and spoke quietly. "By the main gate is a rose bush. Spread the ashes there."

"Yes, Herr Colonel."

"And when that is done, I need maps. We must become familiar with the French border regions."

Chapter Four: The Battle of France

France
May 9

The car lurched and dropped into another of the potholes that dotted the track. Dan Malone rubbed his shoulder, bruised from an earlier jolt. Matthew Barret, another reporter, was shaken from his sleep. "If we go much further, we'll need reservations in Berlin."

"Not long now," the press liaison officer, Richard Ingram, said, glancing at his map before retrieving a flask from the glove box. "A quick nip?"

Barret willingly accepted the invitation.

Malone instead studied the countryside. A few houses and barns, the occasional farmer working fields for spring planting, a pastoral view perfect for a travel brochure but not the copy he needed. Two weeks in France produced a handful of dispatches: a report on the massive Maginot Line, where French soldiers stationed deep underground stood ready to repulse any attack; a feature on a French field hospital with no patients; a tour of Paris that could have been filed in 1938; and a series of interviews with British officers, which were all routine but mercilessly hacked by the censor.

"I say, Barret," Ingram squirmed around to face him, "Ration the liquor."

Barret ran the back of his hand across his lips and reluctantly surrendered the flask. "Take it," he laughed. "I've had enough to drink in the last few weeks. Every mess is well supplied. Even the Duke of Windsor was impressed."

"Met the former King, did you?" Ingram was curious, "I heard he was in France."

"He has one of those quasi-official positions, but no one knows what he does. I didn't see him. My information came second hand. He was usually surrounded by snotty upper-crust types."

"Now, I can't have that kind of talk," Ingram snorted. "Those are officers of His Majesty's forces."

"Oh, forgive me. I wouldn't want to offend them."

"Any news on the Duke's 'paramour', Wallis Simpson?" Malone tried to keep a straight face.

"Now again," Ingram took a deep breath, "That is no way to speak of a member of the Royal family."

"He's ex-Royal family." Barret offered more bait, "The scuttlebutt says the King and Queen want nothing to do with him."

"I don't agree with scurrilous gossip. End it. Right now."

Barret smiled. "I gather the Duke doesn't like the way the war is being run and said there would be no war if he was on the throne. It reinforces the rumors he's pro-German or is willing to make a deal with the devil."

"That is quite enough." Ingram turned to stare straight ahead, "I'll have no more of this kind of talk."

"What are you filing, Malone?" Barrett winked. "Any scurrilous rumors?"

"No, nothing to stir controversy. I was near the Belgium border watching the training for the Expeditionary Force. A few of the poor buggers spent a lovely spring afternoon marching back and forth for the benefit of movie cameras."

"Rather hum-drum," Barret concluded.

"I did have a poignant moment in Flanders. A pioneer brigade was digging a trench and unearthed, human bones, skulls, that sort of thing, remains from the Great War."

Ingram spun to face them.

"A standing order states on discovery of remains the Commonwealth War Graves Commission is summoned."

"Someone should tell the pioneers. They chucked the bones into another hole and kept digging."

"I say that should go in a report." Ingram was aghast. "I want the name of that unit and…."

"We're here," the driver interrupted. "That's the airfield on the right."

The grass covered runway was neatly arranged with planes on either side. A small hangar appeared unused and beside the building a group of men played soccer.

"Another infraction," Ingram sighed. "No sentry on duty."

"But that's an antique on the right," Barret called, "a vintage Renault tank from about 1917."

"Surplus," Ingram told them. "The French use them for security or as anti-aircraft guns."

"The bang might scare the birds," Barrett predicted. "I doubt it would damage an enemy plane."

"I've about had all I can take, Barrett. Clap that mouth shut. Driver! Take us to the Château."

The Château, the billet for the pilots, had seen better days. The paint was faded, and the steps sagged as the men crossed a veranda. A man dressed in a turtleneck sweater and cotton pants, met them at the door. "I'm getting more press coverage than the Air Marshall. I'm squadron leader, Lessing."

"A couple of fresh correspondents," Ingram waved the reporters forward, "Barret is from Birmingham and Malone's a Canadian."

Lessing smiled a greeting and motioned to the soccer players. "We're the front line but everything is quiet. I encourage sports to beat the boredom. It's better than having the men sitting around grousing about one thing or another."

An Angry Sky

"The planes along the runway," Barret asked, "ready for a speedy scramble?"

"Yes and no. A bad guy doesn't have to throw a grenade or shoot from a distance. A touch of sugar in the gas tank can do as much damage. It's easier to guard planes when they're close together."

"Are there any Canadians in this unit?" Malone was hoping for something to make the trip worthwhile.

"One, but he's in the infirmary."

"A flying accident?"

"No, too much time in the mess and a nasty fall. I don't think we'll discuss it."

"I guess not..." Malone began before the sound of an approaching plane caught his attention. The small single engine aircraft grew from a distant speck and circled the field before landing.

"How is the Lysander?" Lessing called as the men approached the aircraft.

"A nice ride but slow," the pilot answered. "I wouldn't want to tangle with a Messerschmitt. We did a reconnaissance into Germany before we turned back."

"Didn't cause any flap, did you? We don't want to start something by accident."

"No, didn't see any German planes but Jimmy thinks he saw trucks."

"Oh yes, Jimmy, the photographer."

Lessing turned to the passenger and grimaced. "Do up those uniform buttons. Proper appearance is important."

"Yes sir."

Lessing waited as buttons were fastened. "Now. This truck?"

"More than one, sir, a convoy and maybe, tanks. I'll know better when the film is developed."

"The flight was over the Ardennes forest," Lessing reminded them. "Intelligence says motorized units can't navigate that ground, too many trees, too many obstructions and

75

the roads aren't worth a damn. I think imagination got the best of you?"

"No. Something was there. If I could fly to HQ I could have the photo's developed and prove it."

"A special trip?" Lessing frowned. "Out of the question. Photo's can go up tomorrow morning. For now, help the pilot with the ground checks."

"Jimmy Russel is new," Lessing explained as they returned to the Château. "We've been assured, time and again, that the Germans can't attack through the Ardennes."

"A moment, squadron leader?" a man in a white apron called.

"Oh, what now cookie?"

"The owner is up in arms. The men have been snubbing cigarettes in the potted plants. Lady Martine demands immediate compensation and reminds us she is friend of Marshall Petain."

"Petain? Hell! He retired years ago but never mind I'll have a chat. I don't want any problems."

"We've seen enough," Ingram interrupted. "I'll show the reporters where to bunk. We'll leave at midday tomorrow."

Lessing nodded, "I'll delay the dawn patrol so they can snap a few pictures. Photography gives better results in full day light."

London
May 9

Evers Chance stepped from the car and glanced at the clear blue sky before tossing the umbrella onto the rear seat. Ideal weather was likely for Whitsun, the spring holiday. War or no war, a holiday would be marked. He walked along the street and sat on a bench beside Martin Downey.

"The Germans will attack within hours."

"Thank you, Cassandra," Downey snorted, "invasion has been predicted every month this year."

"Not by my people."

"Hitler does have to finish with Norway and Denmark."

76

"What's to finish. He took Denmark in hours and the British action in Norway was a fiasco."

"Well, yes...the Norwegian action has...uh, upset...the government." Downey sounded embarrassed. "Oh, I'll be frank. Chamberlain's goose is cooked. His own party turned against him. Opponents are using the words of Cromwell, 'Depart, in the name of God, go'."

"Well delivered, Martin. Have you considered a stage career?"

"I'm don't have time to banter." Downey rose to leave but Chance spoke softly, his voice almost lost in the hum of traffic. "Invasion is imminent. German call ups, leaves cancelled and more troops to the borders. A major advance will come through the Ardennes. They'll bypass the Maginot Line."

"That forest is impassable. I don't believe it."

"Have my reports been inaccurate?"

"No, but we need to know where they come from."

"Why? Is it to bring the new university men in MI6 up to speed, men barely out of short pants? Appeasers have worked them over as have die hard Tories, Socialists and, I'll bet, communist agents. They're so confused they don't know what to think. I protect my people with total secrecy. And, demand a free hand."

"Oh, have it your way. There are more important things on the agenda. Chamberlain is stepping down. He'll meet the King today."

"And the new Prime Minister will be ...?"

"Lord Halifax is the natural choice."

"That's not change! Halifax is a Chamberlain crony. New man, same policies. Why not Churchill? He's been foaming at the mouth since the '30s."

"Churchill?" Downey was aghast. "He was behind the Norway fiasco. He's unstable, a troublemaker. He drinks too much. It won't be him."

"Hmm...I'll try to follow the news," Chance said. "I'm off to the continent."

Al McGregor

"Good lord, you spend a lot of time in France. Is there a French damsel hidden somewhere?"

"My personal life is off limits Martin, another rule that won't change."

Northeast France
May 10

In the dream he was home, a summer morning and the buzzing of a persistent fly. Dan Malone twisted on the cot and pulled the blanket over his head before remembering where he was: the reporter's tour, the Royal Air Force field and based on a throbbing headache, a long night in the mess. He shook his head, but the buzz grew louder. Somewhere in the distance, were shouts and a muted explosion. Seconds later, another blast, much closer, shattered the window and sent glass across the room.

"Air raid!" The shout came with the sound of running feet. He gingerly rose to look through what was left of the window. A fighter parked on the edge of the grass strip burned and the flames reached toward other aircraft. A shadow passed the window and another explosion added to the carnage.

"Get to the shelter!" The warning was almost lost in the shrill scream of a siren. The Château shook, releasing clouds of dust and plaster.

An excited airman identified the attackers. "That's a German dive bomber. A Stucka!"

London
May 10

His shirts were folded to fit neatly in the luggage, while a British officer's uniform, hung in the garment bag. He tucked away army identification before glancing at the clock. The Channel ferry would leave in two hours. The telephone rang as he reached for his civilian jacket.

"Chance?" the caller asked.

He recognized the excited voice of Martin Downey.

"Who else would answer my telephone?"

"Ah good," Downey was relieved.

"What is it, Martin. I don't have time to chat."

"The balloon has gone up."

"Oh, for Christ sake, speak English. It's too early for rubbish."

"The Nazis are moving, crossed the Belgium and Dutch borders before dawn and hit forward bases in France."

"And are we surprised?" Chance asked and slumped into a chair. From the window he noted normal activity on the streets below. Londoners were blissfully unaware of the action across the Channel.

"The first army communique's will, no doubt, tell of the repulse of enemy forces," Downey assured him. "The British Expeditionary Force and the French will move into Belgium as planned and stop the Germans in their tracks."

"And, the war will be over by lunchtime?"

"Don't be so cynical. The Belgium forts will hold. Eban-Emael is a massive new fortress."

Chance sighed loudly. "German contractors helped build the fort. Do you suppose the blueprints reached Berlin?"

The telephone line went silent and it was a full ten seconds before Downey replied. "I didn't know that."

"Shit happens," Chance stood and stretched. "What did you want Martin? I have to go."

"Anything you have, more along the lines of that Belgium tidbit."

"It was in my report a few weeks ago. The university men should learn to read."

"If that's the case, I'm sorry we missed it. Could we have missed anything else?"

"The Ardennes Forest."

"Uh," Downey rustled through papers, "a few dive bomb attacks. Can they really break through?"

"I'm certain."

Downey sounded flustered. "Things are a bit hairy. Chamberlain was to resign but with the attack may hold off, the need for continuity…"

"He's lost the confidence of the House and his party. He might as well go. Let Halifax take a crack."

"Uh, a little surprise there. Halifax feels the new leader should be from the House of Commons and he's in the Lords. He's turned the job down."

"Now there is a surprise."

"Yes. Chamberlain wanted Halifax. King George wanted Halifax. But Churchill gets the nod."

"You made my day,"

"Don't be too happy. Churchill is a mere caretaker. He doesn't have wide support. He can't last."

"I have to go."

"Wait, we'll need anything you find. Can you take a radio?"

"Martin, the Germans will be eavesdropping on every wireless transmission. I'll contact you from the embassy in Paris."

France
May 10

The second wave of German dive bombers destroyed what little remained of the border post. The Château was in flames, the neat rows of planes charred to metal skeletons while amid the wreckage men who escaped serious injury looked for the less fortunate.

"A bloody mess," Richard Ingram surveyed the carnage. "The flight crews are in shock, the ones that aren't dead or dying. Squadron leader Lessing was killed along with the second in command, so decisions fall to a young flight lieutenant."

"How many other bases were hit?" Dan Malone asked.

"We don't know. The communication shack was destroyed and nothing's left of the radios in the planes."

"Our car is intact," Malone said, pointing to the vehicle in the shelter of a tree line. "We can carry the word."

"I'll come," said Jimmy Russel, the photo observer on the previous day's flight had been listening. "I saved my film. If those were tanks, they'll be several hours away. There may be time to stop them."

"Find Barret and we'll go." Ingram decided and cast a nervous look at the sky. "Those bastards will be back."

"Barret won't be coming," Malone tried to sound calm. "The first attack, a piece of glass…a foot-long shard…into the forehead. He never knew what hit him."

"Ah, God," Ingram blanched. "Can you drive? The driver bought it too. We should go before the air force commandeers the car."

An hour later Ingram studied his map. "How far to the main road?" Malone asked.

"Soon, left at the next…and what's this?" A crossroad was filled by people on foot, in cars and battered trucks, on carts and horses. "Boche!" A man shouted and pointed down the road, "Boche! Chars d'assaut!"

"Malone. You speak French. What's he saying," Ingram demanded.

"Germans," Malone edged into the traffic. "German tanks!"

Ottawa
May 13

"And when the casserole is cooked, let cool and season to taste. That's this week's edition of news for women. I'm Sandra Fleming."

Through the studio glass, Sandy saw Frank Willard hold a finger to his lips as he fidgeted over the recording controls.

"Got it," he called. "I'll play back."

Sandy strained to hear her voice as the recording began. "A little low isn't it?"

"The stations will adjust the volume," Willard's voice boomed through the speaker. "This equipment isn't hard to learn. I knew we didn't need to pay for a technician. And 'Sandra' works well, a nice classy ring."

Al McGregor

"The recording sounds, hollow."

"Don't worry. The stations can correct it."

"And we're going to do this once of a week?" she asked.

"That's right, to reach a female audience. Maybe next week something on knitting."

"Women don't just cook and knit," she snapped but realized he had shut off her microphone. Moments later, he joined her in the main office.

"Shouldn't we be filing important news?" she asked. "The German invasion should trump a casserole."

"I'll put out something for the afternoon editions and when our man in France surfaces, we'll have a first-person report." Willard began to clean his fingernails.

"No word from Malone?" She studied her script to avoid his digital display.

"He'll turn up. I'm more concerned about getting this women's feature off the ground. Station owners don't want controversial material, rather something the little lady can absorb as she scrubs the floor. Remember that when writing the scripts. The advertisers won't buy airtime if women are anxious."

"Women do care what's happening. We're not all ditzy dames."

"Hah. Like that, ditzy dames." Willard turned his attention to the nails on his other hand.

"I'll go over to the Hill," Sandy announced. "Maybe there's something new."

"We don't need much," he said. "The latest military communique says the German drive is faltering. The war will be over in a few days."

St. Thomas, Ontario
May 13

The truck driver leaned on his horn until a weary provost guard stepped from his hut. "Lay off the noise."

"We're not all in the army," the driver shouted. "We don't get paid whether we work or not."

The guard glanced at the licence plate and checked his list, "This shipment was expected hours ago."

"Jesus, man. The damn thing just crashed last night."

The guard swung on the running board and lifted the tarp. Only the tail section of a small plane was undamaged. The cockpit was mangled and, wedged along the side, was a section of wing.

"Ok. Building H. Someone will show you where to dump it."

"Oh, thank you, General," the driver spewed sarcasm. "My faith in the air force is restored."

Robert McLaren smiled as gears ground and the truck lurched forward. He had been watching from the street and now approached the guard. "Nice to see the air force and the civilians getting along so well. I'm a reporter. I'm supposed to meet a Sergeant Foster for a tour. This is Number One Technical Training school?"

"Yes, but you'll wait like everybody else."

A full forty-five minutes passed before Foster appeared. "We've one of the few training schools up and running," he explained. "Mitch decided when the war started that training schools were more important than psychiatric hospitals, so he turned this complex over to the military."

"Mitch?" McLaren was taken aback and asked, "Are you a friend of the Ontario Premier?"

"Oh, all the local people know him. His farm is up the road. When the war broke out, someone had to light a fire under Ottawa's ass and Mitch had the matches. He wanted guards on important sites, the power plants and the Welland Canal and after his needling, we got action."

"I don't recall evidence of sabotage."

"A lot of foreigners are in this country. Good people, most of them, but what about their true feelings. Foreigners are a perfect fifth column."

"I don't think there's any evidence of that."

"We have to be on guard, and I don't like your tone. We can end this tour and in a hurry."

"No, no. I want to see the facility. The men are trained for engine repair?"

"Mechanics, metal bangers, fellows that pound metal back in place; airframe people who can fix the skeleton of a plane, or fabric specialists. Today's planes are rugged, but a few are fitted with bits of fabric. A wreck just came in. The boys will see what they can salvage."

McLaren let his eyes wander over the complex of modern buildings. "And, the men use this former hospital, as a barracks."

"Barracks, workshops, fitness facilities, it's all here."

"The men never leave the base?"

"Look, everyone wants leave. The downtown storekeepers expect to cash in."

"But no major problems? No men absent without leave?"

"One of the American papers claimed we had a mutiny. Wasn't so…a misunderstanding. If you plan to write lies, we can stop now."

"No, no. I read the mutiny story too."

"A misunderstanding, an administrative problem, a mix-up over training. A few of the men didn't have permission when they went uptown, and a couple disappeared but came back later. It's all smoothed over. We're up and running. The other training sites are not as advanced. Our next stop is the Fingal base."

The bulldozer nudged a broken branch before pushing a taller, wider tree crashing to the ground. Farmland was being cleared for an airport. "It's going to take awhile," Robert McLaren laughed. "The dozer must have one gear, slow."

"More machines arrive next week," Sergeant Foster assured him. "Don't be surprised if the work takes on more urgency with the fighting in Europe."

"Yes, I suppose. This path will become an airstrip, right?"

"Three runways in all, shaped in a triangle."

"Stand aside," an engineer called and directed a work party. "That stake on the left, marks a hydrant. The plumbers will install next week."

"Impressive, eh," Foster said. "In the next few weeks the boys will have everything they need, hangars, repair shops, a small infirmary..."

"The men might be lured away by the bright lights of Fingal? That hamlet can't have more than two hundred souls."

"Yah, big changes when a couple of thousand airmen arrive and they rotate through. A new bunch every few weeks."

"But this facility won't train pilots."

"Dozens of other sites have flight schools or elementary flying schools with pilot training for Fighter Command, the single engine planes. And, there will be special schools for navigators, radio operators, everything a modern air force needs. Fingal is designated for bombing and gunnery."

"Any errant explosive would only take out a few cows or a barn."

"I've heard that joke before," Foster wasn't laughing. "This is serious business. With targets on Lake Erie there's less chance of accidental damage. Targets will be set up on land later."

"And the training for gunners?"

"A plane will haul a target, a drogue, a glider. Gunner in another aircraft could have target practise."

McLaren watched as the bulldozer attacked another tree.

"Somehow I expected Spitfires and Hurricanes."

"Not here. Bombers are bigger planes, usually with two engines or maybe four. And not a single pilot, a whole crew, six or eight men and trained to work as a team. These bases, by the way, go up fast. Buildings are pre-fabricated and assembled on site."

"And all this also means jobs?"

"Lots of them."

"An upside to the dirty work of war." McLaren knocked a lump of clay from his shoes. "And all of this coming off a grass strip."

"Oh no. Asphalt on the runways, a big control tower, it will be a modern airport."

"And what happens when the war ends?"

"No one has thought that far ahead."

France
May 14

The road was a mass of wreckage. Burned-out cars and trucks, dead horses hitched to overturned wagons and human bodies of every shape and description. Too many bodies to count. Stuka bombers ranged above the roads. The scream of the sirens, attached to their wings, was imprinted for life in the minds of those on the ground. And, if a bomb did not fall, machine gun bullets might trace a deadly pattern through fleeing refugees.

Dan Malone leaned against the car. The spring-time foliage, the leaves from trees in a small woodlot, offered scant protection from above, but was more than those on the road had known.

His mind raced over the last few days: mingling with the first of the refugees, the arrival at an RAF headquarters to find it abandoned, food looted from store shelves and a filling station with enough gas to power the trio to the south and west.

Richard Ingram snored loudly in the back seat, sleep the only escape from the continuing nightmare.

"Hey!" Malone jumped as Jimmy Russel banged on the hood of the car, "Come see what I found."

Ingram awoke with a start. "What is it?"

"Come on, past the trees."

The two followed as Russel returned to his discovery, an abandoned tank in the middle of a field.

"If there's a German tank, the Huns are nearby," Ingram turned back. "Let's go."

"Nah, no one around," Russel strode forward. "I checked. The tracks show a bunch of Panzers but for some reason this one was left."

"And what do you intend to do with it?" Malone looked at the black monster.

"Pictures," Russel lifted the camera. "I have film. Army intel can see what the other side is using." He scrambled up and lifted the hatch to slip inside. "I trained on tanks. This is one of their latest models." He worked his way into a crewman's seat and whistled. "I might be able to start it." The engine growled but failed to catch. A second and third attempt brought the same result. "Out of gas." He flipped another switch and the radio came to life with German voices. "Wonder what they're saying."

"I'm saying get the hell out of here." Malone was halfway through the hatch.

"Don't worry. They're miles away. Come back down." Russel shone a flashlight over the crew compartment. "Headsets," he said. "So there's an intercom system. Our men shout to make themselves heard and wow, leather seats. Most of our seats are cold, hard steel. And, I'll bet it has shock absorbers. No wonder they travel so far and so fast."

The camera clicked as Russel explored.

"I found a few packets of pills." He tossed the pills to Malone. "Stick those in your pocket. A pharmacist might be interested."

Malone climbed through the hatch, "Let's go."

"In a minute." He heard something tearing. From the turret, he glanced nervously about but saw no danger. "Take this," Russel passed the camera to Malone. A puff of smoke followed him from the tank. "Get back toward the trees. I cut the leather and started a fire. Oil and grease will feed the flames. The Nazis won't use this machine again."

Seconds later, smoke and flames burst through the hatch.

London

May 15

"My dear, don't be downhearted. The young man is almost certainly safe." Marcie Eaton tried to smile and prayed that the general was right.

The club rooms were quiet. Men on active service had no time to socialize and only members, like the former general, would spend the afternoon. Retired officers had rummaged in closets for old uniforms. Henry Dalton's had a fresh press.

"I haven't heard a word since before the invasion," she half whispered. "He was in France."

"So, as the BBC says, 'Somewhere in France'. I wouldn't worry. In my day communication lines failed but men muddled through."

"I hope so. Can I bring you anything?"

"No. Stay and chat."

"We're not supposed to but I've no one to talk to."

"It must be difficult for the weaker sex." The general lightly tapped her shoulder and for an instant fingered the strands of blonde hair. "The young man, a reporter, didn't you say?"

"Yes. He's Canadian. We only met last year and we've grown close." The general might be shocked at how close. The earlier generations disapproved of unmarried couples living 'in sin'.

"Things were different in my day," he smiled, "The little woman stayed at home and minded the household. That was the Boer War."

"Bore War?" she asked. "Isn't that what we just had?"

"Huh," he chuckled, "no, no. The South African affair at the turn of the century. Don't schools teach history?"

"I was never good in history. Dan was. He was doing feature stores and went to the Maginot Line."

"That's probably the issue. Damn French don't speak English. Too much time is lost in translation."

"Dan speaks French. I doubt that would be a problem."

"In my day, we tried to keep the press away until the fight was won. I suppose reporters were well intentioned, but their blasted dispatches caused no end of headaches. What a pain in the ass young Churchill was."

"The new Prime Minister?"

"Yes. Isn't that a joke? In South Africa, the man was a rogue, a glory seeker, a publicity hound. And, anytime I met him, in the last few years, he's been drunk. He should rally the people but frightens them with talk of blood, tears, toil and sweat."

"I thought he was being honest?"

"Honesty doesn't work in war time but don't worry. Lord Halifax will keep him under control. Thank God for Halifax. When, I hunted with him, a fox didn't have a chance. A former Viceroy of India, a pillar of the Anglican church, a member of the aristocracy, a natural leader. He'll take over when Churchill is dumped."

"Miss Eaton." The manager strode across the club. "Please don't annoy the club members."

"Oh, go away." The general squared his shoulders and glared. "This member is enjoying a pleasant conversation with an attractive young lady. Men of my age take advantage of every opportunity. Leave us be!"

Paris
May 16

Automobiles and horse drawn wagons fought for space on the streets. Mattresses were strapped to car roofs. Suitcases and boxes were piled high and ropes snugged across the jumble of luggage. A policeman with a megaphone urged Parisians to remain calm but the roads to the south were jammed.

Evers Chance entered the British embassy as a line of cars departed, closely followed by a truck filled with armed troops.

"Did you see him? Churchill just left." A young secretary excitedly continued, "I waved but he didn't see me. He's off to meet the French leaders."

Chance offered his credentials. "Has the embassy announced arrangements for evacuation?"

"Nothing official." She took a moment to glance at the papers. The gentleman dressed in fashionable English tweeds showed no sign of the anxiety displayed by other travellers. "The rumors," she whispered. "I don't know what to believe. It must be a relief to be a mere civilian."

"Yes. My concern is finding a decent hotel. But first, Rutherford? Is he still the Passport Control officer?"

"Room 14, down the hall, if he's here. A few men dashed off to the front, where ever that is."

In Rutherford's office, he found a phone and in moments had Martin Downey on the line. "Uh, good," Downey sounded anxious. "What do you have for us."

"A complete mess. The French are in full retreat."

"We feared as much. Our men and a few tanks are regrouping around Arras and the old Vimy battleground and...."

"Careful. Telephone lines are not necessarily secure."

"Ah, I see. That makes for difficult conversation."

"Speak in general terms, and of what, we expect the German's know. For example, the French government will flee the capital. Paris will be declared an open city."

"Rotterdam was an open city and the Luftwaffe bombed it. Hundreds are dead. Churchill is working to buck up the French spirit and may offer more RAF squadrons."

"I saw his cavalcade. The French need more than planes and Churchillian bluster. Clouds of smoke are rising over the government complex."

"Are firefighters on strike? I'm not surprised. Paris is riddled with communists. They could take advantage of the confusion and stage a revolt."

"Not the buildings, Martin, files, secret files that must be kept from the enemy. When they burn files, they don't want the fire brigade."

"Oh my. It's come to that."

"Martin, the army report circulating, the one titled 'a Certain Eventually'? Have you seen it?"

"It's defeatist, a bunch of malarkey."

"We don't need to discuss details but have a close look at the recommendations. Britain may soon stand alone."

For an instant, Chance thought the telephone link was severed but Downey's voice came through, with a tone of measured resignation. "I'll pass the view along."

"A couple of other points. See what we have on two German generals, a Heinz Guderian and Erwin Rommel. That pair are spearheading the attack."

"Wait, you said not to discuss specifics."

"Martin. The Germans know their generals. We're the ones that don't."

"Oh, I see. Guderian and Rommel. I'll have a look, but we probably will never hear of them again. There's chatter of an armistice."

"And, what would that look like? Ah, never mind. I have work to finish in Paris and plan to see the Channel Ports."

France
May 21

The car inched through the long streams of refugees. "We're low on gas," Malone said from behind the wheel. "We may have to siphon fuel from an abandoned car."

"Good luck," Jimmy Russel lowered the passenger window and reached to adjust the outside mirror. "No one leaves a car unless there's a breakdown or it's out of gas."

Richard Ingram leaned from the back seat to peer at the gauges, "Fuel for a couple of hours, I'd guess."

Malone tapped the car horn as a woman pushing a wicker baby carriage stepped onto the road. The reply was an angry glare and a raised finger. Two young children joined her and walked on either side of the buggy. Both had small bags strapped to their backs.

Russel wiped at the dust on the mirror with the sleeve of his tunic. "Something is happening," he called suddenly, "People are running…" Before he could say more a Messerschmidt fighter appeared, firing into the lines of refugees."

Malone cranked the car to the right, into a shallow ditch. It slammed to a stop as the plane roared overhead. "Oh, sweet Jesus." He swallowed hard. The baby carriage was on its side, the mother and two children, lay on the road. He pushed the car door open and ran to the victims, but a glance was all that was necessary. A priest stopped and made the sign of the cross over the mother and children. He knelt by the baby carriage but found only a few pots and pans.

"Nothing we can do," Ingram joined Malone. "See if the car will start."

Russel sat in the passenger seat, his face grey from shock. "Can't get free." His arm was pinned between the car and the bank of the ditch.

"Rock the car!" Malone pushed against the frame but stopped when Russel screamed in pain.

"We need something stronger!" Ingram appeared lost but then shouted, "That one."

A farmer jogged by, leading a team of horses, an extra set of harness, jingling from the back of one animal. He slowed momentarily, just long enough for Ingram to wave a fistful of francs. "Non!" The teamster took a few steps before he felt Ingram's pistol.

"Oui!" Ingram ordered, holding the gun with one hand, while tugging at the harness with the other. The extra harness became a safety rope.

"Allez! Allez!" The farmer urged the horses forward, watched as they took the pressure, heard Russel's scream but saw the car lurch from the ditch. Ingram holstered the gun and stuck the cash in the farmer's vest.

"Try the car." The engine fired on the first attempt. As Malone steered back onto the road, Ingram fashioned a rough tourniquet. "Russel has passed out. That arm is bad shape." He slumped in the rear seat. "Another lesson is to keep bullets in a revolver."

"The gun wasn't loaded?"

"No. I thought the damn thing might go off accidentally."

The first aide station was a delipidated house, easily identified by the stretchers in the yard and a Red Cross hanging from a wash line. An hour later, a British army nurse came to where Malone and Ingram waited.

"He shouldn't travel immediately but he'll recover. The tourniquet stopped the bleeding, a handy piece of medical work. He might have bled out."

"I once worked as a medical orderly," Ingram told her.

"We could use help. The other men I've asked turn white at the sight of blood. We'd need you for one night. We evacuate tomorrow." She turned to Malone, "And, we could use a car. Other reporters, with transportation are in the house on the left. One came by earlier. A fellow named Philby from the *Times*. That should be good company."

"Yes, ma'am. That will be fine."

He offered his hand to Ingram. "Look out for Jimmy?"

"I'll take care of the bugger and his Nazi treasures. The pills and film fell from his coat when we lifted him to the stretcher. Silly bugger thinks they're important. He'll expect a medal."

Calais, France
May 22

"A lovely little hotel," the British officer appeared impressed.

The owner managed a worried smile. "We do our best but in today's conditions…"

"Not to worry. I'll take a room. I'm not expecting anyone, but the name is Chance, Major Chance. Can't say more. Secret Mission and all that."

"Very well. The porter will run a hot bath?"

"Yes, things are dusty on the road. Telephone service?"

"Calls are difficult. Perhaps a refreshment?"

"Not yet. I'll try the call first." The French telephone system was on the verge of collapse and it was an hour before the switchboard operator handed him the receiver."

"Bascom's Flower Shop," the voice of a bored shop clerk came through from London.

"I can handle it from here," Chance smiled and passed several francs to the attendant. "Go have a drink."

"Bascom's Flower Shop," the clerk repeated.

"I need to speak with the florist," Chance said. "My order for Marigolds failed to arrive."

After a short pause, Martin Downey was on the line.

"I'm in a bit of a rush," Chance told him. "Calais is hotter than I remembered and German tourists are taking over. I won't stay long."

"I see."

"However, I came through Dunkirk. A good skipper could bring a boat in."

"Uh- huh."

"And I had time to walk those marvellous beaches. Remember when we sailed across. Just the two of us on a little boat. The fun we had frolicking on the sand. And later, we picked up guests and sailed back to England. A bit crowded but we made it?"

"I must dig out the pictures. As I recall, others talked of making the trip."

"Yes, fine memories."

"And the present excursion? Almost over?"

"No, I'm going to stay a bit longer, can't be sure when I'll see the continent again."

Near Dunkirk
May 22

"Nothing unusual, Herr Colonel," the radio operator reported. "The British are hard pressed. They've abandoned their codes. Panic stricken messages go out in plain English."

"Very good," Karl Munster, smiled.

"And as we advance, we tap the telephone lines for military or civilian conversations. I listened this afternoon as an Englishman reminisced about French beaches."

"Ah, chasing the young ladies?"

"No, Colonel. He had been sailing with a male friend. I felt sick when I imagined the two men on the beach. The English are such degenerates."

"That issue is solved in the Reich," Munster laughed. "Homosexuals are in the camps. We'll need large camps for the deviates and the weak-minded when we take Great Britain. But first, we must eliminate the remnants of their army."

A few feet away, in a makeshift work yard, mechanics worked to service and repair the Panzers. "Machines break down, but not the soldier," Munster addressed Corporal Heinzman. "You look tired. Are you taking enough Pervitin? The courage pills boost energy and keep the mind clear."

"Yes, Colonel."

"Then what is it? Is something wrong? Speak freely."

Heinzman clenched his fists. "The prisoners, the prisoners of war."

"Corporal, war is hard. I take no prisoners. Other commanders waste time collecting a disorganized mob."

"But the coloured?"

"The French Colonial Forces. Is that it? Yes, they surrendered and put down their weapons, but they were black, racially inferior. Those men must be controlled or, as I ordered, destroyed, to protect the master race. No one enjoys it but the Reich grows stronger each day. The British shoot prisoners too."

"But it's...."

"No more, Corporal. I thought better of you. I will hear no more."

"Colonel Munster. A message." Another orderly brought a dispatch. Munster read the note and seethed with anger. "Fools! A stupid order."

"Herr Colonel?"

"Relieve the repair crews. We're in for a delay."

95

Munster slammed one gloved hand against the other. "We should push the enemy into the Channel and drown every one of them but some fool in Berlin has ordered a halt."

London, May 25

"Winston has gone too far." The general stomped into the club rooms, eyes brimming with martial fire.

"What is it, Henry?" another elderly member called.

"Bugger seized my boat, the *Victoria,* my thirty-foot yacht. An admiralty panty-waist came by, said the navy needed her and wouldn't say why."

"My brother-in-law had his boat taken too," another man spoke. "Same thing, no rhyme, no reason."

"Winston 'Bloody' Churchill," Henry Dalton spat the words. "Power has gone to his head."

"Take a deep breath, Henry. Don't burst a blood vessel."

Henry's voice carried around the club room, "This type of chicanery wouldn't happen if Halifax was Prime Minister. No gentleman would act this way."

"I was in Whitehall this morning," another member spoke. "The German advance stopped outside of Dunkirk. The German's have made their point and may be ready to talk."

"An armistice?"

"No one is sure. But the tanks have stopped."

"Finally, a smart decision," another member suggested. "I thought we should negotiate. The Germans will see reason."

"But what about my bloody boat," Dalton demanded. "What does Winston want with her?"

"Perhaps, a refreshment would be in order." Marcie Eaton had entered the room at the sound of the raised voices and asked, "A gin and tonic, General?"

"What's that? Ah yes, a glass would be welcome."

"And, you were right, sir," she offered a big smile. "You said not to worry, and my man came back last night. He's safe and sound."

An Angry Sky

The general admired Marcie's swaying hips as she returned to the kitchen. Only when the door closed behind her, did he speak again. "Best to get all the bloody reporters out of the way. On a battlefield, a reporter is nothing more than another useless mouth."

Dalton drained the glass and slumped into a seat. "Maybe the reporters can put an effort to this boat business. I won't rest until *Victoria* is safely back in harbour."

Le Havre
May 30

The sound of a car alerted her to a visitor. She looked out to see Evers Chance carrying a black briefcase and suitcase toward the house.

"Are you moving in?" she laughed, greeting him with a light kiss on the cheek.

"I'm not used to such attention," he said as he set the cases down and took her hands. "A delight to find you safe. I wanted to leave some clothes in case they're needed in the future. And, I've brought provisions for you."

"Don't worry so. I've built my American resume in the last few weeks. A few articles for the Washington magazine and the neutral passport should keep the Germans at bay."

"Security services are persistent. Don't let the guard down."

"What's is in the case? I love when gentlemen bring gifts."

"I should have brought flowers," he laughed and followed her inside. "What I did bring won't wilt as fast."

He flipped the cover to reveal neat rows of currency. "An American magazine would pay in U.S. dollars, so the greenbacks raise no suspicion. The pounds are more problematic. Deal them out slowly or wait until a black market develops. And when the Nazis arrive, slowly dispense the Francs and Reichsmarks."

"All business today," she smiled.

"It's not safe to think of other than business. The German advance will start again. There's a desperate attempt to rescue the army from Dunkirk and thousands of men are making their way to southern France. The outlook is bleak."

"Except for a neutral," she told him. "Thanks to you I have the papers and cash to survive."

"Communication will be difficult," he explained. "But I've arranged access to the U.S. embassy. A consular official named Dobbins can slip any urgent message into the diplomatic bag."

"So, the German's won't see it?"

"Every security service wants to access the diplomatic pouches so assume the Nazis will try. I also brought a new code book and invisible ink. Letters might tell of what anyone in occupied France would see. Use the special ink to write on the margins or between the lines and add what you shouldn't have seen."

"And who am I writing to?"

"The letters will be sent to your cousin, Helen Cummins, in Detroit."

"I don't have a cousin…" she began. "Oh, I guess I do now."

Reality slowly began to sink in. She fought sudden tears and wrapped her arms around him. "How long can you stay?"

"Only an hour or so." Reluctantly, he broke the embrace. "I need help on another matter. I need to test your memory?"

"I'll try."

"A restaurant in London, in South Kensington called the Russian Tea Room?"

"The Tea Room?" she asked, regaining control. "When I felt the need for Russia food, I'd stop by. It's owned by an Admiral, who knew my father. The old fellow expected a Romanov would be restored to the throne. I didn't have the heart to tell him that was impossible."

"And did you meet his daughter?"

"Yes, of course, Anna. She was a bit pretentious but always interesting, And, her boyfriend was around, an American…Ted…no, Tyler Kent. I'm not sure what he saw in Anna. She's rather plain."

"Did you know he worked at the American embassy?"

"No. Why?"

"They've been arrested. He was stealing confidential documents and she passed them to Berlin."

"Berlin? Oh, of course. Any good white Russian dreams of the day when Hitler will overturn Stalin. It's improbable but that's what some believe."

"Anything else?"

"Humm...It wasn't much of a restaurant, kind of dingy and the food wasn't great, but you don't care about the borsht." She was silent, then... "The American, Kent, passing secrets to Berlin? I wonder? He had too much vodka one night and started to praise the communist system. Anna shut him up, but he did work in Moscow."

"Probably nothing," he told her, "but we want whatever we can get."

"Everything is confused. Old names keep cropping up. I read the *Times* and saw the byline for Kim Philby. Another old acquaintance, a Canadian actress, from the silent era, used to speak of him. Philby is now at the heart of the British conservative establishment, but my friend said his first wife was a communist and Kim helped in her work. Isn't it amazing how people change? I'm sorry, I'm running off at the mouth."

"Don't change," he smiled. "Sometimes little bits of information become important."

She stepped closer, threw her arms around him and felt his hands stroke her hair. "I have to go."

"Chance?" she asked as she studied his face. "My letters? Will someone reply?"

"Yes. They'll be routed to me. And I'll be thinking of you every day."

Ottawa

June 1

"What an incredible turn of events," Sandy Fleming brushed her hair and peered into the small mirror on her desk. "A month ago, Mr. Willard assured us peace was at hand."

Robert McLaren flipped through a stack of U.S. newspapers, noting that each day, the maps showed a further German advance. "If England falls, would we be next?" she asked.

"I doubt the Fuhrer cares about Canada," he said, "but he may come for the Americans."

"Mr. Willard thinks Germany will launch air attacks on the east coast from aircraft carriers." She set the brush aside and turned to face him.

"Sandy. Check the facts. Hitler has no aircraft carriers."

"He says the Royal family, the crown jewels, and important works of art are coming to Canada."

"That's premature. Flight would indicate the war is lost and judging from the tough talk, Churchill is not ready for surrender."

"But what if the entire British government came, what if the Empire was run from Canada?"

"Wouldn't that be fun," McLaren laughed. "Can you imagine King trying to lord it over Churchill or for that matter, Toronto businessmen fighting for influence? And, the Americans would want a say. President Roosevelt believes the royals should go to Bermuda. He doesn't care for the idea of a monarch ruling from North America. Americans like to remember their revolution."

Sandy glanced again at the mirror and patted an errant strand of hair.

"Do you think Mackenzie King will be replaced?" she asked. "He doesn't fit the image of a wartime leader. I've tried to imagine the Prime Minister as a military hero but it's hard. I picture a Roman centurion, a roly-poly little fellow, plodding along in sandals. It's not pretty."

McLaren began to laugh.

"Ah, Sandy, that's the stuff for satirical cartoons. Thank you, I haven't had a good laugh in weeks. "By the way, where is Mr. Willard? Buying up houses to rent to the royals?"

"He said he had personal business and I shouldn't worry my pretty little head about it."

Washington
June 2

"Children! Behave." The elderly teacher was losing patience. "The Lincoln monument is the highlight of our trip. Billy, put the stick down and pay attention."

Brad Wilson chuckled, one of the few times he had relaxed in the last few hours. His effort to obtain a passport had been mysteriously delayed in a State Department office. He should have lied, he thought, and not confessed the Canadian visit was anything more than a vacation, but the clerk had been disarming and Wilson told of his interest in training with the RAF or the Royal Canadian Air force. The casual conversation ended abruptly with orders to wait. Two hours later, a sullen clerk returned with instructions that led him to the Lincoln Memorial, a park bench and another long wait.

"Billy. No more shenanigans," the teacher shook a finger. "Or no more class trips."

"Billy is in deep shit," a man spoke softly as he took a seat beside him. "And, you sir, are dangerously close to a sewer."

Wilson tensed. The stranger wore a dark suit and hat but what he noticed most were the piercing blue eyes. "Those kids should pay attention. Lincoln was a war time president. He handled a lot, including different factions inside his government." The voice was deep and carried the weight of authority. "Roosevelt faces a similar challenge. Our ambassador to France demands aide for our oldest ally. But our man in

London, says, don't bother, the Germans are going to win. Quite a dilemma."

"Who in hell are you?"

"We know who you are. A visit to the State Department for a passport application, a flyer who intends to join a belligerent air force while America remains belligerently neutral."

"This is a bazaar way to deal with a passport."

"An observant clerk thought the request, unusual and sent word to his superiors, who contacted me. Your name is on file."

"What file?" The questions stopped as the man produced a badge and Wilson focused on FBI.

"I'm Bert Laramie, special agent with the New York office. By luck, I was in Washington. A friend is playing a dangerous game and it could reflect on you."

"I don't understand. What does this have to do with Canadian Air Force?"

"We don't care about that. This country is neutral, but we understand not everyone agrees. We're more concerned about men that use the isolationist camp as a cover for German sympathies. Know anyone like that?"

"No. I don't...unless...are you investigating Fulton? Tim can be a pain in the ass but he's harmless."

"Not all of his friends are innocent."

"Innocent of what? He carps about staying out of the war but since when is that illegal?"

"As long as it's talk, no laws are broken, but he's been with German agents. We want to know more?"

"Do you expect me to rat on a friend? What if there's nothing to rat about?"

"Then off to Canada. But first, we want to know what he's up to."

"I don't like this. I'm no spy."

"We'll guide you along."

"I need to think."

"Of course, give it careful thought. You have until 4 o'clock."

London
June 3

"Why all the fuss over an American leak," Evers Chance demanded. His temper was growing short after long days of travel. And, in a matter of hours he would return again to France.

Martin Downey stood by his side watching boats on the Thames River. At least on cursory inspection two old men were killing time.

"The Map of Continental Europe is being redrawn before our eyes," Chance said. "While Whitehall is agog over this Kent and a floozie."

"More to it than you know," Downey said knowingly. He rarely had more information than Chance and intended to make the most it.

"Rubbish," Chance hissed. "A disaster at Dunkirk. Thousands of men rescued but thousands more are prisoners. France is on the verge of collapse and intelligence chiefs worry about the Russian Tea Room."

"Good of you to look into that. Is the information reliable?"

"What else do you want, the recipe for stroganoff. She was only there as a customer."

"Oh, a she. I always imagined your network peopled by dark, muscled and relatively unintelligent, male foreigners. But look, we want to help a potential ally. This Kent fellow had access to hundreds of confidential documents. The American Ambassador, Joe Kennedy believes England will lose this war, so if his image suffers, we don't really care. The problem is what's in the files."

"Come on, Martin. I don't have all day."

"Churchill and Roosevelt had private communications. Churchill asked for help, guns, ammunition, planes and ships. The President replied with sympathy, a problem because

American public opinion is so divided. If those messages leak, they could affect the Presidential election."

"So, keep it quiet."

"Oh, we will. A secret trial and a long prison sentence. We wouldn't want Kent deported to face an open trial in the United States. It could all be terribly embarrassing."

"Very clever, Martin."

"We also considered your observation that those files might have been passed to Moscow," Downey said. "I ran it by Philby, the former reporter. He doesn't buy it. Moscow isn't learning anything from us."

Chapter Five: An Alliance in Tatters

Dover, England
June 5

Dan Malone almost tripped over the legs that protruded from under the army truck. "Keep the eyes open, bud," the voice called. "I don't want wrenches scattered all over hell."

"Sorry, didn't see you," Malone answered and stepped around a toolbox. He had been distracted by a giant grassy parking lot, by rows of trucks, cars and half tracks."

"Everything all right, under there?" The question was a polite afterthought.

"Everything will be fixed properly," the mechanic called. "Stop disturbing me."

"Don't mess with an artist," Reg Oliver cautioned and rolled his eyes. Oliver was a press officer assigned to the First Canadian Division and had orders to brief the reporter. "The Brits left their equipment at Dunkirk and no one knows when new gear will arrive. Canadians are the best equipped in Great Britain. We could see action soon."

"After what I saw in France, everyone would be smart to simply enjoy the English countryside."

"Tough was it?"

"Tough is an understatement. The Panzers', terror bombings, thousands of civilian refugees and a wild retreat to the Channel. I turned away from the worst scenes, don't want to dwell on them. But the images keep coming back."

"The Canadian division was almost caught up in Dunkirk," Oliver confided. "The Brits wanted to insert a fresh force, but General McNaughton went for a look and decided it was no use."

"And now?"

"Couple of options…" Oliver began but stopped immediately. "Look this has to be secret or we'll both be in the stockade."

"What I write has to clear the censor and from personal experience very little gets through."

"Ok. Our infantry is in good shape, green, but well supplied. If the Germans try to invade England, we're the first line of defence. But it might not come to that, if the French keep fighting. Suppose a few regiments, were moved across the Channel, to buck up their morale. The Royal Canadian Regiment, the Hasting and Prince Edward and the Royal Canadian Horse Artillery are making preparations."

"When would they go?"

"Soon! The French can't last long without us. If you want to come, I can make arrangements."

"Only Canadian troops?"

"That's what I hear."

"Then save me a spot."

New Jersey
June 10

"Why have we stopped," Tim Fulton confronted the conductor. "This train is supposed to be an Express."

"Sorry. Army gets top priority."

"Army specials?"

"Two of them, under special orders for the mainline, a hurry up shipment." The engine of the first train whistled and passed the passenger cars. Minutes later the second train slowed and stopped.

Fulton lowered his window to watch uniformed men sprint along the track. Two stopped below him and opened the door of a freight car. Inside were large crates marked 'Lee-Enfield' and others labelled 'Danger-High Explosives'.

He called to an officer, "Are we going to war?"

"No sir. The army is saving taxpayer money. This material is surplus. A steel company bought the whole she-bang."

"What on earth for?"

"The rifles could be melted for scrap," the officer stepped to below the window. "Explosives might be extracted from the ammunition and resold, maybe to a mining operation. The buyer turns a tidy profit."

"Where's that leave the army?"

"In a few weeks the armouries will be refilled with new stock. Some of this, dates from the Great War."

Fulton watched as the men checked the cargo before closing and padlocking the door. "Where is it going?"

"Raritan, New Jersey. After that I don't care. I'll be on leave in New York."

"We'll be rolling soon," the conductor tapped Tim's shoulder. "We'll make up the lost time."

Fulton nodded. "Say, where is Raritan?"

"It's the marshalling yard on the New Jersey coast. A lot of material for Europe goes through there."

Fulton returned to his seat before the reality struck him.

Those weapons aren't scrap, he thought. The American government has made an under-handed deal. A private company can resell them without the kind of questions the government would face. The army and, or the President, are playing tricks to re-equip the Brits.

Ottawa
June 10

"The gloom over Italy is thicker than I would have expected," Robert McLaren said as he and Sandy crossed Parliament Hill. "Mussolini is a German ally. He invaded France, it's natural he'd want a share of the spoils."

"And, will Canada declare war on Italy?" Sandy Fleming asked.

"The External Affairs Department will be dotting the i's as we speak," McLaren speculated. "President Roosevelt calls the invasion a stab in the back which is pretty strong diplomatic language. But that's as far he goes. The Brits and French need more than moral support."

"I know, it's important," Sandy adjusted a broad brimmed hat. "But everything seems so far away. We're isolated. The world is at war and we're about to fight over free food at a political reception."

McLaren jumped aside as an army staff car sped up the driveway and screeched to a stop by the Peace Tower. An officer and aide bolted from the car to rush inside.

"Someone is busy," Sandy laughed. "The RCMP should nail that driver for speeding. But, maybe it's too nice a day for the police to work. Spring makes the Hill so pretty. Although, if a woman was in charge, we'd have more colour, more flowers. Imagine how it would look with maybe...tulips."

As they neared the steps to the Centre Block, a small group emerged, including several members of Parliament. "The reception is cancelled," one told them. "A sad day for Canada."

"Why, what's happened?"

"Norman Rogers is dead."

"The National Defence Minister?" McLaren understood their shock. "I didn't know he was sick?"

"No, a plane crash. He was on the way to Toronto, a speaking engagement. The plane went down near Trenton."

"Mr. King is beside himself," another MP confided. "The Prime Minister had urged cancellation of the trip. He thought Rogers needed a rest."

"King's cabinet was rebuilt after the election," another MP joined the conversation. "And now he'll have to shuffle the deck again. But that comes later. He's gone to break the news to the man's wife."

"Should we return to the office?" Sandy asked. "We'll have to get this out."

"You go. I'll see what else I can dig up."

"Awful," she said. "And a few minutes ago, I thought anything war related was far, far away."

Bordeaux, France
June 16

"We'd be better off without the French."

"I think that's coming," Evers Chance tried to calm the foreign office specialist. "Are you ready to leave, Mr. Porter?"

"I haven't unpacked since the government fled Paris."

Chance, wearing the uniform of an army major, had arrived on a special government plane, an aircraft that would carry non-essential staff from the latest temporary French capital. Bordeaux too, would soon fall. "Is Churchill coming over?" Chance asked, knowing the growing confusion on both sides of the Channel.

"No, the trip was cancelled, and his ground-breaking offer rejected. Think of what might have been, a formal union of France and Great Britain. The earth would have shaken as old soldiers, enemies for centuries, rolled in their graves."

Porter tossed more papers into a blazing fireplace.

"Everything is falling apart. Marshall Petain is expected to form a new government and seek an armistice."

"All the more reason for the British nationals to leave."

"And what will you do?

"I'm going by road. Someone in London believes we can maintain a Breton redoubt. I doubt it's feasible. An awful lot of wild ideas have surfaced in recent days. A Canadian brigade is heading toward Le Mans, as if a few hundred fresh soldiers would make a difference."

"Haven't you heard? The Canadians were ordered back to Britain."

Saint-Malo, France
June 16

Dan Malone woke as the train slowed. His rest disrupted by a ragged chorus of singers at the back of the rail car.

"Mademoiselle from Armentieres, she ain't been laid in twenty years...."

Having exhausted the most ribald lyrics, the troops started over and shared more of an illicit supply of alcohol.

"Where are we?" Malone asked as the press officer Reg Oliver returned from the front of the train.

"Saint-Malo," Oliver pushed Malone to a sitting position and dropped into the seat beside him. "Our last stop."

"Any word from the rest of the force?" Malone asked.

"It's a mess. The troops sent to Le Mans had to turn a gun on the engineer to make him reverse course. Luckily, one of the officers was a railway man. He rode in the cab, gun at the ready, to make sure the engineer made for the Channel. They'll make it back to Dover."

"And what about us?"

"We're on the wrong track. We weren't supposed to embark from Saint-Malo, but the Admiralty agreed to hold a couple of ships. We'll get away, but our equipment, including brand new trucks will be abandoned. The men coming by road will meet us after the equipment is wrecked."

"I read this story before. It was called Dunkirk."

"Be a smart-ass, but the Canadians will leave in better shape than the British. We've had only one causality and that was a from a motorcycle accident."

"Only one?" Malone found it hard to believe.

"Ok, a half-dozen or so are missing, but they may turn up. You do realize, you won't be able to file a story. I can't pass anything on this debacle."

"Maybe we can negotiate a few paragraphs. The Canadians came, saw, but were not allowed to conquer."

"General?" A soldier swayed through the car and addressed Oliver. "You being the best dressed officer on this car…"

"You're drunk. I should put you on report."

"Be that as it may. This place, this Saint-Malo. I've heard of it."

"Ah Lord. Collect your kit. We get off here."

"But why do I know it?"

"History and a poem. Jacques Cartier, an explorer of New France, set sail from Saint-Malo…*From the seaport of Saint-Malo* and so on and so on. Canadian school children recite it."

"Damn. I remember now." He pushed to the open door of the carriage. "Cartier," he bellowed, "Cartier, we have returned!"

Malone, shook his head in amazement, "Do you suppose he's confused Cartier with the American love of Lafayette?"

Oliver nodded. "If we get lucky, he'll fall off the boat. It may be the only way to sober him up."

Saint-Nazaire, France
June 17

Jimmy Russel winced, the pain knifing through the arm, as a man brushed against him.

"Sorry mate," the soldier glanced at the sling. The jetty was full of men: walking wounded, men on stretchers and hundreds more who wanted only to go home. The line moved slowly toward small boats that would ferry them to evacuation ships and to England.

A medical officer carried a battered notebook and made a notation on each man's condition.

"Broken?" he asked and lightly touched Russel's arm. The pain that never went away grew more intense.

111

"No, crushed."

"With that arm you'll be a burden and we can't take any more on the hospital ship." The doctor hesitated before he called, "Nora, take this one in tow."

A young brunette stepped toward them, a once-white blouse stained with blood and grim. "Another one for the *Lancastria*?"

"Yah. Cram a few more aboard."

"I'm Nora Field," she said and helped him into a boat. He grunted and tried to protect the arm.

"We'll get that fixed when we get you home," she assured him. "And don't worry about missing the hospital ship. The big Red Cross on the main deck no longer means safety. German dive bombers use the cross as a target. You and me are going in style. The *Lancastria* is part of the Cunard line and converted to a troop ship. She ferried men from Norway and if the captain can navigate a fiord, the Channel will be a piece of cake. She's too big for this harbour. They had to anchor four miles out."

Despite the pain, Russel found the chatter comforting. "Are you army?" he asked.

"Lord, no. I was a private nurse with an old lady in my charge until her family whisked her to Switzerland. I've made myself handy to get a lift home."

"One of my friends did the same thing, a press officer who became a hospital orderly. But, a few days ago, he was killed on the road when the Luftwaffe came by. I'm going to look up his family."

"Seen too much, I guess." Her green eyes offered sympathy.

"We're told not to think about it. I was an RAF observer, taking aerial pictures. My unit was destroyed."

"I hope there's food on this ship," she changed the subject. "I could eat a horse."

"Not me." His mind flashed back to a scene on the road as civilians, desperate for food, cut apart a dying horse. "Reach into my tunic," he said. "We'll have a smoke." He waited while she retrieved the pack and lit two cigarettes.

"Good old fashion looting," he told her sheepishly. "I lifted them from an abandoned store. Other men went for the booze and a few got new boots."

She took a puff, smiled and blew a smoke ring.

"Lord, she's a big one," Nora admired the ship as they approached. "Five decks, two swimming pools, a library, and if we're lucky, a real bed to lie in."

"No more." Someone called as their boat unloaded, "We must have close to six thousand aboard. Send the next boat to another ship."

"RAF," an officer glanced at what was left of Jimmy's uniform, "Your lot are crowded in below."

"He can't be banged around," Nora intervened. "We'll find a place on deck." She took his good arm and lead him to shelter near the bridge. Her flashing green eyes convinced a steward to produce deck chairs and moments later she wrangled two bottles of beer. "I'm going to make the most of this." She raised a bottle, "Live it up. La-DI-da."

"Another cigarette," he said and as she reached into his jacket two packages dropped to the deck."

"What's this?"

"Ah, film I shot inside a German tank. Army intelligence might want to see it. The other packet contains pills."

"Pills?" Nora studied the package, "Wish I could read the language."

"Each of the tank crew had a supply..." Any further explanation was cut short as anti-aircraft fire erupted from ships around the harbour.

"Shit! Air raid," he screamed. "Get down." He pushed her to the deck as the plane grew closer. For an instant, he thought the bombs had missed, but heard the explosions, saw smoke billow up and felt the giant liner shudder."

His nurse lay on the deck, apparently unconscious. "Nora...Nora?" With his good arm he slapped her, hoping to shock her to consciousness, poured beer across her face and gulped with relief as her eyes began to flutter. Only then did he notice the screams and shouts of other passengers. The *Lancastria* began to list adding to the horror around them.

"Jump," a ship's officer pointed to the rail. "She's going down." A few lifeboats were swung out and crewmen tossed chairs, lifebelts and hatches into the water.

"Jump, swim to anything that floats," another sailor scurried by.

Nora shook her head to clear the cobwebs. "Get these off," she said tearing at the laces on Jimmy's boots and more gently removing his tunic, shirt and pants."

"Can't swim." He was remarkably calm.

"The good arm will keep you up, nothing wrong with the legs."

"No. Can't swim. Never learned."

"I'll hold you up." He watched fascinated as the skirt and blouse came off and she stood in a bra and a set of snug men's briefs. "I looted too. Women's undies had been picked over."

"Take this," he ordered, passing the film and a packet of pills."

"No time."

"Make time," He tugged on elastic band of the underwear and dropped the packages inside."

Nora would never remember all of what happened. She did recall pulling him from the ship and clinging to wreckage as bodies floated by. The few life boats were dangerously overloaded and other rescue boats were slow or never left the dock at Saint-Nazaire.

She had a dim recollection of *Lancastria* rolling, slowly and then faster until the hull faced the sky; men climbed the hulk and sang and she wondered if the courage came from alcohol or a grim patriotism.

"I'm glad I met you Nora," Jimmy's strength was fading. "We might have been an item."

"We still can be," she told him before she screamed and waved to a small boat, praying the crew would see them. But the next thing she remembered were rough hands and soapy water cleaning thick oil from her body.

A day later, the road leading to the west was surprising quiet and with a British army corporal at the wheel, Evers Chance had time to reflect. He had watched as Marshall Petain, a legend of the first war, took control of the French government. His first broadcast to the people and the German army, was a call for negotiations. On leaving Bordeaux the refuse of war littered the highway: wrecked cars, abandoned weapons and goods that soldiers and civilians agreed, were of no immediate value. The highway had been packed with civilians, hoping for safety in what would be called Vichy, the part of France controlled by the Petain regime.

Beyond, Saint-Nazaire traffic grew lighter, with only a few cars, trucks and the last of the fleeing British units.

The mission for 'Major' Chance had been fruitless. Fortifying the base of the Breton peninsula, might once have been possible but events overtook the war planners. The French general, Charles de Gaulle, concluded the idea was impractical. The peninsula could serve as an escape route for the few British left in Europe. "Did you need a break, Corporal Wheeler. I can take the wheel for a few hours."

"No, sir. I need to be doing something. I keep thinking of all that's gone wrong in these last few weeks. I lost a lot of friends, men I served with for years and I wasn't looking forward to a prison camp."

"And, I wasn't looking forward to the drive on my own. The Michelin Guide shows a village ahead. Let's try for a meal."

The lunch was barely adequate and the owner of the small café less than hospitable.

"Run," he sneered as Chance paid the bill. "The British drag us into the war and run away."

Chance turned to leave but Wheeler reached across the counter. "Nervy bastard." He grabbed the man's smock. "The French army collapsed. The vaunted Poilu threw down their guns and raised their hands." He released the smock and shoved him backwards.

"The British ran," the Frenchman yelled but stayed out of reach. "Our men held the line in Belgium. The English ran to Dunkirk and saved themselves. These are Allies?"

"You little toad!" Wheeler leveraged himself to jump the counter, but Chance held him back.

"Some of it is true," Chance admitted. "We saved our own men at Dunkirk, but the ships did go back for thousands of Frenchmen. Most returned to fight in France, but it wasn't enough. But now it's done. C'est Fini!"

Outside the hotel was another surprise.

"English?" A man, gun in hand, stepped from behind the building.

"Steady, Wheeler," Chance ordered.

"Ah, bonne." The gunman lowered his weapon. He whistled and four other men appeared, each holding a corner of a heavily weighted blanket. Inside was a young woman, her mouth gagged, hands and feet tied."

"She's crazy." The gunman tapped his head. "We find her on the beach, where the current flows from Saint-Nazaire. She wears a cover on her breast and men's underpants. She's coated with oil. We try to clean but she goes crazy. If Germans are about, we have to keep her quiet."

Chance saw the appeal in her eyes and unravelled the gag.

"I know a British uniform. Get me away from these men."

"What's this about?"

"My name is Nora Field, I'm a nurse. I was on *Lancastria* when it sank."

"Sank?"

"Sank! And, thousands of men went down with her. I guess I drifted until I hit a beach. That's when these outlaws grabbed me. I do not appreciate having my breasts rubbed by pigs. They spoke French. I understand French."

Chance looked at the gunman.

"Ah Monsieur, at first, we thought she was dead and when she came around, we agreed she had a lovely set and things may have been said."

"Thanks for the compliment," she strained against the ropes. "But they weren't going to see more."

"Oil, Monsieur. She was covered in oil. We wanted to remove it. Her privates must be well lubricated."

"That's enough," Chance undid the ropes. "We'll take her with us."

"Be careful. She has a nasty mouth and, Monsieur, she wears my wife's dress. I would like it back."

Nora started to sputter but a glance from Chance silenced her. "Get in the car. A few francs will cover the expenses of these gentlemen. I won't need French currency for a few years."

The highway showed no sign of bomb damage and Wheeler sped toward Brest. Nora lay in the back seat and closed her eyes, but the restless sleep was haunted by what she had seen. Finally, after drifting in and out of nightmares, she gave up.

"What happens in Brest?" she asked.

Chance twisted from the front seat to face her. The woman was pretty, not a striking beauty, but definitely attractive. "With luck, a British ship and England."

"It can't happen soon enough," she said and scratched at her underwear.

"What do you do?" she asked. "Cleanest men I've seen in weeks. My guess is staff officer and batman. Men from headquarters seldom get dirty."

Chance smiled. "How do you know so much about headquarters?

"Oh, I don't really. The men talked while we waited for the boats and didn't have much nice to say about the officer class. I was a private nurse and until I arrived in Saint-Nazaire, didn't have anything to do with the army."

"And what will you do in England."

"Look for a job, I guess. I'm qualified to be a nanny but have a nasty temper. I might beat the little urchins."

Again, he smiled. "Nurses will be in demand."

"Oh grand! I'll spend my life changing bedpans."

Wheeler added speed and blew the horn as he sped by a truck.

"In a hurry, are we?" Nora glanced behind to see the truck driver shake his fist, "I'm waiting to hear what you do?"

"Corporal Wheeler is regular army. My work is more, irregular, which means you shouldn't ask."

"Ah, come on," the answer tweaked her interest. "Clean officer's uniform, well spoken and carries enough cash to free a lady from captivity. Are you a spy? A German in disguise, a fifth column agent intent on bringing mayhem to Blighty?"

"You've read too many tabloids. No, I'm a collector. I gather information."

"Special Branch," she guessed. "A London Police Dick? Maybe you could help. I have to find someone in intelligence. Jimmy gave me some stuff. He was an RAF guy I met on the ship. And, since he didn't make it, I should pass it along."

"What kind of ...stuff?"

"Who wants to know?"

He slowly pulled credentials from his pocket. Nora whistled. "Holy shit! Military intelligence? I did hitch a ride with a spy."

"Want to tell me about the stuff?"

"Sure. Jimmy took pictures inside a German tank. He thought someone should see them and he had a packet of pills that the Germans use. I doubt it's aspirin."

"The army will want evidence and not hearsay."

"I've got them."

"What? Where?"

"Turn around, face the front." Chance saw Wheeler take one hand from the steering wheel and rest it on his side arm. "Eyes front, plee-eese," she ordered.

Chance saw the corporal's eyes lift to the rear-view mirror as she wiggled to the edge of the seat.

"The Frenchie said she was crazy," Wheeler whispered. "Maybe we should tie her."

Nora rose, reached down and slipped something from her underwear. She tossed the water stained film and pill packet onto the front seat."

"You hid them all along?" Chance laughed.

"Wasn't going to let those men inside my knickers," she began to scratch again. "Those things have rubbed so much I have a rash."

Saint-Malo
June 20

Jurgen Heinzman shook his head in disgust. Dozens of trucks sat in a makeshift wrecking yard. A few vehicles had burned to bare metal, others showed evidence of where a fire burned out. And, he suspected, trucks that appeared intact would be missing parts or have engine damage. "Like Dunkirk," he stepped to where Karl Munster was completing a personal survey. "The Canadians learned from the British. Almost everything is damaged. Bullets fired into the radiators and engines or sand in the fuel tanks. Most of this will be junk."

"Don't be too hasty," Munster lifted his cap and rubbed his shaved head. "Germany can use scrap metal but first let the Reich mechanics work. Spare parts may fit trucks we salvaged at Dunkirk and the odd one may still run."

Across the yard, an engine caught and a young mechanic waved in triumph.

Munster laughed, "The Canadians are not as efficient as they believe."

"But scavengers have been here," Heinzman led him to a truck. "The battery is gone. A farmer has an extra battery, or a shop keeper is selling parts from the back door."

"We are too lenient." Munster growled. "I would treat the French as we did the Poles. Shoot the leaders and send the others into forced labour, but I don't make the decisions." He walked

119

to another truck and banged his fist against a wheel. "Salvage the tires," he said. "Rubber is in short supply."

"Now, that we've beaten France, will the fighting stop?" Heinzman asked.

"Don't be an idiot. The first of the big guns from the Maginot Line have been moved to the coast. Those guns can send shells across the Channel. The English won't know what hit them."

"Will we invade?" Heinzman asked, thinking of friends who died in France.

"I doubt our war is over."

Brest, France
June 20

Night was falling as the fishing boat left the harbour. "Good thing, we connected," Brandon Young adjusted the speed. "Only a few of us take the risk and in the last few weeks, we sail at night."

"I'll make it worthwhile," Chance leaned against the side of tiny wheelhouse. The cargo section behind them was filled with bags and crates. Fishing gear was stowed below where Wheeler and Nora Field slept on narrow bunks.

"The weather is fine," Young smiled as the boat wallowed in what Chance considered rough seas.

"What's the cargo?" He hoped conversation would distract from a growing feeling of seasickness.

"Odds and sods. I don't ask a lot of questions."

"Then, we're kindred souls," Chance pulled his tweed jacket tighter. He had returned to civilian garb. The uniform was at the bottom of the Channel. "I thought we might find the Royal Navy at Brest?"

"Most left a week ago," Young told him. "Chaos! Every man claimed priority. The best was the Canadian Horse Artillery. The men were told to abandon the guns, big guns, not rifles. Their commander demanded time and space to load and pulled it off."

120

The sensation of sickness faded, and Chance began to relax. "Have you been at sea long?"

"I was born to it. My ancestors knew all the inlets and hideaways off the Channel and naturally turned to smuggling."

"I may need someone who knows the coast."

"Smuggling?"

"People might call it that. I can't get into details, maybe in a few weeks."

A flash in the night sky drew their eyes to the west.

"Could be anything." Young peered into the darkness. "Gunfire from a ship, a night fighter or an explosion on land."

"We'll leave you at the first port with a rail link," Chance decided. "Cornwall by morning?"

"If all goes well. The weather has been on our side. I've never seen the Channel as calm as during the evacuation of Dunkirk."

"Did you go?"

"No, I'm not that brave. I put to sea when the admiralty showed an interest in small boats. I didn't want to lose this one."

"I'm going below," Chance decided. "I can send Wheeler to keep you company."

"That would be appreciated and would free up a bunk unless you want to slip in with the lady."

"No. I need to sleep and for the record, she is a lady. She's had a rough time. She was on the *Lancastria* when it sank."

"*Lancastria*? I didn't know. But I'm not surprised. We've lost a lot of ships. A friend in the navy says we've a shortage of destroyers."

Philadelphia
June 27

"Finally, I thought you weren't coming." Tim Fulton scowled at the young woman. The convention hall was filling for the final hours of the race to choose a Republican candidate for President.

"Let's see that smile, Wendy and undo a couple of buttons on the blouse." He waited impatiently. "One more. Don't be modest. Do it for the country."

Finally, he nodded approval.

"Vandenberg for President," she called and held up a brochure. "Elect the Senator from Michigan."

"I'll take one," Brad Wilson gave her a big smile. "No self-respecting gentleman would refuse an offer from a pretty girl."

"Thanks mister," she winked and faked a southern drawl, "Y'all remember to vote," before whispering, "Tim's in a bad mood."

Wilson was not surprised. Fulton's candidate was fading. "Senator Vandenberg is the only candidate with experience in foreign affairs," Fulton collared an Ohio delegate. "He's run the Senate Foreign Relations Committee and he'll keep us out of war. He'll stop Roosevelt."

"Haven't you paid attention? Old Franklin is tired and won't run again."

"No President should even consider a third term," Fulton countered. "Which shows what he thinks of our traditions."

He turned to another delegate, "You sir. Vandenburg is the man for the hour."

"A lot of people, like this Wendell Willkie," the delegate had to shout to be heard over the crowd, "He'll avoid a war."

Fulton put his hand on the delegate's shoulder and spoke in his ear, "A few weeks ago, I saw a trainload of American weapons destined for England, but no one will admit it's happening."

"You don't say."

"I do. Roosevelt and the banks want us to fight the Germans. Why would we do that? Vote for Vandenburg." Fulton saw Wilson approach.

"The fix is in," he fumed. "The party is moving behind Willkie. The polls show the delegates don't know much about him but suddenly he's the people's choice."

"He is a fresh face. It looks like toss up between Willkie and Dewey. Vanderburg can't win."

"Since when are you an expert? Pass out brochures and keep fighting."

It was after midnight when the final vote showed Wendell Willkie was the Republican choice. While Fulton remained in the convention hall, Wilson had moved to the adjoining commercial museum.

"Incredible." He said as he watched the live pictures from the convention floor.

"First time you've seen television?" another spectator asked. "I saw a broadcast at the World's Fair in New York. American ingenuity at work again."

"Incredible," Wilson repeated and stared at the box.

"Yes, it is," the voice was familiar, and Wilson turned to see his FBI contact. Agent Laramie wore a dark blue suit, white shirt and tie and could easily pass for a convention delegate. "Except, the television is not an American technology. The Brits had it first."

Wilson found it hard to turn away but eventually followed Laramie to a quiet corner.

"Is the FBI investigating the Republican Party?"

"No. I'm only curious. Fulton must be disappointed."

"Tim talks a good story but I'm not sure he liked Vandenburg. He keeps hoping that Charles Lindbergh will run. He loves the story of the solo flight over the Atlantic. And, he thinks Lindbergh is right about superior German air power."

"Mr. Fulton appreciates all things German."

"If he could stomach a Democrat, he'd support Joe Kennedy."

"The ambassador won't be running." Laramie smiled. "What's the latest on Fulton?"

"He has more money than he used to and spreads it around. I don't know where it comes from. Look, he's a loudmouth but I think that's all."

"Stay with it. You can't fly off to Canada yet."

Al McGregor

"Now wait…"

"A little longer. Keep those ears open. And by the way, Fulton is telling the truth about arms for Britain. But it's odd, we monitor radio signals. The Germans knew it too. We had to make last minute changes for shipping."

"Tim told them?"

"Was it him or some other German agent? Keep those ears to the ground."

Vimy Ridge, France
June 29

German patrols and gas shortages made travel difficult and a thick fog compounded the problem. Maria drove slowly but almost missed the signpost for the Vimy Ridge Memorial. A German officer lounging by a staff car came to life as she entered the parking area.

"Lieutenant Gunther Webber?"

"I am," he clicked his heels and bowed.

"And, you speak English. That makes my job easier."

"I spent summers in England, but art rather than language brought me here. I've also read the articles from your magazine."

"My job might be easier if I worked for a better-known magazine, maybe *Colliers* or *Life*."

"It doesn't matter, Germany tries to maintain good relations with America." He led the way along a path, "I have something to show before we go the monument."

A wood stove warmed the small office where Webber had arranged a series of photographs. A rumor the monument had been destroyed set off a storm in Canada and German propagandists had released photos showing Adolf Hitler inspecting an intact memorial.

"As you can see, the Fuhrer was here," Webber said. "At heart, he is an artist, a painter before his natural leadership qualities were discovered."

"Were you here?"

"No. But, it was on June 2nd. The Fuhrer came at great risk to himself. Our troops had not yet taken Paris and the enemy was close."

"I ask, of course, because of the claims the photos were doctored, and we know other monuments were damaged."

Webber appeared genuinely sad. "In Paris, the statue of Edith Cavell was destroyed. To Germans, she was a notorious English spy. Another, honoring Black French Colonial soldiers of the Great War is no more. It was in obvious conflict with the racial policies of the Reich."

"Canadians believe the so-called 'brooding soldier' monument was wrecked."

"The battlefields of the first war have become battlefields once more. It may have been damaged in the fighting."

She saw he was uncomfortable and tried to explain. "People in North America are anxious to know the truth."

"Do Americans really care about Canadian monuments?"

"My magazine has subscribers in Canada."

A breeze began to clear the mist and the sun broke through as they walked to the memorial. She could see no obvious sign of damage.

"Assure the readers the statue is intact," he told her. "I would not presume to speak for the Fuhrer, but he may see what I do. The memorial does not glorify war or a victory. Canadians focus on the fallen, but I see an impressive work of art. I studied the career of the sculptor, Walter Allward."

"You are way ahead of me," she laughed.

"The stone came from quarries in Croatia," he told her. "He was obviously dedicated to the project."

"I didn't know that either. I do know Canadians will be relieved. I won't need anymore. I must thank you for your patience. My editors will be satisfied."

"Your home is near Le Havre?" he asked. "I expect to work in that region."

"More monuments?"

"No, something more difficult. The Air Minister, Hermann Goering, is an art collector. I am to search for works that may have been overlooked."

"Won't you enjoy browsing galleries and museums?"

"Yes, but dealing with owners can be difficult," he said. "Private ownership must give way to the needs of the Reich or to the demands of Mr. Goering."

The English Channel
July 2

"Spitfire," Marin Downey smiled, and a distant drone was followed by the roar of an aircraft. "Hear that Rolls Royce engine." The plane flashed above and in seconds vanished into the clouds over the Channel.

"Do you think we pass for birders?" Downey asked and raised a set of binoculars to his eyes.

"More like a couple of odd ducks," Evers Chance answered. "But it's lovely to be out of the city and away from your office crowd."

"I've never understood your refusal to keep an office. It makes it hard to know where you are."

"Precisely, Martin. We never know who may be watching. Besides, offices are prone to clutter, dirty, dusty, little chambers. Most of my files are in my head."

"But if…"

"No, my habits won't change. By moving about, I see more of the changes in the country. Those cliff top towers, for example, are a disgusting blot on the landscape."

"They're important for the war effort. Radar. It's top secret."

"A man would be blind not to see them and I'm tired of secrets." Chance let his binoculars fall to his chest. "We may have lost as many men when the *Lancastria* went down as were lost in all of the Battle of France, but the people haven't been told. Our leaders are covering up a naval disaster."

126

"Do you want a lecture on morale?" Downey asked. "The government isn't sure the people can take it." He scanned the horizon, "But that's not why I wanted to talk. What do you hear of the French fleet?"

"The odd vessel is in France or Vichy but most of the ships are in North Africa. Why?"

"We face a showdown with our former ally. They'll be offered a choice. Scuttle the fleet, send the ships to remote French colonies or face the broadsides of the Royal Navy."

"That's no way to treat a former ally or a future friend."

"The fleet would be a potent weapon if Hitler seized it. It has to be neutralized. And, there's a second aspect. The Americans aren't sure Britain has the stomach to continue the war, alone. An attack on the French would show our determination."

"Any attack could come at a high price."

"Churchill is prepared to pay."

Le Havre
July 10

Maria's neighbor brought the tragic news. Raymond Gregoire and his two sons had helped renovate the house and barn, until, the oldest son had been conscripted for the French Navy. "Maudits Anglais!" Raymond shook his fist as he stood in her doorway. "Danielle is dead. The British attacked our fleet in Algeria. The *Bretagne* is no more and my son is gone with her. Twelve hundred French sailors died."

"Oh, Raymond, I don't know what to say. Danielle was so young, so vibrant."

He had clenched his fists, the callused hands ready to strike. "Anything to do with the English goes badly for us. You should be very careful."

"What are you saying?"

"I want revenge, but I won't take it out on you. Others may. An American passport may not be enough. Stay away from the towns and villages for a few weeks. And if you must go, speak French. The danger is real."

"Is there anything I can do for you?"

"No, nothing you can do or say can help."

And, she had watched as he returned slowly toward his own home.

Her next dispatch for Weatherbee Magazine told of the French reaction, the shock and anger at apparent British deceit. On the margins of a private letter were details of new German air strips, of more planes and of large barges, potential landing craft, arriving in channel ports.

Chapter Six: Britain and the Blitz

Near London
July 29

The country lane was blocked. The nose of a Spitfire rested in a dense hedgerow, the rest of the fuselage blocked the road. A half-dozen men hacked at the greenery while a second crew attached chains to the wreck. "Pull it up," one man yelled as an improvised pulley took the strain. "We're not going to do any more damage." With the scream of tearing metal, a section tore loose and was lifted to a waiting truck.

"The cockpit is a mess," a workman attached another chain. "We'll have to wash the blood away to see if the gauges can be salvaged."

"Do that at the yard. Get a chain on the engine. And, someone tell the men in the car, the road will be re-open in fifteen minutes."

Martin Downey nodded his approval and tapped his fingers on the steering wheel. "Those are Beaverbrook's men. He's stepped up production at the aircraft plants and arranged for these recovery crews. Our planes are removed smartly but no one rushes to move a Junkers or Messerschmidt. Wreckage of a German plane proves the RAF is doing a bang-up job." The workmen began to sweep away the last of the glass and metal debris.

"That fuselage will be taken apart and anything that can be repaired will be," Downey explained. "The aluminum will be melted down and used in a new plane. Nothing goes to waste."

"I wonder if doctors can salvage the pilot?" Chance asked. "The ambulance wasn't in a hurry. That's a bad sign."

"Pilots are a concern," Downey admitted. "We'll find more planes. I'm not sure who will fly them. It will be months before large numbers arrive from the Canadian training program."

"And do you think we have a few months? Hitler assures us he is coming."

"Yes, I saw the translation of his latest peace offer. Clever of Winston to have Halifax deliver the reply. The old appeaser sounded decidedly militant."

"The Halifax speech was a nice change of pace but where are the great orators? Halifax has a lisp. The King stutters. And Churchill sounds drunk?"

"Rest assured, he's had a few nips."

A road supervisor whistled and waved traffic forward. Downey slipped the car in gear and drove slowly past the wreck site. "I wonder," Chance began to speculate, "have we listened too much to Charles Lindbergh and other men enamoured by German airpower? Maybe we've closed the gap between the RAF and the Luftwaffe."

"We'll know soon enough. But look, this is what I wanted to show you."

Chance looked along the road to the distant outline of buildings, a control tower, and hangar. A plane appeared ready for takeover, but there was no sign of life, no sentries, pilots or ground crew. "A decoy airfield," Downey said proudly.

"Are there many of these," Chance was intrigued.

"Enough to attract tons of German bombs. Set designers from the movie industry built phoney airfields and imitation factories to fool the bombers."

"Very clever. But what if spies get close enough to see the ruse."

"The timing of the question is perfect," Downey braked for a farm wagon blocking the road. "These are Home Defence Volunteers."

An elderly man, carrying a pitchfork, approached the car. "Purpose of travel," he demanded. "But, oh, it's Mr. Downey." He relaxed the grip on the fork, "Showing off the handiwork, are we?"

"Good day, Bert. Busy?"

"No. People aren't moving about much. A troop convoy came through, Canadians on a training exercise."

"We're off to Dover," Downey smiled. "I can vouch for my companion."

"Sorry, sir. I need more than that. Let's see identification."

Downey smiled broadly as Chance produced his documents, waited as the sentry plucked glasses from a case and squinted until he was satisfied. "Off to Dover then."

"Yes. We're birders. We haven't had a chance the last few weeks."

"A lot of seagulls," Bert predicted. "Watching the shit hawks over the white cliffs of Dover don't seem exciting. But have a good day."

"Bert is ok." Downey explained as he drove on. "The men are local and notice anything suspicious. They'll fight with everything from Molotov cocktails to booby traps. If England goes down, we'll go down fighting."

"A real people's war, is it?"

"That's right," Downey nodded. "And look over to the left, the farm equipment in that pasture. A German glider would be ripped apart if it tried to land."

"But the volunteers are armed with forks?"

"With the losses in France, we're hard pressed to re-arm the army but eventually we'll have weapons for the home guard. We're taking anything, even Ross Rifles from Canada. They had a bad reputation in the first war but we're desperate."

Chance shrugged. "It beats repelling the Wehrmacht with pitchforks and pointy sticks?"

"There you go again," Downey complained. "We're doing our best. The invaders won't simply waltz into Whitehall."

"I wonder," Chance looked across the fields. "An agent tells of barges and tugs moving to the Channel. Everything points to invasion, but the Germans would face enormous losses. Hitler would be smarter to wait. If he could destroy the will to fight, we might give up."

"No chance of that," Downey snorted. "Think of Bert. He's ready for action."

"But is everyone so full of piss and vinegar? How many people believe the Nazi propaganda broadcasts? According to them, fighting would be useless."

"I've heard...ah what's this."

The road ahead was blocked by another farm wagon and several men. "More of the Home Guard?" Chance smiled. "Test them. Drive through and I'll shout, 'Sig Heil'."

Downey grimaced. "Keep your mouth shut and let me do any talking."

Stanmore, England
August 7

For Nora Field, a day full of promise turned to frustration. The bus was delayed, and she was an hour late for the interview at Bentley Priory, a fact a prickly officer, warned must never happen again. He briskly directed her to join other young women, the new members of the Women's Auxiliary Air Force.

"Watch your step," someone warned as they descended a long flight of stairs. "The operation room is deep underground."

The staircase ended at a large room where several women worked at a plotting table. Each wore a headset and microphone. The male commanders watched from a platform several feet above. The tour guide spoke in a whisper, "Each of the markers on the table represent an enemy flight. Radar spots them before they reach the coast. An air observer on the ground identifies the type of aircraft. The information is collected, filtered, plotted and fighters are scrambled. The women at the table must always be on their best game."

A radio speaker came to life as a pilot called a warning, "Bandits…four o'clock."

"We'll go now," the guide began to hustle the trainees from the room, "Things get frantic. Besides, there's another briefing scheduled."

Up the stairs and in a large classroom, a middle-aged man in an air force uniform waited by a blackboard. "I'll do a quick run through on radar." And with that the lights went out and photographs appeared on a screen. The first picture showed radar towers, but Nora was soon confused by jargon. An hour later his lecture, mercifully, ended. "Now, you can see why radar is considered 'Most Secret' and why you were required to sign the 'Official Secrets Act'. That's it for today." She waited as the other women left the room before approaching the officer.

"Excuse me," she offered her sweetest smile.

"I'm not repeating anything," he told her. "Learn to pay attention."

"I was, but it's beyond me and nothing was said about driver training."

"What?"

"I signed up to be a driver, a chauffeur. The radar is interesting, but I don't see how it applies to autos."

"A driver. How do you get in?"

"Walked in with the rest of them. I was a little late and followed along."

"Walked in? Where was security?"

"A soldier at the gate was chatting up a blonde girl and I didn't want to intrude."

"Have you signed anything?"

"No. What's that Official Secrets Act you went on about?"

"Come with me," he grabbed her arm. "A top-secret facility and she walked in. The shit will hit the fan over this one."

Al McGregor
Northolt Air Base
August 17

Black smoke rose like a beacon. A hangar blazed and on the runway was the wreckage of an aircraft. The enemy was no longer content to focus on channel convoys, the targets shifted to RAF bases.

Dan Malone was forced to leave his car and walk to the base entrance.

"Who in hell are you?" An air force sergeant ordered Malone into a guard hut. "Army uniform, no insignia and too damn fresh and clean for active service. Better talk fast. The prison cells are calling."

"I'm a correspondent, Canadian," he flashed the press credentials. "And yes, the uniform is new. I was ordered to wear it."

"You picked a hell of a day. An hour ago, we were under attack. What do you want?"

"I guess I should see a press officer."

"Fat chance of that. The two of them ran off when the first bomb dropped, the chicken shits."

"Perhaps, I could see a squadron commander...I'm looking...." He stopped and listened. Despite the bedlam, he recognized a familiar sound from his days in France, the wail of an air-borne siren. "Stuka!" he shouted and looked frantically for cover. The sergeant didn't hesitate. With Malone in pursuit he galloped to a makeshift shelter, a circle of sandbags rising from bare ground. An instant later a blast showered them with debris. As the dust settled, they saw they were not alone.

"Sir." The sergeant saluted an officer and began to stand.

"For Christ sake, stay down. You'll get your head blown off."

The officer brushed dust from his uniform before glaring at Malone. "Can't the army take care of its own?"

"Only wearing what I'm told," Malone, too, brushed at the dust and hoped no one would notice his shaking hands. "I look better in air force blue, but the press office made me wear khaki. I'm a correspondent."

"We can't all be perfect." The officer said, waving as a staff car rolled up.

"No real damage," the driver called. "Big hole in the runway but we can fix that."

"Good show, I'll be back at headquarters in a few minutes." A wisp of smoke brought the odour of burning oil and spent ammunition. He turned to Malone. "Obviously this is not a day for tours."

"I was looking for Canadians. #1 RCAF is supposed to be here."

"Not yet, although the sooner they arrive the better. That squadron flies Hurricanes. A Stuka is slow especially coming out of a dive. A few more Hurricanes or Spits and we'll blow them from the sky."

"I'll come back...later?"

"Maybe you should look up 242 squadron. Commander Bader has a few Canadians or better yet, find the Poles. They can't speak English but are damn fine flyers."

Ogdensburg, New York
August 17

Sandy Fleming almost tripped crossing the railway yard. The Presidential train was on a rear siding and the engineer was raising steam. A sharp whistle and the rail cars began to move. She raced forward, glanced up and sucked in her breath. Franklin Delano Roosevelt sat by a window, a broad smile, the trademark cigarette holder and then he was gone. Her heart sank. The big story of a hastily arranged meeting between the President and the Prime Minister was speeding away. But, the passage of the train revealed a small group of men watching the departure. "What did I miss?" She crossed the track to join fellow reporters.

"Hello Princess," the bureau chief for a Montreal paper greeted her. "FDR was sorry he missed you. He'll send flowers but don't tell Eleonor."

She smiled in spite of her irritation.

"There's nothing to see Sandy. No drama, no pathos. Only a joint statement. Boring as hell and not worth sweating out a hot Sunday."

"Do you have a copy?"

"Get one from the Prime Minister's group," someone suggested. "He hasn't left yet."

Sandy trotted toward a private railway car, arriving as several men descended. "I'm a reporter, I'm late but is there a press statement?"

"Oh, by all means give one to Miss Fleming." The Prime Minister ordered as he stepped down. "Tell the readers, it is a great day for Canada." King had removed his jacket and red suspenders stretched across his stomach. An aide carried his jacket and a briefcase.

"Is it the destroyer deal?" she asked.

"Destroyers? Franklin and I did discuss ships, but the real news is a Joint Defence Agreement. The full details must be worked out, but Canada and the United States will co-operate on North American security."

"We must go, Prime Minister," the aide opened a door on a limousine.

"I can't say any more, Miss Fleming," King smiled. "I'm sure you understand."

The press statement written in ponderous civil service language added to her frustration.

"Need help?"

She turned to face a young man wearing a short sleeve shirt and a battered hat. "I'm Mark Ryder of the Monument News Service. I know the feeling of arriving late."

"I've had one of those days, a flat tire and an overbearing border guard," Sandy explained. "The tire I could handle but the guard flummoxed me. He thought a Canadian woman might be taking work from an American male. I'm Sandy Fleming from the Willard Agency."

"I did a stint in Ottawa before I landed in Washington. I'll bet Frank Willard assigned you late and forgot expense money."

"Our reputation is growing," she laughed. "And he didn't give me any background."

"Officially," Ryder began to explain, "the deal allows for more co-operation between American and Canadian Forces, at the command level, joint planning and that sort of thing. Eventually, it could allow more integration of the supply chain. Unofficially, your Prime Minister is worried about Great Britain and what happens if the old country goes down. Mr. Roosevelt worries too."

"And that's why King calls it 'a Great Day for Canada'?"

"Yup and it probably is. Although, if I was an opposition politician in Canada, I would say King has surrendered sovereignty and I'd question how deep the co-operation will go. Will Americans now make Canadian defence decisions?"

"Will they?"

"We'll have to see."

"What's in for Roosevelt?"

"His northern border and the east coast are safer. The isolationists won't like it and will say the U.S. is choosing sides. The British may not like it either. Their former colony is drifting deeper into the American sphere of influence. But don't expect a public fuss. No one wants to upset Washington when America may be the ultimate saviour."

"I think I see," Sandy folded the statement. "I'll track down reaction when I get back to Ottawa. I wish I had a way to thank you."

"Maybe you do. You mentioned destroyers. What's that about?"

"Rumors," she told him. "The British desperately need ships. A half-dozen Canadian destroyers were sent to England. And, a colleague picked up a hint of negotiations over old American ships."

Al McGregor

"Is the colleague, Robert McLaren?"

"You know him?"

"I know of him. He's has a reputation as a good reporter. I'll start asking questions in Washington."

"Then we're even," she smiled again.

"No. We'll meet for dinner or drinks the next time I'm in Canada."

New York City
August 22

Erich Schmidt didn't walk. Instead, with ramrod precision he marched the pathway of a New York City park. And, when he reached the bench where Tim Fulton waited, he performed a perfect, if unintentional, right wheel.

"Good day, Tim," he said and precisely aligned his briefcase on the ground between them. For a few moments he was silent, content to watch the passing crowd.

"Were you in the army long?" Tim Fulton asked. "It shows as you walk, the erect posture."

"In Germany, boys and girls go to Hitler youth camps. And in the army, we competed to see who was strongest and who could endure the most. The lessons stayed with me."

"I've picked up something that may be important," Fulton whispered.

"Please don't talk about that silly Canada-U.S. agreement. The two countries are already in bed together."

"No. Ships. Roosevelt may give the British surplus destroyers."

"This too is trifling. A few old ships will not change the course of the war."

"Not a handful, as many as fifty."

Schmidt took a moment to consider the news. "Fifty is a larger number than I would have expected," he said. "When would they sail?"

"The first will go almost immediately. American crews would take them to Halifax where the Royal Navy would take over."

"And, what do the Americans get from this? The U.S. has demanded cash or gold for anything they sell."

"The British will make land available for American bases, in the Caribbean and Newfoundland."

"Another signal Roosevelt is waging an undeclared war."

"That's how I see it. The election is two months away and FDR publicly claims he'll keep us out. But he won't be able to control the campaign as he did the Presidential convention. The Democrats acted like a bunch of sheep."

"Perhaps, the Republican, Mr. Willkie, will oppose the deal or maybe the American Congress?"

"Willkie will go along, and the White House legal team will find a way to get around Congress."

Schmidt shook his head in disgust.

"Your country has too many lawyers, but we will win in the end. I was delighted to hear of the new 'America First' Organization. Anti-war groups are finally working together."

Schmidt rose. "I will leave my briefcase. As before, we ask for no accounting. The American political system is so very expensive."

North Weald Airbase, England
August 26

"I thought every reporter worth his salt would be beating down the door at Bomber Command tonight." The RAF press officer was only weeks away from college, another of the bright-eyed young men who planned a career in the air and found himself on ground duty. "Everyone is waiting for news on our raid on Berlin."

"This reporter's salt depends on finding the Royal Canadian Air Force," Dan Malone replied. "I'm not reporting on Berlin; I came looking for Canadians."

139

Al McGregor

"Stay here," the young lieutenant said. "I need clearance from the base commander."

The damage at North Weald was visible to the naked eye, with damaged hangars and wrecked planes but, as at other bases, the flying operations continued. "He mentioned Bomber Command and Berlin," a young man in a leather flying jacket stepped closer to Malone. "No one can tell me how many planes went but I'll bet we sent a bunch. The Nazis deserve it after an attack on London. We had to pay them back."

Malone had skirted the city in pursuit of the Canadian squadron. A hurried phone call assured him that Marcie was safe and German bombs had fallen on another part of London. Damage was heavy and a hundred were dead.

The airman kept his voice low. "I hope our navigators are on the ball. Bomber Command could miss the broad side of a barn. Bombs fall miles from the target. Maybe it's the same story with the Luftwaffe. They had been avoiding the cities. Maybe a German pilot made a mistake."

"Malone?" The press officer motioned him to the door. "No interviews and no statements on the #1 RCAF. The commander has laid down the law."

"Wait. What if I do the story and hold it?"

"Won't work."

Malone sensed he was holding something back. "What's going on. The squadron was in action. Did they take major casualties?"

"Uh, yah, there were losses, but I'm not supposed to say more."

"Give me a hint," Malone persisted.

"No one knows what to say. The squadron spotted bombers over the Channel and shot down a couple."

"But that's great…"

"No. The planes were ours. The army would call it 'friendly fire'. The causalities were British. We're working to determine how many men were lost."

Halifax, Nova Scotia
September 6

"And those ships with the four smokestacks are the new British destroyers?" Robert McLaren asked, studying the vessels from a Halifax pier.

"New is hardly an apt description," his local associate laughed. Brian Potter had been filing occasional dispatches for the news agency since the war began.

McLaren shaded his eyes with his hands. "Tell me what you know."

"Fifty ships, built in 1918-1919, out of service and mothballed," Potter explained. "Washington claims they were destined for the wrecking yard and worth a few thousand dollars as scrap. In return, the American's get ninety-nine-year leases for bases in British colonies. I don't think it's land grab. Roosevelt thinks Newfoundland is only good for raising sheep. The other bases are in the Caribbean."

"What happens now?"

"The British will fit the ships with Asdic, that's anti-submarine gear, and use them as convoy escorts. That's if the old engines hold up and nothing breaks down. A couple almost collided when they entered the harbour. The steering may be deficient. And, with those stacks, the destroyers are top heavy. I'd expect a nasty roll in rough seas."

"But it shows how desperate the British are for ships?" McLaren continued to study the harbour.

"Yup, all kinds of ships but especially destroyers. The losses have been climbing but navy censors kept a lid on. And remember, these ships are fighting the North Atlantic. The weather is awful except in fall, winter and spring when it's worse. That old metal could spring a leak."

London
September 7

"Bandits…two o'clock," the voice carried from the speaker and another marker went on the plot display, "Messerschmitt 109's, a dozen or more."

Evers Chance saw a woman nod at the confirmation of what the air observers reported minutes earlier. Beside him, Martin Downey sighed as more markers, representing more enemy planes, were pushed onto the table. "This can't go on much longer," Downey whispered. "Hugh Dowling at Fighter Command is out of reserves. Pilots are worn out, flying sortie after sortie, dawn to dusk."

"He's on your tail, Billy," the voice came again. "…Billy, I see smoke."

"Fire in the cockpit!"

"Bail out, Billy."

"The canopy is jammed. Jesus, it won't budge."

"Use the crowbar by the hatch. Smash the canopy. Break the blasted thing and get out."

A blood curdling scream filled the air waves then ended abruptly.

"No sign of chute," another pilot called. "He's in the Channel."

Chance saw a tear slide down the face of a young woman. "Poor bloody bugger," Downey sighed again. "Let's get a breath of air. I hate to think of what's happened."

"And that's the trick," Chance told him sadly, "don't think. Accept the danger but don't think of what may happen. The boys are told not to think." Downey coughed as they stepped outside and into a cloud of dense smoke.

"Pray for rain," Chance advised. "A few days of bad weather would buy time."

"Time for what?" Downey spit to clear his throat, "The RAF is exhausted."

Chance plucked a pipe from his pocket and struck a match.

"Jesus. Watch the match, you'll cause an explosion!"

"Anything that hasn't blown isn't going to. Just as Hitler is unlikely to invade."

"What are you talking about? All the signs are there. The air attacks. The barges on the French Coast, practise sessions to load troops and supplies. The information comes from your agents. Don't you trust them?"

"I trust what they see but not what it means," he said. "Hitler hopes for an armistice."

"A fat chance of that. Appeasers are gone."

Chance tapped the tobacco and struck another match.

"Hitler needs to weaken morale, destroy the RAF, and control the Channel before an invasion. He won't get all three."

"Mr. Chance? Mr. Downey?" a woman from the operations centre called. "You should see this."

Inside quiet calm had given way to a marked sense of anxiety. The plotting table was black with markers. "Bombers," she explained, "on course for London."

Forty miles away, Marcie Eaton pulled a sweater over her blouse. "Stay and sleep. I'm going for a walk."

"The beach may be off limits," Dan Malone lay stretched on a bed. The hectic schedule was wearing him down. Pilots were fighting fatigue and the reporters who followed them, were in the same condition. By the time she laced her shoes, Malone was asleep. Their hotel was busy. Cars, filled with families, had been arriving since early afternoon. The new air-raid shelters might offer protection, but many Londoners preferred a safer country retreat. The road to the beach was as she remembered, except sign posts had been removed and the narrow track had a new manmade obstacle at every turn. The white caps and stiff wind would have deterred bathers in peace time but in war, the lines of barbed wire eliminated any access to the water. Still, she walked, meandering along the beach. Sunset was approaching but she felt no desire to stop.

"Don't move an inch," the voice came from behind and was joined immediately by another.

"She's been sashaying about for no good reason, probably sending a signal out to sea."

"Don't move," the first voice repeated. A hand roughly grabbed her shoulder and spun her around. Two elderly men, one armed with a handgun, the other carrying a thick, walking stick, confronted her.

"She's blonde, must be German," the first man spoke, "one of those Aryan she-wolves."

"I'm no German." She wanted to laugh at the ridiculousness of their conclusion.

"Were you scouting the mine field?" the second man demanded.

"Mine field? I was walking on the beach."

"Another twenty feet and you'd have met your maker, blown yourself to hell."

"I didn't know. There was no sign and …"

"Do you think we'd be stupid enough to warn where mines are planted? Let's see the I.D."

"It's at the hotel," she began to explain. "I was only out for a walk."

"Come with us." The men produced a coil of rope and tied her hands together.

The man called Harold appeared to be in charge while the other, Ron, tugged on the rope.

"Sorry miss," Harold grudgingly apologized, "we're Home Volunteers and we can't be too careful. I'll send Ron ahead to check your story."

"Could you undo the rope?" she asked. "I promise not to escape." and sighed with relief when the knot was undone.

For the next few minutes she followed him toward the village. Then in the distance, she heard an explosion, followed moments later by another. Harold was instantly on alert and Ron came trotting back. The short run from the public telephone left him short of breath and he was able to spit out only a single word. "Cromwell!"

144

"Are you sure?" Harold demanded, as the bell in the local church began to toll.

"The bells and the explosions. The lads are blowing the bridges. It's Cromwell."

"What is Cromwell?" she interrupted.

"Invasion! Your Kraut friends are coming ashore." Ron retrieved the rope and again, looped it around her wrists.

"In case we don't make it, it's been an honor serving with you, Ron." Harold squared his shoulders and shifted the gun. "A little too convenient that we find this one on the beach on the night of the invasion. We'll have to shoot her if the Germans come before our men."

"I put a horse down once. I guess I can do it."

Four hours later, Dan Malone arrived.

"Claims he was asleep," Ron sneered, "As if anyone could sleep through bells and explosions. But I called London and he is a what he claims."

Harold pointed to where Marcie was tied, "I was about to gag her. The woman won't shut up."

"I can vouch for her," Malone tried to hide a smile. Marcie's eyes shot daggers across the room. "She left her papers by mistake."

Harold studied the documents before finally loosening the rope.

"I'll take over," Malone helped Marcie to her feet. "She'll be more careful in the future." Once in the street, he began to laugh. "If they did that to you, imagine what would happen to the enemy."

"It wouldn't be so funny if you were tied to a chair." She pretended to be angry, "What took so long to rescue me?"

"A big security flap, getting a phone line to London was almost impossible."

"Something about Cromwell and the invasion?"

"A big snafu," he told her, "Cromwell is the warning signal for invasion. Someone sent it by mistake. The church bells were supposed to alert the countryside. A few bridges were destroyed

to slow the German advance, except, there was no invasion."
Marcie laughed. "And, we came to the country to get away from war."

"It's best we came," Malone told her. "Look toward London."

A steady red glow, punctuated by huge flashes, gave evidence of fires and a city under attack.

"The Luftwaffe is pouring it to the east end," he explained. "The gloves are off. Hitler is bringing the war to the people."

London
September 19

The blaze consumed one building and, despite the efforts of the firefighters, threatened to spread. Towering flames from an inferno, a block away, lit the surrounding streets.

"We won't get through," Dan Malone shouted and saw his fellow reporter nod and double back. Both men stepped aside as an ambulance snaked through the debris.

Malone lifted his helmet to wipe the perspiration from his forehead but only for a moment. A shower of hot metal bounced on the pavement and sent both men racing to a recessed doorway.

"Shrapnel, coming back down." Steve Carter yelled over the sound of the iron shower. "Anti-aircraft guns fire blind. The crews can't see a target. The noise is supposed to show we're fighting back." The two reporters teamed to witness the Blitz at ground level. Carter, a local reporter from a London paper, was familiar with the area and Malone was content to follow.

"There's not much left to burn," Carter said a few minutes later as they passed the ruins of a line of buildings. "This goes on night after night. No one knows how many have died. Most people appear stoic although what else can they do."

A giant searchlight came to life and waved across the sky. "The chances of catching a plane in that band are pretty small. Again, it's meant to reassure the public." Another search light came to life as the first blinked off. "How bad was the damage to the docklands?" Malone asked, knowing Carter had been on the streets since the attacks began.

"Houses and shops were hit hard and a few warehouses, but ships continue to load and unload. A few people took shelter in the tube, which is the last thing the authorities wanted. The stations aren't equipped for crowds or for long stays. Have you been down there?"

"No," Malone confessed. He had watched the attacks from a rooftop several miles away. "The tube is deep enough for shelter but there aren't enough toilets. The stench gets worse every night. The city administration was slow to build deep shelters, which is odd. We've been warned for years that the bombers would come."

Malone recalled what Marcie told him. The basement below the club had been reinforced and a few members spent the night underground. He hoped she was with them.

"Hear that," Carter shouted as the roar of aircraft engines grew in intensity. "Another wave. Make for that church. There may be a basement." But the church door was locked. The only shelter was under a carved stone entrance way.

"What's this?" Malone watched a rain of small projectiles.

"Incendiaries," Carter backed tight against the building. "Fire wardens douse them with sand. Spray them with water and the things explode. Any new fire offers another brightly lit, target. And, the Luftwaffe use high explosives to increase the damage. I spent a night with an air force specialist. He was looking to see what tricks we could copy to attack Germany cities."

Another ambulance passed, the driver using the light from the fires to navigate. "More trouble ahead," Carter predicted. They moved cautiously until the deluge of cannisters stopped. "What's this?" Carter shook his head in amazement. There was no fire or bomb damage, but glass was smashed from the windows in a line of small shops. A mannequin, from a menswear store teetered over the sidewalk, a hat still attached to the head, but the other clothing was gone. Next door, the remnants of a jeweller's display littered the sidewalk. "Looters," Carter concluded. "The authorities try to keep it quiet."

Malone heard raised voices and rounded a corner to find an ambulance surrounded by a small, angry mob. The medical team cowered inside.

"We'll beat the hell out of you," an angry man shook his fist.

"We're trying to do our job," a nurse answered. "Maybe, we can help." She tried to open the ambulance door but men in the street pushed it shut."

"Four bodies were in that house," a woman yelled. "The other ambulance crew went to look and now each body is missing a ring finger. The scavengers didn't try to work the rings loose, they cut off the fingers."

"Maybe we should go," the nurse decided. "Nothing we can do. The police can deal with it in the morning."

Malone pulled Carter from the crowd. "Is there much like this?"

"No," Carter shook his head. "Looting...yes...but this looks organized. I haven't seen this before but don't expect to publish anything. Bad for morale."

London
September 25

"Get a move on. The car was expected an hour ago." The lieutenant berated the driver. "I came as a fast I could," Nora Field stuck her head from window, a few strands of hair escaping the cap of the Women's Air Force Auxiliary.

"Aw, for Christ sake, a woman driver. Well, beggars can't be choosers but drive carefully. The other passenger is the top man in the Canadian army, Andrew McNaughton. Can you find the road to Aldershot?"

"Maps are right here," Nora patted the seat beside her. She didn't mention the delay was the result of a wrong turn.

"Let's go," a middle-aged officer said as he sprinted from the building.

148

An Angry Sky

The lieutenant loaded several suitcases before he slammed the door. "The trip will take a couple of hours," he told the general. "I thought you might want to catch up on paper work and, I have the outline of the latest training exercise."

"And who is this?" The general leaned over the seat to peer at the driver.

"Corporal Nora Field, sir." She noted the grey in his moustache and hair.

"In future, Corporal Field, will suffice," the lieutenant set the rules. "This is General McNaughton, and I am Lieutenant Jeevers."

"Yes, sir," she put the car in gear. "And, I will speak only if spoken to."

She heard the general chuckle but kept her eyes on the road. "The Luftwaffe is right on schedule," Jeevers starred through the rear window. The red glow offered mute evidence of another night of bombing.

"The transport arrangements," McNaughton ignored the scene. "The last exercise was a mess. I can't have the division lurching across three counties."

"Home guard units got in the way," Jeevers reminded him.

"In the future, prepare for that," the general grumbled, "but keep the home guard happy. That Cromwell alarm showed how much training needs to be done." McNaughton set the paper aside as a large limousine, honked and swept past. A small American flag waved from the fender.

"I'll bet it's Joe Kennedy," McNaughton laughed. "He flees the city each night. First, he was an appeaser calling for a negotiated settlement. Now, he predicts England will lose and each night protects his hide and runs from the bombs."

Jeevers watched the limousine weave through traffic, "I've never seen the man in person."

"And you won't have many more chances. He's begging to be recalled to Washington and, according to the talk, he'll get his way."

Al McGregor

"I have the list for promotions," Jeevers extracted another paper from his briefcase.

McNaughton scanned the list and squirmed to get comfortable. "Corporal, are there no larger cars in the fleet?"

"This was all they had," Nora answered. "Staff cars are at premium."

"Everything is at premium," he shrugged. "Basic equipment is hard to find. Do you have a gas mask?"

Nora winced. "In the boot, in the back," she confessed.

"It's supposed to be with you, on your person, part of basic kit. Stop the car and get it."

A glance in the mirror showed a scowling officer and she pulled off the road. It took several minutes to find the mask. She waved it for the general and climbed back behind the wheel. The car was in motion before he spoke. "Do you think it's a silly precaution?"

"Oh no, sir."

"I've seen men after a gas attack. In the first war, chlorine gas. Nasty stuff. I'm surprised Hitler hasn't used it. And, if he does, we'll respond in kind. Keep that mask handy."

McNaughton turned to his aide. "Make a note, a message to Dr. Banting, Fred Banting. He's been working on chemicals. I want to know what's become of the chemical test facility in Canada. It was somewhere remote, Alberta, I think. The work started when I was at the National Research Council."

"And driver," McNaughton turned his attention to Nora, "nothing said in my car is to be repeated."

"Right sir. Official Secret it is. I've been primed for that."

"That's a good girl. You'll do well."

Le Havre
September 27

Maria's first trip to the small shop on the harbour had been exhausting. Today, after building stamina, the bicycle ride was easier. Evers Chance had made the initial arrangements. Farm products could be exchanged for other supplies. Maurice, the

150

owner, managed to find scarce commodities. In the shop, she manoeuvred past bicycle parts, shovels, a half-dozen car batteries, a few sacks of grain and a rack of dresses before reaching the counter.

"The hens are doing well," Maurice gently took the eggs she carried and placed them below the counter. "What do you need?"

"Sugar," she laughed. "I'm desperate for something sweet."

"Wait," he slipped through a door and returned moments later with a tiny bag. "Not much, but these are difficult times."

"Anything is welcome."

"I have news," Maurice said. "The Germans are sending tugs and barges back where they came from."

"Are they all going?"

"Only a few, so far, but others will go soon. And, the troops are preparing for a change of scenery."

"Is this only happening in Le Havre?"

"I don't know. My contacts are from this area. Will you go to Paris soon?"

"I think so. Chance will want to know." Outside, she mounted the bicycle, peddled from the dock and with time to spare took a different route home. In a shopping district she saw windows, once filled with merchandise, almost empty. After only a few months, the German occupation had begun to bite.

"Maria Dickson?" A German officer stepped into her path. She felt a twinge of fear. "Gunther Webber," he smiled a greeting. "We met at the Vimy memorial, a few weeks ago."

"Oh yes, Lieutenant. I remember now."

"Call me Gunther. I'm in uniform but trying to forget the army for a day. There's a café on the next street. Join me?" A woman in the company of a German officer might raise eyebrows but to refuse would be an insult and Webber had been courteous at their earlier meeting. "I don't like riding in the dark," she told him, "But I have a couple of hours before dusk."

Webber took the cycle and pushed it between them. "The café is on the left. Do you want to go inside or sit by the street?"

151

"Inside." Fewer people would notice them in the dim light of a restaurant.

"How is your work," Maria asked when they found a table. "Is it as you expected?"

"Yes and no," he signalled to a waiter. "The French hide the better artworks."

"I suppose with the fear of bombing, owners try to protect them."

"Let's be candid," he said. "It's fear of confiscation, and the fear is well placed." The waiter arrived, and they were silent as the glasses were filled.

"I saw a painting a few weeks ago," he told her, "The model looked like you."

"No, it couldn't be me...unless...I met an artist when I came back to Europe. I sat for him, but he never finished the painting. I had completely forgotten. But it's probably someone who looks like me."

"The eyes and the face were familiar."

"I don't think so. Pierre was a struggling artist. He would flit from project to project and seldom finish one."

"Perhaps I was mistaken. Are you still writing?" he asked.

"The odd article for the Washington magazine. I have another to send shortly. I'll go to Paris and send it from there."

"I'll be based in Paris," he smiled. "We could tour the galleries."

She tried to hide her uncertainty, "That could be pleasant."

"I'll give you a telephone number," he said as he began to write. "I will look forward to this."

Later, she reconsidered his invitation, deciding an innocent meeting should present no danger.

The sounds as she cycled home were harder to dismiss. Hundreds of bombers and fighters flew above her. Le Havre and the barges in the harbour had been the target for RAF attacks but the Luftwaffe was aiming at civilians.

London

October 15

Another explosion, the latest in a series, created a shower of dust. Marcie Eaton nervously glanced at the ceiling and slipped a napkin over a tray of glasses.

"Good thinking," Henry Dalton congratulated her. He sat in a broad easy chair relocated from the club rooms to the basement shelter. She carefully placed a glass on the table beside him.

"Where's the young man tonight."

"He was off to watch the Americans. I hope he doesn't do anything stupid. Radio reporters get so close to the action."

"Oh, I wouldn't worry." The general placed his hand across the rim of the glass as another shower of dust fell. "But what about you?" Marcie had appeared for work each night since the Blitz began. "What about a break?"

"No where to go." She slipped another napkin from her pocket and dusted the table. "Dan wants me to go home but I want to stay. Life is pretty slow in a small country village. And truth be told, I'd soon be bickering with my parents."

"Humm," the general nodded. "Sometimes I think Dan is lucky." She said. "He's an orphan, no family at all."

Another explosion sent more dust and tiny fragments of cement through the shelter. "Reinforced concrete," he wiped at his shoulder, "keeps the bombs out but pushes up the cost of cleaning. Has your family complained about the riff-raff fleeing the city?"

"My mother wrote of children arriving when the war began but most went home a few weeks later," she said. "I wonder if they've evacuated them again."

"The bleeding hearts will be bending over backwards. But, children from the poor neighborhoods don't know how to behave. One would have to keep a close watch or be stolen blind. Little buggers have light fingers."

"Oh, it can't be that bad," she wiped her hands. "Did you plan to eat tonight?"

153

"Later. I don't want to swallow a layer of dust." She could hear more explosions but further away.

"It must be hard for children," she said. "Parents with money or friends in North America can send them to safety."

"Safety? Didn't you read of the *City of Benares*? Almost eighty children on that ship bound for Canada. Eighty young lives snuffed out by a torpedo. It would have been better to take their chances in London."

"I suppose the parents felt they had to try. And, what about the other refugees, the children who came from Europe?"

"We're stuck with them. The North Americans prefer pale, white, English speakers. If the parents don't turn up, their governments would have to support the children and governments do not want that."

"That's cruel...heartless."

"The way of the world. The authorities wanted my neighbor's country house for shelter, but he refused. He had a devil of a fight and pulled a lot of strings but refused to deal with the lower classes."

"But if people need shelter..."

"We can't take care of everyone. The Russians tried and look where that led."

"Don't you think the war will bring change. The Labour party is taking a larger role."

"Labour will pick your pocket. No, this war is to preserve the society as we know it."

A few blocks away a radio engineer signalled to the man standing before a microphone.

"This is London," the voice was deep, mellow and the speaker was calm, in full control, *"For yet another night the air attack continues..."*

The engineer dropped the sound to a background level before turning to the guest. "Can't say I've heard of Willard?"

"We're small," Dan Malone answered. "We service about a dozen small papers and are building a radio division. That's why

I wanted to see this operation. CBS and Edward R. Murrow get a lot of attention."

"Ain't that the truth," the engineer touched a knob and watched as the needle swung to the optimal setting. "*Again, today I walked the streets and talked to Londoners. I met a child, a boy who couldn't have been more than ten but showed the character of those twice his age....*"

"An easy broadcast," the engineer said, settling back. "Ed and his observations and no sound to mix. We wanted to use the recordings from the Balham Street Tube Station, but the censor refused. That's him in the other studio. He has a copy of the script and if anything is changed, he can flip a switch and kill the broadcast."

Malone nodded, "I saw a picture of the bus that dropped into the bomb crater in the blackout."

"That's the visible part. About sixty people below ground were killed. Hopefully, the blast snuffed them. Imagine being underground when gas mains or water lines rupture."

In the next few minutes, the engineer explained the workings of the production facility, the link with America and distribution to stations across the country. "CBS has the money to arrange it, but Ed Murrow gives it the magic."

"And so, good night from London."

Murrow stood frozen for a few seconds before he lit a cigarette. After a deep drag, he collected his notes and entered the control room. "We're good," the engineer assured him. "But I want to check the cables. I heard a minor glitch near the top."

Murrow nodded before he noticed Malone.

"The Canadian. I forgot you were coming."

"Mr. Murrow," a woman said, bursting in from another office, "a transatlantic call. New York on the line."

"I'll have to take this," he apologized.

"The bosses in New York forget the time differences," the engineer explained. "It's after midnight. We've worked all day and we're not done. I need to check the mike."

155

Al McGregor

He led the way into the studio, lifted a cable and snarled. "The connection is loose. A sharp vibration, a bomb close by and we'd have lost the broadcast."

"Fix it tomorrow," Murrow smiled from the doorway. "Call it a day. And, I'm sorry Mr. Malone, we'll have to chat another time. I've got to get back on the phone with New York."

Chapter Seven: A Waiting Game

Boston
October 30

L ate again. Sandy Fleming fumed as the cab driver manoeuvred through heavy traffic. She had missed the start of the President's speech. "Is the auditorium far?"

"Lady, I'm doing the best I can. Maybe music would help." He switched on the radio and loud cheers filled the car before he could reduce the volume. "Sorry, I get the best signal from this station but tonight they're doing another election broadcast." He switched the radio off.

"No. Turn it on. That's why I'm here. I'm to cover the President's speech."

The radio came back to life and Sandy heard the voice of Franklin Roosevelt. She searched her bag for a pad and pen.

"The same old story," the cabbie complained. "I spend a lot of time listening to these guys and they say the same thing over and over. Wendell Willkie repeats himself too. The only guy saying anything different is Charles Lindbergh and that outfit called America First."

"I have to listen," Sandy leaned forward, "I've come from Canada for this."

"Can't be much happening up north," the cabbie laughed. Sandy wished she had paid more attention to the American election. McLaren had been following the campaign and expected to make the trip until he had a fall. He would be off his feet for several days. "FDR is in good form," the cabbie said as more cheers erupted.

"And, I say again, your boys are not going to be sent into any foreign wars!" The cheers were louder and sustained.

"Nobody wants to get tangled up overseas," the cabbie said. "We had enough of that in the last war. The Irish in Boston don't care for the English. Course, they don't much care for Hitler either."

Sandy strained to hear Roosevelt's conclusion but missed his final words.

"About ten minutes and we'll have you at the rally," the cabbie found a break in traffic and drove faster. The last of the crowd was moving through the exits as Sandy entered the building. An usher pointed to the section where reporters were gathered. "Hey sweet heart," a man called, "Don't you remember me." A hand touched her shoulder. She turned, ready to swat the hand away. "Don't you remember our rendezvous in Plattsburg? A man shows a girl a good time and she snubs him. I'm Mark Ryder of the Monument News Service and you're from Ottawa. Can't recall the name but I would never forget that face."

"Sandy Fleming," she blushed.

"Are you always late?" he laughed. "The meeting was over when you arrived in Plattsburg too."

"I've a different excuse this time but it's a long story. I heard most of the speech on the car radio. Did I miss much in the hall?"

"Not really. A big crowd, a lot of nervous Democrats but he reassured them. They left happy."

"He promised to stay out of the war?"

"He's said all along that he'll keep our men out but usually qualifies that with something like 'unless we are attacked'. He dropped the qualifier tonight. Clever move, with the election race tightening."

"Could Roosevelt actually lose?"

"The President carries a lot of baggage after eight years in office. He wasn't planning to campaign but in the last few weeks, he's been on the trail slugging it out. It shows the race is closer than he expected."

Sandy scanned the auditorium. "I wanted to pick up a few interviews to round out the story."

"I can introduce a couple of the party faithful."

"That would be great. I'll owe you, again. I have to file for the morning papers and then I'm off to Washington."

"Call my office when you arrive. I can show you the sights."

"Will you have time?" she asked.

"For you...I'll make time," he smiled and waved to a pair of well-dressed men, "Gentlemen, meet Sandy, a Canadian reporter."

London
October 31

"Get it, Willie. Bite right into it." Willie struggled to heed his mother's advice and raised his soaking head with an apple gripped between his teeth. The church hall was filled with children and parents. A few glanced anxiously at the clock hoping to be home before the nightly Blitz began.

"Who's next to bob for apples?" the pastor asked then jumped back as Willie shook his head and sprayed water. "Whose next. Alice? Give it a try."

Martin Downey slipped into the empty chair beside Evers Chance. "You've outdone yourself. No one would expect us at a children's party."

"I thought you'd be amused." Chance laughed as Alice dove for an apple. "The children need a break from the tension. They won't be able to mark Guy Fawkes Day. The blackout puts a damper on bon fires."

Downey snickered as the girl lost her footing and fell head first into the tub. "But you have no family. Why meet here?"

"No one can hear us over the sound of the children's laughter. And we have a lot to talk about."

Downey folded his trench coat over his knees. "What do you have?"

"An agent tells of major construction and big demands for cement. The Nazis will fortify the French Coast."

Chance grew silent as a woman approached with a tray of cookies. "Oh, my favourite, gingerbread," Downey laughed.

"Don't take too many, Martin." Chance warned. "Don't spoil dinner."

The woman hovered as the men made their selections. "The donation box is by the door," she told them. "We welcome guests but in these times, guests should contribute."

"Oh, we will. Martin is very generous," Chance assured her as she turned to move on. "I could have told her my friend is on the government payroll," he whispered to Downey, "but, the government is not that popular."

"The government is a little busy. Now this concrete the Nazis are ordering, what are they building?"

"Mr. Hitler feels barbed wire isn't enough. He's ordered pill boxes and gun emplacements as a wall to face the Atlantic. Todt, the big German construction firm, has been ordered in and it doesn't work on simple projects."

Downey shook his head. "It would take years to protect everything along the Atlantic."

"Start with the areas most susceptible to landings, probably the beaches, low lying areas. They can expand later."

"Anything else?"

"The U-boat bases could be moved to the Channel and the Bay of Biscay. That would give easier, faster access to the North Atlantic and our convoys."

"U-boat bases could be a job for Bomber Command."

"I don't think so. Pilots might aim for the Channel but hit Paris. Anyway, a few bombs won't do the job. The concrete will be too thick."

"Children…Children." The pastor clapped his hands. "Time for pin the tail on the donkey." The room exploded with exuberant laughter.

"Be thankful, Martin. I could have volunteered you as the ass."

"Must you be that way? Can't we just have a conversation? I haven't even asked if the information is reliable."

"I have complete confidence."

"It would help if we knew the origin."

"Not going to happen." Chance shook his head, "My network. My way."

"I'm not sure how much longer I can protect you. The new Special Operations staff are all gung-ho and want contacts on the ground. Winston believes we must set Europe on fire. He doesn't want the Nazis to get comfortable. And, the Americans are showing interest."

"Fat lot of good they will do. Neutrals don't play offence?"

"A fellow named 'Wild Bill' Donovan was sent by Roosevelt. He was to assess our abilities to survive a German onslaught and the conversation drifted into what could come next. Men on the ground could hit railway lines or blow up bridges. All we need is the tools and people on the ground."

"I told you. My people are observers and has anyone thought of who will get the guns and explosives? Right wingers? The Communist left? Fighting Nazis is one thing, but those factions could turn on each other and once that starts, it's hard to stop."

Downey smiled as a blindfolded youngster with a large hat pin spun in search of a target. "Lord Lothian has come home for meetings. What do you think the ambassador to Washington will tell the next American administration?"

Al McGregor

"Hmm...that we can't continue without more help and we can't pay anymore. A Canadian friend was telling me of the fish trains from Halifax."

"Chance, what are you talking about?"

"Short, fast trains get fish to market before there's spoilage."

"I don't see where this is going."

"More of the trains have been running the last year or so and he wondered why armed guards were needed to protect fish? So, he concluded it was gold, gold from the Bank of England, shipped to North America to pay for arms. But he hasn't seen those trains lately. He thinks we're out of gold."

"So," Downey rose to leave, "Lord Lothian will tell the Americans we're broke?"

"Or, stand outside the White House and rattle a tin cup."

Washington
November 2

"No sign of moving vans," Mark Ryder laughed. "FDR doesn't panic as an election race tightens." He and Sandy had walked the streets of Washington and a stroll along Pennsylvania Avenue would finish the tour.

"The White House is smaller than I expected." She peered up the driveway. "And, the President, is he always in a wheelchair?"

"Oh, he can stand with support for major speeches, but the chair is always close. By an unwritten rule, press photographers shoot only the upper part of his body. The administration doesn't want to admit the President is an invalid."

"Leaders manage to keep secrets." Sandy watched a police patrol car pass. "In Canada we have censorship and the War Measures Act."

"And, a compliant press. When I worked in Ottawa, most of the Press Gallery preferred not to rock the boat. Besides, your President, Mr. King isn't an awe-inspiring character."

"He's the Prime Minister, not President." Sandy corrected him.

"I keep forgetting and provinces as opposed to states."

Sandy took a last look at the White House. "I'd have missed this if I was on my own."

"The tour is not over. I have to check in at the office but tonight we can sample the nightlife."

The club was packed on a Saturday night, but Ryder managed to book a table. He smiled to acquaintances as he guided her across the room.

"Hi Ken," he shook the hand of a very tall man.

"Another Canadian," he told her a moment later, "John Kenneth Galbraith. He tutored one of the Kennedy boys. He's an economist, a whiz with numbers."

She glanced back to see Galbraith leaving the room.

"I'd like to have met him," she said. "I could work up a profile."

"That would be boring. Find a body with a knife in the back. That's what people want from newspapers."

"We don't have to look in the gutter for material." Instantly, she regretted her words but something in his tone and attitude had annoyed her.

"Boy, have you got a lot to learn." He held her chair and didn't notice the hint of anger on her face. "I'll order for you. I know my way around."

Later as they danced, she whispered, "I love the saxophone. In fact, I've loved the entire day."

The orchestra picked up the pace and by mutual agreement they returned to the table. The plates had been cleared, replaced by glasses and a bottle of champagne. Over dinner she had learned more about him. Ryder was born in Richmond which explained the hint of a southern accent. He had travelled in Europe before drifting into newspaper work, and he confessed he had been engaged once, but the relationship soured. Women, he told her, must know their place.

163

Al McGregor

"I have a confession," he announced. "I was prepared to abandon you this afternoon but now, I hate the thought of the night ending."

"It's early." She touched his hand. "Can we stay longer?"

"I'm free until Monday. That's when the press pool moves to Hyde Park for election night. By early Wednesday morning we'll all be hammering out theories on the results."

"What do you expect?"

"Let's assume FDR wins. He's got three choices: commit to war, send more help to the British and let them do the fighting or drift along as he has since 1939. I'd bet on drift."

He topped up the glasses. "But listen to me. If there's anything I should have learned, it's not to have opinions, or at least, not to spout them and spoil an evening."

"Oh, you haven't." She decided to overlook his views. "Listen that's a slow waltz. Let's dance."

It was past one when he guided her along the hallway to her room. She raised the key in mock celebration and slipped it into the lock. As the latch clicked, she turned to face him and found herself in his arms. The kiss was long and passionate. She felt him push the door open. "I don't invite men into my room," she tried to sound stern, "but one is already here."

In what seemed only seconds their clothing littered the floor.

Ottawa
November 6

"Sandy," Frank Willard called, "Sandy. What is with you? My God. You are in a kind of fog."

"Sorry. What did you want?" she asked absently.

"The story on President Roosevelt's victory and what, if anything, it means for Canada. Add a touch of background from the Washington trip and, I almost forgot. A telegram came this morning."

She grabbed the envelope and tore the flimsy cover.

164

"Gorgeous!" She read and felt tears forming. "Wrong again. FDR won easily. I thought he had three options but there was a fourth, a vacation. I'm to follow him to Florida but would rather be coming north. Let's plan to meet in the New Year."

New York
November 12

"I'm disappointed Wilson," the FBI agent scowled.

"I'm a poor snitch," Brad Wilson admitted, "but Tim Fulton is all talk. He doesn't toe the administration line and he's not alone. Thousands of Americans don't like to think of war."

Wilson pointed to the people passing on the sidewalk outside of the restaurant. "Everyone has an opinion. Will Mr. Hoover want a report on who they talk to and what they say? Do we create a nation of informants?"

"So, you want out?" Laramie nodded. "That can be arranged. I'll have your passport re-instated. In fact, if you plan to join the Canadian Airforce, I can grease the wheels."

"And no problem on the border crossing or any hints of the work I've done."

"Nothing," Laramie assured him, "Besides, you didn't produce much."

"And what becomes of Tim?"

"We'll keep watching."

A few blocks away a temporary canteen drew a constant flow of seamen. A former store had been transformed into a recreation centre with a small kitchen offering sandwiches and coffee.

"Coming or going?" Tim Fulton put the question to a young sailor. His most distinguishing features were tattoos beginning at the wrists and disappearing under a dirty jacket at the elbows.

"Going," he answered. "I was booked on a steamer for the Caribbean but the paper work was fouled up and I'm bound for Liverpool through Halifax."

"Take it up with the captain." Fulton poured a cup of coffee.

"He won't do nothing."

165

Fulton reached under the counter and produced a sandwich. "Others have had this problem," he said quietly, "A few have jumped ship."

"I have a record in the States. If they caught me, I'd be put away."

"Have you a record in Canada?"

"No," the young man said.

"Jump ship in Halifax. The Canadians hold jumpers for a week or so and release them if they volunteer to return to sea. All you have to do is find a ship going south. No one in his right mind wants to join a slow convoy on the North Atlantic in the winter."

"Sometimes ships are herded into a convoy without touching land. How is a man supposed to get away?"

"Accidents happen or you could make one happen. The ship might put in for repairs. Maybe a slight oil leak is ignored and gets bigger. Maybe a piece of chain slips and fouls a gear. All kinds of things happen. What is the ship carrying?"

"Steel and pieces of machinery. The holds are full of crates, but I don't know what's in them."

"Ammunition would be my guess," Fulton stoked the sailor's uncertainty.

"Give it some thought." He topped up the coffee and slipped a small card across the counter. "Contact this fellow in Halifax. He can help."

Halifax
November 16

A thin layer of ice made the street slippery and Robert McLaren moved carefully. The cane, once a major part of his life, was back in his hand but with luck for only a few weeks. The fall at the Ottawa office had aggravated the injury suffered in the first war. The doctors had reassured him. In a few weeks, he would regain full mobility. Inside the newspaper office, he heard the presses rolling and felt the vibration through the floor. Another edition would soon be on the streets.

"Anything exciting?" he asked as found Brian Potter. The freelance reporter had picked up a few weeks of regular employment.

"It's always exciting in Halifax. Is Ottawa too dull?"

"I needed to get away; too many people tut-tutting over a little limp."

"How did you do it?" Potter asked. "Originally I mean. Did you fall into a trench?"

"Forgot that I was to ride the horse, rather than have the horse ride me. It doesn't matter. The leg is getting stronger every day."

"This is great place to rest. One of the big German cruisers shot up a convoy. The Germans know it and half of Halifax knows it, but we aren't allowed to work on it."

"It won't be the first convoy to take losses." McLaren pulled a chair closer and stretched the leg.

"That's only the half of it," Potter began to thread a new ribbon into a typewriter. "We make do with merchant ships that should have been sent to a wrecking yard years ago. And, that doesn't play well with a crew. A ship limped in from New York today with an odd oil leak. It can be fixed but, mark my words, after a delay for repairs, a handful of seamen will be missing. Some German agent in New York is suggesting ways to avoid convoy duty. Bombs are no longer necessary for sabotage."

The ribbon replaced, he wiped his hands on a page of newsprint.

"Wow. Listen to you," McLaren laughed. "No wonder censors are clamping down. The only thing missing is a white flag."

"How long are you here for?"

"A couple of days."

"That's enough," Potter said. "Listen to the talk. We're losing this bloody war."

London
December 27

"I wish our fighters could shoot down a few more of the bastards." The blackout curtains in the loft were open, and Martin Downey stood with Evers Chance watching the sky a few miles away.

"A pilot can't see much in the dark," Chance said as a sheet of flame rose in the distance. "If a night fighter gets lucky, he sees a flash of the exhaust from an enemy plane and sends it down. If he's unlucky, he's hit by our flack or in the confusion, one of our aircraft hits another.

"So much for a Christmas truce," Downey muttered. "Adolf was kind enough to give us a holiday reprieve but we're back in it now."

"Despite the Blitz, Churchill is having a very good month." Chance began to pack his pipe. "Shame about the death of Lord Lothian but appointing Halifax as the new ambassador to the U.S. takes the last opposition from his cabinet. The Prime Minister must be secretly pleased."

"He is and this new American Lend-Lease arrangement will mean millions of dollars in supplies. However, while I don't like to look a gift horse in the mouth, someone should take a close look at the fine print. Yankees drive hard bargains."

Chance nodded, turned from the window and struck a match. "I half expected an American declaration of war, after their election but instead, we're still alone. They appear prepared to fight to the last Englishman. Just as those across the Channel believe we were prepared to fight to the last Frenchman...or the last Pole."

Downey starred off at the flaming horizon. "The financial district is catching the brunt of it tonight."

Chance finally had the pipe going. "I'm going away for awhile. I expect to be back but in case of an unforeseen difficulty, I've made arrangements to provide my list of contacts."

"Finally, we're making progress."

"Not so fast. I said *if* I don't come back."

"Come now. We helped finance your extra-ordinary intelligence service over the years, but conditions have changed."

"Nothing has changed. We both fear the Special Operations Executive will do more harm than good. The people in the occupied countries are more concerned about food and safety than setting Europe ablaze."

"Where are you going?"

"I haven't decided, but I need to talk with my people."

Chapter Eight: Secret Lives

Le Havre
January 5, 1941

Thick fog shrouded the sailboat, but Evers Chance had decided, dinghy was a more appropriate description. The craft had been stowed aboard a fishing trawler and offloaded in the dead of night. A sail was raised, the canvas dyed as black as the night sky.

"About a mile from the French coast," Brandon Young kept his voice low, "I'll land you near a small stream. A hundred yards inland is a rough path. Hide till dawn and watch for a farmer with a cart."

"And how will I know he's the right man?" Chance asked.

"He talks to his horse. Her name is Christelle. You won't miss him."

Young made a slight adjustment on the tiller and said, "I haven't thanked you. The business opportunities have been most welcome."

"I suspected a man with a family history in smuggling would see the possibilities. There can't be much difference between revenue collectors and a German patrol. Avoid one and you can avoid the other."

Young raised his hand. "A patrol boat," he whispered. It was several minutes before he spoke again. "I've decided to stay with your organization, if you want me."

"Oh, I do. And, I'm glad you are staying although other customers might pay better."

Young chuckled. "The Special Operations Executive promises to pay more and has all kinds of wild plans. Money is available, the ideas are there but I'm not sure the local population is onside."

"Nothing says you can't work for them too."

"And I will, but you have priority. Now, we're very close. Good luck."

Christelle was aging, and Chance was amazed the animal could pull the cart and two men. The driver maintained a steady stream of conversation with the horse while ignoring the passenger. At the end of the journey, he turned the cart back the way he had come. Chance produced a few francs and received a cold nod in return.

The shop was as he remembered. Goods were stacked in odd positions, but he noted there were more empty spaces. Maurice broke into a wide smile when he saw his customer. Chance gripped his hand. "Time is short. Is there anything I should know?"

"Have you the correct papers? The wrong document can raise an alarm at a checkpoint." Maurice inspected the identification, a ration card and a pass for temporary travel.

"Good," he announced. "And, the clothes are fine except for the shoes. I've a pair of old boots. No one has seen new shoes in years."

"Life has been hard?"

"No harder for me than for anyone else. I found a suitcase that should work. It's sturdy but has seen better days."

"Haven't we all," Chance laughed and pulled a wallet from his pocket. "Maybe you could dispose of this."

Maurice smiled happily as he ran his fingers through the bills. "This is very generous."

"And have you decided whether to continue with my operation?" Chance asked.

"I am satisfied with our arrangements," Maurice explained. "And it's safer than what I hear from others. A few men have been approached for sabotage, but I have a family. An act of violence and I'm off to the work camp or worse."

"The time for sabotage may come," Chance said and pulled his pipe from a pocket, "but not through my operation. Still, it's a decision you may face in the near future."

He struck a match and saw the instant scowl. "No!" Maurice snatched the matches and sniffed at the tobacco. "That match box is English and so is the tobacco. I'll give you a fresh supply. These things arouse suspicion."

"A good warning." Chance smiled. "Now the suitcase and I'll be on my way."

"A suitcase carried by a French farmer? Why not wave a British flag?" Maurice shook his head in disgust. "We sent supplies to Maria recently. She has the suitcase. And, this is the key. The lock works."

"You don't trust her?"

"These are strange times. One must be careful. She was seen with a German officer."

The showers turned to a cold, steady rain as Chance approached the farmhouse. Maria answered the door on the second knock. She remained the beauty that haunted his dreams.

"Get out of the wet clothes and sit by the fire," she instructed. "I'll hang them to dry by the stove in the kitchen."

"A fireplace and stove," he laughed and undid the jacket. "Life in France is better than expected."

"And, I'll put a chicken in the pot. I'll forego a few eggs in honor of the visit."

Chance rubbed his hands together and leaned over the flames. "I won't stay long. I'm off to Paris tomorrow."

"Oh." Her tone suggested sincere disappointment. "Our time is always so short."

"I'll need the suit I left last summer, and the suitcase Maurice sent." In the case were several well used shirts, a pair of ragged trousers, a shaving kit, a pen and paper, two bars of chocolate and a bottle of Canadian whisky.

He hoisted the bottle. "I leave this for you, or we might share. How are you?"

"Lonely, at times but not tonight. As to work, the Germans approve most of what I write and sending the articles gives me a chance to travel."

"But friend or foe, someone is always watching," Chance warned her. "Maurice says you have a German friend."

"What? What? Oh, he must mean Gunther. Remember, I wrote to you of the artworks and Goering's private collections. Gunther Webber is a good man. He's not arrogant or brutal. But yes, I saw him in Le Havre. And he's to show me a gallery in Paris."

"Could you write something for the magazine to make this easier to explain."

"I can. And, my articles may appear to be soft on the Nazis. But compliance is the only way to get the articles past the censors."

Chance settled in a chair by the fire. "We need a new way to communicate. The German's are reading the diplomatic mail. In the future, Maurice can get a message through."

"I sell firewood through him. He has a man come with a horse and wagon, but the man is a bit 'touched'." She rapped her knuckles on her head. "He only talks to the horse."

"Haw. I met Christelle yesterday."

She laughed and for the first time he saw the easy smile light up her face.

"Thank God for the cash from the wood. Last fall, the Germans confiscated the livestock. The chickens are all that's left."

"Is it time to leave?"

"No. I don't feel real danger. The American passport helps. Hitler won't annoy America."

"Anything else?"

"Fewer troops are around. One unit was moved to Poland. The Luftwaffe bases have fewer planes than last fall. But bombers fly every night, headed for London, I guess."

"London and the other major cities. The damage is severe. We can't stop them."

"I've tried to get close to their radio towers." She brushed hair from her eyes. "But the compounds are well guarded and 'verboten'. The German equivalent of radar?"

"Questions again, that's the Maria I remember."

"So, you won't tell me?

"Honestly, I don't understand the technology. I'm better with people."

"The people here keep their heads down to avoid attention which usually works. Except for Jews, it's getting worse for them."

"I do have good news. Your Polish friend, Anna and the children, will be off to America soon. One might expect official government help for refugees, but the most successful effort comes through back channels."

Maria rose to stir the fire. "I saw Anna in Paris. She was worried about the children. People—Jews and non-Jews—simply disappear. No one knows why or what happens. They just disappear."

"It's a form of terror. What's called, 'night and fog', which covers many disturbing possibilities."

"And what are we to do?"

"At the risk of sounding cavalier, I think we should have a drink."

Later, Maria reminisced of happy times in Canada, of life on her own on Europe, and of meeting Chance in 1917. Chance didn't tell her that he had been captivated from the moment he saw her, or that he hoped the candlelight was as kind to him as it was to her.

"Listen to me," she said, laughing, "I've laid out my world in front of you, again. And, after all these years, I don't feel I know the real Chance."

"I thought I explained. I dappled in intelligence and discovered business and government would pay for what I learned...and...."

"...No, no." She moved to sit beside him. "Why isn't there a little woman, a kind lady to darn socks and turn the bed covers down. Or, do I have it all wrong?" Her eyes were laughing. "Have you spent so much time with men you prefer a male companion. Female intuition says no...but?"

"Trust the intuition. In the past, I was attracted to beautiful women, but nothing was permanent." He hesitated. "I have no family and didn't think I needed anyone close. It was easier to think solely of myself."

"Has something changed?" She asked.

"I'm not sure. I am in the company of one of the most beautiful women in Europe, a woman who is also charming and intelligent."

"I don't know what to say..."

"Then don't say anything."

Maria spoke softly, "We've been friends, long distance friends for many years. And each time we meet the years drop away. It's so comfortable. We're able to pick up where we left off."

Washington
January 6

"Have you been to Florida," Mark Ryder said and flipped the light switch on.

Sandy pulled a pillow over her eyes. "That's too bright."

"Imagine a tropical sun," he laughed and tugged at the bedsheets. "Time to check for an all over tan. The ladies in Key West are often bleached."

175

"My hair colour is natural." Something in Ryder's attitude in the last few hours had again annoyed her. She still felt a psychical attraction but was finding him brash and outspoken.

"I didn't mean that," he laughed. "I've seen the proof."

"Don't be a jerk! Talk about something else. Did you follow the President through the Caribbean?"

"No, the press corps were marooned on the beach. But everyday or so we'd be briefed by his staff. That's how we knew about the private letter from Churchill. His message must have been bleak. Why else would Roosevelt create the Lend-Lease Act? And what a deal: whatever the Brits need and no payment until after the war."

She pushed the pillows behind her. "But the American army is on the sidelines."

"I can't get confirmation, but the army planners may be working alongside the British. If the White House says 'go' the armed forces must be ready."

"When?

"At least a year and probably longer. Equipment that should be going to Americans will now go to England. But if or when the moment comes Yanks will lead the way as we did in the first war."

"Now, wait a minute. We were fighting for three years before the Americans woke up. The British wore the German army down before the first dough boy appeared."

"Hey, we don't have to spar. Time is short. Your train leaves at nine."

"Oh, I know. I'm in a sour mood. I can't measure up to the Latin ladies of the south."

"Is that it? Jealousy?" He began to laugh and pull on the sheets.

"Stop it!"

"Isn't this why you came?" His hands reached under the sheets.

"No!" She slapped at his hands and aimed toward his face, but he caught her wrist.

"Let me go," she hissed.

"I don't know what I did wrong."

"I don't either." she rolled from the bed and began to dress. "But this isn't working. Maybe I'm not ready for a relationship."

"Honey child. We're not serious, we're having fun."

"Not anymore."

As she dressed, he watched with amused detachment from the bed. "Sandy…"

"Goodbye, Mark. Have a good life!"

Paris
January 7

For most of the train journey Evers Chance had a compartment to himself. He claimed a place by the window, feigning sleep, until a sharp poke brought him to reality. A German officer stood above him. "Move the case." He pointed to the luggage on the seat. Chance smiled and dropped the battered case to the floor.

"And move your body. I will sit there." Again, he smiled and obeyed. The German began to sniff, "What is that smell?"

"It may be my suit. My wife locked it away and stuffed the pockets with mothballs."

"Do all French live in vermin infested houses?"

"No…no, I don't often wear a suit. I'm going to Paris for my cousin's wedding and want to make a good impression."

The officer reached and ran his hand across the suit. "Hmm…good material, expensive…once."

"From before the war. The tailor is no longer in business. He was a Jew, but I beat him on the price."

"Hah. That doesn't happen often. Perhaps you are Jewish? It takes one to know one."

"Oh no." Chance replied, "I am Beauchamp, a well-known family in Normandy, no Jews in our closets. Here are my paper's. And, I should apologize. On the farm, I seldom see officers. I don't know the ranks. Are you high command? Do you control tanks? Those magnificent machines, big tractors covered with steel."

"I suppose a simple farmer would be impressed. But no, I command trucks, fuel tankers, army transport."

"What a responsibility! I have two old horses. In all honestly," he dropped his voice, "I am hard pressed to pay the bills."

"I'm not surprised. In the Fatherland, farms are well maintained but in France, I see broken fences, weeds, barns and houses falling apart. You must learn from us."

"Oh, I hope so. The Third Republic, the last French government, was a disaster. Those at the top were corrupt or communists. Marshall Pepin in Vichy is taking the right steps. Soon, he can control the occupied territories, too. German work will be done, and you will be able to go home. We'll all be part of a new Europe."

"Don't expect too much, too fast."

"Our people are lazy." Chance pointed to a small farm beside the track. "Imagine what those fields could produce if managed properly."

"France will produce more. The Fuhrer demands it. The British believe their naval blockade will starve us into submission. What a joke! France will produce more food as will the other occupied lands."

"Yes, Belgium and the Netherlands have excellent soil. Their crops are important to the new Europe."

"And other territories will bloom. My unit is being transferred to the east. We'll teach the Poles to work. And, if Russians cause trouble, we'll teach them, too."

Chance slowly shook his head. "All too much for a poor farmer. Help me understand? Germany could take Russia as it has taken France?"

"Yes, and soon. France is decadent but once had a great culture. That can't be said for the inferior races, the Jews, the Poles, the Slavs and Russians. They have no place in our world."

London

January 10

Dan Malone was a happy drunk. Marcie heard him singing as he climbed the stairs.

"Roll me over…in the friggin' clover. Roll me over and do it again."

The singing stopped and she imagined him, slapping at a coat pocket in search of the key. She waited a moment before opening the door. He teetered on the landing but offered an awkward bow. "The gallant knight returns to the fair damsel."

"You, sir, are pissed!"

"Not for the first time, Marcie my pet, and not for the last time either."

She reached to steady him and guide him to a couch. "It must have been quite a night."

"Working my dear. Nose to the grindstone. Toil never ends."

"It never ends when someone has the cash for the bartender. Who was it this time? Ed Murrow buying a few rounds? I hope it wasn't you because we can't afford it."

"Never fear, my pretty," Malone reached to touch her cheek, "I'll always keep something for us. But yes, it was Murrow and a new American friend, a man from FDR's inner circle."

She bent to untie his laces and remove his shoes. "The whole city smells of soot, but those shoes are the worst of all. I'm surprised Americans don't turn up their noses. You reek of whisky and soot."

"They don't care," said Malone as he leaned back on the coach, "and for the record my new friend lives at the White House."

"Who is it, one of the President's sons?"

"Better than that. The top advisor. Harry 'bleeding' Hopkins."

She set the shoes by the door.

179

"Roosevelt's right hand," Malone told her. "He's been the President's confidant for years, worked on the New Deal. Everyone knows him."

"I don't."

"Marcie, pay more attention. Hopkins is a big shot. He crossed the Atlantic in a flying boat, a Pan Am Clipper. And what's the first thing he wants in London? A bar. So, we got blitzed in the Blitz."

"He's come to London on a lark?"

"Hell no. Serious business. He's meeting Churchill. The Yanks need to know what to send under the new Lend-Lease scheme. He's the one that will open or close the tap."

"What tap?" She shook the jacket and placed it in the closet.

"The spigot," he answered, "the great valve on the pipeline that will flow from American factories and across the Atlantic."

"I hope Hitler doesn't find out. Be careful, Mr. Malone, loose lips sink ships."

"And you are right again." He lurched to his feet and balanced against her as she led him to the bedroom, "Can't give away secrets."

"Don't worry," she told him. "By morning you won't remember any secrets."

Paris
January 12

The woman was dressed in black, her face covered by a veil. She stood in silent prayer before lighting a candle and joining parishioners streaming from the cathedral.

"Don't turn Nicole," the voice came from behind. "Walk toward the river."

"I know that voice," she whispered, "Welcome back, Mr. Chance. I've missed you."

"I wish we had more time. I was sorry to hear of the death of your son."

"In war mothers suffer, and after we grieve, we seek revenge. The Nazis killed him. I'll get even."

She walked slowly and Chance felt safe enough to move beside her.

"A new organization will be taking over," he told her. "I can give them your name. The new men are aggressive. They want more than information. They'll want action."

"I'll do what I can."

"Good luck, Nicole."

"Wait. Our other old friends? Will I see them?"

"The baker will join. Terresa as well. I'm yet to see Philippe."

"Be careful." She rung her hands together. "Philippe swings with the wind. And as for Terresa, she is a godless whore, but I will work with her if need be."

"Be safe," he said and slipped away.

Two hours later, Chance rapped on the door of a butcher shop.

"We're closed," a man called from inside.

"A special order for an English cut." Seconds later the door swung open.

"This is dangerous. The Boche may be watching."

"Bonjour, Philippe," Chance smiled, entered and leaned on the counter, "It's been a while."

"Not long enough."

"What's happened to my friendly butcher? As I recall, my payments are accepted."

"The local police watch everything and pass the information to the Gestapo." Philippe dabbed at drops of sweat on his forehead.

"I wanted to talk but I understand the danger," Chance told him. "In fact, I'm leaving, soon. I have a ticket on the night train to Verdun."

"I'm sorry," Philippe dabbed again at his face, "But I can't go on. I must ask you to leave."

"I'm sorry too," Chance said extending his hand, but the butcher turned aside.

181

The train station was busy, but Chance moved easily through the crowd. A railwayman studied the ticket and directed him to the southbound train, for Marseilles. The commotion began as he boarded. Armed soldiers and guard dogs surrounded the carriages on a neighboring track."

"They're after someone on the train to Verdun," another passenger whispered. And Chance knew another name could be struck from the list for the new resistance.

Ottawa
January 28

The door slammed and the two men could hear Sandy stomp toward the stairway.

"She's in a mood," Robert McLaren said as he glanced up from his typewriter. "Did something happen?"

"No, nothing out of the ordinary," Frank Willard replied. "She's been a proper bitch since she came back from Washington."

"Wonder why?"

"Maybe her monthly visitor is about to arrive." Willard smiled. "Or, maybe it hasn't."

"Jesus. Don't talk like that. Has that American tossed her over?"

"Hah, I'll bet he's tossed her a few times and...."

The rest of his words were interrupted by a ringing telephone.

"Willard Agency," McLaren said, picking up the phone. "Oh, Officer," he laughed. "How are Ottawa's finest on this winter day?" His face tightened. "That's up the street. Are you sure he's dead?"

McLaren had begun to scratch on a notepad. "Only sixty-two? But yes, the job takes a toll."

Again, he grew silent and tapped his pen against the desk. "We'll keep you out of it and we'll see there's a little something coming your way. Does the Prime Minister know?"

He listened before speaking again.

"King went to the morgue? Why on earth? Can't he take the word of the Ottawa Police?" He lifted the receiver from his ear and Willard could hear the laughter across the room.

"Yes, he is odd. But he's the only Prime Minister we have."

McLaren returned the telephone to the cradle. "Oscar Skelton is dead. A car accident on O'Connor Street but not enough damage to cause a serious injury. Police think it was his heart."

"Another personal blow for King." Willard began to root through the files for background. "Here we are. Officially Skelton was deputy minister at External Affairs but unofficially the government's muse on foreign policy. Considered independently minded, often suspicious of British intentions."

McLaren rolled a sheet of paper into the typewriter. "Give them a couple of hours to reach the family and we'll release the story."

"Don't go too heavy. The bureaucrats know him, but I doubt the average citizen has a clue who he was or what he did."

London
January 31

"Mr. Downey. We haven't met. I'm new, name is Nick Trent."

"And what can I do for you?" Downey sat behind a desk stacked with folders.

"Kim Philby said you know Evers Chance. Philby is away but we've had word of Chance and I thought someone should know."

"Hmm, good of you. I hadn't realized Chance was the object of our surveillance?"

"Oh yes sir, since he went to France. Mr. Philby ordered a watch right after Chance reported on the German forces being moved toward the Russian border."

"Hmm. Missed that one too."

"Yes, well, he disappeared in Paris and we feared he'd been arrested. Mr. Philby was concerned," Trent said as Downey rose from the desk, stretched and walked to the window. "But he turned up in Lisbon," Trent continued, "He was helping a woman and two children board a ship for America."

"Why would he be do that?" Downey turned back from the window.

"Not really sure. It is strange. Is he Jewish? The woman and children were?"

"No. Chance is at best a lapsed Anglican. He's not the church going type."

"Why send them to America?"

"I don't know. Both Canada and the U.S. have been reluctant to take Jews, afraid of opening the flood gates, I suppose. Rest assured Chance will have thought it through. Did he go with them?"

"We don't think so."

"Think? Don't we know?"

"He managed to drift away in the crowd."

"Drift away, Mr. Trent? What kind of agent can't track an aging Englishman?"

"I'm sorry, sir. That's all I know."

"Not very satisfactory, I'm afraid." Downey slipped back into his chair. "Let it rest. You must have other business."

Lisbon, Portugal
February 2

The café was almost empty with only a few customers lingering over a noon meal. Evers Chance set his derby on top of his briefcase and opened a newspaper, but before he could begin to read, a well-dressed man slipped into the empty seat beside him.

"It's been several years," he said, his English tinged with a German accent. "Italy, as I recall."

"Yes, Taranto," Chance remembered. "I was trying to buy steel."

"Such a shame," the man said. "The smelters were damaged in a British attack last fall when torpedo planes attacked the Italian fleet. The Japanese, for some reason, asked for detailed reports on the action."

"I've never understood the oriental mind. I do know these are not good days for the import-export game. Do you still dapple, Mr. von Ronstadt?"

"No. I have too much other work, mostly through Admiral Canaris. He sends his regards. And please, call me Otto."

"I have something of interest." Chance opened his case and retrieved a photograph of a young man.

"It's Ernst," said Otto and smiled.

"He's in an internment camp in Canada. A work camp but conditions are much better than in Germany. Your son has worked as a farm labourer since his ship was seized."

Otto ran his fingers across the picture. "His mother will be relieved. The Reich has greater concerns than the fate of a single merchant sailor. And, what might I offer in return?"

"Today, I am interested in observations, in conversation. For example, the popularity of the Fuhrer. A few months ago, we heard he could be replaced."

"But not now." Otto slipped the photo in his pocket and signalled to a waiter, "Schnapps?" The waiter nodded and the men were silent until the glasses appeared.

"The Fuhrer is firmly in control," Otto began. "Those close to him are certain the breakthrough in the west came through his military genius. Any who doubt his greatness, keep silent and wait for the inevitable mistake."

"Does anyone know what he plans next?"

"The Fuhrer has many options. He could move on the Balkans or help the Italians in North Africa? He might convince General Franco to allow our troops passage across Spain and attack the fortress at Gibraltar, or... he could move east. The uncertainty is caused by Britain. Will the English see reason and negotiate a peace?"

"That's not likely with Churchill's promise to fight on the beaches and so on..." Chance fingered his glass.

"And the Americans?" Otto asked.

"Stronger every week. Bigger factories, more planes, more tanks, more ships. Hitler is wise not to provoke them. I just put

185

three people on an American ship because your submarines have orders not to attack the U.S vessels."

"What you say is true. But I'm curious. Who did you send to America?"

"Three lowly Jews of no political significance. Not scientists, or great thinkers, not really important, only a family I offered to help, and I try to keep my word. They might have been safe in France but…"

"It's wise to be cautious. Germany strives to eliminate any Jewish influence. I've never understood the pathological hate for the Jews. The drive for racial purity distracts us from other goals."

"Including Lebensraum."

"Germany does need more living space, more territory for future growth."

"How much more? You have Western Europe."

"Why not Eastern Europe? It's an option. Russia has rich soil plus Slav's, Ukrainians and other lesser races for heavy labour. Understand, this is not my view, but what I hear. Joe Stalin is not a long-term ally. The Fuhrer hopes the British see reason and give him a free hand against the Bolsheviks."

"I can't see that," said Chance shaking his head. "Besides we can't accept the word of the Fuhrer."

"As I suspected. But conditions, even leadership can change. It might be valuable to maintain contact. Of course, we must use extreme care. Did you know you were being followed?"

"I suspected as much when I arranged this meeting."

"Ah, but my men are not alone."

"As in Germany, there are conflicting interests in Great Britain," Chance said smiling. "I might give away secrets. I might tell you that that Churchill is in control and, despite what you might hear, will remain in power."

"And, the same is true of the Fuhrer and he is obsessed with Russia. Thank you for the news on my son." The German rose and concluded, "Some day, I may return the favour."

Washington
February 5

Tim Fulton stood in front of a large map and pointer in hand tapped America's eastern shoreline. "Roosevelt is spoiling for a fight. He's ordered more ships into the Atlantic, to help his British friends. And…" The pointer swung to the west coast. "I don't think we have to worry about the Japanese but the new home base for the Pacific fleet will be Pearl Harbour."

"Tim," a middle-aged man had raised his hand. "I'm sure we all appreciate a lecture on naval affairs, but we came to talk about the Lend-Lease hearings. Can we concentrate on how to stop the legislation and leave the oceans for another day?"

"I…I…thought you should know," Fulton stammered. "A clash in the Atlantic could bring us into the war before the bill reaches the Senate."

"I'd like to hear about Pearl Harbour," a young woman interjected. "It's a great name. Is it a quiet lagoon, pretty, as in the movies?"

"I'll explain later Wendy. But yes, let's talk about the hearings. Blocking the legislation may be the most important thing America First can do. The bill would give Roosevelt more power and he could offer a special deal to any country he considers vital to American interests."

"He'll bankrupt us," the middle-aged man spoke again. "We can't afford to support the British. And, I think most people agree with me."

"Don't be overconfident," Fulton warned. "We weren't able to swing the election. And, I'd feel better if Lindbergh was playing a larger role."

"Oh, don't go there," the middle-aged critic spoke again. "Lindbergh does more harm than good. He has fascist tendencies and his ideas on eugenics, the superiority of the white race, that sort of thing, is all counter productive."

"Lindbergh, a fascist?" Fulton snapped. "Nonsense. Concentrate on the dictator in the White House. Every Senator and Congressman must be convinced Lend-Lease is a mistake. We'll start with a visual demonstration. That's where Wendy and her friends come in."

"All set, Tim," she smiled. "The mothers of future wars will appear, dressed in black, in mourning. One of the girls made special dresses and veils. The halls of Congress will be like a funeral parlour."

"That's great," Fulton sounded reassured. "And Wendy if you recruit a few more girls, I can pay them."

"Wait," the critic demanded. "Where does the cash come from?"

"Never mind. Bring as many girls as possible but don't put them all under veils. The pretty ones can smudge their makeup. Mascara should run as the little darlings cry their eyes out. Let the politicians see the future and stop shipping arms to Britain."

Goderich, Ontario
February 10

"Where's the know-it all American?" A flying instructor thrust his head through the canteen door, "Where's the bugger who claims Yankee know-how will win the war? Eat later. Your elementary flying school initiation awaits."

Brad Wilson pushed the food tray aside and followed. His two months in the British Commonwealth Air Training Program had been spent on the ground. Despite his earlier flying experience, the air force demanded a full training regime with weeks of classroom and theory. Goderich finally promised time in the air.

"Ever flown with instruments?" the instructor asked.

"No," Wilson admitted, "my flying was in an old biplane, so definitely visual flight rules."

"That's about to change. That big blue box with the wings and tail is a flight simulator. With the hatch closed, it will be darker than crap and you won't see much. If you crash, we haven't lost a plane. And don't worry about the smell. The last guy threw up. A devil of a job to clean."

An Angry Sky

"What do I do?" Wilson ignored the scent and settled into the seat.

"Listen for my command. I have a repeater outside for every reading in the cockpit. Put the headset on and close the hatch."

Wilson found himself in complete darkness.

"Ok, see the altimeter," the instructors voice boomed through the headset.

"Don't yell," Wilson called.

"Then adjust the volume. God damn rookie."

Wilson fought the urge to shout back but before he could speak the instructor was feeding him a course, altitude and wind direction."

He suddenly felt the sensation of flying but flying in deep unending blackness. The voice in his ears was the sole contact with the outside world. Fear suddenly gripped him, a sense of being totally alone. The faint glow of the instrument panel was the only light. Instinctively, his hands rose to open the hatch.

"Get your hands on the yolk. Keep the nose up," the instructor yelled. "Watch the air speed! What the hell are you doing?"

Wilson fought for control. Was this flying box right side up? Again, his hands rose to the hatch."

"Oh hell. I've already seen enough," the instructor called.

As the instrument glow faded, Wilson fought panic and the urge to escape his dark prison.

"Claustrophobia!" The instructor lifted the hood and welcome light flooded in. "A fellow can be a fine pilot in daylight but when the sun sets and the darkness comes, he's not worth a damn. Maybe, we'll ship you to radio school or a bombing and gunnery course. We've too much invested to give up completely."

"I've never had a problem before," Wilson's voice was shaky.

"Problems show up in training. That's why we train. We want to avoid an accident."

189

Al McGregor

Ottawa
February 24

"Sergeant Smith," Sandy Fleming said, flashing her press credentials. "I'm to pick up a picture of Dr. Fredrick Banting for the afternoon papers. It's so sad. He survived the plane crash but the weather at Gander delayed the rescue and he died."

Smith leaned across the desk to give the reporter his full attention.

"Every paper in the country wants a picture. But there's only one left. *The Journal* asked me to hold it." Despite bulky winter clothing, the woman was very attractive, so he added, "But first come is first served."

"How kind," she answered with a smile. "I don't suppose there's any recent biographical material. I mean, we have the important stuff, how Banting discovered Insulin and won the Nobel Prize, but we don't have much on the last few years."

"I'll look." Smith disappeared into a nearby office and returned with a thick file. "I can't let you take this but have a quick look. And as a reward, maybe we could meet when I'm off duty."

"That would be nice," Sandy offered another smile.

"A flying suit?" she spoke out loud as she leafed through the papers, "What's a flying suit?"

"At high altitudes, the air grows colder so pilots need insulated clothing, flexible, not too bulky. Pilots need oxygen, so that is taken into account and uh…it's kind of…well…on a long flight, the crew have to relieve themselves and no one wants to drop his pants in below freezing temperatures…"

"Alright, Sergeant. I get the picture. I'm surprised he was working on futuristic clothing."

"He was working on all kinds of things. Take a glance at page 27."

Sandy flipped the pages to read, "Present Situation regarding biological warfare."

"What on earth is that?" she asked.

"Banting was working on chemical warfare, along the line of the gas attacks from the first war. And, biological warfare, that's attacking the enemy by spreading sickness, typhus maybe, diseases that kill or put the enemy out of action."

"Surely we wouldn't use such weapons."

Smith nodded knowingly, "It's war ma'am and all things are fair."

"That will do Sergeant." Neither Sandy nor Smith had seen the officer approach.

"I was helping the lady," Smith said. "She needs a picture of Dr. Banting."

"Then give her the picture and get back to work."

"Yes sir!"

As Sandy left, the officer leafed through the open file.

Only minutes after she returned to her own office, another army officer appeared. "You spoke with a Sergeant Smith?" he demanded.

"Yes..."

"And took notes from a confidential file?"

"I took notes. No one said the file was confidential."

"A violation of the Official Secrets Act, miss. I must inform you that the material is subject to strict censorship. Publication would bring the most serious consequences."

"Well, what am I supposed to write?"

"Feel free to write of Bantings' earlier life and achievements. Or, study the Prime Minister's statement. I think he said something about an important wartime mission. Don't mess with any of these rumors of secret orders."

"Have I no option?"

"Not unless you want to face the consequences. Sergeant Smith has volunteered for reassignment."

"Plus ça change." Robert McLaren shook his head in disgust when the officer was gone. "I fought and lost on censorship in the first war and will lose again in this one."

"We won't even fight," Frank Willard said, showing a rare display of determination. "They'd shut us down or make life so difficult we'd lose anyway. All we have is Sandy's recollection. This Sergeant Smith is probably already on a train to an obscure post on the prairies. We can't win."

"A story making the rounds in Newfoundland says Banting was unto something important and his flight was sabotaged." McLaren leafed through his note pad. "But another pilot says engines act up in cold weather and Gander has cold in abundance. He thinks it was an accident and is surprised there haven't been more. The Airforce uses Gander and the Atlantic as a ferry route to get planes to Britain. It's faster than sending them by boat."

"That's another story we can't touch," Willard said. "Anything connected with Gander will be off limits for now."

"What brought the censors down on you?" Sandy asked McLaren.

"I wrote the truth about the battle of Passchendaele in 1917."

"The army didn't think it was the truth," Willard chortled. "Our Robert spent a few days in the brig and was sent back to Canada, persona non grata to the British army."

"Was it really like that?" she asked.

"Close enough. I thought the armed forces and the government had grown up, but I was wrong. No one objects to restrictions on reporting troop movements or ships at sea, but the censorship rules can be used to cover all kinds of secrets. That's not what they were meant to do."

Paris
March 5

In the thick mist, only the lower levels of the Eiffel Tower were visible but the huge banner that translated to "Germany is victorious everywhere" defiantly penetrated the gloom.

"It's not a great day to see Paris," Gunther Webber said as he led Maria from a gallery. "But as a German officer I can cut through any queue."

"It's not necessary." She fastened her coat. "I've seen the Tower."

"It's sad. Music plays and good food is available, but the City of Light has lost its spirit."

"Did you visit before the war?" she asked thinking it would explain his knowledge of the museums and galleries.

"As often as possible and I was delighted when posted here. However, it's not the same. Our demand for order conflicts with the natural charm. But enough gloom, I have a surprise, and can I take you to dinner, perhaps the Moulin Rouge?"

"Gunther, I can't. I've a reservation on the evening train."

"Only my surprise then and I'll take you to the station."

He stepped into the street and motioned for a taxi. With the shortage of gas, bicycle powered rickshaws competed for business. "Driver, 84 Avenue Foch."

The cyclist hesitated. "Gestapo Headquarters?" Webber nodded and sat beside Maria.

"Gestapo headquarters?" she repeated the driver's question.

"I have a small office, not much more than a closet. And, despite the perception, not everyone in the building is a thug."

"Heil Hitler!" An orderly sprang to his feet as the couple entered the building.

"Heil Hitler," Webber responded with a limp Nazi salute. "A busy night, Bruno?"

"The usual," he smiled. "One of our soldiers was discovered in the throes of ecstasy with a night club singer. He should have been more discrete. The woman is coloured. And a few teenagers were writing graffiti. The fools painted the English "V" for victory slogan on a garden wall."

"Will they be executed?" Webber laughed, failing to notice the shock on Maria's face.

"I wish!" the orderly threw his hands in the air. "French police believe a few nights behind bars is enough punishment. Will you be long?"

"No. I'm taking this lady to identify an artwork."

"Go quickly," he winked. "We'll save the paper work of signing in and out, and oh, a message came."

Webber tore it open, read quietly, and laughed. "Don't worry about missing dinner, Maria. New orders will take me to Le Havre in a few weeks. We'll have dinner later." She tried to appear pleased and followed him to the stairway. The hallway on the second floor was empty, scrubbed and polished for the next day. The only sound was their footsteps until a piercing scream came from above. Maria froze but he gently pushed her forward. "It is better not to notice." Webber opened his office door and felt his way toward the window to ensure the black out curtains were in place before returning to twist a switch. The light revealed a small office with a desk and single chair but propped against the walls were dozens of paintings and containers.

"These are not valuable, forgeries or lesser works but I wanted to show you a portrait." He stepped to a large carton and began to lift a frame. As a head appeared, Maria gasped.

"Oh, my God, it's me." She starred in silence for a few seconds. "I posed when I came back to Europe. I think I told you. I thought it was never completed."

"The eyes are impressive, the hair, the face, the colouring, a portrait of a beautiful woman."

Maria continued to stare, secretly pleased with the creation. "However, that's not all." He lifted the entire frame. Below the head and neck was a full, voluptuous and naked body.

"No." She recoiled in shock. "I didn't pose nude. What has he done?"

"If it's not you, the artist had an active imagination," Webber laughed. "I've seen this before. A painter produces the face of a woman and adds the body later. He might sell it to a

194

brothel. At the neckline, I detected a subtle difference in the paint."

She blushed. "I don't know what to say."

"One woman was striking," he said as he touched the head, "and another striking in different ways."

"Oh God," she stammered, "what's to become of it?"

Again, he laughed. "In the coming weeks everything in the room will be burned."

"Couldn't we destroy this one tonight?" Her mind was racing. A knife, a pair of scissors and the painting would be in shreds.

"No. I must note where each work came from and when it was destroyed."

"Can you hide it somewhere, at the back or under a carpet?"

"Don't worry, no one will see it."

She waited as he slipped the portrait back in the container and placed it behind other paintings. "I'm so embarrassed."

"It will be our secret."

London
March 15

"I've ordered tea," Martin Downey announced. "Had I known you would finally grace us with an office visit I'd have made other arrangements."

Evers Chance flipped the workman's cap from his head, slipped off his overcoat, and shook it allowing water to pool on the floor. "Lisbon was wonderful. I had a pleasant journey as you know."

"I didn't order surveillance," Downey explained. "But it was silly to enter occupied Europe."

"I needed to reach my people. Most are willing to work for the Special Operations Executive, despite my personal reservations. A few agents have disappeared, a handful prefer not to engage in sabotage or, ...have changed sides."

Chance produced a sheet of paper. "Names, addresses, contact information. I don't have to warn of the danger if this falls into the wrong hands."

Downey slowly ran his fingers down the list.

"Is this the end of your network?" he asked.

"No. I will keep a few private connections. I'll pass along anything important."

"Hmm…" Downey studied the list. "We may have immediate work for these people. Some of our pilots shot down over France reach the ground safely. We're working on an escape route to bring them home. Agents on the ground are at a premium but we may not need them for long."

"And what does that mean? Oh no, not another peace feeler?" Chance shook his head in dismay. "Haven't we learned anything?"

"I'm afraid I don't know much, mere speculation, but Hitler appears to want to preserve a British Empire."

"For Christ sake, he's been bombing the hell out of our cities. That's not the action of a bosom buddy."

"The German's may have had enough of war."

"Nonsense." Chance slammed his hand against the desk. "Hitler will open a new front."

"Now take it easy. The war has to end sometime."

"But it won't end soon. German troops are moving east. That may be a relief for us, but this year will not be remembered for an armistice."

Le Havre
March 21

Something woke her. A nightmare, Maria thought, until she heard another thump. She stumbled from the bed, grabbed the overcoat that doubled as a robe and fastened a single button. The noise came again. Whoever was at the door was persistent. She considered lighting the oil lamp but instead felt her way down the stairs.

"Miss…Maria…It's Maurice."

"I'm coming." As she slipped the latch, the door flew open to show Maurice and another man silhouetted in the entrance. "I had no where else to bring him," Maurice helped the man to a chair. "German troops are searching houses on the edge of the city. He's an English pilot."

"Damned parachute wasn't packed properly," the Englishman tried to stand but collapsed back into the chair. "We got him a doctor," Maurice picked up the story, "His leg is damaged. We have nowhere to hide him."

She felt along the mantle for an oil lamp and a match. In the flicking light, she saw a young man, in his twenties. His blue uniform was caked with mud. A boot was ripped to expose a dirty bandage. "He needs shelter for a day. A courier from Comet will come."

"I don't know what you are talking about?"

"Comet, the new network for escaped flyers. We spirit them to the coast or sometimes through Vichy and to Spain..."

"I don't know about any of this."

"But I thought you were part of it."

"They don't tell me everything, Maurice. You must know that."

"Sorry to be a bother." The pilot squirmed and looked beyond her. "Maybe I can hide in the barn?"

"No. The Germans are coming for wood today. That won't work."

"I have nowhere else to take him," Maurice too appeared to look past her.

She spun but saw nothing. "What are you looking at?" The overcoat flew open. And the cool night air reminded her of the short cotton shift she wore to bed. She hurriedly fastened more buttons. "Is that better? Really gentlemen, a women's night time attire should not bring a rescue to an end."

Maurice began to laugh.

The pilot shook his head. "They told us the French were different..." he began.

Al McGregor

"Don't worry," Maria interrupted, "clothing and appearances are our last concern. The cave in the forest, Maurice. Take him there. The Germans come after daybreak. I'll bring food when they're gone."

That morning it took forever to load the firewood and to make matters worse, the sergeant in charge demanded breakfast for himself and two privates. But finally, they left. She waited another full hour and had finished wrapping bread and cheese when a young girl on a horse appeared.

"Maria?" the girl swung lightly to the ground.

"Yes…"

"Maurice sent me for the parcel."

"Who are you?"

"A friend of Maurice." The girl was young, probably in her teens, but her attitude and tone suggested someone much older. One day, the pretty face and blond hair would turn heads. "Where is it?"

As they made their way the hiding place Maria tried to make conversation but was rebuffed by a stony silence. The girl finally spoke at the cave entrance. "Hey. Wake up. Time to go home." A moment later the pilot appeared in the shadows.

"One, I recognize. Good day, Maria. Who is the little friend?"

"English talk too much," the teen interrupted. She reached into the saddle bags and extracted clothes: pants, a tattered shirt and jacket and worn shoes. "Wear these."

"I won't change in front of you. I'm more modest than Maria."

"I brought food," Maria laughed and pushed the pilot toward the cave. "Eat while you change."

Minutes later, a French workman emerged with the air force uniform in his hands, "What about this?"

"I'll destroy it." Maria took the clothing.

"My name is Claudia," the teen checked his appearance and scooped up a handful of soil. Before, he could object, she rubbed dirt across his face and clothing. "Your name, is Jules Robert." She produced a set of papers, "Your identification."

"A little dirty," the pilot glanced at the forms, "Someone spilled gravy on them."

"The dirt should fool them. Especially, when I explain I am the little sister and my brother is a half-wit. Can you drool? No? Maybe you learn. The papers describe a mute. If you have anything to say, speak and say no more until I deliver you to the next safe house."

"Yes, sir!" he laughed and turned to Maria. "A half-wit thanks you."

Fingal, Ontario
March 26

The wind sock above the control tower showed a strong breeze from the south and doors across the air force base were open to welcome the hint of spring. The troop approaching the parade square faced an obstacle course of ruts and puddles.

"Frigging mud. I can hardly lift my feet," a man complained.

"Yah, let's hope, they did a better job on the buildings."

"Hey Yank!" Brad Wilson turned and recognized a face. The name escaped him.

"Gibson. Eric Gibson," the man prompted. "We were at the manning depot together. Did the gifted American wash out of pilot training?" Wilson was about to retort when Gibson laughed, "A bunch of us did, so there's no shame. How far did you get?"

"Elementary flight training," Wilson opted for honesty. "Goderich may be nice in summer, but I don't recommend a winter visit. The air force thinks I am better suited as a wireless/ air gunner or a bomb aimer. I've yet to be told which."

"Ah, the brass will set you straight, soon enough." Gibson said. Then he cleared his throat and spit. "Have you seen anyone else from our group?"

199

"Don't think so," Wilson glanced at the other men on the square.

"Hear about Skippy?" Gibson asked.

"Skippy, the big gangly kid?" An image flashed in Wilson's mind. An awkward teenager, only days removed from a prairie farm. "Is he here?"

"No. He won't be coming. Damn fool lost his head."

"I'm not surprised, what with his temper, always on a short fuse."

"No. He lost his head. He wasn't paying attention and walked into a propeller."

"Jesus."

"He'll be a paragraph in a flight instructor's manual. Accidents happen. They lost three men here just after the base opened. Live fire can be deadly."

Any further conversation was drowned by the roar of a plane flying low overhead. "That's an Anson," Gibson announced, "a flying coffin. The RAF lost so many in combat, they turned them into trainers. And, all the birds shipped to Canada have seen better days so pay close attention in parachute training."

"I'd rather fly single engine fighters, a Spit or a Hurricane."

"Put that out of mind, fella. We washed out. In our new career, we'll rupture an ear drum to hear Morse code or freeze our butts in a gun turret. Or both."

"What a cheerful thought."

"Only being honest."

"Save the honesty," Wilson said, looking to a brighter future. "The Ansons and other old kites are being retired. A Boeing Fortress may be next. Or, Ford is building a Liberator plant at Willow Run, near Detroit. Hell, we could drive over and fly one back."

"No, we'll fly British planes," Gibson predicted. "The Halifax maybe, a big four-engine heavy bomber, lose an engine or two and still make it home."

"Do they build heavies in Canada?" Wilson asked.

"Our factories build smaller planes. But that could change. Where there's a war, there's a way."

Ottawa
April 5

"This country is screwed. Mackenzie King and gang led us on the road to ruin."

"Take a deep breath, Mr. Willard," Sandy warned. "Watch the blood pressure. Don't get too excited."

"Someone in this God-forsaken city should care," Willard continued to rant. "The Liberals keep hiring friends. The size of the civil service grows by leaps and bounds and all they do is pass paper back and forth."

Sandy held a newspaper in front of her face and winked at Robert McLaren, who smiled and said, "Come on Frank. The war effort is in better shape than a year ago. Give King credit."

"For what? First, he tried to keep us out and by the time he got serious we'd lost the edge. I'm not talking about soldiers, although two divisions are sitting on their asses in Britain. And, I'm not taking anything away from the flyboys, or the sailors. But modern wars aren't won by brute force. Brains are needed and, in that category, King is sadly lacking."

"Frank," McLaren tried to sound serious, "have you been reading conservative newsletters again?"

"What if I have? What's needed is a national government, a coalition with the best minds. Bring back the former Prime Ministers. R.B. Bennett is available. Arthur Meighen is in the Senate. Form a coalition. Instead, do you know what King is planning?"

"No," Sandy answered meekly, covering her face with the newspaper again.

"He's going on holiday, off to Florida, again. The country is at war and the Prime Minister shelters under a beach umbrella."

"A little harsh," McLaren suggested.

Willard shook a fist in the general direction of Parliament Hill. "Our radio division is primed for growth, but King is pumping money into the CBC, which is nothing but a government propaganda mouthpiece."

"Is that it?" McLaren asked. "Are you miffed the CBC spends money and covers the country as opposed to our little operation?"

"Not just that," Willard answered. "We could be leading the way with factory production."

"But the country is working, flat out. We're building ships in the harbours on the Great Lakes. Men are back at work in Collingwood and Kingston. The car plants are churning out trucks in Windsor and Oshawa."

"It can't last," Willard snapped. "The Americans are offering handsome financing through Lend-Lease. British aren't fools. Why buy in Canada if the U.S. offers a better deal? And, what did we get for backstopping England? They dithered over whether to send the specialized drawings and tools our plants needed, and their selfish attitude slowed the war effort."

"Someone is in a bad mood," Sandy whispered to McLaren.

"What's got into you?" McLaren asked.

"I've been going over the books," Willard admitted. "Things aren't looking good. Another bad month and we'll be trimming hours."

The newspaper crumpled to expose Sandy's worried face. "My rent has gone up. I'm barely scraping by."

"Don't panic," McLaren shot an angry glance at his partner. "It can't be that bad. A few good stories would get us back on track. What about a series on those shipyards?"

"Not my idea of exciting."

"What about the strikes? Work up an angle on organized labour and war production?"

"Only if you tie the strikes to socialists and communists."

"Come on, Frank. Working men have legitimate concerns."

"Yah, well, businessmen have suffered in the last decade and every bit as much as the worker."

"Ok, that's it." McLaren rose and strode from the office. "We'll talk when you're in a better frame of mind."

London
April 22

"Good lord, Willard is cheap." Dan Malone grimaced. "He sent story ideas by regular post. A phone call wouldn't bankrupt him."

"I've heard this complaint before," Marcie responded, laughing. "It reminds me of a recurring serial."

"He asks for more exciting copy, but his suggestions would bore readers to death."

"Maybe I can help with excitement." She dropped the housecoat and slipped into the bed.

"Oh, I'm sure you can." He laughed.

"I didn't mean that. I picked up hot gossip at the club. Churchill's wife is sleeping around and reporting the pillow talk to the Prime Minister."

"What? That's crazy. Clementine must be over sixty."

"No, not Winston's wife, his son Randolph's wife, Pamela. She's a really good-looking woman and the men say she's using her...wiles...on the Americans."

"Where's Randolph in this?"

"Who knows. He was elected to the Commons last year but is often away on secret war work. He came to the club a few times. He's arrogant. He drinks too much. And when he's drinking, he's more arrogant. And, oh, he has wandering hands."

"Great story. Do you think the censors would pass it?"

She laughed and patted the bed beside her. "It's lonely and cold in here." Twenty minutes later she stirred and asked, "The stories from Willard. Will you have to travel?"

"Not very far. Old Frank wants a puff piece on the former Canadian Prime Minister. He thinks R.B. Bennet can play a role in a new Canadian government and wants an item extolling his virtues. Although, it's odd. The Agency has never directed me on what to write but he was emphatic on what he wanted with this one."

"Is Bennet interesting?"

"Yes and no. He got a bad rap during the Depression, but most politicians failed on that file. He's been doing war work in England and bought a country estate near Lord Beaverbrook. And King George is ready to make him Sir Richard, or Sir R.B. or Sir Dick or whatever he wants."

"Sounds like the story will write itself."

"Yah, but I won't rush it," he said. "Don't want Frank to think I'm not busy."

Chapter Nine: Bombers' Moon

Near London, Ontario
April 23

Eric Gibson drove slowly to avoid the deepest ruts. "A truck would be better, but this jalopy was all the motor pool had. We've lots of time, the first bombing runs aren't scheduled for an hour."

Brad Wilson sat in the passenger seat, glad to be away from classroom activity at the Bombing and Gunnery school and curious to see the targets from the ground.

"This is as far as we drive," stated Gibson and stopped the car. "The observation post is about a half mile ahead. That thing that looks like a duck blind. From there we can see how close bombs come to the target."

The pair reached the edge of a field where trees and shrubs had been cleared.

"And, that's the target," Gibson said pointing to a pile of logs. "The bombs let off smoke, there's no explosive. But keep your eyes open. The sergeant says the first runs are really bad. The safest place might be on top of the target."

"Which explains why we're in the middle of nowhere."

"Actually, we're not that far from the city but that should be obvious from the air. Someone came too close to a farm house on the range near Dutton and knocked down a chimney. The brass were not impressed."

"And there's a target on Lake Erie?"

"Observers can sit on the cliffs and use binoculars. But for a cushy job, I'd go for a crash boat. Those men do nothing but cruise about in case a plane goes down."

"I wouldn't enjoy the lake on a rough day."

"But at the end of the day a billet is waiting in Port Stanley. Food, drink, and in the summer, scantily clad women. What else could you ask for?"

Le Havre
April 29

"I feel guilty." Maria smiled at Gunther Webber. "I don't know when I've had so much food."

The restaurant was almost empty. A few men stood at the bar. They sat at a table in a quiet corner.

"Good and plentiful food is one of the perks of dining with an officer," he told her. "I'm glad you came. Many French no longer appreciate what friends can do."

"But you understand why they feel that way?"

"Yes, the occupation, the ham-handed police actions, the shipments of food and men to Germany. My brother officers are less sympathetic and say to the victor goes the spoils."

"I doubt you could change the situation."

"I complained but no one listens. The treatment of the French Jews is horrible. And, the foreign-born are deported. Trainloads are shipped to the east, but few know the destination and fewer care."

"I don't notice the changes in the country, but more businesses were shuttered the last time I came to the city. The owners were Jews."

"Scowl when speaking of them," he said, wiping his face. "That will make you appear more German."

"I'm comfortable as a neutral."

"But you must also be careful. A female, identified as a friend or seen with a German officer, could be a target for violence. I won't be able to offer protection."

"Are you leaving?"

"I finished my work in Le Havre this afternoon. I wanted to see you before I left. I'll soon order the destruction of that artwork."

"Oh, thank you." She grasped his hand. "I have enjoyed the company, too."

He smiled and helped her with her coat. "I'll walk you to the city limits."

He pushed her bicycle and they talked as night began to set in, until he finally said, "You should go, the curfew is approaching."

She lightly kissed his cheek. "Thank You for everything."

A movement in the nearby bushes caught her eye. "Someone is there," she whispered but before she could say more a rough hand closed over her mouth and she was forced to the ground.

"Frigging Boche!" The insult was almost lost in the sound of a struggle.

She tried to rise but was held down. Finally, after what felt like hours, a man wrenched her to her feet.

"Have a good look!" He pointed to the body of Gunther Webber.

"What have you done?" she screamed before another hand covered her mouth.

"Quiet bitch. That German bastard sent a train load of stolen art to Paris today."

"Fools," she wrenched free and dropped beside the blood covered body. "Gunther," she cried but there was no response. "He was no Nazi. He was an art lover and simply following orders."

Again, the men dragged her to her feet. "A German whore. Do you want to join him?" She stared at the assailants, each with a scarf wrapped around his face. One of the men pushed the bike toward her and hissed, "Don't look back."

She lost the battle with her tears as she pedaled to safety.

The next day Maurice came to the farm. The house appeared deserted. The only sign of life, a badly stained coat dropped near the front door.

He knocked for several minutes before Maria answered. She appeared to have aged overnight. "I heard what happened," he told her. "How are you?"

"What do you think? I witnessed a murder."

"The men are hard to control," Maurice tried to explain. "The attack should not have happened."

"That's lame. An innocent man is dead."

"To those men, no German is innocent."

"What about the police?"

"The body was found on the railway track. Wine bottles were everywhere. The investigator believes he was drunk and hit by a train. Case closed."

London
May 10

"Imagine, Saturday and a night off." Marcie Eaton sat on the bench in front of the mirror. Dan Malone slouched on a couch. "We could go out. Make a night on it."

She ignored him and stood to pull at her dress. "I'm gaining weight." She twisted to study her reflection.

"Is that why you don't want to go out?" Malone asked. "Afraid of being considered fat? That, my lovely, will not happen."

"I'd rather have a night to ourselves."

"Your wish is my command."

"What's with you?" She spun to face him. "Something's up. You've been acting like the cat that swallowed the canary. What are you hiding?"

"I've a new job. Willard can stick it."

"Something steady. With a future?"

"I think so. The Ministry of Information. Honestly, it would be little more than writing propaganda but could lead to important work, later."

"Whoop-de-doo," she laughed and threw herself into his arms. "A future, that's not tied to a tightwad and a job when the war is done."

"That's what we hope, so I can afford to take you out."

"We'll eat at home." She spun away. "The kitchen is well stocked except for eggs. I tossed them. They made me sick this morning."

"I'll eat later. I've other things planned."

"Don't be naughty, sir…I…" The thought was interrupted by an air-raid siren. "Oh damn. I thought Adolf had given up. The raids haven't been as bad in the last few weeks."

"Douse the lights," he ordered. "I'll open the curtains."

Seconds later she joined him by the window.

"Full moon, a bomber's moon," he sighed. "The Luftwaffe uses the Thames as a marker and fly right into the city. We should go to the shelter."

"No. Not yet. I don't want to waste a night together."

Search light beams punched into the sky as anti-aircraft guns began to bark in the distance. The A-A guns positioned down the street added to the growing chorus and the sky, a few blocks away, erupted in flames. "We should go." He clasped Marcie's hand.

By morning rescue crews had completed their work. "The fires are under control," a police officer announced, "But this building will be condemned. A strong breeze could take it down."

"A bomb right through the centre," said a warden as he pushed aside debris. "We found a young couple upstairs. The concussion, the shock wave, would have killed them. Damn shame! The girl was a real looker and she must have seen something in the fella."

"Bodies to the morgue?" the police officer asked. "Already gone and a busy day for the morticians. The raid was the worst this year. The House of Commons was hit and Westminster Abbey. Makes you wonder what message Hitler is trying to send."

Ottawa
May 12

"This is the best yet," Frank Willard laughed and set down the phone. "London has one of the worst nights of the Blitz and the staff at Canada House are given a new mission. The Prime Minister dashed off a coded message. He wants stones from the wreckage of the British House of Commons shipped to him for the ruins at Kingsmere. My God, what will that man do next?"

Willard stopped as an ashen Robert McLaren entered the office. In his shaking hand was a telegraph form. "Dan Malone and his lady have been killed."

Sandy's gasp was the only sound. "What happened?"

"The Blitz. A bomb…"

She reached for a handkerchief. McLaren appeared lost in thought. Only Willard appeared unaffected and lifted an envelope from his desk. "Malone's dispatch on R.B. Bennett came in yesterday's mail along with a private note, saying he doubted Bennett would be part of any Union Government. That's a pity." He dropped the envelope on his desk, "Malone was leaving anyway. He had another job."

"Does he have family?" Sandy asked. "We should send a note or flowers."

"A note," Willard decided. "Flowers are expensive."

From the corner of her eye, Sandy saw McLaren squeeze his hands into fists. "Don't worry, he had no family."

"This may be a blessing in disguise, "Willard carried on, "We'll save the money from Malone's salary. But we have to decide what to do with London. My first thought is to close the bureau, but a few papers consider us their exclusive British source." He began to scribble figures on a notepad. "Or, we could shut down radio and raise money by selling the gear. And, send Sandy to London. Imagine a female view of beleaguered Britain."

"It's not safe," McLaren said, interrupting, "and she doesn't have the experience."

"We can't send you," Willard retorted. "The Brits remember you from the last war. And, I have to cover the business side of the operation. If I pull a few strings, I could get her on a troop ship and arrange free passage."

"You can't be serious?"

"Damn right, I'm serious. Sandy, start packing."

"And, what if I don't want to go?" She finally found her voice.

"Wartime, young lady," Willard declared. "My way or the highway. Take your choice!"

London
May 12

The air was foul, a mixture of smoke and a scent that no one wanted to consider. Evers Chance watched as more bodies were carried from the wreckage and loaded onto a waiting truck. "An ugly sight," Martin Downey sighed, "But we're grown used to it."

"Let's move on." Chance turned down a street that was relatively undamaged.

"Don't walk so fast," Downey said as he struggled to keep up. "The smoke affects my breathing."

"Getting old?"

"Aren't we all. Rest by those sandbags. No one will pay attention to a couple of old geezers."

"Why did you call?" Chance picked at a ragged thread on a bag. "What's so urgent?"

"Did you ever meet Rudolf Hess?"

"No. But did you want me for the interrogation? I'd love to speak with the Deputy Fuhrer."

"How did you know?" Downey slumped against the bags.

211

"I have sources, Martin. A man who claims to be Hess, slips past the Luftwaffe, mysteriously eludes air defences and crash-lands in Scotland. The silence from Whitehall is deafening."

"A press statement will come in a few hours," Downey stammered. "We wanted to be certain of his identity."

"Bull! You want to know if he was invited. Was he expected and if so by whom? The Germans know Churchill won't negotiate but may believe he can be ousted. A new government might stand aside as Hitler deals with Russia. Or, Berlin may think Britain will join the effort and finish the Bolsheviks."

"If that's what they think they are badly mistaken."

"Oh, there are people in Britain who see Communism as a greater threat than National Socialism, fewer than in 1939, but they exist. Did Hess bring a message?"

"Apparently. I don't know the contents."

"So, secret meetings are underway with unnamed officials and no written record. What do we do? Lock him away? Welcome him to England? My guess: Lock him up and interrogate the hell out of him."

"You're not helping."

"And you wonder if a rogue department or agent has been sending signals to the other side. Was the weekend Blitz a message? Over a thousand dead, the city in flames. Look what we Germans can do. Listen to what Herr Hess proposes."

"We wouldn't negotiate. Not now."

"Grasp at straws then. Could the Hess visit be a sign Hitler will be replaced? I doubt it. I do think it's time to warn Stalin the Wehrmacht is coming. Although, Moscow knows as much as we do. Our agencies are peppered with communists."

"I'll pass that along, but you have no proof."

"No, but strong suspicions." Chance started to leave but turned back. "What's happening with the Americans?"

"Oh, we keep giving them another nudge. More propaganda, planting pro-British stories in the papers, a few tricks to make the isolationists look bad. The British Security

Co-ordination bureau has a growing operation in New York. Bill Stephenson runs it. Remember him?"

"Yes. I do." Chance shrugged and added, "I find it amazing that we need undercover operations in America."

New York City
May 23

Tim Fulton pushed to the entrance of Madison Square Garden. Twenty thousand people were expected for the America First rally and millions would listen on radio. The movement had grown in strength despite the passage of Lend-Lease and new aid for the British.

"Don't push. Lots of room inside," he reached to help an elderly man.

"Thanks, young fellow. These people have no manners. I hope it's not a reflection of the movement."

"I assure you, it's not," Fulton with a smile and waved to an usher. "Help this gentleman to a seat." An appearance by Charles Lindbergh had stoked interest in the rally. He would present the arguments against any American military role in Europe.

"Tim, we have a problem," an associate caught his arm. "Phoney tickets." He waved a stub. "We didn't print this. If we can't organize seating for a public event how do we maintain any credibility?"

Fulton threaded through the lines to where another organizer stood beside the two men blamed for the confusion. "Where did you get the tickets?"

"I didn't do nothing wrong," one answered. "A guy gave it to me on the subway."

"And, I got mine outside of Rockefeller Centre," the other volunteered. "Two guys were passing them out on the street."

"What did they look like?"

"Ordinary guys except one had a British accent, an upper-class limey type."

"And the other?"

Al McGregor

"He wasn't a New Yorker."

Fulton drew his colleague aside. "A full house?"

"Yah, turning people away."

"Someone is trying to make us look bad, but what a stupid game. It won't prove anything."

A wave of cheers erupted from the auditorium as Lindbergh rose to speak.

"Listen to that! The people are with us."

Quebec City
May 24

The sun broke through the low clouds as Sandy Fleming reached the bridge. The former passenger ship had moved into the Saint Lawrence minutes after she came on board and an hour later, an entire convoy stretched over several miles. On one ship she saw the fuselage of an aircraft, on another the snout of what appeared to be a tank. All holds were full and extra cargo was chained to the decks.

"What is a woman doing on my ship?" A bearded man, dressed in navy blue, shouted and strode toward her.

"I'm Sandy Fleming, a reporter...."

"The reporter," he said, his face blanched, "is a woman?"

"I have a letter from Defence Headquarters," Sandy began. "I'm to observe..."

"A woman. That's all I need. Hundreds of horny soldiers aboard and a woman. What in hell was the navy thinking?"

"It was all arranged..."

"Arranged my ass. The captain did not give his permission."

"If you would take me to the captain, we might straighten this out."

"I am Captain John Treadwell and I make the rules. I've a mind to unload you at one of these Quebec villages."

"Captain!" A crew man called, "Signal from Raccoon."

The captain lifted his own binoculars to peer at the flashing light and swore. "No, damn it. I will not reduce speed. Reply.

Tell him to take station at the rear." A minute later the light on the Raccoon blinked again.

"Acknowledged and good night."

"What does he mean by 'good night'?"

"The Raccoon is an armed yacht," the signalman answered, "only a few small guns. Her radio is down so he'll signal again in the morning."

"Bloody wonderful. I can't communicate with her except by Aldis lamp. Shit. Order him to follow Tarragon but stay well back. That old freighter is loaded with ammunition. The rest of the convoy will maintain speed."

Sandy wondered if he'd forgotten her. He hadn't. "Look, Miss," Treadwell lowered his voice, "we can launch a small boat and put you ashore."

"Perhaps, if you read the letter from Defence Headquarters?" she suggested politely.

"Give me the damn letter."

Treadwell took a long time reading the few short paragraphs. "Captain. Urgent message," another sailor appeared. Treadwell squashed Sandy's letter into a ball and fired it overboard while reaching for the latest message. As he read, his anger grew.

"Bloody Hell," he turned toward her and spoke with a low growl, "I do not like women on a warship. It's bad luck. And worse since you plan to document every little detail. Return to your cabin. You will be allowed to move about only when an officer is available."

"I'm supposed to have the run of the ship…"

"Not my ship!" He motioned and spoke to another officer, "Take her below."

The captain turned to the officers on the bridge. "Admiralty reports the *Bismarck* is loose and has sunk the *Hood*. Only three survivors from a crew of fifteen hundred and our course runs close to her last known position."

For two days, Sandy made no attempt to leave the cabin. Instead, she staggered from the bed to the toilet and back again and again and again.

"Getting the sea legs?" a sailor asked on third morning. "We'll air out the cabin, dog the door open for a few hours."

"Uh…," Sandy turned her head into the pillow. "Breakfast." He set a tray beside her, "The cook used extra lard with the bacon. Bread soaks up the grease."

The smell produced more dry heaves.

"Take it away," she begged.

"Don't want to waste food."

"Eat it yourself."

"Ok. Captain wants to see you this afternoon. I'll come back with lunch. We're having shepherds pie."

"Oh God. Leave!"

She awoke as a cold wind blew into the cabin. Through the open door she could see clear blue sky and for the first time in days felt better.

"I brought coffee with a touch of ginger," the sailor said upon his return. "Being sea-sick is bad enough. Don't dehydrate."

"I feel better," she sat up, "Does the sickness always pass quickly."

"Everyone is different. Some never shake it."

"Is there a place to do laundry?" she asked sheepishly. "The clothes and blankets smell."

"We'll take care of that. And uh, I'd suggest something warmer than those pyjamas. It's cold on the bridge."

"The convoy can spread out in the Gulf," the first officer pointed to the distant ships. "A pair of corvettes are up front, two more in the rear, a destroyer on one side and we handle the other. We're making good time, but the met staff predict rough seas."

"Isn't that something to look forward too." Sandy snapped and more gently asked, "Where are we? I've lost track of time and space."

216

"In the Gulf of Saint Lawrence. Newfoundland is to the north. To the south are the French islands of St Pierre and Miquelon."

"Miss Fleming," Captain Treadwell appeared in a doorway. The uniform was gone. Instead he wore slacks and a thick woolen sweater. "We'll talk in my cabin." The cabin was sparsely furnished with a desk, two chairs, and a bunk. A leather case brimming with papers lay open on the desk.

"If you hadn't been sick, I'd have you put ashore."

"All of the arrangements were made in Ottawa," she said, thinking of the hurried meetings at Defence Headquarters before passage was approved.

"Yes, I've had a message from the minister's office. I am to assist as best I can."

"That's what my letter said, too."

"Oh. That letter that was lost in the wind."

"If you say so," she laughed. "Captain's prerogative."

He opened a desk drawer, removed a bottle and two mugs. "Rum. We take it neat."

The alcohol burned and she feared a bout of nausea, but the feeling passed.

"I'll give you an outline," the captain spoke. "I've a ship loaded with troops but have also been ordered to escort this convoy toward Iceland. And, we have to move slow. Several of the older ships can't make good speed. So, it may be a rough trip and not only because of the weather."

"The major risk is submarines?"

"We think so. While you were sick, the German battlecruiser *Bismarck* was on the prowl, but the Royal Navy got her. She's been sunk. Our guns can stop a sub but are no match for a warship."

Ottawa
May 28

"It's like pulling teeth," Robert McLaren exclaimed. "The navy routes Sandy not to Halifax, but to a convoy from Quebec City and refuses to say what ship she boarded or the destination."

"War time regulations," Frank Willard was unconcerned. "She'll be fine. If I were a captain, I'd maintain radio silence."

"If you were a captain, the crew would mutiny."

"Still miffed? Sending her overseas solves a financial problem. And, no one else has a woman on the front line. And, let's get something else straight. We created a partnership, but I put up most of the money. And since we're bleeding cash, I'm exercising my option to take financial control."

"You can't do that."

"Then buy me out. That's the other option." McLaren was silent. "I thought so," Willard snapped. "So let's get back to business. The competition is playing up the Bismarck. Ship sunk, heavy loss of life, revenge for the Hood. Anything to add?"

McLaren scowled but reached for his notebook.

"British ships picked up Bismarck survivors and could have saved more but there was a U-boat scare. The navy left the rest of the enemy to the mercy of the sea."

"What are we talking about? Thousands of men?"

"No one is sure but there's a touch of irony when a submarine scare claims German lives. And, we got a break with the *Bismarck.* A vast ocean to search, and a slow-flying aircraft stumbled across her."

"Too bad Sandy wasn't already in England. She could have tracked down the pilot."

"He wouldn't talk."

"Killed in action?" Willard wet his lips. "Makes a better story."

"No. He's alive but he's American, officially an observer. Washington doesn't want publicity."

218

An Angry Sky

"Good story," Willard beamed. "Put it out under your byline."

"No! No confirmation!" McLaren smirked. "You may have financial control but under the partnership agreement, I've the final say on journalistic standards."

North Atlantic
June 2

"Wear the tin hat, miss. We're at battle stations. It pays to be safe." Sandy Fleming adjusted the helmet. The captain had provided coveralls and gloves and with the added bulk of the life jacket she could barely move. After hours of argument, he grudgingly agreed to let her spend the night in the radio room. "I'm Monahan," the radio operator introduced himself, "but call me Sparks." His helmet rested within easy reach beside the radio set. "Things could get interesting tonight. The Yanks can't take an active role but do broadcast warnings, in plain English, and they spotted a sub."

"U.S. ships are near the convoy routes?"

"More every month," he told her. "The rumor mill says Americans will replace the Canadian troops occupying Iceland. A contingent has been there for a year waiting for Hitler to invade."

"I forgot about Iceland. The military thought Hitler might leap frog to Iceland and Greenland and attack North America. It must have become a boring assignment."

"Boring, but a damn sight safer than being at sea."

He pulled the headset over his ears and pressed his hands against them. Moments later, he scratched a note and bent to the voice pipe to the bridge. "A transmission on the Kraut wave lengths. It's close."

"U-boat?" she asked.

"Maybe a wolf pack, a bunch of them. The Royal Navy has special sub-tracking gear, but the admiralty hasn't seen fit to install the technology on all the Canadian ships. Our gear is out of date."

"Stay sharp, Sparks," a voice carried from the bridge. "Aldis signal from a corvette reports a periscope."

"The radios on those corvettes aren't worth a damn." He continued to twist the dials as he talked. "Corvettes are wet boats. Water splashes all over them. Men can't get food from the galley without it being wet. And, in winter when the ice forms, it's worse."

"Corvettes are the small ships?"

"Yah, fast and turn on a dime. Dozens are under construction, except when the workers go on strike. We're fighting for our lives and the buggers on shore strike for more money."

"Explosion to port," the voice from the bridge was excited. "Shit, she's on fire. Hopefully, someone remembers the fuses."

"What's that mean?" Sandy asked.

"If they don't pull the fuses, the depth charges can explode and blow the life boats all to hell."

"My God."

"You DID see our lifeboat drill, the second day out."

"No. I was sick."

"Ok, the boats are one deck down. No one survives long without a boat."

"Flare to starboard!" a voice shouted on the bridge. "Torpedo, 500 yards. Heading right for us."

"Ah shit," Sparks slapped the helmet on his head, "Brace yourself."

The bridge went silent. She shivered and imagined the explosives streaking through the water.

"Dud!" Someone shouted in exhilaration.

Sparks took a deep breath. "Thank God for German inefficiency." He plopped the helmet on the desk and resuming his listening post.

"Bridge!" He didn't wait for a response, "Tarragon under attack and on fire."

"Can't they see that," she asked.

220

"Not if it's a small fire, she's miles behind."

He sat silently and then. "Bridge! Tarragon will abandon ship."

"Christ! Look at the size of the blast." The crew on the bridge saw a distant explosion. "No one is getting away from that."

"Tarragon was loaded with ammunition," Sparks murmured. "At least it was quick."

"Will we go to help?"

"Help with what? No chance of survivors from something like that." The headset was again clamped tight to his head."

"Bridge!" He called again. "A tanker reported a fire but no further signal."

The cabin was silent except for the hum from the radio equipment. Sparks pushed the headset from one ear and enlightened Sandy, "Men don't waste time leaving a tanker. Oil or aircraft fuel goes up like ammunition. What doesn't burn off coats the water. Anyone who gets a mouthful is in a bad way. And if oil on the water catches fire, well…then it's ugly."

"Doesn't anyone try to find survivors?" Sandy had to ask.

"One of the rear corvettes will have a look," he explained. "Captain Treadwell has to protect the troops aboard this ship."

"Sub on the surface. Port side," a voice called from the bridge.

"Flares!" Captain Treadwell's voice sounded calm, "Fire at will."

The bark of guns drowned all other sound and continued for several minutes. "She's diving. Maintain course. Stand by to ram!"

"She's gone under sir!"

"Fire depth charges!"

The ship shook from underwater explosions. Sparks suddenly called, "Bridge. British destroyers. Ten miles out and pinging on a target."

He turned to Sandy. Was her white face the result of the battle or a recurrence of seasickness?

221

"We're safe. The Royal Navy can take over. The captain will soon order full speed and race for Glasgow."

Washington
June 2

"Hello, gorgeous," Mark Ryder said as he pushed the door open. "Oh, sorry. I thought a Canadian reporter was using this office."

"He is," Robert McLaren answered.

"No. A woman."

"Sandy, couldn't come, transferred to England. I'm Robert McLaren. And I've never been called 'gorgeous'."

"I'm…I'm sorry. I know Sandy and assumed that…"

"Make do with me. I was looking for you anyway…Mark Ryder, is it? They tell me you have a handle on the American military."

"I have sources," Ryder smiled. McLaren appraised the American. Brash, he thought, and handsome. No wonder Sandy had fallen for him, if only briefly.

McLaren waited as Ryder pulled an office chair from the corner.

"Did Sandy enjoy the Clipper?" Ryder asked. "I've heard the service is great."

"She didn't fly. She's with a convoy."

"That's not safe. Why send her by ship?"

"Money. The same reason I slept in a train coach instead of a sleeping compartment."

"Ah. Sandy said the guy running the shop was a skinflint. She had nice things to say about you, though."

"That's good, but I doubt we'll click as the two of you did."

"She's a real knockout. You…uh…put the make on her?"

"We have a professional relationship."

"Just curious," Ryder leaned back in a chair and raised his feet to the desk. "What do you want to know?"

"I'm trying to understand American policy. A lot of cheers went up over Lend-Lease but the actual shipments are barely a

222

trickle. And what is President Roosevelt's declaration of an "Unlimited National Emergency?"

"The White House is backing off on that," Ryder said. "It gives the President more power and he could do an end run on Congress, but he hasn't tried. He wants to be sure the people are with him and the people don't want war. He'll sell material to Britain but keep our men at home."

"Canadian army planners have been spending a lot of time in Washington. Any idea why?"

"A lot of Brits are here. Buggers insist on wearing uniforms and stand out like a sore thumb. Even the men in our war department wear civilian clothes."

"Aside from dress codes, what are they talking about."

"I can't pin it down or I'd have the front-page story. The code name is ABC1. The Americans, British and Canadians are deciding what to do if America joins the war. They'd concentrate on Hitler but some of our people worry about the Japanese. I'm not sure why. We could beat them with one hand tied behind our back."

"How do they plan to beat the Germans?"

"More ships, more planes, more tanks and make 'Arsenal of Democracy,' a fact, rather than an empty slogan."

"I wish I had better connections in Washington." McLaren stood to stretch and relieve the cramp in his leg. The cramp disappeared when he heard Ryder's next words.

"The Willard Agency could have had access to our material and reporters, a sort of joint venture, but your partner wouldn't agree."

"What?"

"I heard it from the managing editor. We offered a deal, but the Ottawa guy wanted a major say. That wasn't going to happen."

McLaren tried to control his feelings. His partner had ruined a chance to grow the agency.

Ryder pulled himself to his feet. "Sort of like the war plans. Canadians will be involved but won't have control. If or when, the Americans come in, your country will drop lower in the pecking order. I'm pretty sure the war planners make that clear. Just as I'm sure my boss saw the Willard Agency as a poor country cousin."

Off Scotland
June 6

Relief washed across Captain Treadwell's face when the Scottish hills appeared on the horizon. "I confess, Miss Fleming, you were less trouble than expected," he said. "The troops won't disembark until tomorrow, but a pilot launch will be alongside shortly and take you ashore."

"Thank you, Captain. I have a better sense of what the navy is up against, and, well, you read my dispatch."

"The writing appeared factual," Treadwell said. "But someone else can decide how much can be told."

"Were there many survivors from the ships that sank?"

"A few men were rescued but the subs came back. Four more ships went down."

"And that would be eight ships in only a few hours?"

"I won't confirm numbers, but we do need stronger escorts and more air support. Talk to the censors about what can be said. The same with those interviews with the troops. From what I read, a few of them opened up too much."

"Thanks for allowing me to talk to them. My editor would have gone berserk if their story wasn't included."

"The army may have something to say. It's not my department."

A heavy mist formed along the shore and in minutes the welcome site of land was obscured. "Will fog cause a delay?"

"No. A pilot boat will find us. And a message came through, you have a seat on the Ghost train."

"The what?"

"A train that is hidden under layers of secrecy. A special, no schedule, no notifications, but the railways ensure a right of way to London. VIP's and foreign guests use it. It's another war time secret."

"I'll keep mum," she smiled. "I'd better pack."

"Only room for one suitcase. We'll ship the rest later. Someone at Canada House should know how to find it."

London
June 12

London shocked her: the devastation, rows of ruined buildings and the lines for daily necessities. An air-raid siren sent her frantically in search of shelter, arriving to find people streaming out, as the all clear sounded. And, the blackout was frightening. Londoners might navigate but a visitor from aboard was soon lost.

"Miss Fleming?" A man stepped from the darkness. "I'm Evers Chance."

Relieved, she almost hugged him. "Mr. McLaren speaks highly of you."

"I hope he does; we go back a few years. Come we'll talk at the pub."

The Ploughman's Rest was nearly empty. Idyllic scenes from the countryside adorned the walls but years of tobacco smoke and grime dulled the lustre.

"Have you eaten?" he asked.

"Yes," she said.

"Just as well. The menus grow thinner each day. English farmers once fed us," he said gesturing to the paintings. "Now we rely on the Dominions. I hope, the ships on the convoy carried food."

"I don't know," she said, embarrassed to admit she hadn't asked about all of the cargo. "One ship had ammunition, and another carried oil."

"Good, we can use that."

"They sank." She saw no need for details.

"Hmm…tough crossing."

Chance admired the girl, a good-looking woman. She was likely in over her head but ready to tough it out.

"I brought books from Ottawa," she told him. "Histories of England, books on the Royal family, Churchill on the first war, and a travel guide for Great Britain. But my luggage has disappeared so...."

"If it turns up, treasure the travel guide. Most were destroyed lest road maps fall into the hands of phantom invaders. As, for the other books, don't waste time. Churchill writes well but of the world according to Winston. Have you read Hitler, *Mein Kampf*?"

"I was afraid to be seen with it."

"Too bad. He lays out his plan. Your people will be looking for a Canadian angle, although, honestly, very few people really care about Canada right now. Try to grasp the big picture. That's where I can help."

"That would be great."

"For a start, learn about Russia. You'll see why in a few weeks. Now I have to cut this short. I've another meeting."

Martin Downey arrived minutes later and immediately glanced at the décor. "Always intrigued by your haunts. Is there a message in rustic art?"

"Yes, Lebensraum, new lands for German farmers."

"Another warning?" Downey slid into a chair.

"The Germans will attack in days."

"We've heard this for months. Nothing has happened. And, Moscow has been warned, repeatedly. Even the Americans, dozy as they can be, raised an alarm. But Stalin won't trust the west."

"Maybe he's too busy pacifying the Baltic states," Chance mused. "The Russians have been active since they seized those lands. Forced migrations, destruction of the intelligentsia, that sort of thing."

"And what am I to do with that?"

"Kick the intelligence gurus in gear. If nothing is done, Latvia, Lithuanian and Estonia will be lost for a generation.

Stalin won't want to surrender those countries. He's using Hitler's playbook, destroying anyone that offers the slightest hint of resistance. And the hell of it is, we'll soon be working to save him."

Chapter Ten: The War Goes East

Western Russia
June 21

"Don't be nervous, Jurgen. I've crossed into Russian territory before. The Red Army is docile as a kitten when it sees the swastika."

Karl Munster was giddy with the adventure. The German staff car carried a flag on the front fender and left a cloud of dust on the track from the border. He tapped the driver's shoulder and pointed toward a small village and men carrying sacks to a rail car.

"Comrades," Munster used a smattering of Russian to address the workmen. "What are you loading?"

The Russians looked on in silence until another man approached. "I am Bulanov, Red Army Commissar. What do you want?"

"Only pleasant conversation," Munster said and smiled. "Heinzman. Gifts for the comrades." The corporal produced two bottles of vodka. "To friendship," Munster passed the bottles. "We are lost and stumbled across the village. The men are hard at work."

The commissar opened a bottle before he spoke. "The bags are full of grain, wheat for Germany. In a few weeks our people will reap another bountiful harvest and send more supplies."

"That is very kind."

"It is an obligation under the Russia-German friendship agreement."

"I learn something every time I cross the border," said Munster, still smiling. "Could you direct me to the nearest airport?"

Heinzman unrolled a map of the border region. "Here," Bulanov poked a dirty finger at the map, "across the river."

"Understood, Heinzman?" Munster asked.

"Yes, Colonel, a few kilometres."

"We're off then." Munster smiled and bowed to the commissar. Out of sight of the village, he began to laugh. "The fools. Peasants won't live to see another harvest. Instead, next year, German settlers will produce magnificent crops. Have you marked the location?"

"Yes, Herr Colonel."

"Jurgen, are you well?"

"I am tired. We don't have time to sleep."

"And what about the pills? Are you taking the courage pills?"

"Sometimes, I double over from a pain in the gut. I blame the drug."

"Nonsense. The pills clear the mind. I take two each day."

"The airstrip should be just ahead," Heinzman said, trying to change the subject and made a show of checking the map.

"What a sight," Munster called as they crested a hill. Dozens of Russian aircraft lined a runway. "Honk and wave," he ordered. "Comrades. We are lost. Where is the border?"

Sullen airmen were soon smiling, sharing vodka and offering directions to the German lines.

"Everything is so well organized." Munster appeared impressed. "Are the planes always parked, wing tip to wing tip?"

Al McGregor

"When there is no drill, they are parked this way," a Russian said.

"And is a drill planned soon? I'd like to watch. I could come back tomorrow."

"No, nothing is planned. But you are welcome to return with vodka."

"Perhaps, I shall," he smiled and tapped the driver's shoulder. "Home. Our friends have shown us what we need to see."

A few minutes later Munster again began to laugh.

"The Luftwaffe will destroy the airfield before the Russians know what's happened. This will be the greatest invasion of all time. Millions of men, the Wehrmacht, the Luftwaffe, the Panzer's, all poised to smash Russian lines. The Fuhrer uses the code name 'Barbarossa'. Tomorrow will be a beautiful day."

New York
June 23

Tim Fulton easily found a vacant seat on the subway. A copy of the latest *Herald-Tribune,* telling of the invasion of Russia, was tucked under his arm. The wheels screeched as the train rounded a curve and the overhead lights faded.

As the light returned, Erich Schmidt appeared. "I hope the dramatics weren't too much. Hoover's men are persistent. Did anyone follow you?"

"I don't think so, but I don't ride the subway much, too many coloureds, foreigners and Jews." He glanced anxiously around the car.

"And what would they see? Two gentlemen talking and one carrying a mouthpiece of British propaganda."

"It was the only paper left at the newsstand. Have you any idea of what later editions will say?"

"Newspapers will tell of a great German advance with the Red Army in full retreat," Schmidt said. "Hundreds of their planes were destroyed on the ground. We'll capture Moscow in a few weeks."

230

"I never liked the commies, but several unions have communist or socialist backing," Fulton said. "I had suggested more strikes and slowdowns but with the invasion they'll want to boost production and help the Reds."

Schmidt reached for Fulton's newspaper. "One of the Fuhrer's first steps was to suppress German unions. And this press report is wrong. The shortwave broadcast from Berlin says Stalin attacked us."

"That's not the story reaching the west."

"Tim. The British and the Jews control your media. But never mind. Churchill, once said, the Bolshevik movement should have been strangled at birth. He was right. Germany will finish it."

"Only days ago, the Russians were German allies. Their oil and raw material powered the drive into Western Europe."

"And, now we'll have access to those resources without the middlemen. Eventually people will understand. Charles Lindbergh could work with Germany. He sees where American interests lie."

"But I keep telling you he's not in power. He has what we call a bully pulpit, to sway public opinion. Roosevelt and the Democrats have control and are considering Lend-Lease financing for the Russians. And, Churchill promises British support."

"What can the British offer? The country is bankrupt. Their Empire is teetering. It's why they beg America for supplies. And, Russia is beaten. Stalin had a nervous breakdown or perhaps was deposed. He's disappeared." Schmidt folded the paper and set it between them. "When Russia is conquered Germany will deal with England. America would be foolish to join a losing cause."

As the train began to slow, Schmidt rose. "We won't meet again. Washington has decided that peaceful Germans and Italians are no longer welcome. Roosevelt is closing our diplomatic missions. I am ordered home."

"I didn't know."

Al McGregor

"We will find ways to communicate," Schmidt said as the doors opened. "Stay on the train for a few more stops. Read up on the news."

As the train began to move, Fulton opened the paper and a bulging envelope fell in his lap. Schmidt was gone but the work could continue."

Port Stanley, Ontario
June 29

"A lake full of women. Check the babe in the blue bathing suit."

Brad Wilson laughed, "Use that skill finding targets and you'll be an officer."

A half-dozen men lounged in the sand enjoying a rare day of freedom. "Nothing like a day at the beach," Eric Gibson grinned. "Those tarts or, I should say, those young women are office staff from the technical school. I prefer the red-head in yellow. That bigger one would crush me if she rolled in bed."

"Safety first," Wilson agreed. "That's what the instructors tell us."

"And wear a condom to prevent a communicable disease." Gibson reached back to pat the trousers, discarded in a heap behind them. "One in each pocket. I'm ready for action."

Gibson snickered and began to rebuild an abandoned sand castle. "This should be an easy week. Dominion Day on the first, a parade in full dress but it won't be bad, unless it's hot. And we get the word on what comes next. I've been kissing up to the officers. They may keep me to around to do odd jobs."

Wilson closed his eyes and lay back in the sand. "I've taken to bomb aiming. I don't like confined spaces but if I see the ground or the sky, I'm just fine. And, I've hit more targets than the rest of you. They may send me overseas."

"The radio says the Russians are in full retreat," Gibson patted a turret and began to dig a moat. "Think there's any chance of being sent to Siberia? My uncle was in the Canadian force that went to Russia after the first war. He didn't care for the experience."

232

An Angry Sky

"Afraid it's out of our hands," Wilson said and sat up. The sand was uncomfortably hot. "Let's go swimming."

"I never learned. But I'll follow you to the water and get a better look at those women. If they ask, I'm a pilot."

"Yah and I'm a general."

Smolensk, Russia
July 10

Jurgen Heinzman felt a desperate urge for action, to run or wildly fire his rifle, instead he slowly followed a single prisoner. The Russian spoke German and something about his story demanded closer attention. The pair walked through the wreckage of a small village. The houses and barns lay in ruin and bodies of men, women and children were sprawled along the street. Mute evidence, he knew, of the orders of Colonel Munster. Heinzman stopped twice on the short walk to the headquarters, both times to relieve himself and to fight recurring nausea. Pills wouldn't help. His mind was clear, but his body was wracked with pain. He turned the Russian over to a guard at the prisoner compound. If, the intelligence officers believed the story he might survive. If not, he would join the other causalities of the invasion.

"Jurgen, you are back," Munster said and rose as he approached. "Come show me where you've been."

A map of the Smolensk region was spread on the table. "Another small village ahead," Heinzman pointed as he responded, "with only a few old peasants."

"Artillery rounds before the Panzers move," Munster decided, "and we'll wipe out the pestilence."

"They have nothing to fight with. No food or water. They'll surrender."

"No need. All will be dead within the hour." Heinemann wanted to protest but the pain in his gut returned.

"And you brought us another useless prisoner," Munster shook his head in disgust. "What reason can you offer for his survival? Stalin's cousin?"

Al McGregor

"He claims to have witnessed a massacre."

"Why bother with that? We've dealt with those who attacked our men."

"No. This was before our invasion. Polish officers, prisoners of war, were taken into a forest and executed by the Russians. Hundreds, he says, maybe thousands."

"Why would we care? The Russians did our work for us."

"If true, the Russians are guilty of war crimes."

"War Crimes! Jurgen what is to become of you? We didn't come to bring justice. We're nearing Moscow. The war is almost won. I won't hear foolish talk."

Heinzman staggered, tried to stay erect but doubled over with the searing pain in his stomach.

The bark of a bullet ended his agony. "Sniper," a guard screamed.

Munster ran forward, waving a luger and scanning the horizon before the second shot. Blood flowed from his head as the gun slipped from his grasp.

London
July 15

"Need a lift, mate?" Nora Field laughed and stuck her head from the car window.

Chance was momentarily confused. "Nora? A lovely surprise."

"Ride up front," she smiled. "Only the real toffs want the importance of the rear seat."

"How have you been?" he asked. "Our paths haven't crossed since, what, last fall?"

She slipped the car in gear. "I've been learning skills for the post war. What firm wouldn't hire a woman who can double clutch, change a tire and keep position in a convoy. I can maintain 30 miles an hour in a blackout with a forty-foot separation between vehicles."

"Great skills for a cabbie," he said. "I'm not sure why the military cares."

234

"Oh, how fast can we get where we don't need to go? Or, how fast can we return? Check out the dabs of white paint under an army three tonne. At night, we focus on that paint and stay close."

"I learn something everyday."

"I'll bet you do and mostly official secrets." She hadn't changed, and he was certain her irreverent chatter would frustrate her superiors."

Nora floored the gas pedal, and the car shot onto a busy roadway. "I'm not in a hurry," Chance told her.

"Why didn't you say so." She smiled and slowed. "I like these American cars. The V-8 engines are great. This is one of the first from this Lend-Lease business. We need tanks. Yankees send a classy roadster. And it had to be repainted to drab olive. It came with big white stars. I guess the Yanks aren't acquainted with low-flying Nazi fighters. The only problem is the gauges act up." She slammed her fist against the dashboard. "Yeah, that looks better."

Chance shook his head and decided not to worry. "Who have you been driving?" he asked.

"Ah, come on. I'm not supposed to say. But since you ask, a general or two, a couple of American VIPs, but mostly men from Bomber Command. They're chatty when they're off to London on leave but miserably quiet on the drive back."

"And have you made new friends?"

"Looking for naughty tales?" she laughed. "A lot of the boys are fun, but I keep a distance. I got close with one, and he didn't come back from a raid on Bremen. I jinx them. Remember poor Jimmy in France?"

"Yes, the young fellow from the *Lancastria*," Chance said. "The admiralty still hasn't admitted that ship was lost, a case of stupid government secrecy."

"What happened to the film and pills that Jimmy found?"

"Hmm. The film was too damaged to develop, but the chemists are intrigued by the pills. Our people are looking for something similar. The German dose gives a psychical lift,

235

allows them to stay on their feet for hours but could be addictive. The side effects may range from stomach and digestive problems to mental issues."

"Lovely. A psychopath with deadly farts," Nora said, smiling. "A lethal gas attack could stop the Russians, but from what I hear, they're on the run anyway."

"The so-called Eastern Front is a disaster," Chance admitted. "But don't put all the blame on the Red Army. During the '30s Stalin purged the command. The best generals were shot or sent to gulags."

"Gulags?" The car sped past a group of bicyclists.

"Work camps. The same idea the Germans use. Men are destroyed mentally or are worked to death. Very few come back."

"I drove some Poles the other night. A lot of their people are in Russian prisons."

Chance glanced at the instrument panel and prayed the speedometer was broken.

"The Polish government in exile…hopes…the men are in Russian custody," he told her. "The communists won't talk about them. Thousands vanished when Stalin claimed his slice of Poland."

"And what is Mr. Churchill doing for the Russians? Will he pull a Roosevelt and sit back to watch?"

"Very little he can do. We don't have the men to invade Europe and open a second front. We'll send more supplies, but the air force will have to carry the load."

"That's already happening. Bomber Command has been busy the last few weeks."

London
August 3
"Watch it," a photographer bumped Sandy Fleming, a jolt strong enough to ruin her picture. She tried to re-focus, but Winston Churchill slipped through the door at Ten Downing Street. "I need another shot," she called but none of the Prime Minister's

staff paid attention. A young woman with the flag, the prop who posed with Churchill was leaving too and Sandy's hope for a British Flag Day feature went with her.

"Miss the photo?" A Ministry of Information co-ordinator asked.

"Got bumped," Sandy said casting an angry glare at the other photographers.

"Don't worry. We'll get you a copy."

"I should have been set up but I'm new to London and hadn't seen Churchill in person."

"At least, he was well dressed. Oft times, he wears that silly siren suit, a one-piece coverall that makes him look like a bus mechanic. I'm Collins, by the way. Stop by the M.O.I. office Tuesday morning. The picture won't be released immediately anyway."

"That would be swell."

"From the sounds of that accent, you aren't a native."

"No, I came from Canada a month ago. I did get good shots of the American, Harry Hopkins last week. He's so thin. Is he well?"

"Oh, come on miss. We don't answer questions like that. He's had health issues, but the doctors don't share a prognosis."

"Guess he's well enough or he wouldn't have gone to Moscow?"

"Miss. That's a matter of national security. I'll overlook it but watch what you say in the future."

"Anyone could make a guess. The Russians want a share of the Lend-Lease supplies. The U.K. isn't sure what it can give up so Hopkins will sort it out."

"I wouldn't know. I came to watch over the Flag Day pictures. You appear remarkably well informed."

The image of Evers Chance flashed in her mind.

"I was taught by a master. Oh, by the way. Is the Prime Minister going away? The pictures were taken so far in advance. Is he unavailable for a few days?"

"No more questions," Collins cut her off. "Come by the office Tuesday."

Ottawa
August 13

A short holiday did nothing for Robert McLaren's temper and another shouting match with Frank Willard didn't help. He replayed the argument in his mind, a fight over a delayed message.

"A guy named Francois claims something is happening in Newfoundland," Willard told him. "The only thing happening in Newfoundland is at the American naval base and we know about that."

"How many times did he call?"

"The first time was three days ago, then yesterday and about an hour ago. I told him to stop bothering me."

Several hours later McLaren tracked the caller, a source who had access to the highest levels of government.

"What do you have?" he demanded.

"Churchill and Roosevelt had a face to face meeting, in Newfoundland."

"How do you know?"

"Hell, the world could have known," the man said with a shrug. "Even German radio has speculated on a meeting of the western leaders. A navy friend mentions the largest British battlecruiser is on the North Atlantic and wonders why a flotilla is escorting *Prince of Wales*, then an American says a U.S. Fleet is showing the flag at the new base in Newfoundland. That's when I called the first time."

"And then?"

"The air force went in a tizzy. A special flight was cleared for Gander and ground transport was arranged to the new base at Argentia. It was for a film crew and it turns out special orders came from the top, from the very top. That was two days ago."

"And since then?"

238

"Not much until today. The fleets have separated. One back to the U.S., the other moving at top speed for Great Britain."

"That's all."

"Think about it. An out of the way base crammed with ships from the British and American navies. I doubt it was for a picnic. Tell your office to pay more attention. I tried."

Ottawa
August 14

Frank Willard tried to break the conversational ice. "Maybe, a follow on this story of the car made from soybeans. Henry Ford's latest idea. Henry is pushing for an organic model T while his son, Edsel, pours his soul into the monster aircraft plant." Robert McLaren maintained an icy silence.

"Look, I'm sorry," Willard shrugged. "I didn't realize the man was reliable."

"Leave it. The press statement has been released on the Atlantic Conference."

"I only read a summary," Willard confessed. "Is there much to it?"

"Americans love to talk about freedoms so there's a lot of that. A cynic might say this 'Atlantic Charter' supports motherhood with the promise of a future apple pie."

"So, we didn't miss much?"

"President Wilson had great aims in the first war and very little came of it. This time the Allies stress they don't want territory. They promise freedom of religion, freedom from want and the right for people to choose their own government. It sounds nice but we'll have to wait and see."

"What about Mackenzie King? His nose must be out of joint since he wasn't invited?"

"He may feel left out but he won't criticize the President or the Prime Minister. By the way, the meeting was supposed to be top secret, but Churchill brought three reporters with him. That's why the Americans rounded up a film crew. Roosevelt wasn't about to allow an English-only slant on the story."

London

August 15

"The emotional highlight of the conference would have been the church service. The hymn begins *'Eternal Father, strong to save'*," Evers Chance kept his voice low, "But I can't remember the rest."

"'For those in peril on the sea'," Sandy Fleming prompted.

"Ah yes, we'll hear the hymn sung by lusty British and American sailors when the film of the Newfoundland meeting is released."

"Have you discovered religion," she asked, "or, is there another reason to meet in a church?"

"It's quiet," Chance said and motioned to the empty pews. "I like that."

"I'm trying for a new angle on the Atlantic meeting," she spoke softly. "And I'm not finding much."

"The British are playing things close to the vest, which makes me think, the meeting did not go as hoped. Churchill waits for a declaration of war and Roosevelt refuses to commit. Hopkins did present a shopping list of arms after his Moscow journey. Without new supplies, the Russians could collapse or negotiate an armistice. Neither Churchill nor Roosevelt want that."

"Why can't they just come out and say it. It would be simpler."

"Oh, don't be too harsh. The leaders mean well." Chance rose slowly. "Religion is based on faith and trust. The Atlantic Charter is like that. But did you note, there are no formal signatures on the accord. Signatures imply a treaty. I'm not sure Roosevelt is ready for that."

"Was it all only a show?"

"It was a fine performance. I'm sure, it was valuable. The two leaders met face to face, and I'll bet the discussions were chalk full of things we'll never know. But I have something special for you. Your Prime Minister is planning a visit to England."

London
September 4

The eyes of the Canadian Prime Minister darted over the room. The British establishment, the military leaders from the various Dominions and his own Canadians had come to hear his address. The location, Mansion House, the residence of London's Lord Mayor, was a sign of official respect.

Mackenzie King completed a review of the two years of the war and moved toward a vision of a new world order shaped by British and American influence. *"This new world order seeks neither to divide or destroy. Its aim is brotherhood, its method, co-operation."*

"Mr. King delivers a better speech than expected," a British reporter whispered to Sandy Fleming, "Not bad for a man considered bland and boring."

She nodded and scratched more notes. "Churchill is to reply. Do we expect anything important?"

"I think not. Praise for your Prime Minister, we're all in this together, that sort of thing." King wrapped up to a generous round of applause. Churchill rose and made his way to the podium.

"Mr. King suggested Britain could negotiate a truce. Is he right?" Sandy asked.

"As he said, the risk would be too high. The Germans would use the time to re-group. A negotiated settlement might have been possible during the Phoney War but not now. And, your PM issued a veiled warning for Japan, the reference to Singapore is a polite way of telling the Japanese to give up expansion plans. But my deadline is near. Don't you have to file?"

"No. I have an interview with the Prime Minister."

"Oh, fresh material?"

"I hope so. The speech was broadcast to Canada. By tomorrow it will be old news."

241

Al McGregor

Mackenzie King offered a bright smile when he saw her, but a political veil fell in place as he answered her questions.

He hadn't felt left out of war planning or the Newfoundland meeting. Spending time at Churchill's Chequers estate had been memorable. He enjoyed the flight across the Atlantic especially since the air force installed an easy chair in a new Liberator aircraft. And he emphasized, several times, that there was no need for Canadian conscription. And with that, the official interview was over.

He sat silently as she gathered her notes, lost in his thoughts until his eyes began to water.

"Miss Fleming. Did you know Pat died?"

She was confused and tried to remember a Pat.

"He liked you. I could tell when you stroked his stomach."

"The dog," she thought.

"His loss hits me when my official duties are complete." He rubbed his eyes. "And I feel guilty. I was at a reception and stayed for a refreshment. I should have been home. Poor Pat," He sniffled again. "He's in a better place."

"I'm so sorry," she said finally finding words. "He was a delightful little creature."

"I thought you saw him that way." He turned aside and loudly blew his nose. "Pat and I were close. In fact, he was all I had. Make no mistake. I grieve for each man lost at sea or in the air. But when death is close, it's harder."

"Yes. I can see that. I mean, I know."

"Miss Fleming. Have you talked with the troops?" His mood abruptly changed again.

"No, I haven't spent much time with the Canadian divisions. I'm not very popular. The military objected to something I wrote. Two soldiers I met on the convoy, spoke of hard times, of the Depression. You see, they felt there should have been more government help. Their commanders decided they were likely troublemakers. They were demoted."

"The army can't be too careful, can't have a lot of bellyaching, or so, I'm told." King was silent for a moment before he began to ramble. "More help was needed during the Depression, but those decisions were made under R.B. Bennett and the Tories. The people tossed him out and re-elected me. And, I wonder if the Tories were behind the recent incident with the soldiers."

The sour reception for the Prime Minister had drawn the attention of writers on both sides of the Atlantic. A chorus of boos had erupted as he addressed the troops.

"I heard about that. I wasn't there."

"The men were upset about standing in the rain. The boos weren't meant for me. The Tories are making too much of it."

King rose, pushed the handkerchief into his pocket and surprised her with his next question.

"Would you join me tonight? We'll set aside official duties."

Mackenzie King and Sandy Fleming rode in the rear of an unmarked army car while a lone RCMP officer in plain clothes sat beside the driver. The Prime Minister's staff urged extra security, but King dismissed their advice.

The driver stopped outside a depilated single-story building where the sign advertised a local pub. "The former establishment was destroyed in the Blitz," King explained, "but she has a private room. Constable Anderson, go to the bar and tell them Rex is here."

"I'll wait inside," the constable said when he returned, "just in case."

The pub was crowded. The patrons were well dressed, office workers relaxing after a busy day. One man smiled at Sandy as if they had met before, but there was no time to stop.

"This way," a barman led them to the rear and knocked loudly before opening a door. Inside, a dozen men and women sat in a semi circle.

"You must be Rex," a woman greeted them and pointed to empty seats, "We've started, and Jane has made contact."

Jane, a short thin woman, stood with eyes closed and arms spread wide. Her words were delivered with a hint of Parisienne French. "General Bonaparte says Hitler will not capture Moscow and his forces will be destroyed by the winter snow." Her voice changed to an English accent. "Another spirit has arrived. Is Jerome here?"

"Is it Mattie?" an elderly man asked. "I'm Jerome. I lost Mattie a month ago. We were together for forty-two years."

"She is at peace but misses you."

The man's eyes welled with tears. "Mattie," he whispered, "I'll come soon."

"No." Jane's arms raised to underline the command. "Mattie says to wait and there's more, eat properly and visit cousin Ken."

"I will, Mattie. I will!"

"Oh, it is a busy night." Jane wiped perspiration from her forehead. "A message for Rex."

King tensed. "Sir Wilfrid predicts a safe flight home."

King considered himself a close friend of the late Prime Minister and began to fidget. "And, more from Mr. Laurier," Jane grew animated as she continued, "Hansen is no threat, but Meighen may return." Sandy was surprised by the reference to the present Canadian opposition leader and to the former Prime Minister, a bitter opponent of King. Odd, she thought. King was absorbed. On this night, the spirits had a special word for almost everyone. Sandy smiled at the woman's increasingly erratic movements but suddenly another thought struck her. The man in the bar. She had seen him before. He was a newspaper sketch artist.

She slipped away to find the police escort. "An artist and maybe reporters are here," she told him. "We should get the Prime Minister away." Back Inside the room, Jane run her hands through her hair.

244

An Angry Sky

"Another message…oh…I don't understand…I don't know…it sounds like… Woof-Woof."

King sprang to his feet. "Pat. It's Pat." Before he could say more Sandy grabbed his arm and forced him toward the back door. "Reporters," she hissed. The door opened to the welcome face of Constable Anderson. And all three hustled through an alley, across the street, and into the waiting car.

"What's happening?" King was confused.

"A sketch artist was in the pub," Sandy explained. "He freelances for the *Daily Express*. Someone tipped him you were coming."

"The *Express*. That's a Beaverbrook paper." King clenched his fists. "The Tories put him up to it."

"Or maybe Jane and the séance crowd," she suggested. "How well do you know them?"

"I'd never met her or the other people," he said. "An old friend recommended them."

"I'd suggest making that old friend—a former friend," Anderson said.

"Yes, that might be wise." King reluctantly agreed before turning to Sandy. "But, Miss Fleming. Didn't you think Pat sounded happy?"

"He's bizarre," Sandy Fleming said, explaining the experience later. "One minute he's a devious, extremely partisan but capable politician. The next minute, he's a lonely old man who communes with ghosts."

She flipped the collar on her rain coat and handed the umbrella to Chance who said, "And, you are trying to decide whether to keep silent or spread the details over the pages of Canadian newspapers."

"Other reporters and politicians must know. Surely, his staff see something amiss. But no one says anything. What if he's blackmailed? Or, what if Genghis Khan orders him to invade…Portugal?"

245

"Actually," Chance sounded unconcerned. "He's guilty of nothing but poor judgment, a common enough malady. Hugh Dowling, the former master of Fighter Command talked with dead pilots. Churchill drinks too much and endures bouts of severe depression, what he calls the black dog. Hitler studies horoscopes and doesn't eat meat. The vegetarians keep that quiet lest the idea ruins their movement." Sandy began to smile as he continued. "All of the leaders have secrets. Roosevelt has lady friends…"

"What? He's paralyzed."

"Mobility doesn't stop him. If we expose them all we'd have no leaders."

"Should I keep silent?"

"That's your decision but I doubt Willard would publish. Even larger news organizations would be careful. And what proof is there? The recollections of a young reporter? Will the security guard or the others at the séance back up the story? I doubt it. Besides, King is a political success, at least so far. The people keep electing him. And he appears to keep his 'interests' separate from official duties."

A gust of wind caught the umbrella and Chance fought for control.

"He's gone anyway," she said. "He flew to Montreal this morning. And, I may be called back too. Willard is watching the pennies and doesn't expect much to happen here in the next few months."

"He may be right. Our meetings may be over. I hope I helped."

"Definitely!"

"And at least write the King story. Secrets have a way of emerging, weeks, months or years later."

Le Havre
September 10

Maria felt a bite in the wind as warm summer breezes gave way to the autumn gales. Dark black clouds blew from the Channel.

An Angry Sky

The angry sky, the changing weather, added to a growing feeling of isolation. The local underground had severed contact after the death of Gunther Webber, and she had seen no more of the group helping rescued flyers. The house became her refuge as the farm was converted to a German work camp. The barn was transformed to a rudimentary shelter for the men building Hitler's Atlantic Wall and scattered across the field were weather-beaten tents. The prisoners were slave labour, marched to the worksites each morning and returning at night fall.

The appearance of one man was fixed in her mind. He was badly beaten, with several teeth missing and was a mass of ugly bruises. She had been ordered to perform first aid and learned he spoke English. And, only last night, Ivan Mikhailovich, a teacher from Smolensk, had slipped her a handwritten note.

A terse account told of how a student reported strange events in Russia's Katyn Forest in the early months of the war. The story was so unbelievable he went to see for himself and watched in horror as men in Polish uniforms were systemically murdered. One by one, a single shot to the head, and the bodies tossed into a mass grave. Too many bodies to count, he had written, and the murders were the work of his own people. His beating came at the hands of fellow Russians, who felt it better not to talk of such things.

The sound of a motorcycle signalled the return of the prisoners from the day's work. But Ivan was not among them. Dead, a guard explained, later. He failed to hear a warning when another Russian prisoner detonated an explosive charge.

Chapter Eleven: Air Wars

Southern England
September 14

Nora Fields leaned against the staff car and lifted her cap. The breeze was welcome after a stuffy cross-country drive. The small depot was an hour drive from the Bomber Command base. A few civilians stepped from the train before a man in a Royal Canadian Air Force uniform dropped a duffel bag on the platform. Her passenger had arrived.

"A woman driver?" He shook his head in disgust.

"I hear that a lot. Are Canadian's allowed to travel alone?" she answered. "Probably a rash of pregnancies will be reported along this line."

"I'm Wilson," he said and smiled as she swung the car door open.

"And I'm Field...Nora...WAAF." Handsome, she thought. Tall, well muscled, pleasant features but probably a pompous ass who believed he was God's gift to flying.

"Men in the RCAF call me Brad."

"Say that again."

"Men in the RCAF call me Brad."

"It's not strong, but I hear a trace of accent. You're a bleeding Yank."

"I've been told I sound like a Connecticut Yankee."

"American girls may not read much but I know my Mark Twain."

"Are we going to the base," he asked, laughing, "or shall we discuss literary masters?"

"This could be fun," Nora slid into the driver's seat, "I don't usually get classy chatter from fly boys, usually questions about pubs or do I have a big-busted sister?"

"And do you?"

"I'm an only child. Sorry." In minutes, they were old friends. She offered a glimpse of her role as air force driver. He told of drifting into the RCAF and a recent transfer to the RAF Bomber Command. "I've been at an O.T.U.—an operational training unit—where..."

"I know what this is, you don't have to explain. It's a flyer's finishing school."

In open country she pushed the accelerator to the floor. "Not bad," he said. "If someone maintained this car, she'd go faster."

"I maintain it." She whipped by a cyclist. "And, I do a damn fine job." She slowed and swung off on a parallel road to extend the journey.

Over, the next hour, Nora told of her days in Europe and her escape from France. He spoke of life in America and long cold flight over the North Atlantic. "I like meeting new people." She turned back on the main road. "But the brass, fear we spill secrets."

"Quite frankly, enemy intelligence is better than we think. I had an American friend who worked with what I think were Germans, or as he would say, worked to keep America safe, but I'm not sure it amounted to anything."

"We do keep too many secrets."

"I couldn't agree more."

"I should warn you," she added, already feeling a need to protect him, "pilots and crews don't welcome new men. It's

249

painful if something happens. So, new men are ostracized. Air crew become a band of brothers but not right away."

All too soon she brought the car to a halt at the entrance to the base.

"Nora. If things work out. I mean after a few missions, if I get back and get leave, could we get together?"

"Definitely, Mr. Wilson." She smiled. "And, when...not *if*...WHEN you get back."

With Bomber Command
September 16

"Who the hell is this? On the wrong bus, mate?"

"Digby. Shut up!" The order came from the pilot, Captain Higgins. Eight men were wedged onto the cargo box of aging half ton truck. Their destination, a Stirling bomber, a half mile away.

"For everyone's benefit," Higgins spoke, "Wilson, is a bomb aimer, an observer on tonight's show."

"It's hard enough to get the bird off the ground without the extra weight of another man," an airman said as he grinned and nudged his companion. "We might have to abort."

"That's enough." The pilot snapped. Wilson looked to where the ground crew was bombing up, loading the last of the explosives. Under the pilot's window was the ship's name, "*Foxy Lady*." His eyes roamed to the four huge engines and to the tiny piece of glass that would protect the bomb aimer.

The co-pilot caught his eye. "Not an officer, are you?"

"No. Non-commissioned, a flight sergeant, definitely other ranks."

"I find officers to be more effective. Have you flown in a Stirling?"

"I worked on heavies at the O.T.U."

"He's along for the ride," the pilot repeated as he clambered aboard the plane. Wilson stood with the actual bomb aimer, Rollins, who puffed nervously, on a cigarette. "There's not much room but we'll get you a peek, providing, we're up long enough. The captain has a habit of pulling the plug at the first sign of trouble. We haven't reached the target for the last four missions."

"I missed the briefing. Where are we going?"

"Jesus, didn't anyone tell you?" He threw the cigarette to the tarmac and ground it out before lighting another. "All the way. Berlin." Wilson's stomach tightened. "And while the captain has issues, he'll push on this one. Another abort and he'll be tagged with L.O.M.F." 'Lack of Moral Fibre' was the air force catchall for men who had had enough. It included an instinct for self preservation, extreme fatigue, shellshock or, in some eyes, a coward. The stunning losses among flight crews could destroy the nerve of the strongest men.

"Let's go," the flight engineer called as the first of the engines spun to life and both men sprinted to the plane. "Follow Rollins." The engineer helped them into the Stirling. "I'll show you around in a few minutes, if we don't turn back." Vibration shook the aircraft as the four engines powered up.

Rollins yelled over the noise. "These birds are great in the air. They're less reliable on take off and landing, so hang on." A few miles over the English Channel the headsets crackled to life.

"Pilot to Engineer."

"Go ahead.

"Engines sound rough."

"Gauges are normal…"

"Ok, long as you're sure. Pilot to gunners. Test the guns."

Machine guns rattled and seconds later a re-assuring voice called, "All good!" Time in the air flew by, a glance and a wave from the men in the cockpit, a glimpse of the gunners in position and for a few moments, he gazed at the stars, the only lights above a dark continent. The intercom came back to life. "Pilot to chief engineer. Number four, sparking."

Wilson saw Rollins roll his eyes.

"Gauges normal. Probably exhaust."

"Don't tell me what I'm seeing. Watch those engines."

251

"Will do." Wilson could imagine the smirk on the engineer's face.

"Rear gunner to pilot."

"Go." Captain Higgins sounded tense.

"Never mind. Thought I saw something. Can't see it now."

"Don't bother us with useless chatter."

"Aye, sir."

Rollins unrolled maps on the navigation table. "We may catch flack in the next few minutes. Be ready to hang on tight if we twist and turn. Or, we may drop fast, if a search light finds us."

Wilson could see the silhouettes of other bombers in the stream for the night's attack. He revelled in a rush of adrenalin and settled in to enjoy the flight. The quiet was shattered when bullets ripped into the Stirling. Through the punctures came a blast of cold night air.

"Fighters! Eleven o'clock!" The rear gunner's warning was almost drowned by gunfire.

"*Liberty Wings* is hit. He's on fire," someone called. At the same moment the cabin was flooded with light from an explosion.

"I can't see chutes," a gunner called a few seconds later.

"Forget chutes," Pilot Higgins screamed. "Look for our fighters. Wireless. Anything on the Hurricane escorts."

"Nothing. Not a sound."

"Bastards are lost."

"Fighters ten o'clock and two o'clock." The Stirling shuddered as gunfire struck from both sides.

"Feather four," the captain called. "Engineer. We've lost an engine."

"He can't answer." The wireless operator sounded frightened. "He'll never answer again."

"Jesus!" Rollins screamed in pain as another burst of gunfire ripped into the cabin. "How bad?" he asked as Wilson bent over him.

"A scratch," Wilson lied. "Hold the pack against your stomach to stop the bleeding."

"Number two engine on fire," the pilot called.

The fuselage was illuminated by raging fires on both sides.

"Feather two." Higgins voice steadied. "Pilot to Crew. This bird is finished."

"Number one engine on fire," the co-pilot called.

"Pilot to crew. Bail out. Bail out."

Wilson bent to lift Rollins but saw he was dead. He slipped a parachute over his own head, kicked an escape hatch open and jumped. The Stirling began a death spiral in a sea of flame. Bits of debris fell from the plane but no other parachutes. His leg gave way as he hit the ground, but he was able to free himself from the harness. A gust of wind carried the silk to drop like a shroud over the remains of the burning Stirling.

Four new crewmen arrived on the morning train. Nora saw no need to delay and sped through the countryside to the base. The men, excited to be close to the action, collected their baggage and dismissed her without even a nod of thanks. With extra time she drove to the sergeant's mess. A handful of men were at breakfast. The American was not among them.

"Nora, Nora Field. What a surprise," a middle-aged lieutenant called from a corner office. "Stanfield Preston, our fathers were friends."

"Uh...yes." She remembered the Prestons. Their estate was near her family home.

"Slumming it, are we?" he asked.

"I was looking for someone."

"Best to search in the Officer's Mess, a better class of people."

"I'll remember that," she answered, remembering too his family reputation for pretension and snobbery.

"I'm a mite too old to take to the sky," he told her. "I handle base intelligence. The job can be sad. We had a bad night."

"If it helps, I drove four new men from the railway."

"All helps, I suppose. But we lost three crews last night."

She calculated, knowing a Stirling usually carried a crew of seven, "My God. Twenty-one men in a single night."

"Actually, twenty-two. An American went along as a trainee. His plane went down. No survivors."

The room began to spin. "The Yank. Was his name, Wilson?" She tried to keep her voice steady.

"Something like that." He returned to the office and a moment later called. "Yes, that's it, Wilson, B.

"I did wonder, Nora," he said, stepping back into the main room, "have you thought of selling the land. Your father's gone and those estates are the very devil to maintain."

"No," her voice choked, "I haven't thought about it."

"Oh, I've upset you." Preston saw the tears. "Running the properties can be a strain, supervising servants and dealing with tenants but don't let it get you down. When the war is over life will return to normal."

"I suppose it will."

"Keep me in mind when you decide to sell. Those big houses aren't worth what they once were, but the Prestons could make a reasonable offer."

Brad Wilson had burrowed deep in a hedgerow. His knee was swollen to twice the normal size. He heard machines and voices and tried to stand but the pain was too much, and he passed out.

The sun was high in the sky, the rays striking through the undergrowth when he awoke. He heard a rustle nearby but was unprepared for the hand slapped over his month.

"English! Shut the fuck up!" The command came with a heavy French accent. "Aero?" the man asked. Wilson was confused but nodded.

An Angry Sky

"Shut the fuck up," the French man repeated, and he took his hand away. "Boche." He pointed toward the wreck. "Seven bodies. Any others?"

Wilson tried to comprehend. He must mean the Germans had found the burned-out Stirling. His thoughts flashed back to the final moments in the sky, the gunfire and the confusion."

"Moi et sept autres." He managed to recall high school French.

"Hoh-K," the Frenchman slapped his back. "French speaks shitty. We talk Anglais." Instead, he pointed to the west, made a motion of the sun setting and held up five fingers.

"English. Shut the fuck up." He hissed again and made a motion of sleeping. The linguist and three other men returned at sunset. One offered water and as Wilson drank, the men spread a blanket on the ground. He nodded and rolled. Each man took a corner. As they began to lift, the linguist shook a finger.

"I know." Wilson braced himself, "English! Shut the fuck up." He had no conception of how long the journey lasted, only flashes of sunset, the night sky and recurring bouts of pain.

He awoke on a bed, but not a bed, more a cot. A bright light faded to a smoky oil lamp and a doctor transformed to a teenage girl. "Awake now," she said, leaning forward. "Sleep." And he felt the sting of a syringe.

Maria moved cautiously toward the cave, stepping carefully on rocks so worn grass would not betray the track. Inside, an oil lamp sputtered but provided enough light to see the cot and a man, who appeared fast asleep. Confirmation came with a gentle snore.

Claudia, the teenage guide, had reappeared to ask her help with a 'damaged package,' an airman rescued from a crash. A doctor had set a broken leg but warned the airman might have other unseen injuries. The flyer stirred. The eyes opened, startled, at the sight of Maria. "Who are you?" he groaned.

"It's safer if you don't know…but call me…Maria."

"Where am I?"

"Where German's can't find you. Men will come in the next few days and start you to England. Stay quiet and save your strength. It may be a rough trip."

"Can't be much tougher than coming in." This time he propped himself with his elbow. "You speak English. The others speak Neanderthal."

"I don't know who they are, and I hope they don't know me. I brought food. Keep the lamp low. A German work camp is very close."

"Guess I'll need luck. A bum leg will slow me down."

"The men will figure it out. But there's something else. I have an envelope that must go to England. I've written the name and address. If the German's find it, things would be very bad for you."

"I'm game."

"Thank you. No one else needs to know."

London
September 19

"We need help." Martin Downey replaced a volume on a bookstore shelf. The small shop was almost empty, but the aging proprietor monitored every movement.

"Glad to be of assistance," Evers Chance smiled and replied, "but this shop doesn't carry erotic material."

"Damn it, be serious." Downey retrieved a Hornblower novel.

"Good choice," Chance said, "Once a reader is past the hrrrmping, Forester tells a rollicking sea-faring yarn."

Downey glanced toward the front desk. The shop keeper had turned away.

"It's a quick extraction from France. Two airmen. One is a Spitfire ace and we need every pilot. The other is an American and it could be embarrassing if he's captured."

"Let me guess. Fellow in the Spit was taken down during one of those 'circus episodes' which Fighter Command loves. The raids don't amount too much but keep the Germans on edge.

The American, probably one of those souls who surrendered to the romance of the RAF."

"Background doesn't matter. The Comet line has both men. We need to get them across the Channel."

"I know a man for the job, but it can't be set up overnight. Give me a couple of days."

Downey slipped him a piece of paper. "Names, descriptions and locations. We need to move fast. That Comet line is run by amateurs. That women friend of yours may be involved."

"Damn! She should have been left out of these things."

"Is there a problem, gentleman?" The book seller, hearing raised voices, leaned over the desk and peered down the aisle.

"I wonder," Chance answered, "is there a theology section? My friend wants to study sins leading to hellfire and damnation."

"Sorry, no. Try a Christian bookstore."

"We'll do that," Chance called. "I'll be in touch Martin, but I don't like my people used this way."

Dover, England
September 21

Chance stopped on the pier to speak to the ambulance attendants before returning to where Nora waited in the car. "The boat may be delayed, and Brandon Young won't break radio silence."

"The same fellow that brought us from Britany last year?"

"Same guy."

"Bit of a highwayman, a smuggler, as I remember, a good man to know on a dark, bleak night."

"The danger grows with every operation. He says this is his last mission and we can only hope the rendezvous was a success." He became obsessed with his pipe, fishing through pockets for tobacco, tapping the bowl full and finally striking a match. Nora pushed the seat back and stretched her legs. "I thought of calling you," she said, "I needed to talk."

"Talk away," he said and cracked the car window open. "We've lots of time."

Al McGregor

"A bloke," she said sadly. "I lost another one. We hit it off, magical, a fairy tale. But ..."

"Bomber Command?"

"I checked at the base. The intel officer says no survivors."

"That's better than false hope. We only rescue a few, like the men coming tonight. It sounds harsh but that's reality."

"I'm a jinx. Three men I wanted to know better and all three dead. I didn't have much time with this one but there was something between us. And, it wasn't for a simple romp under the covers, we had a connection." The tears began to flow. "I've tried to put it behind me." Nora sniffled and said, "When I talk out loud it sounds silly. We were together for only an hour or so..." She starred through the windshield and into the blackness of the Channel. "I guess it's hard to understand. A person has to live it."

A minute passed before Chance spoke. "Personal attractions are often strange, a look, a smile, a passing touch and we're smitten."

"Where's that come from? Are we talking about me or you?" Her mood seemed to lighten. "It sounds mysterious. Does Chance have a woman...caught in the spider web of war, a prisoner in a Sultan's harem...in...in Istanbul."

"You always had an overactive imagination."

"Ah, come on. Spill it. Misery loves company."

"Nora, Prince Charming will come."

"Quit changing the subject. I don't like to cry alone. Tell me about her."

"Not much to tell," he began reluctantly. "I've been on the periphery of her life. She's an amazing woman, independent, smart and very attractive."

"A fantasy, a Princess Charming?"

"Maybe she is. Or, maybe she's a shrew. I don't know her well, but she's stuck in my head."

"Does she know? Does she care?"

"Two good questions. We connect when together but we're not together often. A few hours are the most we've had. I don't want to spoil a friendship. She may not want anything more."

"That's a lousy excuse. Does she have a family? A muscled husband? Seven bratty kids?"

"No, nothing like that."

"Then what are you afraid of?"

Chance looked at the waves. He had run a similar conversation in his mind, many times.

"Well, for a start, an age difference." Nora sat up straight.

"Bugger. Are you snorting after a sixteen-year-old? Cradle robber!"

Chance broke into a smile.

"No, she's of legal age but I've a few years on her, quite a few. An aging companion would slow her down. She'd play tennis. I'd play checkers. She might like Jazz. I prefer the music of Harry Lauder. Any thought of a relationship doesn't seem fair or realistic."

"Oh, what's the worst that could happen? She rejects you. No more fantasy. Move on with life."

"Have you trained as a psychiatrist? Nora, I don't know what she thinks. She might explode in laughter or flee for the hills. It's best to leave things alone."

"Ah, I'll come with you and put in a good word. Where's she live?"

"France."

"Oh, now, that could be a problem." Nora glanced up as a hooded flashlight approached the car. "Boat coming in," a sailor announced.

As the trawler tied up a young man jumped to the pier. "Is the bar open?" Two airmen stepped forward as an unofficial welcoming committee, "It is now, Fred. You gave us a scare."

"Wasn't all that bad. I'm better off than that other chap."

Four dock workers lifted a stretcher and carried it toward the ambulance.

"Is he bad?" Chance asked the attendants, but the answer came from the patient.

"Bad? Mad is more like it. The only thing worse than dealing with British is trying to understand the French."

"I presume you are the American."

"Yank! Call him Yank," Nora said, beaming as she bent over the stretcher.

"Nora?" Wilson strained his eyes in the dim light. "I've been thinking of you." He reached for her hand. "How did you get here?"

"I'm a driver, Yank," she rubbed his cheek. "I drive. Mr. Chance orders a car and here I am."

"Wait," Wilson stopped the stretcher crew. "Did you say Chance?"

"Evers Chance at your service."

"Of Carnington Way?"

"Yes."

Wilson reached into his jacket for the envelope. "A woman named Maria sent this."

Chance held it in his hand. He'd read it later. "How is she? How did she look?" Wilson thought for a moment. "Healthy and, for an older woman, very good looking."

Nora began to laugh. "Yank. We've found his mystery lady."

"She'll fill you in later, Mr. Wilson, with facts or fiction." Chance chuckled. "But doctors and intelligence officers will want to see you first and maybe a few weeks in hospital."

"No," Nora interrupted, "No hospital. I keep a cottage on my dad's estate, and I trained as a nurse. I'll take care of him. I won't let him out of my sight."

Paris
October 5

The orderly snapped to attention. "Herr Colonel. We're still cleaning. We didn't expect you so soon."

Karl Munster tapped a gloved hand with a riding crop. "Then, someone has failed in his duty. Take me to my office."

"Yes, Herr Colonel." The sergeant spun away, Munster's face frozen in his mind. A wide scar festered from the jaw to the hairline. One eye was half closed.

"What is your name?"

"Sergeant Bruno Wiebe," he said as they climbed the stairway.

"Hmm. Paris is soft." Munster growled. "Life is harder on the Eastern Front. I was wounded by a sniper."

The sergeant tried not to stare and kept his eyes forward as he opened the door. The painting of a nude woman reclining on a couch greeted them. "This was Lt. Webbers office. He planned to destroy these paintings. He said they were junk."

"Decadent is a better description. Clear this trash away." Munster kicked a canvas to the floor and a domino effect revealed several more of the same style. "Webber kept a record," the sergeant lifted a journal from the desk, "And accounted for everything he found."

"What happened to the lieutenant."

"Killed in an accident. The police say he was drunk but I never knew him to drink much."

Munster flipped through the journal. Each line contained a number, an artist name and other details.

"Keep this book," he ordered. "Eventually we'll track down the so-called artists. Jews most likely. France is infested."

He continued to flip through the pages.

"An officer I know was ordered to clear the Jews from Kiev. He told them to be at the train station in the morning and like lemmings many came early to get a good seat. But there was no transport. Instead, they were marched to a ravine and ping, ping, ping." Munster made the motion of firing a revolver. "Each one was dispatched. Such a waste."

"Yes, Colonel. Life is precious."

Al McGregor

"No, a waste of time. German soldiers had to shoot each one and deal with remains. We must move faster. I am to study new ways to erase this pestilence."

"Yes sir. I see."

Wiebe felt ill. Munster snapped the journal closed, "And I can't start until this office is cleaned." Again, he kicked at a painting and more pictures clattered to the floor. The last one caught his eye. A portrait of a woman with dark eyes, long dark hair, a perfect face and beneath the neckline, huge, pendulous breasts. He shook his head in disgust before a second, closer look. Something was familiar. He consulted the dead lieutenant's journal, began to chuckle and finally laugh out loud. "This one, Sergeant, we'll keep this one, a portrait that may prove entertaining. Cut it from the frame and roll it."

Chapter Twelve: Home Fronts

Above the North Atlantic
October 12

Sandy Fleming pulled the heavy coat tighter. The flight had been longer and colder than she expected. The Liberator was not designed for passengers, but the air force filled the fuselage with pilots and more slept on the mail bags packed in the bomb bay. All available space was filled. The men would have a few hours rest before flying another new bomber to England. "Miss, the facilities are free," a pilot told her. A blanket, hung from the cabin ceiling to a foot above the floor, sheltered a stainless-steel pail, the primitive amenities provided by Ferry Command. "St. Hubert, is six hours away," he informed her and laughed, "and from experience a full bladder makes the trip uncomfortable."

If only he hadn't spoken, she thought. She had been fasting and refused even a glass of water. Reluctantly, she fought the plane's vibration and made her way to the facilities."

"I want to see this!" a man called. She pulled the blanket closed and squatted on a toilet seat, thoughtfully positioned over the pail.

"All I see, is army boots and heavy trousers," someone called. "I've seen more titillating sights in a public washroom."

263

"Stuff it," a harsh voice ordered. "That could be a someone's wife or sister."

The reply was lost in the rumble of the engines.

"Warm enough," an older man asked when she returned to her place.

"Not really." She squirmed deeper into the heavy coat.

"Gets colder the higher we go," the man explained, "but we're at our maximum. We don't need oxygen but there's other danger, engine failure, ice on the wings, storm fronts, you name it. But the trip home is a milk run because we don't have to worry about meeting the Luftwaffe."

Sandy twisted to the small window and looked to the water below.

"The white specks?" she asked, "Icebergs?"

"Yah and once in a while we see a convoy."

"It must be hard to spot a submarine from up here?"

"With the naked eye, yes, but the new planes have better technology, air-borne radar and ways to track radio transmissions."

"Are you a senior officer?" she asked, "No offence but the other men are younger."

"I'll be a senior officer soon," he smiled and continued, "This is my last ferry flight. I'm an American. My contract is up. The other men can take the planes over. This old codger will soon be teaching American boys how to fly. We'll soon have training bases to rival anything in Canada. Now, I have a question? What's a woman doing here?"

"I'm a reporter and my boss wanted an article on Ferry Command," she said and paused. "He arranged this flight so he wouldn't have to pay for my passage."

"And what happens when you get home?"

"I wish I knew," she said. "Ottawa and Canada are going to seem awfully quiet."

Ottawa
October 17

"Glad to be home?" Frank Willard began to massage Sandy's shoulders.

"Don't! Please." She shifted her body to escape his touch and pounded on the typewriter. "I'm finishing the piece on Ferry Command."

"Don't let me disturb you." She felt his breath on her neck and shuddered. Seconds later she announced, "Done. I can drop it with the censor."

"Leaving early?" He sounded disappointed. "Still looking for new lodging."

She reached for her coat. "I can't afford an apartment and the weekly rate at the boarding house rose while I was overseas. But, I've a line on a room in the Glebe."

"I was going to offer a raise," Willard's words surprised her. "But unfortunately, I can't. The government has introduced wage and price controls. Your salary is frozen and I'm a stickler for rules. Be sure and get rest on the weekend. McLaren has gone west. You'll have to carry the load."

She thought of the message McLaren had left for her. The sealed letter, left on her desk, warned the agency was on the verge of failure and suggested she search for a new job.

"I've tried to calm Robert down," Willard droned on, "but he's headstrong, too damn stubborn for his own good. I've been writing of the need for conscription, his reporting implies a draft isn't necessary."

"The Prime Minister doesn't think conscription is needed."

"Sandy!" Willard spoke sharply. "King dodged the army in the first war. Do you think he'd champion the cause now? He'll have to go, although he's stubborn. He'll be dragged from office kicking and screaming."

"Are you advocating a coup?"

"No, well, he should be replaced. We need a national government, a coalition, as in the first war. Bring in strong

Al McGregor

conservative voices and get the war effort on track. We'll need good thinkers especially with the dispatch of the Canadians to relieve the British in Hong Kong. It's time we shared more of the war effort."

Toronto
October 20

The clothing store manager broke into a wide grin when he heard McLaren's request.

"We don't sell much tropical wear but keep a small supply on hand. The usual necessities and I have a couple of light suits that should fit, good quality linen. However, with an order of this size, we'll need a deposit."

McLaren smiled, "I'll give you cash and an Ottawa address for the final bill. Oh, I need a hat, something fashionable, price isn't an issue."

McLaren smiled as he stepped back into the street. Willard had resisted the expense for a trip to Vancouver and would be angry when the bills arrived. But McLaren planned to go first class on his last assignment for the agency. If his partner didn't end the partnership, he'd sever ties himself. A half hour later, he entered the library of a mansion. Shelves of books covered the walls and a fire burned in a fireplace. As he warmed, a nurse pushed a man in a wheel chair into the room. "It's been awhile," the man waved the attendant away.

"Good day, General Barnes. Thanks for taking the time."

"Your request provided an interesting challenge for an old soldier, Robert. I haven't tapped my sources for years, thinking with the war, I shouldn't bother them. It gave me a chance to poke around. Drink?"

The general rolled to a low table to pour two glasses. "I've never seen Hong Kong," he began. "I was with British army in Singapore when I had the car accident and was retired. Hong Kong was considered a soft post, designed to show the flag and keep the Chinese in check, but lately the Japanese have been nosing about."

266

"Will the sudden appearance of two Canadian regiments frighten them?" McLaren asked.

"Not likely. The Royal Rifles and Winnipeg Grenadiers are coming off light duty. The Rifles were glorified sentries at the Gander Air Base, the Grenadiers are back from Jamaica. In both cases, the men need additional training."

"It doesn't look like a rough assignment," McLaren sipped on his drink, "A bastion called the 'gin drinkers' line', can't be unpleasant."

"I asked about that. That fortification isn't complete. The army will want to rebuild. Until a few weeks ago, no one thought much about it."

"What changed?"

"Fear of the unknown. Our leaders hope they can deter Japanese expansion. The British and Americans embargoed shipments of key supplies to Japan, scrap metals, aviation gasoline and oil. The Emperor could say he's been misunderstood and please end the embargo? Or, his military, could look at their dwindling supplies, the natural resources available across the South Pacific and seize whatever they need."

The general wheeled his chair to the fire, grasped a poker, and stirred the flames. "Popular opinion portrays the Nip as a half blind, yellow, pygmy. Don't believe it. The Japanese have been fighting in China for several years. The men are battle hardened, tough, sometimes ruthless. Our men are green and inexperienced. The Canadian command built an impressive army, on paper. It hasn't been tested."

"The Canadian Corps did well in the first war."

"Ah yes, and armchair generals would like another Vimy Ridge."

"I was there," McLaren said. "The men itching for a fight today didn't see the aftermath."

"Still, it was a great victory, Robert. A few old soldiers think we need another one. I fear the blowhards are getting us into something dangerous. Men could be sacrificed.

267

Al McGregor

Reinforcements or a rescue mission for Hong Kong will be out of the question. I'm not sure Ottawa grasps that fact."

Vancouver, British Columbia
October 26

"The Ottawa call, Mr. McLaren," the hotel desk clerk called. "We'll put it through to the booth, on the right."

McLaren nodded and slowly made his way to the telephone.

"Collect calls are expensive. Keep it short," Willard snarled, and McLaren could imagine his scowl, "What's the latest on the troops for Hong Kong?"

"Frank. Nice to hear you too. And I'm fine."

"This is costing money."

"I'm not sending a dispatch. The military has imposed a blackout."

"Which means the troops are at sea?"

"Guess away," McLaren answered. "No reporting on troop movements."

"A rumor in Ottawa says several men deserted when they heard where they were going."

"That's crap. The men weren't told where they are going. A few may have taken a wrong turn and ended up in a bar."

"Another rumor says all the transport was left behind."

"Ottawa is having a busy night. I heard the story too. I'll try to send something tomorrow."

"And what about the morning editions."

"I can't move a censor."

"All right, we'll rehash a story from here."

"And Frank, I'm going to meet a couple of our customers. I'll be sure to tell them what a joy it is to work with you."

"Bugger off!" The line went dead.

Morning found the Vancouver censor in a foul mood.

"Give it up McLaren. If I can't approve Canadian Press copy, I'm not going to approve yours."

"Do we wait till the men arrive in Hong Kong? That could be weeks."

268

An Angry Sky

"Maybe we will."

"What if I want to file a story on army vehicles left on a dock. Or, the transportation foul up in getting trucks to Vancouver? How about a story on the army failing to properly measure for cargo space?"

"Write what you want. I won't approve it."

"Any suggestions on what I could do?"

"Yah, but I don't think it's medically possible."

Near Fingal, Ontario
October 28

"Try the switch," Eric Gibson watched a single headlight come to life, "Shut it off."

"I don't work in the dark," the farmer told him. "Horses don't have lights and I managed to get the work done."

"This won't take much to fix," Gibson said, running his hand along the wiring, "A new tractor, might as well use everything it has."

The farmer nodded in agreement and leaned back on the seat. "I was glad the air base agreed to release men to help with the harvest. Labour on the home front is as important as toting a rifle. I'd hate to have lost any of the crop especially when prices are good."

"Try her again," Gibson ordered and swore under his breath as the light flickered and went out. He disconnected a wire, wiped it with a dirty cloth and said, "Once I know the principal, I can make it work. Electrical jobs or radio, doesn't much matter. The base has tools and manuals and I use them when the no one is looking. What we used to call science fiction is becoming fact."

He rubbed again at the connection.

"A few years ago, scientists were working on a death ray, a weapon to fry electrical circuits. That might sound dangerous but imagine what a guy could do if we control that energy. A fellow could sit at the kitchen table, push a button and start a tractor, a car or what ever."

Al McGregor

"Bit too complicated for me," the farmer tapped his head. "Too many new gadgets. I'm better working with the livestock. I understand bacon for Britain, although condensed milk and powdered eggs are beyond me."

Gibson walked around the tractor, examined the light that worked and returned to adjust a connection. "Good livestock prices this year?" he asked.

"After the Depression any increase is good, but city folk complain. Factory workers are making money hand over fist but object to paying a few cents more for a roast."

"Try the switch." Gibson took a step back. A broad smile crossed his face as both lamps illuminated. "I'll take a look at the living room radio. With a simple aerial, you could listen to broadcasts from all over."

"Don't think I'd notice," the farmer said as he swung down from the tractor seat, "but the wife and daughter would enjoy it." As his feet hit the ground, he faced Gibson. "Don't get too sweet on my daughter. Joan's a child. I've been watching. I also know about the health lectures at the base. Why should airmen learn about birth control?"

Gibson thought of Joan and his package of condoms. At nineteen, she was more attuned to modern society than her father."

"Joan's a fine girl," Gibson told him. "But I'm not about to settle down. I've an idea to make one of those remote-controllers. If a man could produce something like that and get the air force or army interested, he'd be set for life."

"Fine, go to it. I'll drive you to Fingal. I'll feel better with a few miles between you and my daughter."

"Yes, sir. That's probably for the best." Gibson glanced at his watch. "I'm on duty in the tower in a couple of hours."

Night duty was slow, and Gibson was soon playing with the radio sets.

"*The shooting has started,*" the voice of Franklin Roosevelt came through static on a control tower speaker.

"Gibson. Tune in that station."

270

The airman twisted the dial and the broadcast stabilized. *"America has been attacked."*

"What's that?" the captain called. "Was there a surprise attack?"

"No sir. It's just another gung-ho American speech. I was listening under the headsets and he said something about a map showing Nazi plans for South America. That's a long way from us."

"Ok. I'm going off duty. Make sure that radio is off when you leave."

"Ok, Cap," Gibson turned the radio lower, "Uh...do you have a second?"

"What is it?"

Gibson took a deep breath. "I've worked up a device, a radio beam that can control electrical circuits."

"Interesting." The tone suggested he didn't think it was.

"I'd like to do an experiment. I'll install my receiver and bounce the beam from the tower to a truck."

"Be sure nothing is damaged."

"Oh, sure. And, can I get someone to help? Hanlon knows what I'm doing."

"Just don't cause problems."

"Thanks, Cap," Gibson called and adjusted his headset. Roosevelt was closing his address. *"We Americans have cleared our decks and taken our battle stations."*

Gibson waited to be sure the captain was gone before spinning the dial in search of music.

Fingal
October 30

Gibson and Hanlon trotted across the tarmac to where the lights of the control tower glowed in a light mist. "I know, I shut the lights off. No one was here an hour ago." Gibson said as they climbed the stairs. Inside the radio speakers had been cranked to the maximum.

"American One. How do you read us?"

271

"Hey, Cap," Gibson said, surprised to see the captain and other men in the tower, "my experiment worked. I switched the device on and the lights came on in the truck. Hanlon saw it."

"Gibson, shup up." The captain starred at the radio.

"American One. Do you read?"

"Toledo, calling American One. Toledo calling Flagship Erie."

"Detroit tower...calling American One."

"What's going on."

"A passenger plane is missing, a flight from Buffalo to Detroit."

Across the room, an officer used binoculars to scan the night sky and a ringing telephone added to the confusion.

"Fingal Tower," a sergeant picked up the receiver and a moment later called, "Captain. A call from Lawrence Station. A fellow thinks a plane crashed and is burning in his field."

"Damn! Call out the security detail. I want everyone ready in ten minutes. And, monitor the radio. The flight is probably down but let's be sure."

"American One. This is Buffalo. Can you read us? American one, Flagship Erie. Please respond..."

An hour later flames showed a small crowd clustered around burning wreckage.

"Hanlon. I want a wide perimeter. No unauthorized entry. This is a pasture field. It shouldn't be hard to control." Captain Leforge watched as the security detail fanned out. "The flight was an hour out of Buffalo. He'd have almost a full load of fuel. Order up the foam truck. Douse those flames."

"What do we know?" Leforge turned to a local police officer.

"The markings on the tail show it's the missing flight but with the fire we can't get close." The policeman glanced at a notepad, the first of what he expected would be pages of notes. "The airline says there were seventeen passengers and a crew of three and we've found no survivors. We have one body, a woman and based on the uniform, a stewardess. The rest must still be in the wreckage."

"Planes don't just fall from the sky," the captain's face was lit by the flames. "Did anyone see the crash?"

"A couple of people saw the plane, thought it was out of control, rising and falling, turning and then a whoomph!"

"Constable. Think about what you say. The Americans are going to raise questions. They won't accept a mere whoomph."

"What else can I say? The airline says everything was normal leaving Buffalo. The flight checked in on schedule at Jarvis. Strathburn, the next checkpoint, has an emergency strip but no one heard a distress call."

"For the record, Constable, the Fingal base shut down early tonight. No planes in the air. The mist was going to hamper landings."

"Could fog have caused this."

"No, this is light mist. That plane was above it until the very end." The captain mused of other possibilities. "No reports of storms or lightning so rule out weather. Migrating geese have been an issue the last few days. A goose could have hit a prop or caused other damage. Beyond that, mechanical or electrical failure?"

"With the war," the constable hesitated, "I guess we have to consider sabotage, maybe a bomb on the plane?"

"That's an issue for the Americans. The plane never landed in Canada. Baggage and passengers were cleared through Buffalo. Let them worry about that."

"So, you aren't going to claim authority over the site, air force, government orders or like that?"

"I see no need. This is a civilian crash. The air force helps out in the recovery. And that's it."

"I thought, it was suspicious, the Bombing and Gunnery school close by…"

"No constable, not our problem. Civilian Police can deal with any officious Americans. I can make security details available but let me repeat, this is not an air force problem."

Al McGregor

Dawn showed smouldering wreckage, the tail intact, but most of the DC-3 fuselage in a small blackened heap, the nose buried in the soil. "This is going to be a big story," a photographer said and began to snap pictures. "Requests are coming from all over. This may be the worst aviation disaster in Canadian history."

Captain Leforge turned away. A long grim night was ending and he saw no need to remain. "Gibson, drive," he pointed to an air force car. "Back to the base."

The drive was slow with the growing traffic of investigators and sight seers on the rough country roads. "Captain, I better tell you something," Gibson said as they approached a highway. Leforge was pre-occupied, writing impressions for his report. "Captain?" Gibson repeated as he turned unto the asphalt.

"What is it?"

"I may have caused the crash."

"What are you talking about?"

"That device I made, my experiment to turn lights on and off. I was working on it when that plane went over. What if the radio waves went astray and fried the circuits on the plane? The witnesses said it was out of control. Maybe the waves, destroyed something, like…like a death ray."

The captain looked on in shock.

"I set the beam toward the truck and the beam was pointed northeast. That's where that flight was." Gibson's voice cracked and for a moment the car swerved onto the gravel shoulder.

"Slow down." Leforge yelled.

"I only wanted to turn the lights on and off. And Hanlon saw it. He was beside the truck when the lights came on. But the beam must have carried into the sky…"

The captain starred at the driver.

"I didn't mean to hurt anyone. I thought my device would help the war effort or make life easier for people. I didn't mean for a disaster."

Leforge took a deep breath as the car approached the air base. "Ok, tell me again."

Gibson repeated his story, finishing as the car reached the base gate. Leforge didn't hesitate, "Sergeant!" he shouted to the duty officer. "Arrest this driver. Take him to the cells and he is to have no communication, I repeat, no communication with anyone." He raised his voice as a flock of geese flew above them. "Hold him until you hear from me." Gibson was alone throughout the day. No one spoke as a sandwich was delivered or when he was escorted to the toilet. All he heard was the constant rumble of engines. Bomb and gunnery training did not stop for a civilian tragedy.

Night was falling when Leforge returned. "I've had a bitch of day. I should have you shot!"

"Cap, I'm sorry. I keep thinking of those passengers. I didn't mean to do it."

"Two hundred men scoured the fields, looking for any evidence from that wreck. I had them looking for feathers or bits of goose. That would be a sign the plane hit a bird and might save your sorry ass. But they didn't find anything. No geese, in fact, nothing from the plane."

He let the news sink in. "Our phones have been ringing all day. Do we know anything about auto pilot systems? Do we test aviation fuel for contamination? Was anything unusual happening at the base?"

Gibson anxiously rubbed his hands together.

"I retrieved your device," the captain said with a scowl. "All day the engineers have been experimenting. They took it to pieces. Thank God, there were no classified parts, or you'd have opened another can of worms. And what do you think they found?"

Gibson tensed.

"The damn thing doesn't work. It doesn't turn lights on or off. It doesn't emit any kind of signal. It's a dud, a worthless little piece of shit, like the inventor."

"But Cap, it did work. The lights on the truck went on and off. Hanlon saw it."

"Ah. Hanlon, another great innovative mind. He flicked the lights on and off to fool you. A great little joke."

"But Cap…"

"Face it. The little device didn't work. It was crap. The engineers found no basis in science. Investigators will have to find another cause for the crash. But, that wasn't the only way you ruined my day."

Again, Gibson waited in silence.

"The farmer, the one you worked with this fall came see me. His daughter confessed to diddling with you. As he says, the girl is a child."

"Ah, she's no child. She's nineteen going on twenty. And she wanted to try sex."

"Idiot. The girl is big for her age. She's fifteen. The farmer wants you punished, castrated slowly, before hanging."

"She said, she was nineteen."

"I convinced him that publicity would ruin her life. And he finally agreed but only after I promised a transfer to where you could do no harm."

Gibson waited.

"An hour from now a flight will take you to Toronto and on to new base that's under construction. The work will be hard, clearing land and erecting buildings and by special order, no contact with the outside world. No one will hear from you for a long, long time."

"But…"

"Silence. You are going to disappear. This new base doesn't even have a name. The transfer documents call it Camp X."

Vancouver
November 2

The photo of the plane crash dominated the front page.

"The pictures came from Canadian Press," the publisher said and tossed the day's paper on a table. "The Willard Agency didn't offer anything. We're not getting our money's worth."

276

Renton Agnew ran a regional paper and had been a client since the service began.

"We are short staffed, and we made mistakes," Robert McLaren admitted. "Radio was a distraction which cost time and money but we're back on track. I'm working up a series on west coast issues."

"We do that pretty well from here," Agnew shook his head. "I'm willing to give it a few more weeks but if the service doesn't improve, I'll do what Bob Pearce did. He cancelled."

Pearce ran another small daily and was the next on McLaren's list. "We couldn't afford the Willard Agency," he explained a few hours later. "And, we save money when we don't have to pay for teletype machines and line charges."

McLaren had surveyed the newsroom. A single reporter and a receptionist indicated an operation stretched to the limit. "So, when Mr. Willard offered his 'B' service, I jumped at the idea."

McLaren stiffened. "I don't understand?"

"The "B" service," Pearce smiled. "Willard warned to keep it quiet. 'B' articles are a rehash of what's already published. No bylines and a few days old but the cost is lower. A big thick envelope comes through the mail each week and I use whatever feature I need."

McLaren managed to contain his anger. "Yes, simple, the way it's supposed to work, I guess."

"And, he's patient. A cheque bounced and he was sympathetic. Write another one, he said. Make it out to the Frank Willard Corporation and I won't give it another thought."

"He's a believer in good customer service."

"Must be a pain for the accountants," Pearce said, "running two corporations and keeping everything straight. But I expect the "B" service will take off."

"I can't say," McLaren smiled. "Confidential sales information." As he left the office McLaren put it together. It was simple. Willard was cheating him.

Chapter Thirteen: Betrayals

London
November 4

"Evers Chance to see Martin Downey."

The receptionist said nothing but pointed to an empty chair.

"Tell him I'm here." He demanded.

The woman lifted a telephone and said, "Mr. Chance has arrived," and an instant later, "I'll bring him back."

Music grew louder as she led him down a dark hallway and pounded on an office door.

"Enter," Downey shouted. He stood moving his arms as if directing an orchestra to the finale. A few seconds later, he lifted the needle from the record player.

"Rimsky Korsakoff, Song of India," he motioned Chance to a seat. "A relaxing break, brings back memories of the Punjab and Delhi."

"Yes, you were a file clerk in India as I recall." Chance smiled.

"I was the bloody chief of station and never forget it."

"Oh, forgive me. I have trouble with civil service appointments, never know who to kow-tow to. For example, this

278

latest summons. Is it from you or one of the other bright sparks in this building?"

"It's about the apparent massacre in the Katyn Forest. I gather the report came from that woman."

Chance shrugged. "That was six weeks ago. Why bother now?"

"We're doing our job. Odd, that a massacre escapes wide attention. And, the one witness, the person with first hand knowledge expires suddenly after approaching this agent?"

"She didn't claim to know much. I made that clear."

"The issue is sensitive," Downey said and rubbed his hands across his face. "The Poles have a long list of missing men."

"What does this have to do with me?"

"She is your agent. An atrocity charge could damage the relationship with the Soviets. The Nazis have planted counterfeit intelligence in the past. Kim Philby, here at the office, ordered inquiries. The French think this woman collaborated...uh...'horizontal collaboration', if you get my drift. Hopefully, she closed her eyes and thought of England."

Chance let his fingers drum against the arms of the chair.

"So, we wondered what more there might be?" Downey continued. "Easy enough to imagine her position. Alone, lonely, and attractive or so I'm told."

The fingers drummed harder.

"We wondered if there was something we didn't know," Downey paused, "or a past dalliance. I wondered if there was any...uh...other history?"

"I've told you everything I know," Chance said and rose, "and I trust her. I don't think she knows anything. And quite frankly, I'm surprised. A few dead men in a war? We've come to expect it."

"But not thousands and men who were potential leaders of a post war nation. What will the English people think if we send supplies to the Russians while they eliminate democratic opposition. Philby is trying the discrete back channels. We're wondering what the German's know?"

"Asshole's! You are putting her in danger."

"She's done it to herself," Downey snapped. "The underground cut ties months ago but she wormed her way into the Comet line. And, Comet may have been infiltrated. The Nazis have made arrests. And, strangely, that woman remains free. It's odd?"

Paris
November 7

Karl Munster tightened the handkerchief over his nose. He could avoid the smells but not the groans that came from the cells in the Gestapo headquarters. Those he ignored.

"Is she enjoying the comforts of Avenue Foch?" He peered into a cell where a naked girl lay curled in a corner.

"Open." He demanded, and Bruno Wiebe, his new assistant, produced a key. Munster entered the cell, bent, and jerked the short blond hair and stared at her face. A moment later, he let the head fall to the cement floor with a hollow thud.

"She's not going to say much." He stepped back. "The fools went too far. A proper interrogation would have produced better results. Do we have anything, Wiebe?"

"She was known as Claudia. The English airman she was guiding was dressed as French civilian. He was killed. The girl tried to take a suicide pill. Our men smelled the arsenic and pumped her stomach. She refused to confess despite...repeated interrogations."

"Nothing more?"

"The British escape line was called 'Comet.' An airman would be passed along the system by a series of guides. We caught her but no others."

"Hose her down," Munster decided. "Send her to the women's camp. Ravensbruck can do the paper work when she dies. I've other work to complete but this case intrigues me."

Ottawa
November 11

"Yes, operator. We'll accept a collect call." Sandy Fleming waited as the lines were connected.

"You sound happy. Frank must be out of the office," Robert McLaren chuckled.

"Gone for the day," she answered. "He's been out a lot lately. Are we doing a special series on rubber? He's doing research on tires."

"Lord knows what he's doing." McLaren laughed. "Did you find my letter?"

"Yes, but I don't know what to do. Reporting jobs for women are few and far between."

"If I hear anything, I'll let you know. I have evidence Willard has been cheating the partnership. The agency can't last long. I'm sorry."

"No, I understand. I can see it everyday. He sent me to the Armistice Day ceremony and wanted me to a build a pro-conscription story around it."

"And?"

"I lucked out. Lady Byng was there. I've a fresh retrospective on the Great War."

"Anything else happening?"

"I thought we'd do more on that plane crash at Fingal, but Frank vetoed that. I'm not sure what I should do anymore?"

"Get a message to the Prime Minister. He appears to have a soft spot for you. At the very least a letter of recommendation would help."

"I hate to do that, but you're right. When are you coming back?"

"Frank doesn't know but I have booked first-class accommodation to Hawaii and expect to be in Hong Kong by mid-December. After that, I'm not sure."

281

Al McGregor

Washington

November 13

"Tim Fulton?" Tim raised his eyes to see who was asking: a middle-aged man, a swarthy complexion, dressed in a light summer suit and clutching a battered hat.

"Occupied at the moment," Fulton responded, nodding toward his companion and the steaming food on the table. "Please excuse us. This was a special order."

"Erich Schmidt sends his regards."

Fulton's spoon froze halfway to his mouth. "Wendy." He turned to his companion. "Powder your nose."

"No, I'll fix my makeup after lunch—"

"Go and powder that pretty little nose. This won't take long." She had barely left the seat when the stranger took her place. He produced a passport, but Fulton saw only a flash of a Colombian stamp before it disappeared in his coat.

"I am sorry to interrupt," the stranger said, and Fulton detected a hint of Spanish, "but Mr. Schmidt asked me to bring a message. The mail is safer going to South America. Anything coming to America is opened and read. Our delivery system is slower but more secure."

"Erich is in Berlin?"

"I think so, but what's more important is the message. The President's claim about the map showing German designs on South America is a fraud. There are no plans to seize the Panama Canal."

"Tell Erich the message rings hollow. If I am to counter it, I must know more."

"Which...is why I came. Our officials tried to find a similar German 'map' but failed. We think it was created by the British, by a special intelligence unit that forges passports and other documents. The code name is Station M. It's in Toronto."

"The President was duped?"

"Perhaps he knows the origin but wants to incite the nation against Germany."

An Angry Sky

"I'd need more than conjecture. What else do you have?"

"Roosevelt referred to a Nazi Church to replace other religions. This is a lie. He's trying to incite Catholics."

"That kind of talk fires up the Evangelicals too. Organized religion is stronger here than in the Reich."

"You will help then?"

"I'll do what I can, but Americans have short memories and the speech was several weeks ago."

Le Havre
November 24

Maria ignored the sound of vehicles. The work on the Atlantic Wall had been given a higher priority and more men arrived each week. Trucks were bringing more prisoners, she suspected, men recruited for the project or more likely slave labour. She ignored the sounds until the door burst open and armed soldiers stormed inside. "She's here," one called and roughly ran his hands across her body in a futile search for weapons.

"What is this? What are you doing?"

"Their duty." The answer came from the doorway. "Search the house. Top to bottom. Leave nothing untouched."

From the kitchen she heard drawers crash to the floor and the sound of breaking china.

"What are you doing?" she cried again. The question was lost in the tramp of boots above them as furniture on the second floor was overturned and ransacked.

"Do men still find you attractive?"

"Karl...Karl Munster?" Something in the voice triggered the recognition. Little remained of the face she had known.

"Ah, the lovely Maria." He lifted her hair, ran his hand around her neck and without warning, gripped her jaw, forcing her mouth open. His fingers probed around her teeth. "No pills. No poison. We wouldn't want that." The noise of the search intruded again and what sounded like an axe pounding on a wall.

"Karl, what's happening?"

ble liar and too stupid to grasp the truth. It's
happened before. I used you as the war began. Did you really
believe I would turn against the new Germany?"

"Karl, it's been so long. I can't remember…."

"Maybe more recent events. Wiebe, the photo."

The aide produced a small photograph. The badly beaten
face of Claudia seemed to cry for help.

"Do you know her?"

She felt tears form. "No."

"I know about the escape route. And, I have other evidence
against you."

"Karl…I…."

"Those gossipy letters to the cousin in Detroit. How the new
aerial tower obstructs the view? How the planes from the nearby
base make it hard to sleep or how the new fortifications make it
difficult for walks along the shore?"

"I was writing to…."

"Fool! Did you think we don't know?"

"She's a cousin."

"Don't play with me. I know you were born in Russia. You
had no North American family. You claimed to be part Arab.
Maybe instead you have Jewish blood?"

"I…I…"

A hard slap stunned her. "We can do much more?" He
hovered above her.

"Herr Colonel?" A soldier called from the doorway. "We
found a passport, an American passport."

"She's no American. Give it to me." Munster studied the
document and rubbed the paper between his fingers."

"It's genuine." She told him.

Another harsh slap brought tears to her eyes.

"Take her to Paris. A few days in the cells and she'll talk.
American relations are at a sensitive stage and we don't want
any complications, but we'll hold her on the painting. Creating
decadent material is a crime against the state."

Ottawa
November 26

"Ernest Lapointe died," Sandy Fleming announced as she returned to the office. "Another blow for the Prime Minister. Lapointe was the top Liberal in Quebec. King's friends and associates keep dying."

She should have known not to expect any hint of compassion.

"Wonderful," Frank Willard laughed. "A blow to King and a boost for conscription. Work in the angle that Liberal unity in Quebec will splinter. The army could tap a whole new crop of men."

"Now wait, Quebeckers volunteered in the last two years."

"English speakers volunteered," Willard told her. "Francophones played a minor role and Lapointe wasn't about urge them forward. A few Quebeckers who opposed the war are behind bars. There's room for more and if we break a few heads, it's for the good of the country."

"But we don't need the men."

"We do if we fight on two fronts. Talks with the Japanese aren't going well. Men will stand against the yellow peril, a different colour and culture. That's the trouble with Germans, white men, who in the past, were Christian."

"Would you make it a race war?"

"That's what it will be. And, watch how King twists in the wind when the going gets tough. He'll weasel out of the no-conscription promise."

Willard swung his feet up on the desk.

"In a few months, the country will turn to men like me to get us on the right track."

Al McGregor

London

November 28

"What is it now Martin?" Evers Chance blew the foam from the beer glass. "A few days ago, I was welcome at the office and now we're slumming again."

"I have a problem."

"That's a first step. Admit to addiction. Get help. Other men beat it."

"No, not drink, damnit. Quit being so sanctimonious. It's about that woman. Maria Dickson has been arrested."

For a rare moment Chance was too shocked to speak. He waited as Downey continued.

"She's been taken to Paris. The Germans were looking for what was left of the Comet line but we're not sure they connected her. The arrest was over decadent material."

Chance appeared to recover his composure. "Surely that's not enough to condemn her to the Gestapo."

"There's another risk. That document on the massacre. The Russians want the issue to go away. Granted, she didn't do much, but for the Reds, the fewer people who know the better? They might incriminate her."

"So, the communists, our allies, could use our mutual enemy to do their dirty work?" Chance shook his head in disgust.

"I thought you should know," Downey said.

"Is your office on good terms with the Americans? She has a U.S. passport. Their embassy could lodge a complaint? Officially, Germany and America are at peace."

"I'll send an urgent message."

"At this stage, try anything."

Ottawa

December 1

"Another shot, barkeep," called Sandy Fleming and tapped an empty glass on the table. Her afternoon shopping trip took an unexpected turn. A man lurching from a beverage room, sent her

286

groceries crashing to the sidewalk. He helped corral the squash and cabbage before offering his company. "My boss is a jerk," she said, leaning toward him, "but he's not as bad as what you had to contend with. Why should a man be fired because someone doesn't like his manager?"

"Pressure from Washington, that's what." Her companion appeared in his mid thirties, a touch of grey in his hair and with an early start on a midlife paunch. Bill, he wouldn't give his last name, professed to be an expert on radio signals. In a hushed tone, he told of his work for the Examination Unit, which he touted as a secret intelligence operation. But, he complained, when the American who ran the bureau was fired, Bill too was sent packing."

"This unit intercepts Japanese Navy transmissions?" she asked and took a small sip, the thirst tempered by the need to remember all she heard. "And, the listening post is at Uplands, the Ottawa airport?"

"That's right. Who is going to question another set of aerials? And the men trying to break the codes work from an apartment in Sandy Hill."

"Where?" she asked, thinking of the leafy streets near the Parliament buildings.

"Next door to the Prime Minister, beside Laurier House."

"What? Does he know?"

"He'd be pretty dense not to. Men coming and going at all hours. I met him once, on the street when he walked the dog."

She frantically tried to remember the summer. King told her the dog, Pat, died in July. "This has been going on for months?"

"Yah," he admitted, "but I don't know what'll happen now."

She felt his hand squeeze her knee. She grasped the wrist and lifted. "Maybe later. Does anyone know what these messages say?"

He moved closer. "The Navy Department in Washington may read them and maybe London broke the codes. I'll never know. Co-operation isn't a strong suit in signal intelligence."

"But what can you learn if the code isn't broken?"

The hand returned and fingered her thigh.

"Let's finish the conversation first." She forced a smile.

Dismayed, he signalled for another round.

"What can you learn from a radio signal?" she repeated.

"Where it comes from, how long the message is and if the sender is on a regular schedule. If it moves it might be a war ship."

"A bunch of bleeps can't tell you much."

"Ok, think of this," Bill explained. "What if a regular sender, like an aircraft carrier suddenly goes silent. That might be suspicious."

"Has that happened?"

"Yah, a few days ago. A whole bunch of Jap ships went silent. Maybe the signals resumed but I was kicked to the street before I could check."

"Bill, would you be willing to go on the record for me. I'd need strong proof before I write a story."

"Story? Lady, we're having a chat. Leaking that material could mean a prison term. A succulent little wench is not worth that risk."

Later at the office, she repeated the story for Willard.

"Did the interview end in the bedroom?" he asked. "I don't believe a word of it. And, no editor would accept copy from a broad reeking of whisky. You should know better."

Paris
December 2

A rubber hose connected the exhaust pipe to the sealed cargo compartment of the truck. When the engine started, carbon monoxide gas would kill anyone locked inside.

"We used this in Poland and in Russia," Karl Munster said, explaining the lethal process for a small group of officers, "but it takes too long. Death comes in minutes, but we can only eliminate a couple of dozen at a time, and we have to dispose of the bodies. We need a quicker, more efficient method. Germany has reduced the number of Jews, but France still has far too many, as do Hungary and Czechoslovakia. We'll explore the options at the conference in Berlin."

"The Reich does need workers," an SS officer cautioned. "The Atlantic Wall is not finished, and the factories beg for labour."

"Use Russians, Slavs or Ukrainians. Those men have more brute force than a Jew. The Fuhrer demands a 'final solution'."

"Chemical companies could, no doubt, develop a better gas," another officer spoke, "and crematoriums at remote camps might work, the more remote the better. People may be squeamish about this sort of thing."

"Excuse me, Herr Colonel," Bruno Wiebe hurried across the courtyard, "an urgent matter?"

"Everything is urgent," Munster snarled. "Thank you, gentlemen," he dismissed the officers. "In a few days we'll have chemical industry contacts, the transport details and so on. I have more meetings in Berlin, but I am confident the project will move forward. Now Wiebe, what is so urgent?"

"An American diplomat demands to see Maria Dickson."

"How do the Americans know we have her?"

"He didn't say. He only demands access to the prisoner."

"What have you told him."

"Nothing. Herr Colonel."

"Tell him there must be a mistake. We have no such prisoner."

"Yes, sir."

"And have you looked in on her today?"

"Yes, Herr Colonel."

"And..."

"She is no condition for visitors."

An hour later he saw for himself. "Maria. What a mess. Did you fall?" he asked.

Her face was badly bruised. She wore a tattered prison issue dress, soiled with her blood or that of a prisoner who had worn it earlier. Guards lifted her to a seat, fastened handcuffs to her wrists and shackles to her ankles.

"That will do," Munster ordered. "Wait outside."

As the door closed, he stepped closer.

"Are you ready to talk? Tell me about the escape line, about Comet."

She appeared to shift in the chair.

"The girl…" he scanned a notebook, "Ah yes, Claudia. An unfortunate accident. She died in transit to a camp." He wasn't sure if her shiver was a response or an involuntary movement.

"We found another participant, a communist partisan. We're bringing him to Paris." Her head sagged. "Ah Maria, I think you hear me." The response was a low groan.

"The partisan is talking. He says you 'fraternized' with Russian prisoners and led poor Lt. Webber astray. And, that portrait, a woman who poses nude will do anything."

He bent and roughly raised her face. "Beautiful once. Men fell at your feet. An exotic mixing of the races but Aryan society has no room for half breeds. And no one will come to the rescue. The Americans sent a junior diplomat. He didn't learn anything."

Munster let her head fall back. "I have a new chemical I may try. A truth serum..."

There was no reaction. "Guard," he called. "Take her away. Feed her, force feed if necessary. Keep her alive for a few more days."

Washington
December 4

Tim Fulton clapped his hands in glee at the thick, black newspaper headline. **FDR WAR PLAN.**

Wendy stirred in the bed beside him. "Tim. I'm not getting up."

"Don't miss this, baby. Everything we've suspected. Roosevelt wants a ten-million-man army. He lied when he said he wouldn't send American boys into a foreign war."

"Mumm... too early."

"So much for peace and negotiation. The plan is called Rainbow Five. Air strikes against Japan, an invasion of Europe in 1943. It's all here."

"Let me sleep."

"Roosevelt is finished. He'll be impeached as sure as hell. Whoever leaked this deserves a medal." Fulton jumped from the bed and minutes later was deep in a telephone conversation. "The *Chicago Tribune* published it first and other newspapers will pick it up. It can't be ignored. I'll come up in an hour or so," he said. "We can talk strategy."

The phone call finished, he re-read the article. The leak would cause a major storm. On the radio, announcers were already repeating the details. "Wendy. I need breakfast."

She finally appeared. The short house coat momentarily distracted him until the telephone rang. "Yes, I read it. If a house committee starts an investigation all kinds of things will come out, illegal surveillance, Hoover wire taps, all of it. The administration is finished."

He motioned for her to start breakfast.

"Would Roosevelt himself approve the leak? I mean he's itching for a fight. It wasn't America First although I wish we had done it. We'll talk later."

Wendy balanced two coffee cups and a plate of toast as she came from the kitchen. "Why call it Rainbow?" she asked.

"Colours are code names for countries, so I guess he'll make a lot of enemies."

"Ok. One other question. What's selective service?"

"That's the draft, the organization that forces men into the army."

"A letter has come from the selective service administration. It's addressed to you."

Chequers Estate, England
December 6

The door opened before he could knock.

291

"It's been a few years, Chance."

"And nice to see you, Walter. I tell friends not to worry if Thompson is on duty."

The bodyguard smiled and led Chance down a long hallway. "Winston is in bad mood, I'm afraid. A Japanese fleet is nearing Malaya, and the Americans won't commit to action."

"I'm surprised he left London."

"We have communication apparatus at Chequers. A weekend in the country is good for him."

"Sir. An urgent message from Whitehall." A uniformed officer held a paper.

"I'll take it." Thompson dismissed the messenger and rounded a corner to tap on a heavy door.

"Come," a voice called.

"The old scalawag has arrived," Thompson announced, presenting the message at the same time as he ushered Chance forward.

Winston Churchill wore a one-piece siren suit. A burning cigar rested on an ashtray alongside a bottle and a half-filled glass. His cat Nelson occupied the chair closest to the fireplace.

"Hmm…good." He scanned the message. "Russian counter attacks may save Moscow. Stalin has moved soldiers from the far east. He made a deal with the Japanese a few months ago." He carelessly tossed the paper into the fire. "The years have flown by." He gave Chance his full attention. "I haven't forgotten your help during my years in the wilderness, when all but a very few abandoned me. But not you. Toss the damn cat to the floor. Take a seat."

"No, I won't stay long. I've something planned and thought you should be informed."

Quickly, he explained Maria's situation. "I may be able to get her out, but I need a bargaining chip."

"Which would be?"

"The report on Katyn Massacre."

"That's sensitive. The Poles are doing valuable work. I need them to work with the Reds. We mustn't piss off friends on the word of one man?" He puffed on the cigar. "This woman, I gather she reported to you. What has she done for...us?"

Chance outlined what Maria had seen. The Atlantic Wall, sites for airfields, the radar towers, the conditions along the beaches and recent rumors of submarine bases on the Bay of Biscayne."

"Can we get details on the wolf packs?"

"We won't know until we get her out."

"Nicely played, Chance. I'm between a rock and a hard place. I can't sanction the release of that document but if it were to inadvertently reach the Reich, what could I do?"

"I may need more."

"Don't make too many demands."

"Rudolf Hess. The world knows the Deputy Fuhrer flew to England last May but doesn't know what message he carried."

"He's like all Nazis, as crazy as a shit-house rat."

"Might his majesty's government be holding him for the day the Fuhrer falls and keeping him safe while he assembles a new team to lead Germany?"

Churchill chuckled and topped up the glass. "Might keep them guessing? Make them look for boogie-men under the bed. What else?"

"Lovat's Commandos are training on the Channel. My private contractor is out of business. I need help getting to France."

"I'll send a prayer." And, with that he scratched a handwritten note. *"Pray give Evers Chance all possible assistance. Winston Churchill."*

"One last thing," Chance said. He knew he was pushing the limit, but there was little choice. "In twenty-four hours, order my arrest. Some files will be missing. Circulate word through the intelligence channels."

"That could finish you."

Chance nodded. "I've thought of that," he said. "Give me a few weeks. If you haven't heard anything, it won't matter."

Al McGregor

"Thompson!" Churchill shouted. "Order transport for Mr. Chance."

"Dover," Chance said to the driver as he slipped into the car. The plan was in motion and he began to mull the next steps.

"Are you ignoring an old friend?" Nora Field glanced over her shoulder. "Nice to see you, too."

He laughed and reached to squeeze her shoulder. "To what do I owe this bit of luck."

"To Whom. I drove Churchill up and went to my dad's estate. I wasn't expecting to be called back but ..."

"And the Yank, be damned if I can remember his name."

"Brad. He's becoming a country gentleman. He's has an idea Americans will visit English estates after the war and pay for the privilege."

"And his leg?"

"He gets around, but the armed forces don't want him anymore. I'm pleased about that."

"All working out then?"

"Seems to be. This is going to be a slow drive. You must be tired. I'll wake you when we're close."

"Ah, I always listen to Nora."

"Wake up," she called and when there was no response began to weave across the road.

"What the hell?" Chance was shaken from sleep.

"Thought that would stir you. We're a half hour out. Did you want to fix that pretty face?"

"It would take a good deal more than half an hour," he said and began to rub the sleep from his eyes. "Take me to Lovat's HQ."

"Oh commando's, big brawny Scottish lads. English girls swoon over them. Why there?"

"I'm signing up."

"Touché! You're not going to tell me."

"I don't want anyone to talk me out of it." She let the silence fill the car but a few minutes later tried again.

"Is this about the woman? That vixen who has you…besotted?"

She heard him chuckle. "Do it," she urged. "Sweep her off her feet."

"It's not likely to happen." His tone changed. "I made the mistake of looking at a recent picture. I've grown use to my face in the mirror, the fellow who doesn't change day to day. But this photo showed an older man. The annoying type that refuses to admit his time has passed. It was quite a revelation."

"Should I run by the retirement home?"

"Ah, Nora. If I can only keep you close to brighten my day. And no, I'll keep going, one more grand adventure."

"That's better. Drop to a knee in front of her, offer a glass slipper."

"I'm a little old for a Prince Charming. She sees me for what I am, not one of those brawny lads that thrill the heart. Maybe it was never meant to be, an old man's daydream."

"Let her decide. A friend once told me of strange personal attractions."

"That friend was probably full of shit. Pull over here."

She stopped the car and sprang out before he could slip away. "A big hug," she said. She threw her arms around him and felt him respond.

"That's it," she laughed through tears, "Give her one of those."

"Good-bye, Nora. I wish you only the best."

"That's sounds awfully final, chum."

"We never know, do we?"

Chapter Fourteen: End Games

Washington
December 6

The early Christmas shoppers crowded the streets, taking advantage of the warm fall weather. Mark Ryder glanced into a flower shop with a sigh of relief. No romantic involvement meant fewer bills. And, if he needed a companion, he could easily find one. The growing demands of the government brought a flood of pretty, young, impressionable women to Washington.

"Mark," a friend hailed him. "I'm having a few friends in to listen to the football game tomorrow. The Giants have a shot at the playoffs."

"Sorry, Ralph. I'm on the reporting schedule. Sunday's are slow but I have to be at the office."

A lone patrolman lounged at the gate to the White House where everything appeared normal. The President had cut short a Thanksgiving Holiday but whatever tension forced the return waned in a few days.

He thought of his own schedule. He'd work up something on the investigation of the plane crash in Canada. A Congressional probe into the death of the twenty Americans had just ended but insiders suggested the crash would remain unexplained.

The major story was the leak of the Roosevelt War Plans. The sensational newspaper report had prompted a chorus of demands for a wide investigation, into both the leak and the reasoning behind Rainbow Five. The House and Senate would be in full cry next week, but he would need a fresh story for Sunday.

Ottawa
December 7

"What?" Frank Willard was in his usual fine humour when he answered the telephone.

"It's Sandy. I'm onto something."

"Or, out of a job for bothering the owner."

"It's important," Sandy continued. "The senior staff at External Affairs have been called into work, on a Sunday. The men are legal specialists and my source says they are preparing a declaration of war."

"Have you been drinking again?"

"I'm serious. Something is about to happen. Remember, I told you about the smoke rising from the yard of the Japanese consulate. Maybe it wasn't leaves on a bonfire. Suppose, the ambassador is burning documents, the codes and important papers."

"You are making another mountain out of a mole hill."

"But if there's something to it we'd have a clear beat. The Willard dispatches would be picked up around the world."

"More likely we'd be sued. And the reporter responsible would be out on her ass."

"But it's a major story. What if Canada is the first to declare war on the Japanese?"

"Why? Why would we do that?"

"I don't know."

Al McGregor

"Sandy, take a deep breath. Nothing is going to happen today. King isn't in the city. He's at Kingsmere. Forget it," he said. "I'll try to forget you called."

Hawaii
December 7

"It's too early for breakfast," the desk clerk said and shook his head. "Sunday service is eight to noon."

Robert McLaren nodded, "I should be back by ten. I'd like to settle my bill today. I've on an early flight tomorrow."

"I'll have the bill ready."

McLaren fished a chocolate bar from his pocket and arrived at the hotel entrance at the same time as his navy escort.

"I'm Lieutenant Peterson. Sorry for the hour but it's best to go early." McLaren smiled his understanding and took the passenger seat of the car.

"We'll be on the water by dawn. It's a good day to see the base," Peterson said as he drove onto the main highway, "and, after the tour you'll know why Pearl is our Gibraltar, a fortress of the Pacific." He switched on the radio. "Hmm. This station usually goes off the air at midnight. Pilots use the signal as a beacon, so, if it's on air, more planes are coming from California."

The first hints of dawn appeared as the car slowed near an airport.

"I'd go in," offered Peterson, "but we would startle the sentries. The big concern is saboteurs, lots of Japanese live in Hawaii." Artificial lights sprayed across the runway to show the lines of aircraft. "A few sentries can keep the planes safe. Any fifth columnist will face a nasty surprise."

"I read somewhere that the French had the same fears," McLaren recalled. "And, the Russians worried about sabotage. But surprise attacks from the air destroyed hundreds of planes."

"We'd never be taken by surprise. Although, I did hear about a war game a few years ago that involved a successful attack on Pearl. The war game scenarios are more realistic now."

An Angry Sky

An hour later, the young lieutenant stood at the helm, as a small wooden launch motored about the harbour.

The first rays of the sun touched the water as Peterson spoke. "It's best to be out early. The Captains bring guests for Sunday lunch and things get busy. Shipboard activity won't begin until the colours are raised and that's a few minutes away."

McLaren smiled as the sun rose to promise a beautiful, warm day. Ottawa would be shivering in December cold.

"Battleship row," Peterson said proudly. "These ships are among the most powerful in the world. The *Arizona, Nevada, Oklahoma, West Virginia, Pennsylvania, California.* I can't remember all the other names."

McLaren shaded his eyes to peer at the massive vessels above him. "I've seen enough. If we head back to the hotel, I will buy breakfast."

"Never turn down a free meal," Peterson smiled but cocked his head. "Planes coming in, the flight from the States. We're expecting heavy bombers."

McLaren scanned the sky but saw nothing even as the roar grew louder. Finally, he spotted a plane. Not a four-engine bomber but a smaller aircraft, followed by many others.

"What are they?" he called.

The planes dived toward the harbour and the water erupted in geysers. He saw only puzzled shock as the lieutenant fell to the deck. A split second later an explosion turned the launch into kindling.

Washington
December 7

"The President had all afternoon. When does he make a public statement?" Mark Ryder had joined the reporters in the White House Press office.

"We can't say," a spokesman cautioned. "The Cabinet and Congressional leaders must be briefed. The president may not speak until tomorrow."

Al McGregor

"Oh, come on. Radio has been hammering the attack on Pearl Harbour all afternoon. NBC and CBS are all over it. Give us details."

"The losses appear substantial but don't play that up."

"Did we lose a battleship?"

"At least one and we've lost men too but have no numbers yet."

"The Japs caught us flat footed?" another reporter asked.

"That's the way it looks but first impressions can be wrong. The priority has to be the wounded."

"The declaration of war?" Ryder asked. "Obviously, Japan will be named. What about the rest of the Axis, Germany and Italy?"

"Japan launched the attack. I'm not sure we're ready for a multi front war."

"But Roosevelt has been raging about Germany. Surely, he'll move against Hitler."

"I think Japan will be the priority."

Ottawa
December 7

"Now this is a first," Frank Willard laughed. "The King Government declares war on Japan. The U.S. and Britain have yet to act but our Prime Minister leads the charge. I like the image. The pudgy little devil stuffed in his car for an urgent return to the capital, where he assembles the gallant knights for combat."

"Give it a break, Frank," Sandy worked over a typewriter. "The other countries will follow suit. Tonight's cabinet meeting would have assessed all of that."

"As I predicted, a two-front war," Willard was pleased. "My column will repeat the call for full conscription and a Union Government. King knows it's coming but he'll fight to the bitter end."

"The political consequences hardly seem important." Sandy told him. "No one knows how many died in Hawaii and the

300

Canadian force in Hong Kong is under attack. Set petty politics' aside for a few hours."

"No, it's time to force change. King and company have to go. The whole idea may be too much for a female but not to me."

"Have we heard from Robert?" she asked, fearing without a change of subject, Willard would rage on for hours.

"No. I would have thought the hot shot reporter would file from Hawaii." He pulled on his overcoat. "I'll have a few words when he does check in. Tomorrow we need to work on the west coast reaction. The government should arrest the Vancouver Japs and stick them in a camp somewhere."

"Arrests or deportations could disrupt the whole west coast economy," Sandy warned.

"Hell, no. White men will pick up the slack. The government should seize Japanese boats and sell them to white folks on the cheap. That's the way to get things done."

When Willard left, she quietly considered the events of the day. McLaren's silence bothered her and, on a whim, she reached for the telephone. The call, by a telecommunication quirk, was one of the few to reach Hawaii. The hotel desk clerk was obviously on edge. "We may be invaded at any moment. Fires are raging at Pearl Harbour and my God, the injuries. Men are on stretchers outside the hospitals. Doctors can't keep up."

Sandy began to scratch out notes. "What about dead and wounded. Have you heard any numbers?"

"Far too many to count. The whole fleet is in flames. And, we've no air protection if the Japs come back. Planes were destroyed on the runway."

"But the people are carrying on? As they did in the London Blitz?" Sandy reached for an uplifting angle.

"Not really. My oriental staff are afraid to come to work. White people are spitting at them and threatening them on the street. We can't tell one from another. Chinese, Philippine, Japanese. What's the difference?"

"I know Robert McLaren was to leave tomorrow."

Al McGregor

"He won't be going anywhere. Civilian transportation is shut down."

"Maybe he's returned to the room. Could you try it."

"No. This telephone is the only one working. But I've been here all day. I recall the man, very polite, nice gentleman. He went out for a harbour tour just before the attack. I was working on his bill when the shooting started. He hasn't come back."

"Maybe, he's at the harbour, working on a story."

"I doubt that. Civilians have been cleared from the area. Pearl is a charnel house. There's a pretty good chance he's not coming back."

"You mean, until later, when the situation is clear?"

"No, Miss. He may not be coming back, period."

Paris
December 8

"A companion for the night?" the madam asked politely. "My ladies promise many delights."

Evers Chance chuckled. "No, Teressa. I've other plans but I'm pleased to see the business doing well."

"My German clients have important connections. We seldom attract attention."

"Exactly what I had hoped for." His guest arrived a few minutes later, amused by the meeting site.

"Who would look for you here?" Otto von Ronstadt laughed. "A renegade British agent in the best brothel in Paris. I am acquainted with this house. Well done, sir."

"It's good to see you, Otto. Is the hair growing thinner?"

"The truth hurts." Otto smiled and got to business, "Time is short. Tell me of this mysterious proposal."

"I'm calling in my favours," Chance admitted. "One last effort before I leave the business."

"Bridges are burning as we speak. A little bird reports anger in British intelligence. Missing files...tut...tut...tut."

"Could you identify the singing bird?" Chance asked.

"Not by name, but by colour, a deep red."

"The communists have their own agenda. A certain document would cause great embarrassment. Are you aware of Katyn Forest? It's Russian territory, near Smolensk. The final resting place of thousands of Poles, liquidated by Soviet forces."

"The Poles and Soviets recently signed a friendship accord. The Poles do not know of this incident?" Otto asked.

"They have suspicions."

"The document. What it is?"

"An eyewitness account. Unfortunately, the man who wrote it is dead. He gave it to a woman who is in German custody. She did no more than arrange delivery. I want to trade the document for her freedom."

"Preposterous! I thought we might have a serious discussion…but this…"

"Don't be so fast. Defenceless prisoners eliminated by the Soviets?"

"The Reich has no love for Poles. No one cares."

"We both know the Allies are, at best, in a tenuous relationship. British don't trust the Soviets. The Poles don't know who to trust. The Reds don't trust anyone. I don't like leaking the report, but this was murder. Common decency demands an investigation."

"Tell me about this woman."

Chance took a deep breath. "She's important to me but not the war effort. The communists are trying to destroy any evidence of the massacre. They want her eliminated. She did play a very minor role in a network for escaped airmen. A single agent who doesn't know who else is involved. She can't tell you anything."

"I've already made inquiries. We're talking about Maria Dickson?"

"We are."

"And what is she to you?"

"An old friend."

"Odd. I've never seen a sentimental side. This must be deeply personal. And, because you brought news of my son last spring, you think I will help."

"I hope so."

Otto slowly shook his head. "The cases are different. He's a prisoner of war. The woman is a criminal."

"Her role was minor."

"She has a long list of questionable actions."

"Oh, come on. She wrote innocuous articles on art. German censors approved them. She was a very minor player in the underground."

"A German officer may be dead because of her. And, did you know she posed for indecent pictures?"

Chance was silent.

"A portrait exists that exposes all of her."

"Otto, I don't have the luxury of time. She's on a neutral American passport. War between the U.S. and Germany would complicate her situation. And after Pearl Harbour the clock is ticking. What if I offered something more? The Deputy Fuhrer, Rudolf Hess, is held incommunicado by British authorities. He is prepared to take control when Hitler inevitably falls. And, he's provided a long list of prominent men who oppose the Fuhrer."

"I would need names." the German masked any emotion.

"Admiral Canaris, General Rommel among others," Chance offered. "The list would cause great consternation in Berlin."

"If it was authentic? But perhaps we should see the woman. I'll pick you up here tomorrow."

"I'll need another favour if we reach an arrangement. A safe passage to Lisbon for two."

The German was gone only minutes when Teressa returned, a bottle clutched in her hand. "I need company," she smiled and motioned to a waiter with a food cart, "and can't think of a better way to spend the evening." Teressa had been part of his network since the 1930s, passing secrets first whispered in the private chambers of the brothel. "The Germans are spending the night beside the radio. Roosevelt declared war on Japan but not Germany. They appear disappointed."

"An interesting twist," Chance said. "Hitler could continue with the present state of affairs—a sort of phoney peace. In fact, he'd be smart to do that."

"But pride plays a role," Teressa curled into a corner of a couch. "Men don't like to be ignored. There are also mutterings of setbacks on the Russia front. An SS officer almost killed one of my girls a week ago. His associates claim he was deranged by his Russian experience."

"We'll see more of that before the war is over."

"He was hopelessly scarred and takes pride in being disfigured. And he stank. His stomach must be rotting. I told his superiors that Col. Munster is no longer welcome. He's apparently important and has gone to a conference in Berlin. I hope, he stays there. He frightens me."

"Can the police protect you?"

"They better. I pay them well." From the hall came the sound of raucous laughter, male and female, until a door slammed.

"A busy night," she sighed. "And you look tired? Or worried?"

"Or both, age is catching up."

"Only if you let it." Teressa patted his cheek. "We're only as old as we act."

Ottawa
December 9

"We must do something," Sandy Fleming pleaded. "What if McLaren is lying unconscious in a hospital?"

"No more overseas calls," Frank Willard snapped. "I've wasted enough money. Talk to External Affairs. The department can investigate."

"Do you have any connections in Washington?"

"I haven't talked with the Monument News Service for months. Besides, we've other things to work on. Hundreds of

Canadians are at risk in Hong Kong. We shouldn't have sent them in the first place."

"But you were all for it," Sandy reacted with shock. "Help the Empire! Do more for Britain. You campaigned to send them."

"I assumed the force would be well trained and well equipped. At the very least, this debacle demonstrates the need for conscription."

"Oh, not that again."

"A Union Government is coming. King can't last. The Liberals are considering a plebiscite to ask the nation to release them from the no-conscription promise. Quebec would vote no, the rest of the country, yes. We'd be back where we started. The solution is to replace the Prime Minister."

"Can we talk about Robert? I know an American who might to tell us where to start."

"Fine but don't waste the whole day."

"It's nice to hear your voice." Mark Ryder sounded hesitant when he came to the phone. It had been almost a year since their brief relationship ended.

"Look, we didn't part on the best of terms," Sandy said.

"That's an understatement…"

"…But this is business. Robert McLaren was in Hawaii and we haven't heard from him since the attack. Do you have any contacts that could help?"

For a moment she thought the line had gone dead, but his voice returned. "Pearl Harbour is a mess, worse than first thought, much worse."

"I don't know where to turn." Her voice shook. "The Canadian authorities don't have resources in Hawaii. I thought maybe…"

Again, there was a long silence.

"Ok, telegraph me what you have. I'll take a run at it but can't promise much. Washington isn't functioning well."

Paris
December 9

"Can't say I like your uniform, a tad pretentious," Evers Chance said as he examined the fabric and rubbed the sleeve of Otto von Ronstadt. "On the other hand, I am surprised. The Abwehr, naval intelligence, foreign intelligence, I knew all that, but an Admiral? It's been years since you walked the quarterdeck."

"The uniform impresses junior officers. I regret the need for restraint but that too creates an impression."

Chance rattled the handcuffs that bound him to the German. "A bit too realistic but I'll follow the lead. Please don't lose the key."

Ronstadt opened the car door and jerked Chance to the street. Paris was in blackout, but a dim light glowed in the main entrance to the Gestapo headquarters. Inside, the Admiral startled a guard.

"Heil, Hitler." He clicked his heels with a Nazi salute and before the man could respond, barked an order. "Wiebe, the lieutenant. Take me to him."

The arrival of the short procession was only the first shock for Bruno Wiebe. "I...I...my orders say the woman is to have no contact with anyone."

"A good soldier follows orders," Ronstadt offered a thin smile. "This..." he produced a paper, "transfers Maria Dickson to my custody."

"Unusual," Wiebe read the order. "Colonel Munster has an interest. His instructions..."

"...are over ruled. He was investigating her role in the underground?"

"Yes, an escape route for enemy airman."

"Small potatoes," Ronstadt scoffed. "I can link her to a major British spy network. This renegade Englishman," he said and jerked the cuffs, "will identify her."

"This is so unusual."

"I don't have all night. Must I summon, Colonel Munster?"

"He's at a conference in Berlin." Wiebe stepped closer and whispered to the Admiral. "The Colonel is working on a solution to the Jewish problem. The meeting was ordered by the Fuhrer."

"Then we don't want to disturb him. Take us to the prisoner."

"I'm not sure…"

"More soldiers are desperately needed on the Eastern Front. I would be happy to arrange your transfer."

The reluctance collapsed and Wiebe led them through the prison. Chance shivered, from the chill in the cell block and from fear of what he might find.

"The woman is difficult," Wiebe informed them as he turned the key. "We used all the tools, electric shock and chemicals, without success."

The door swung open to reveal a single light bulb hanging from the ceiling. The only hint of furnishing was a pail by the door. Maria lay in the centre of the floor. Her face and body were a mass of cuts and bruises. The once bright eyes were dim, but she appeared conscious.

"Bastards," Chance tried to reach out but was held back by the handcuff. Ronstadt forced him to his knees by her head. "Do you know him?"

Her head twisted slightly but there was no response.

"Bitch!" Wiebe yanked her hair. "Answer the question. Do you know him?"

The answer was too faint to hear.

"Speak up," he twisted her hair.

"No," she whispered. "No."

"His turn." Wiebe slapped Chance. "Do you know her?"

"Of course. That's her."

"What a brave man." Ronstadt snorted. "A hint of interrogation and he breaks. Bring her to the office. The prisoner will use his free hand. Wiebe, carry the other side."

"But she's filthy, covered in blood and filth."

"Requisition a new uniform later, Lieutenant," Ronstadt said.

Awkwardly, they carried her through the halls, around tight corners, and down the stairs. In the office, Wiebe unceremoniously dropped his side. Chance was barely able to cushion her fall.

"Get me her file," Ronstadt demanded.

"Files are to remain in this office—"

"Everything from her file."

Reluctantly, Wiebe retrieved the folder and counted out several sheets. "Testimony of the communist partisan, interrogations of neighbors, evidence of morale depravity."

He laughed and slowly began to unroll the portrait. First, her face smiled from the canvas and then the rest of the portrait appeared. For a moment there was silence.

"Those breasts aren't hers," Chance said softly. "I saw hers once, a long time ago. Only a flash, but I've never forgotten. Perfect. Pert. The breasts in the portrait were modelled by a Holstein cow."

Maria appeared to stir.

"Carry her to the car," Ronstadt ordered. "I'll conduct my interrogation at a special facility in Vichy. And find a blanket to wrap her. I won't dirty the seats."

"The cuffs," Chance demanded, as the car moved off.

Freed from the shackles, he gently cradled Maria's head. "It's all right," he whispered. "You're safe."

"Don't move her too much," Ronstadt warned. "The Gestapo use rubber hoses. The marks don't show, but she could have other injuries. Teressa will know of a discreet doctor."

"The plane is ready?" Chance asked.

"Yes. And the documents you promised?"

"Will be delivered on the tarmac in Lisbon."

"I have another car a few blocks ahead," Ronstadt explained. "The driver and I will leave you. Hide the car or have Teressa dispose of it. Let the woman rest. We've a few hours to spare. Hitler will convene a special session of the Reichstag.

He's been angered by the leak of the American war plans. He'll likely declare war later tomorrow."

Maria's eyes darted around the room. A bright red couch, a matching chair, a thick blue rug on the floor and above her, on the ceiling, a wide mirror. A stand, against the wall, held towels, a basin and what appeared to be a water jug. Hazy memories flooded back. The cold cement floor, the beatings, but why was Chance there and who was the man who probed at her body? She shook her head to clear her mind but produced more pain, gave up and drifted into an uneasy sleep. She awoke to a whispered conversation.

"Has she been awake?" a woman asked.

Maria opened her eyes. One woman appeared to be a servant, the other, heavily made up, wore a full-length robe.

"The lady comes and goes," the servant said as she rearranged the sheets. "She groans and writhes but in the last few hours slept more soundly."

"Maria. Can you hear me?"

"Where...am I?" Words were hard to form.

"Ah, good. I am Teressa." Confused, Maria tried to rise.

"No. Save your strength. Sleep."

The sunlight that had bathed the room was gone, replaced by an inky twilight, when she next awoke. Teressa sat beside the bed reading a book.

"Water?" Maria forced the word and in seconds felt a wet cloth on her lips. The memories flooded back. Cells. Questions. Accusations. Beatings.

She tried to speak. "There was...a man here..."

"Dr. Forget. He treats social maladies and knows the female body. He predicts a full recovery."

"No...another man...I thought...I knew him."

"Oh, Evers Chance. I've never seen him so concerned. He demanded a doctor and hovered about during the examination. I told him to rest. But he held your hand until dawn."

"Where is he?" Maria asked.

"He'll be back in a few hours. Rest. You'll need strength for what's ahead."

A few blocks away Karl Munster seethed with anger. He had returned from Berlin after the urgent call from his lieutenant. "I contacted the Abwehr office," Wiebe explained, "but when I mentioned Ronstadt a curtain fell. I was warned to drop the matter, a thinly veiled threat. But I found the driver. He thought it strange but didn't know where they went."

"Imbecile! Think. Where did he pick them up?"

"At Madam Teressa's brothel."

"That whore is involved in this? How?"

"Colonel, I don't know...I..." Wiebe watched in horror as Munster clutched his stomach and doubled over in pain."

"Colonel...what is it?"

"The pills. In my office, the courage pills. Bring them to me and call out a security detail. We'll visit Teressa."

Maria was fully dressed in a fur coat and matching hat. A long dress and high stockings hid the bruises on her body. Makeup covered the worst marks on her face."

Chance slipped his arm around her waist and half carried her to a back stairway and a waiting car. "Take care of her," Teressa whispered. "I can see the attraction. I hope..."

"Madam," a maid interrupted from the doorway, "Gestapo! Soldiers at the front door."

"Go! Go with God!" Teressa urged and dashed back up the stairs.

The first of the troops smashed through the doors on the ground level, drawing angry shouts from brothel clients. Karl

Munster glanced at half-dressed men and women before climbing the steep staircase.

"Stop!" Teressa stood on the second-floor landing, "Colonel. You have been barred from this house."

"Bitch!" Munster snarled. The pain struck him as he reached the top step. He doubled over, clutching his stomach.

"Take my hand." Teressa's voice was low and husky.

As he reached out, she pushed hard against him. Munster toppled backwards, striking his head repeatedly as he rolled down the stairs. Teressa ran after him, stopping only when she saw the head, grotesquely twisted to one side. "Oh, my God!" she screamed. "He fell. Someone call a doctor!"

"Who commands the troops?" No one had paid attention to the man wearing long underwear and red suspenders until an aide produced his tunic.

"Who is in charge?" He repeated and Wiebe faced a Wehrmacht general.

"I guess I am. I'm second to Colonel Munster."

"An unfortunate accident." The general looked down on the body. "Close the case. No more disruption for this business."

"But we haven't finished the search. Colonel Munster…

"…died as a result of an unfortunate accident." The general concluded, "Call off the dogs."

Washington
December 11

In four days of war the American capital changed. A week earlier, Mark Ryder would have breezed into Navy Department. Today, armed sailors barred the entrance, reviewing each set of identification. A full hour passed before he was able to reach his navy source. "Thanks for your patience," Commander Peter Stalker led him to a quiet office where walls were covered by maps. "We can't do much for the missing Canadian. He's not on any lists of wounded. As to the dead, some will never be identified."

"I'm not sure civilians have grasped the extent of the attack," Ryder told him. "And, reporters have only a broad sense of what happened."

"Nothing official will come from me," Stalker said. He tapped a paper on his desk, deliberately turned his back and walked to the window.

Ryder studied a large-scale map of Peal Harbour. A series of large red X's appeared to show the positions of ships. He read quickly. *Nevada, Oklahoma, West Virginia, Pennsylvania, California, Arizona...*"

Stalker cleared his throat, made a point of rubbing at a speck of window dust before slowly turning. "The President says we lost twenty-five hundred men."

"Those ships were sunk," Ryder guessed. "What about damage to others?"

"It's extensive. Every repair yard will be busy. The harbour at Pearl is shallow and several of the battlewagons can be refloated. In the meantime, new orders for the Atlantic fleet. More ships are moving to the Pacific."

"Which leaves a hole in the protection for British convoys?"

"The Canadians and the Brits will have to step up. And, I'm not sure it's public yet, but the Royal Navy has taken yet another major blow. *Prince of Wales* and *Repulse* have been sunk."

"How much more can go wrong?"

"Lord only knows. General MacArthur had ample warning in the Philippines, but his planes were destroyed on the runway. Everything we do goes in the crapper."

"Excuse me, Commander," a secretary rushed into the office.

"Damnit, Rita! Knock before entering."

"I thought you would want to know. A report from Berlin. Hitler has declared war on America."

Both men were stunned but Stalker recovered first. "How very interesting. Close the door firmly on the way out and next time, knock."

When the door closed, Stalker shifted the maps on his desk. "War in the Atlantic and we're moving ships to the Pacific. Mr. Roosevelt is going to have to decide on his priorities."

Bay of Biscay
December 11

For Maria, everything was a haze: the high-speed drive from Paris, a vague recollection of Chance guiding her toward a small plane and a German officer, who appeared to help. Dawn broke as the plane left the runway.

"I'm glad to be in the air," Ronstadt turned from his seat beside the pilot. "All night, in the drive from Paris, I expected a Gestapo roadblock. Whatever has happened, they are not coming."

"How long to Lisbon?" Chance asked.

"If all goes well, we'll land this evening."

The pilot interrupted and pointed to the water below. An overturned hull was visible in the water.

"We change course here. The pilots have a location marker," Ronstadt explained. "The wreck of a British ship, the *Lancastria*." Chance starred at the hulk.

"Britain has yet to reveal the extent of this tragedy," he told them. "No one cares anymore. We've more pressing issues."

Maria awoke as the plane began the descent. She stared wildly about the small cabin until Chance squeezed her hand. "Lisbon. Portugal is neutral. The lights are on," and she was mesmerized by an illumination of a peaceful world.

The plane had barely stopped when a van appeared. The markings indicated a private ambulance service, but a British army sergeant stepped from behind the wheel.

"Welcome to Lisbon. Do we need a stretcher?"

"No," Maria shook her head, "I'm not an invalid. I'll ride with you."

"Have it your way," he said with a shrug. "I've a briefcase for a Mr. Chance."

An Angry Sky

"That's me, Sergeant. Take the lady away. Otto and I have business to complete."

Back on the plane, he unlatched the case and removed two files.

"As promised, the report on the Katyn Massacre and the other on, what should we call it? The resistance? It's the one with the red seal."

The German immediately broke the seal and began to read. A few minutes passed before he glanced briefly at the other document. Finally, he spoke. "Searching for a mass grave on the Eastern Front would be like looking for a needle in a haystack. But if the Russian was interrogated, something may be on file. We do keep good records." He tossed the page aside. "The other document is more interesting but what you call 'resistance' is fiction. I know these men and can vouch for their loyalty to the Reich."

"But not their loyalty to the Fuhrer?"

"It doesn't matter," he began to tear the document into tiny strips, "No one will see it."

"A reprieve then," Chance guessed. "Hitler would order mass executions. Is it because your name is on the list?"

"No. We may all be needed...later. I have something more for you. We can simply exchange cases, although mine is better-quality German leather. You'll find Maria's file and a report you might deliver to the proper authorities?"

"What is it?"

"Colonel Munster was not alone in planning for a final solution to the Jewish question. Perhaps if world opinion was brought to bear..."

"I know men who would be interested."

"Good-bye, Chance."

"Good luck, Otto!"

Al McGregor

Lisbon
December 14

"Can I bring a blanket, miss?" The concierge at the small hotel appeared concerned. "Winter can be cold in Lisbon."

"No, I'm fine," Maria smiled as she responded. "I've slept. The sunshine feels good and lunch was excellent."

"I don't mean to pry but the bruises...."

"I was simply in the wrong place at the wrong time. Has a Mr. Chance checked in?"

"An older gentleman? Don't worry, he paid for your room. Is he your father?"

"Oh no," she smiled.

"I see." The concierge removed his glasses and began to polish them. "We do run a proper establishment."

"I'm sure."

"We don't want any improprieties."

"Shouldn't be a problem."

The polishing continued. "Will you be staying long?"

"No! She's leaving tomorrow." Chance strolled across the courtyard. "We're booked on the Clipper but separate rooms on the flight," he added as he touched her shoulder. "We'll have an amorous encounter tonight."

Maria feigned surprise. "Again? You're like a teenager."

"I warn you," the concierge said and popped the glasses back on. "I will remove you both. Money is one thing, but the reputation of my hotel is more important."

"Don't worry." Chance slipped a coin in his hand. "We are discrete, and please, bring some of the best wine." He winked at Maria as the concierge stomped away. "I did get two seats on what may be the last flying boat from Lisbon. The Pan Am fleet is to be refitted for war service."

"How did you manage that?"

"Americans are silly about famous people," he said. "I produced a letter signed by Churchill, begging every assistance for yours truly."

316

"You forged his signature?"

"No. It was real."

"How do you know him?"

"I'll explain later. Have that waiter pull the cork. I need to make a phone call."

In London, a secretary summoned Martin Downey. "An urgent call, on the secure line, at the caller's request."

"Secure line. What's that?"

"A line with special security features. It's hard to tap."

"I didn't know we had one."

"The caller did."

Downey picked up the receiver. "Martin, Evers Chance."

"What? Warrants are out for your arrest. Where are you? No, wait don't tell me. I'd have to report it."

"Martin, there's a leak. The Germans knew about my difficulty, as soon as I did and guess who told them? A red operative inside your office. I'll send a full report. My other request is for a meeting. When can I see Churchill?"

"Out of the question. The Prime Minister is not available."

"He'll meet me."

Downey swore and slammed the telephone against the wall. "Hear that. I'm trying to knock sense into you."

"Martin. Remember the rules about damaging government property. It could lead to a suspension. Now, Churchill. In London or at Chequers?"

"He's...uh...going on vacation."

"What?"

"Travelling."

"He's meeting Roosevelt in Bermuda?"

"Not exactly."

"The States! That would make more sense. With the Japanese in the war, strategy must be reviewed. When's he expected. I can meet him there."

"That's out of the question."

"Martin, arrange a date. And by the way, Lisbon is lovely. Sunshine and bright lights. I highly recommend it. Ta for now."

Over the Atlantic
December 15

"We're past the point of no return," the Clipper pilot explained, "halfway to the Azores and then Baltimore. About eighteen hours to reach the States."

A visit to the upper deck and cockpit was a part of the experience for transatlantic flyers. Maria peered between the two pilots, through the windshield and into distant clouds. On either side the propellers spun effortlessly, carrying the plane further from the European war. "Time for dinner," Chance announced. "We'll return to the belly of this beast. Pan Am chefs are first rate, recruited from the best hotels." He helped her navigate the stairs and the passage to the dining area where the finest silver and china waited. Maria had begun to relax. "I'm glad I had the chance to try this. But it's so expensive. Thank heavens, the government is paying."

"It's not, but let's talk about that later."

While the passengers ate, stewards converted cabin seats to beds. Several travellers moved to the lounge, but Chance followed Maria to the sleeping quarters. He pulled the heavy curtain to bring a measure of privacy.

"What are your plans?" he asked.

"I have none. I'm dead broke, no home, a face that looks like I was in a bar fight. I ache all over and wake with nightmares. The last few days are a blur. Did you say something to the Gestapo, something about that...portrait?"

"Yes. It was gauche but it worked."

"What became of the picture."

"I kept it." Chance snapped the briefcase open. "Or part of it."

Her hand shook as she looked at her face.

"And the rest?"

"Destroyed. Gone forever."

An Angry Sky

"What's left of my reputation is salvaged. My debt is growing rapidly. I don't know how to repay you."

"I have something for you to consider. My friends would remind me, there's no fool like an old fool but I'm in a position to help. The commissions from my business have grown into substantial sums. And, I have no family, no close friends."

"I don't understand."

"A proposal...no... a proposition. Let me provide for you. This must sound awkward. I'm not good at this kind of talk but I hope we can spend more time...together." The only sound was the distant hum of the engines.

Finally, she spoke, "I'm flattered...I...."

Chance could read nothing in her eyes. "Take time to think," he said. "Neither of us has anything pressing."

"I don't know...it's..."

"Take some time." Chance rose and pulled the curtain open. "One other thing?"

"Yes?"

"I want to keep the picture."

Ottawa
December 16

Sandy Fleming gasped as she read.

"Now it can be told. An exclusive account of December 7th by Frank Willard."

The anger grew as she read his account of the bonfire at the Japanese embassy. "A young naïve colleague believed the enemy was burning leaves, but I determined from the colour of the smoke that more than leaves were in the bonfire."

Willard's account extolled his investigative skills.

"Why," he wrote, "did Canadian cryptologists pour through intercepted Japanese messages and, more important, what did they find? Did clues exist that could have alerted the world to the disastrous attacks of December seventh? An anxious country waits for an answer." She felt sick. Willard had sent the dispatch as part of his campaign to discredit the King government and boost his own prestige. All of his arguments on reporting and war time regulations had been tossed out the window. A glance at the clock showed only minutes before the first newspapers would print afternoon editions. She moved to the teletype and began to type.

"Bulletin...Bulletin...Bulletin," she wrote, imagining the bells ringing in newsrooms across the country. "KILL-KILL-KILL-'Ottawa-Now it can be told'-Erroneous-Repeat Erroneous."

She let several minutes pass before she sent the advisory again. The first phone call came seconds later.

"It's Montreal," an angry editor screamed. "What the hell is happening. We had to stop the presses."

"A stupid mistake," Sandy answered as a second telephone began to ring. In the next half hour, she fielded a dozen calls. All demanded answers she couldn't provide.

The man with answers arrived in early afternoon. Frank Willard was in an unusually happy mood, whistling, as he entered the office. A second man she didn't know followed him. Willard took one glance at Sandy's face. "What is it?"

"How could you?" She fought to control her voice. "The bonfire and the secret messages. That was my story."

"Teamwork, Sandy. We're all in this together." He turned momentarily to the stranger. "Joseph, this is what I put up with."

"Now, it can be told," Sandy said, spitting the words. "All you've done is write witless opinion columns. Who knows what damage you've caused?"

"I'm going to consider this professional jealousy," Willard quipped as he moved to the wire machines. "What's this?" he demanded, "Kill...Erroneous. Oh, you've gone too far."

"Yes, I killed it. I couldn't stomach spending time in jail with you."

"Joseph. The decision is yours, but I suggest immediate dismissal."

"Fire me for doing my job?" Sandy asked.

"The last few days have been hell," Willard said to the stranger. "I lost my close friend and partner at Pearl Harbour. I begged him not to go, but he wouldn't listen. And this one," he said, pointing at Sandy. "I brought her alone, mentored her at every step, and she turns on me."

"He's lying!" Sandy screamed. "He stole my story, and when Robert went missing, he refused to do anything. I've been trying to get answers while he was…well, I don't know what he was doing."

"Getting the books together," Willard snapped. "I've sold the business. Joseph Avenatto represents the new owner."

"Sold? You can't. Robert would have to approve."

Willard threw up his hands. "He is no longer with us. I make the decisions. Sandy, for the past two years those breasts, legs and that little ass saved your bacon," he said. "That's the only reason I kept you on."

Willard scooped a few papers from his desk. "I'll wait downstairs. Don't waste time on her."

"Miss Fleming," the stranger said softly when Willard was gone. "We'll talk tomorrow. Carry on as usual."

"Easy enough for him," she thought as he left. "I won't have a job tomorrow."

Tears ran down her face, and she began to sob. Her eyes ranged around the room at the wire machines spitting out copy, at McLaren's empty desk, at the mess Willard had left for others to clean up. And the phone, the damn phone was ringing. Once more with feeling, she told herself and lifted the receiver.

"Hey, Sandy. Who screwed up?" She recognized the voice of a Halifax reporter. "Is the whole story erroneous or only part of it?"

"Parts of it are…uh…no… consider the whole thing one giant screw up."

"Ok, only curious. That's not the reason I'm calling."

"If it's an unpaid invoice, I can't help," she said. "Willard handles, well handled, the books."

"I'm looking to a future pay day. A big French sub has arrived, and by big, I mean *big*, three times the size of a normal submarine."

"We can't discuss ship movements."

"She's not moving. Big sucker. Has a hangar on deck that holds a float plane. Think about that, a plane on a submarine deck. It's that big."

"We've had a bad day here. I don't think we should be talking about anything military."

"Ok, how about political? Her name is *Surcouf*. She's Free French. Check the files. Call me if you need more."

New York
December 17

Holiday shoppers jostled at the store counters, but Maria found the women's department was quiet. Her full wardrobe could be replenished later. For now, she needed essentials. A clerk glanced at what she was wearing and directed her to marked down merchandise. Instead, she moved to racks of high fashion. She might be a refugee but didn't plan to look it. And Chance had offered to pay the bill. She felt momentary guilt. There was no way to repay him. And yet she knew he wouldn't expect repayment.

"How about this," suggested a clerk, holding a floor length gown. "It's a lovely shade of blue. Perfect for an older woman."

"Mmm...yes...we all age don't we. But we must never admit it. Life's too short."

Chance waited on the street. His coat collar was turned up to cover his ears but as she approached, she saw the pain on his face.

"What's happened?" she asked, realizing at that moment she could read his moods.

He took the clothing bags and guided her to booth at a nearby restaurant. "I've bad news. Robert is missing. He was on assignment in Hawaii when the Japanese attacked."

"This is a bad joke."

322

"It's no joke." Chance took a deep breath. "He talked himself into a tour of the harbour early on the morning of December 7. The guide was a young naval officer. No one has seen them since." Maria began to shake, and he gently placed an arm around her shoulders.

"I don't understand," she stammered. "If he was in a boat, he wasn't in the water...it..."

"He was in the middle of Pearl Harbour when the Japanese attacked," Chance said.

"The hospitals maybe..."

"He's not on any list of injured or... of the dead."

"I don't understand. What was he doing?" Maria asked. "Why Hawaii."

"On his way to the Canadian Forces in Hong Kong. I've tried to find out more, but the Willard office doesn't answer the phone. I'll try again in the morning."

Tears began to run down her face. She sat silently shaking her head in disbelief.

Chance held her hand.

"I feel so guilty," she said. "I've felt guilty since we separated. We were happy and..."

"Don't put this on yourself."

"He wrote, several times a year and I didn't always reply. I didn't take the time and now..."

She wiped at tears. "For some reason, he wanted divorce papers signed. I don't think there was another woman. He wanted to clean up loose ends. I sent the forms off, a few weeks ago."

"Is there any family?"

"No. He had an uncle. They fell out during the first war. After Flanders, after what he saw, he refused to have anything to do with the family munitions company."

A waiter brought a pile of napkins and quietly stepped away.

"He knew what he wanted and saw what could be done but...listen to me. I'm talking about his career, not the man.

Robert was kind and gentle and in those early years we were deeply in love."

"I saw that. I know."

"Damn. Why is life so hard?"

"I wish I knew."

"There's so much running through my mind. I faced the Gestapo. This is worse. I can't really think, not right now. But please stay with me. I don't want to be alone."

Ottawa
December 18

Sandy was waiting when Joseph Avenatto arrived, braced for the worst but determined not to show it.

"That was quite a display yesterday," he spoke before she could. "Mr. Willard was persuasive in his arguments. The man in charge has to expect loyalty but I find loyalty can be overrated. Employees who speak truth to the boss are rare."

"I do try to be honest."

"And I'll be honest with you. The agency may continue or may be closed. Head office in Montreal will make the final decision. In the meantime, we'll continue. Except Mr. Willard will join us...infrequently."

"I have a job?"

"At least for awhile. Now, what's in the hopper."

"Uh, an article is ready on Louis St Laurent. He's Lapointe's replacement from Quebec City, a Liberal on the way up and..."

"I'm aware. What else."

"I've been trying to pull something together on synthetic rubber. The Germans use it and we could too. It would take a huge investment but there's a rumor of building a plant at Sarnia."

"Hmm. Keep working on that. Our corporate parent also owns a chemical firm. Anything else."

"I'm hoping for something more on Robert McLaren. I asked a government connection for help."

"Really. Who?"

"It sounds silly but the Prime Minister. I've met him and he knew Robert."

"Do what you think best. I've got to try to understand the accounting system and see what's really here."

Ottawa
December 21

Union Station was quiet and Evers Chance had no trouble finding Sandy Fleming in the waiting room. The cold outside had seeped into the building and she was bundled against the weather.

"Ottawa and Moscow are cities to avoid in winter," he laughed. "Good to see you despite the fact the circumstances are awful."

"That's the truth," she said as her smile faded. "I gather time is short."

"I'm going back this afternoon, but I booked a room. Sadly, the hotel does not rent rooms by the hour."

"I'll let you check in. A man with a small suitcase and a dame might raise awkward questions."

"At my age," he smiled and said, "such questions do wonders for self esteem."

She wrapped a scarf around her face. "They wouldn't be able to identify me anyway. I'll run over to the office and pick up Robert's stuff."

Twenty minutes later she returned. "I'm not sure he planned to come back. The desk drawers were empty. That big legal looking envelope came after he left." Chance recognized Maria's handwriting and knew it was the divorce documents. The envelope went into his case, unopened. "What about you, Sandy?"

"I'm ok. The agency is teetering but I'm working on a big story. I've decided to 'soldier' on. And, maybe you could help? I need to know more about Charles de Gaulle?"

Chance smiled. Her question was a relief. After days of uncertainty and trying to comfort Maria, he was dealing with something more familiar. "Any French who oppose Hitler get high marks. De Gaulle however rubs people the wrong way. Arrogant might best describe him."

"He was in Ottawa last week. And, a massive French submarine and three corvettes were in the Halifax harbour but have disappeared."

"I wonder? A very strong radio transmitter has been erected on the French islands off Newfoundland. A suspicious soul might wonder if the radio could send convoy locations to U-boats or spread Vichy French propaganda."

"It's the Free French who are our side?"

"The French allegiance is complicated, but yes. Now, suppose someone wanted to shut down that transmitter. Canada and the U.S. don't want to upset Vichy. They'd like to keep what's left of France, neutral. The Free French believe it's too late for that."

"And, if De Gaulle tried to seize the islands, the war could come to North America."

"That's possible but more likely it would create only a tempest in a Gulf of Saint Lawrence teapot. And, keep your ears open. De Gaulle may not be the only visitor coming to Ottawa."

Washington
December 22

"What in hell have you been doing?" The chief editor put the question to his reporters. "I approved generous expense accounts. Dinner with General so and so, drinks with State Department minions and I might as well have thrown the cash away. Churchill arrives in Washington and no knew he was coming."

"Ah, come on," Mark Ryder shot back. "Security. The British Prime Minister was at the mercy of U-boats. No one was going to talk until he was safely across the Atlantic."

"Bull shit. He came on the *Duke of York*, the newest, strongest ship in the British fleet."

"And her sister ship the *Prince of Wales* is at the bottom of the Pacific. I understand the silence."

"I think my overpaid reporters missed a big story. To salvage our reputation, I want full coverage each day from breakfast until Churchill slips under the silken White House sheets. And, I want to know what the leaders of the free world talk about."

"I'd lay money on a knock out, drag out fight," Ryder predicted. "The U.S. and Britain had agreed that Germany was the priority. Try telling that to the parents who lost sons at Pearl Harbour."

"Yah," another reporter nodded, "The Japanese are in our sights now. And we'll hear more about arms and munitions. Don't be surprised if factories stop making cars and refrigerators. More tanks and planes will be coming off the assembly lines."

"Finally, we're making progress." The editor scratched a note. "The White House plays a good public relations game. Don't get bamboozled. Don't lose sight of the big picture."

"Mackenzie King is joining them," another reporter chimed in, "and Churchill will address Congress and the Canadian Parliament."

"See what I mean about public relations," the editor snapped. "They'll give the Canadians a pat on the back. The real message is, we appreciated the help but it's time to let big kids run the show."

"We could do something on the future of Empires," Ryder suggested to a chorus of groans.

"Hear me out. FDR is no fan of colonies, but Churchill needs U.S. forces to keep British territories safe. This war could spell the end of the British Empire."

"Maybe save that for the opinion page."

"No. Think about that. If the Brits fail who takes their place? It may bring the birth of an American Empire. We're already

Al McGregor

building the new Pentagon building for the army, maybe we'll play a bigger role in the world."

Ottawa
December 24

A few discordant carollers sang in the halls, a seasonal din that failed to produce Christmas cheer but leaked through thin walls into the Willard Agency office. "No one will talk about St Pierre and Miquelon," Sandy yelled from across the newsroom, her voice barely audible over the carols. "The Vichy Consulate refused to take my call. I got through to National Defence and External, but the spokesmen left early for the holiday. Gosh, who would have expected a civil servant to quit early?"

"I can't help you," Avenatto shouted back. "You've a better news sense than I do."

"We're nearing the deadlines for the eastern papers," she called. "I can rework the statement from the Free French; the landing on the islands were virtually unopposed. The invasion was over in half an hour. I'll finish with the promise of a plebiscite to decide if the islands should be Vichy or Free French and predict the Free French will win."

"Sounds fine. Most of the papers will shut down for Christmas anyway."

Sandy focused on writing and relaxed only when the dispatch was on the wire. At the same time, she realized the carolling had ended. "I couldn't have written like that a few months ago," she spoke in a normal voice. "A little late but bully for me!"

Avenatto looked up from the account books. "I wish I was as successful. I can't follow the money trail."

"Mr. Willard would know every dodge in the book. He's a slippery devil."

"I'm going to talk to him next week. If we're shutting down, I'd hope to get severance for you and something for McLaren's wife."

"That's unexpected but would be appreciated."

328

"I'll see what I can do. Take the rest of the day off and Merry Christmas."

New York City
December 25

Christmas sentiment was spent by mid evening. The band in the night club returned to popular favourites. *Silent Night* gave way to *Moonlight Serenade*. An older man in a white dinner jacket danced with a woman in an elegant blue dress. Her head rested on his shoulder but only for an instant as if she feared an indiscretion.

"What a pretty melody," Maria said, "but so short."

"The shorter the song, the more the dance hall owners collect," Chance smiled, "the old ten cents a dance."

"So much for romance," she said as they returned to their table. "Radio Belgrade played a tune every night and it was haunting, too. *Lily Marlene*? It left me melancholy, but I listened anyway."

"Ah yes," he responded and held her chair, "a rare composition loved by both the Axis and the Allies."

"Chance," she smiled at him as she said, "you've been amazing these last few days. I don't know what I would have done without you. It's been so nice to have someone close."

"I couldn't agree more."

"And yet I have been thinking..."

Something in her voice triggered an alarm. "Not yet," he said. "We're two souls who've been alone for such a long time. Don't rush a decision."

An errant streak of light from the doorway caught her and highlighted a thin streak of grey in her hair. "I haven't made a decision," she assured him, "but we're both so independent. And yet, sometimes when I look to my future, I see a lonely dowager, counting past loves on her fingers. I don't like that image. I'd like another try for happiness."

"Even if only for a few years?" He let the question go answered. "Set it aside, at least for now. Come, we'll dance."

As they circled the floor, she whispered, "You're a better dancer than I expected."

"I had good teachers," he laughed.

"Like who? Tell me?" The question stopped just short of a demand.

"Oh, over the years, a long list, but they're no longer important."

"Cutting in," a voice came from behind. "The old geezer shouldn't have all the fun."

Chance turned to see the smiling face of Martin Downey. "I thought it was you." Downey laughed, "But I don't know the lady."

"Martin Downey – Maria Dickson."

"Oh. I see why you kept her a secret...a very attractive woman..."

Chance interrupted. "What are you doing here?"

"I came over with Mr. C." Downey pulled a business card from his pocket. "We've business with the Yankees. Stop by this office at the Rockefeller Centre. I may have something for you and for the lady. Now, don't be a wall flower. Dance the night away."

"I was glad to get away from Washington," Martin Downey explained the next morning. "And, I wanted to see the British Security Operation. Although with the Americans in the war, Bill Stephenson may be out of work. Churchill, by the way, is taking over the White House, up till all hours of the night and drinking like a fish. He brought his map room where he tracks the events of the war. FDR is allowed to see it and Harry Hopkins, but no one else."

"It sounds like an excuse for him to play military planner." Chance smiled. "He can upstage headquarters daily."

He began to pack his pipe. "I thought the military decisions had been made."

"We did too but the Americans are wavering. The British would be in a stronger position if we could grind out a few victories."

"Don't count on that," said Chance and lit the pipe. "Singapore is not impregnable and if it falls, India could be next."

"And, I'll add to the gloom," Downey confided. "Hong Kong is lost. The official communique will come in the next few hours."

"This does mean new work for political investigators, the type that search for scapegoats. Roosevelt needs to hang Pearl Harbour on someone. Churchill would like a culprit for the disasters in the far east and poor Mackenzie King has to explain sending untried troops to Hong Kong."

"Don't get your hopes up. Those jobs will go to safe choices, a judge or a retired politician. For the good of the war effort major blunders will be addressed quietly or filed away for consideration post-hostilities. I wonder, though, if your expertise might be put to use in other ways."

"How so?"

"The Americans want something like our Special Operations Executive. I'm not suggesting a parachute drop into France, but I thought you and Maria could…consult."

"So, now Americans want to set Europe ablaze? The Brits haven't been very successful. Still, keep me in mind and I'll run it by Maria. She'll make her own decision."

"Winston's schedule is packed." Downey flipped through a calendar. "But he's taking a few days in Florida. We might fit you in there. Is this about those missing files?"

"No, something else he should be aware of. Any luck finding the leak?"

"Still looking, I'm afraid," Downey said. "It's a little sensitive, you know, suggesting our communist ally would feed information to the enemy. And suggesting the information originated with British intelligence."

331

Al McGregor

"Whoever it was is burrowed deep in our establishment. Think of the secrets at risk."

Ottawa
December 27

"I'm not getting anywhere," Sandy Fleming fumed. "Hong Kong surrenders, sixteen hundred Canadians are captured and all we can get is a quote from London, that reads: *So ends a great fight against overwhelming odds.*"

"We need more than a paragraph," Joseph Avenatto agreed.

"National Defence Headquarters isn't any help." She ran her fingers through her hair. "The minister says causalities were high but can't provide names. Weeks may pass before the Red Cross reaches men in prison camps."

"Do your best," he told her. "Why not walk over to Defence Headquarters. Willard is coming by and I doubt you want to see him."

Frank Willard watched as she left the building and waited a few more minutes before climbing the stairs.

"I saw the bimbo on the street, got to admit she's a fetching morsel." Willard smiled and removed his coat. "But don't let the little minx fool you. The sooner she's gone the better."

"No decisions have been made. It's why I wanted to see you. I'm having trouble with the books."

Willard shook his head in disgust. "I told your boss not to worry about a few cents here and there."

"But if we keep the agency going, we have to see how the money flows?"

"Keep it going? That's stupid. I tried to find new clients, but the competition was too strong."

"What is Willard Corporation?" Avenatto asked abruptly.

"That's a private company and will stay that way. Your men bought the agency, not my private company."

"If I could raise cash, I could keep the business afloat or come up with something for Sandy and McLaren's wife."

An Angry Sky

"Let them fend for themselves. Or, sell the office furniture. Split the proceeds between them. And, out of the goodness of my heart, I won't demand an accounting."

Avenatto followed him to the door, "Every business has its problems. My brother-in-law has a trucking company. He's having a devil of a time getting tires."

"I can help," Willard eagerly snatched a pen. "Here's an address for a garage. I can get him a good deal."

"Great. He's going to be in the city tomorrow."

Willard glanced around the office, "Too bad this didn't work out. If people had listened to me things would have been different."

Ottawa
December 30

"There's not much room left in the Commons Chamber." Sandy followed the popular Ottawa photographer, Yousuf Karsh. "I'm to shoot a portrait of Churchill after his speech," he explained. "We'll get in the back way."

The Chamber was packed with the who's who of Ottawa. Two Prime Ministers, Winston Churchill and William Lyon Mackenzie King, stood in conversation a few feet from the microphones. But Sandy wouldn't be filing a story. The agency was closing. Office phones and teletypes had been disconnected, and her credentials would expire in hours. She was a mere spectator as Churchill took centre stage. The rhetoric, the bluster was familiar.

"Hitler and his Nazi gang have sown the wind: Let them reap the whirlwind."

His speech checked all the boxes of the Canadian war effort: Material and men, the air training program, the Hong Kong Force, and he recalled the days before the conflict exploded in Europe. *We did not make this war. We did not seek it. We did all we could to avoid it."*

The Phoney War was far in the past, vanquished by the sweep of events from Poland to Pearl Harbour but he resurrected

333

Al McGregor

a prediction from the days when the British future appeared bleak. *"England will have her neck rung like a chicken… Some chicken…some neck."*

If he had doubts about the future, he kept them to himself and predicted the ultimate victory of the Allied nations.

"United Nations," Sandy silently corrected him. President Roosevelt had begun to use the term and she liked the way it sounded. As the speech ended, she was swept along to the doorway of a private room where Churchill, King and Karsh stood. Karsh and Churchill spared over whether Churchill would be photographed with or without a cigar. King ignored the argument and moved toward her.

"Miss Fleming, I've been very busy but did mean to call. I wish I had better news." He spoke softly. "Mr. McLaren, our friend Robert, has passed over."

"Oh, we feared as much." Sandy sighed. "In a way, I'm glad official enquiries were able to confirm his death. We didn't have much luck getting answers from the government."

"Oh no, Miss Fleming, the government does not have an answer. Officially, he's missing, but you see, I was at the table. The spirits were active, and Robert was with them. He's crossed over and sounds quite content."

"The table rapping?" She tried not to sound incredulous.

"Yes, but I can't say more for now. I must watch over Mr. Churchill. I fear, he drinks too much."

Ottawa
December 31

Pedestrians were forced to wait as two workmen lifted a desk to a moving van while a third man carried a chair. Sandy scurried up the stairway into a nearly empty newsroom.

Joseph Avenatto sat at the sole remaining desk, sorting the last of the files.

"I had to come," she told him. "This room has been my life for the last two years."

"Yes, I thought you'd be here at the end."

334

"And, I've been living out my reportorial dream," she perched on the edge of the desk as McLaren once had. "And, what a shame I couldn't write about it, an off the record briefing from Winston Churchill. An exclusive, me and about a hundred reporters, editors and publishers. And, of course, I can't report that he didn't say much."

"Simply bucked up the morale, did he?" Avenatto smiled.

"I guess. He certainly boosted Mr. King's prestige. And, I'm breaking confidence, but Churchill backs him on conscription. It's not needed. At least not now."

"That must be a relief for King."

"The question won't go away. It will dog him for months or maybe years."

"You don't have to worry about the news anymore."

"Actually, I might. I'm meeting a Toronto Publisher next week. He has a job open."

Avenatto seized her hand. "Good things do happen to nice people. I'm delighted. I'm being reassigned to a job in Toronto too. Our paths may cross again."

"I'd like that."

"And, one other small item that might be of interest." He swept the last of the papers into the waste. "I told Willard that Ralph, my brother-in-law, needed tires and arranged a meeting. What I neglected to mention is that Ralph is with the RCMP. Willard's garage was full of tires, booze and pretty much anything that would turn a profit on the black market."

"The shifty bugger!"

"Yah. I couldn't hang anything on him from the news agency, but he'll need a good lawyer."

"Hey, buddy," a workman said, reappearing in the doorway. "If we don't take the last of the furniture right now, we'll have to bill for overtime."

"Wouldn't want that," Avenatto answered and reached for his coat. "Sandy, it's New Year's Eve? Can I buy a girl a drink?"

"You can buy this girl a double."

335

Pompano Beach, Florida
January 7, 1942

A distant smudge caught his eye, and Evers Chance reached for the binoculars. For a full minute he studied the smoke. The small beachfront hotel was a perfect location to observe activity along the Florida coast. "The Americans have so much to learn," he said. "That's an oil or gasoline tanker belching engine room smoke. If I can see it, a U-boat can. One ship alone, no protection, and tonight she'll be a perfect target, a graceful silhouette against the lights from the shore."

"Can't they see the danger?" Maria asked.

"Apparently not and they won't listen. No convoys. No blackouts. The wolf packs could make their Atlantic coast a U-boat hunting ground."

"But there must be patrol ships."

"Not as many as needed. New construction takes time and much of it is spoken for. England needs help in Asia, the Mediterranean and the middle east. The U.S. needs ships in the Pacific while Joe Stalin begs for supplies and a second front. God help, the first troops to land on French beaches."

"I don't know when I've heard you so pessimistic."

"All of the elements are in place to win but yes, things are very dark right now."

"Are you going to continue the work?"

"I can't just walk away. What have you decided?"

Maria raised her hand to shield her eyes from the sun.

"I feel the same way."

"No matter what they offer, be careful. A few of the Americans are cowboys, long on yee-haw and short on brains." Chance glanced at his watch and bent to retrieve the leather briefcase. "The car will be here shortly. I shouldn't be long. And then we should have that talk."

A short taxi ride brought him to a villa in a strip of prestigious retreats, a winter playground for the rich. The gate was closed but a civilian emerged to check his identification. The dark black suit was an odd contrast to the light summer attire worn by others in the area.

"What's in the case," the man demanded.

"Papers!"

"Open it."

"Secret papers," Chance snapped. "I doubt you have the clearance to read them."

"We'll see about that, buster..."

"Let him pass," a voice blared through an intercom system. "He's expected."

"Thank you." Chance bent to the speaker. "I need protection from junior G-men."

At the door, Churchill's bodyguard waved him in. "That FBI agent is an officious little bastard. Good fun to put him in his place. Have a seat. Winston will see you momentarily."

"How is he doing?"

"Tired. He had a bit of a health scare, but the doctor says it's nothing."

"The black dog? The Depression?"

"No. We thought it might be his heart, but he seems fine."

"Damn right he's fine," Churchill said as he entered the room. "And there's nothing wrong with his heart or his hearing. Good to see you, Chance. Last I heard, the Gestapo had you hook, line and sinker."

"They threw me back." Chance smiled. "The little Hess distraction helped, and I indicated that Britain knew all about the resistance to Hitler."

"Hmm. If they fell for that, there may be more to it," Churchill said.

Chance set the briefcase on a table. "In return," he said, "I agreed to play courier. One of my contacts thinks we should know what's happening. I took the liberty of making copies for the Americans."

"What is it?"

"A meeting in Wannsee near Berlin this week will work on what the Nazis call 'a final solution' to the Jewish issue."

"More persecution? More camps?"

"Not concentration camps. Death camps, the elimination of the race."

"No!" Churchill was shocked. "Hitler is mad but that's too much even for him."

"My man lays out the case. It's already started. Mass murders in Russia, deportations in the occupied territories, brutal repression. The list is extensive."

"But based on the word of a Nazi?"

"I think he's a 'Good German' but we'll need confirmation."

"Chance, this world is full of secrets. Massacres, frightening new weapons, unfaithful allies and only one viable solution. Win the War. No armistice, no negotiations. Unconditional surrender! And then, we'll go after the criminals who started all this. Our people are already building a dossier."

He began to leave but turned back. "That woman. What became of her?"

"We got her out."

"Hmmm…good!"

Maria didn't answer when he knocked on her door. Maybe she's gone, he thought. He wouldn't blame her. They had both faced a difficult decision. They were good together, had grown much closer, but the age difference threatened a long-term future.

He walked toward the beach, which was almost deserted as evening approached. The sun worshippers were gone for the day except for the lone figure coming toward him.

A broad brimmed hat, a light jacket over a short, white swimming dress, a beautiful woman. She stopped a foot away. "I've done a lot of thinking."

"And, so have I," Chance said. "I'd like to sweep you off your feet, but at my age I might drop you."

Maria laughed, and the smile he loved played across her face. "Oh, Chance. You're not that old. We owe it to each other to give this a try."

Al McGregor

A Final Word

The real figures who appear in *An Angry Sky* are subjects of history. Books abound on Churchill, Roosevelt, King and the others who lived through the Phoney War. The choices are endless. Major events including the Blitz, Pearl Harbour, the Katyn Forest or the role of Kim Philby are well documented, but a few surprises surfaced as I studied the period. Jonathan Fenby added a special dimension with *The Sinking of the Lancastria, Britain's Greatest Maritime Disaster and Churchill's Coverup.* For drug use in the German army, Norman Ohlers' *Blitzed, Drugs in Nazi Germany*, added a fresh perspective. And, for Canadians, *Final Descent: The Loss of the Flagship Erie*, by Robert D. Schweyer, provides a factual account of the airline disaster of 1941.

Special thanks to Deborah Phibbs for the cover design, another bit of magic, and to editor and first reader Catherine Rupke for her work and encouragement.

For other background information, visit the website at www.almcgregor.com.

About the Author

An Angry Sky is Al McGregor's fourth book of historical fiction. *A Porous Border, To Build a Northern Nation* and *1917* are available through Amazon, Kindle and Kobo. He speaks frequently on history and about the writing process. McGregor, a former television anchor and reporter, is a self-confessed history buff. He lives on a farm in South Western Ontario.

62371489R00208

Made in the USA
Middletown, DE
25 August 2019